Over the River

TAYLOR HORNIG

First edition

 Formatted with Vellum

For those who dream in such vivid detail, you wake up wondering where the dream ended and reality began.

Contents

Author's Note

First of all, thank you for giving this book a chance.

I woke up one Saturday morning and while I sat with my morning coffee watching the same episode of Bluey for the one thousandth time (Rug Island), my mind wandered to medieval Germany in the Black Forest, as one does. A location I'd been obsessed with since I was a kid and looked a little too deep into the creepy fairy tale Hansel and Gretel.

Don't worry, no children are eaten in this story.

Some scenes and memories in this book may be extremely upsetting. Sexually explicit content and recalls of abuse, sexual assault, and rape have significant roles in the development of this story. **Because of the nature of parts of this book, it should only be read by readers 18+**.

Thank you for reading my baby.

Trigger Warnings:
Rape, Sexual Assault, Physical Abuse, Murder, Death, Trauma, Thoughts of Suicide, Physical Fighting, Breaking Bones, Depression, Anxiety, Bondage, Blood

1 in 5 women are victims of rape.
And that is just what is reported.
This book explores healing, regaining control, and redemption. This one is for the survivors like me.

Prologue

Butterflies are objectively beautiful. Their wings are full of intricate designs, swirling around and holding vibrant colors protectively within their borders, keeping them from spilling over. Nearly weightless, you pray one chooses you to land on, to take a rest from straining their wings on your shoulder.

But if you look closer, past the distraction of beauty, they are clumsy. Each flap of their wings takes immense effort. Their bodies move up then down at least a half an inch, like if they faltered in the rhythm they created they would crash to the ground and break their beautiful capes. Imagine the stress that would take on a heart. Knowing one mistake, one misstep and you die.

What if they don't enjoy living like that? Maybe the pressure and energy it takes to move from one place to another is why they die so quickly. A few weeks being all their little hearts can take before it's too much weight to bear. A flawed design if you ask me, but then again, we're kindred spirits if it's true.

Laying frozen on the plush grass, I tried to summon a merciful death. The blue sky taunted me, fluffy clouds floated effortlessly above. What might it be like to fly with the angels in the sky than walk alongside the evil here on Earth?

"Take me away, please," I whispered to whatever cruel God sits in his castle in the sky.

The God who watches his followers, the ones who visit his home every Sunday morning and pray for the sick, the children, and the prospect of a better life; then pretends not to hear us pleading. He created woman and man and then allowed man to be led by his favorite fallen angel. The one who sings to distract you from the demented ways of his army.

The Palace keeps us hungry, subservient, poor and fearful. Lord Bosque gave his men free rein over Holleberg's women, and you sure as fuck don't fight back if you want your heart to keep beating.

I'm not sure I want that anymore, though. A beating heart, that is. Father is dead, mother may as well be. Rations come far and few between these days, and the three hungry mouths that are now my responsibility to feed are withering away to nothing. Like the butterflies, if I don't keep survival as priority number one, I'll die.

So, maybe fighting back against the wicked world is how I perish, but at least then I can say I fought.

CHAPTER 1

Amelie

Whispers echoed from the Forest that haunted my village, beckoning for me to join the creatures that dwelled there. The dewy August grass was cool and plush under my bare feet as I walked through the haze to meet my friend at the edge of the trees.

The dirt path that always took me on my greatest adventures was alive and well, the sparkling winds brushed the trees as if to welcome me. Creatures of the Forest poked their heads out to say hello, fluffy tailed bunnies hopped along with each of my steps to keep up. Warm sun soaked my summer stained cheeks through the cracks in the Forest's canopy leaves, the shadows of night long forgotten here in my dreams. Butterflies floated atop glowing orbs and birds weaved through the trees on their own special path.

The faceless dwarf accompanied me tonight, I hadn't seen her in a while so my heart calmed when her short arms wrapped around my body. She never spoke in my dreams but when danger lurked, she'd take my hand and give me the tenacity to forge on. Her shoulder length white hair was combed neatly and set in place so the breeze that followed us wouldn't hinder her view.

I used her ear as a diary. Letting her in on all of my darkest secrets. After the day I had, she was just the company I needed.

"So you know my boss, Henrik? He was kind enough to let me go home early because of the pin pricking headache I was fighting. I finished shining up the new shoes we were setting out for display and started for home. I was so close to home, less than three houses away, when two guards stopped me…" I trailed off. After many nights wandering aimlessly through the forest with my friend, she knew all too well how guards treated women in Holleberg.

"The bigger one of them tore my satchel off my shoulder to do an *authorized random search of possessions*," I mocked the greasy man's voice. "When he didn't find anything, he threw my bag to the ground. The loop that I used to cross it over my body ripped into two pieces. When I bent to pick it up, the guard sunk the toe of his boot right into my stomach. Then his counterpart knelt by my side. For some reason, I thought maybe he'd show me mercy." I laughed and looked down in time to see a sob escape my friend.

"He didn't. He grabbed me by my hair and pulled me back to stand. My legs were wobbling, but it didn't matter because he didn't need me to stand as he bent his elbow back and threw his fist straight into my cheek."

I was safe here in the Forest. Here, it was funny what I endured day to day. Because my dreams always showed me that my life was one long, drawn out, cruel fucking joke. I could only hope the punch line would be a hole dug six feet into the ground and a stone with my name carved into it.

"Blood and spit poured out of my mouth, I focused on the spot where the crimson liquid muddied the dirt road." My voice was quieter now, the metallic tang still lingered on my tongue and reminded me of the ever present throb in my face.

The Dwarven woman squeezed my hand repeatedly. The blows to my face could have easily been the end of my life, but not even the Angel of Death would show himself in Holleberg.

It wasn't uncommon for Lord Bosque, Holleberg's wicked leader, to allow his men to abuse women. In fact, cruelty was encouraged to keep us subservient. He wanted all of his villagers to know that the palace was the power. No hierarchy existed here. You were either poor and hungry or one of his demons. At least today it was a physical attack and not one to my womanhood. I wasn't sure how many pieces left of that I had for them to take by force.

To escape this life, I dreamed. There was no time to dream or hope for a better life when I was awake so I used every moment of rest to picture a place far from here. Though my dreams always brought me here to the Forest. The one the elders spoke of that bordered Holleberg and was known to be a purgatory for Lost Souls and all things malevolent. I would never be so stupid to go there when I was awake but in my dreams, it was safe. When I fight evil here, I win. I leave unscathed and with my faith halfway restored in a God I wasn't sure I could believe in anymore.

Then I'd wake up and do it all over again.

Wake up, suffer. Dream, conquer.

Someday, I *will* find sanctuary.

Through the dangling branches, a woman with pin straight, black hair lurked beyond the weeping willows. Like my dwarf friend, her face had never been clear to me. Just skin and her raven locks to frame the sharp boundaries of her face. I didn't know her the way I knew the dwarf, but I knew her routine.

Any time the woman would appear, my friend would retreat. She wouldn't go anywhere near her. I wasn't afraid of her, but I felt her presence the way I feel a storm rolling in on the clouds. Walking alone toward the woman in the willows, I reached for her outstretched hand on my approach.

I didn't like taking her hand, but she always took me to my

prince. Then he would take me to the palace that overlooked the vast sea of deep blue water. But before I could let my palm reach hers, she evaporated into somewhere between awake and asleep.

"Ammy!" A tiny voice cut through the haze of my dream, and I watched the woman and the expanse of the haunted forest fade to black before a new haunt began.

Sticky fingers pushed my cheeks together. I fluttered my eyes open to see my youngest brother sitting criss crossed on my chest, waiting for our morning routine to begin.

I squeezed his body close to mine, trapping him as I forced the best baby giggles known to man out of him. Each day, Tildan woke me up in anticipation of his morning tickles. In his own way, he knew that joy could only be found, not given in Holleberg.

"Hi bug," I said, pressing a kiss into his floppy blonde hair and taking in the distinct baby smell that still lingered at the top of his head. We both looked to the door when the sound of clumsy skips pounded on the creaky wooden floorboards the hallway.

Right on cue, Hansel, the second youngest, bounced into my room and plopped on the bed. "Morning, Amelie!" He didn't wait for permission before he, too, piled his frail body onto mine. "Do you remember what today is?" Stars shone in his eyes. My brothers all inherited my father's pretty brown eyes, I had my mother's deep blue eyes with golden rivers flowing in them. Hansel and Tildan's still had their twinkle, though. Wren, the oldest of my younger brothers, his eyes were darkened now, having taken on the responsibilities of the head of household since father passed.

"Mhhh… Christmas?" I teased, knowing full well what August 21st was. Hansel furrowed his brows and his mouth tilted downward.

"It's my birthday," he deadpanned.

"No, your birthday was last year," I urged, brushing a

piece of his shaggy, light brown waves off of his freckled face. His cheeks were tight, attempting to suppress his megawatt smile.

"Everyone gets a birthday every year." He pointed out.

"I distinctly remember you turning six last year, you don't get to be any older than that. I won't let you."

His body rumbled into a belly laugh. He's talked non-stop about how important his seventh birthday was. Wren's been taunting him that all the big kid things happen when you turn seven, so Hansel's imagination had him counting down the days.

I gave Tildan a plotting look, and his two front teeth peeked through his smile. We tackled Hansel, tickling him relentlessly. Hansel burst at the seams, trying to catch his breath through the laughter.

"Happy Birthday, Hansel." I gave my brother a kiss on the cheek.

"Can I have a cake?" Hansel dropped his hopeful eyes to his fingers. He twiddled them together, anxiously awaiting an answer.

Hansel made every day the best day ever, but I knew it was only a way to cope. Just like dreaming was for me. The best day ever would be the day we escaped this hell.

"I'll try my best, buddy." Knowing that there was little I could do to find anything in our rations to bake with.

"It's okay if I don't get one. Someday I'm going to make so many cakes for all the birthdays we didn't get one for. For me, you, Tildie, and Wren." Hansel promised.

"That's a lot of sugar." I tucked both of my littlest brothers into my arms tight, holding onto their innocence for dear life.

Hansel was a storyteller. His mind went to places not even I could dream of and half the time I felt the need to redirect it back to reality, but then I would be a hypocrite. Someday, I knew the next generations would relay the stories he told.

They'd say *The great traveler Hansel once said…* then tell the most fantastical stories of my little brother's adventures. Even if they are all made up.

"Let's go, boys! I'm running late."

Wren's voice struck us like lightning. All three of our backs went ramrod straight. Tildan and Hansel come to me for fun, but Wren for structure. He was a man in a teenager's body.

Hansel hid under my quilt. Tildan bounced to the edge of the bed to meet Wren at my door.

The expression on my thirteen-year-old brother's face would make a soldier shake in his boots. Wren's brows were pinched and his caramel-colored curls were wet and falling into his face. He stared at the younger two who were still exhaling their morning breath and lounging in their pajamas.

I scooped Hansel up and stepped onto the creaky wood floor below me. It threatened to fall straight into the sitting room below us but held on for yet another day.

"I have to go, Amelie!" Wren motioned to the two boys that were not ready for the day with pure frustration on his face.

"You can head out. I'll get Hansel to school and drop Tildie at Magda's."

Wren's jaw twitched at the lack of control he had. I was the oldest and would turn twenty-five in just a few months, but Wren wanted to take care of the house. He'd tried so hard to fill our father's big shoes since he left, but he was still just a little boy.

"Fine," Wren bit out as he went for the stairs to leave. On a normal day, Wren wandered the perimeter of the Whispering Forest to collect berries and herbs. Only the perimeter. No one would dare to cross the tree line. It was the beginning of harvest season, though, so he would spend the morning foraging, then help the farmers in the fields in the afternoon.

I directed the two younger boys to get dressed and

followed Wren into the kitchen downstairs, where he loaded up his satchel with his Palace issued tools.

"I'm going to find something sweet for him to have at dinner," I told Wren, fidgeting with the back of the chair. I had over ten years on the kid but he wasn't a dreamer like me and Hansel. He'd let his light fizzle out long ago.

"Don't get his hopes up," he replied without looking my way. "You need attention from the Palace like the mice need more holes in our walls to live in."

I looked to the wall in the living room, noting that the mice absolutely did not need another hole to burrow in.

I'd been caught stealing from the bakery a few times, but the guard that seized the goods always let me go. He was older, probably around my father's age. Of all the guards, he was the only one who never hurt me. Even when he caught me committing a crime and most of the guard's had hurt me for doing a lot less.

"I'll be safe, I promise," I lied, and Wren knew it. There wasn't a way to be safe in Holleberg. As ironclad as my heart had become, my body wasn't as strong. Our rations had dwindled to almost nothing, so I always gave the majority of mine to the boys. A few pieces of stale bread, warm slices of meat, cheese that often had mold already crawling over it, and murky water.

"Taven has us off early tonight because of the colder weather. I'll be home around the same time as you," Wren announced as he threw the satchel over his shoulder and walked out the door, not sparing me a glance as his head dropped in submission to whatever his day was about to entail.

Two sets of feet came up behind me.

"Ready." Hansel dramatically swept his arms down his body showing off the outfit he chose for himself.

I turned to see him wearing a striped shirt with holes in the neckline and jeans that had dirt stains all over them. The frayed hem at the bottom threatened to unravel completely if he stepped on them wrong. Tildan was still in his jammies, and I couldn't be bothered to change them.

"Very handsome, birthday boy. Let's get you off to school."

AFTER GETTING Hansel dropped off and Tildan to Magda's, a family friend who watched the baby during the day, I went back home to get ready for work.

I pulled on a skirt that was two sizes too big and already dotted in shoe polish and pulled my cream knitted sweater over my head. My shoulder was entirely exposed in it, thanks to the gaping hole in the shoulder from the time a guard threw me to the ground for no good fucking reason. Grabbing a ribbon from the clay dish my father made for me, I blindly braided my frizzy, dark chocolate hair. If you lined me and my siblings up, it would look like a quill running out of ink on the paper.

In the mirror, I noticed my swollen lip and fresh bruises. Blood vessels had burst throughout my cheeks and added a purple hue to the dark circles covering my right eye. My eyes were the only thing left that had any light to them. The deep blue color accompanied by the streaks of gold that ran through them were the only thing about me that I thought was pretty.

People always told me I looked like my mother when she was younger. *You're a vision, Amelie. Just like your mother,* they'd say. I blocked the thought of being my mother's replica as I stepped into her room to visit her before I went to work.

"Hi mama," I announced only to be polite. Her sickness made her catatonic. She wouldn't speak or even acknowledge my presence. She was a ghost of the woman she once was.

I rolled her each way, putting a clean set of sheets on her bed and throwing her soiled ones in a hamper. Her hair was matted on the side from where she'd been lying since last night. I did my best to brush it and put it into a new braid. Then I stripped her down to wash her body. If I was catatonic, I think my children having to wash all my bits and pieces would be enough to bring me out of it.

She was diagnosed with Melancholia last year by the village healer. After losing father she was distraught, but then she nearly died delivering Tildan. She's been in this bed ever since. The healer said it was common after having a baby for a mother to lose herself for a while. But this was extreme, this was neglect. Not only to us, but herself. My mother was a radiant, lively woman. She and my father could make the air in this home feel like breathing in magic. My father loved to swing her around the house as she accompanied their dancing with her singing, badly, I may add. But nonetheless, their joy drowned out the sounds of our rumbling bellies and soothed the bruises on our bodies.

Now? My mother's body was a vessel. A part of her soul died with my father, whatever she had left was mopped up by the healer after Tildan's birth. Her lack of contribution to Holleberg brought her rations to barely a bite per day. Not enough to share with the rest of us, and not nearly enough to sustain her.

I grabbed a chair and sat in front of her as she continued to stare through the wall of her room. Her hand was icy as I grabbed it and brought it close to me.

"It's Hansel's birthday today." I was talking into an empty abyss. "He really wants a cake, but I know that he'd want you to get up more than any variation of a cake I could come up with."

Tears formed in her eyes, a sign of life I hadn't gotten from her in months.

"I know you're hurting, mama. But we need you. The boys

need you. We miss you and papa the same, but you're alive. That's not right…" I trailed off, choking back the cotton in my throat.

The dam broke. Her tears fell in a steady stream down her cheek. She pulled her hand from mine and tucked it back into her body.

Her rich, dark hair was graying, and her eyes were no longer an exact match to mine. Mine might not hold a lot of hope, but they weren't entirely lifeless like my mother's.

"Please, Mama," I begged her once more. She curled into her body, trying to hide away from my words.

A tear slipped from my eye, but I wiped it away quickly. Everyone here was bruised and beaten. Whether it was one's soul that's been battered or our body, the marks are all the same so there's no use in crying about them.

I shoved the chair back into the corner as I stood and left her with my plea, then strode out the front door with my ripped satchel.

It was a rather short walk to work. I kept my head down and tried to avoid catching the attention of the guards. Since the last time I stole some vegetables from a merchant's cart, I'd been under the Palace's watchful, dangerous eye.

Approaching the bakery, I peeked through the dusty window and noted where the sugar was stocked and exactly where patrons needed to be standing in order for me to swipe it. There were a few smaller jars rationed for the villagers to buy. I'm sure it was cheaper too. My wages from working at Henrik's were still being garnished by the palace to pay back my father's funeral costs, so stealing was my only option. The imaginary pennies I dreamed of in my pockets wouldn't suffice. The rich were getting richer, and the hungry would only get hungrier.

A sinister feeling tickled up my spine, accompanied by the clop of large footsteps and the putrid smell of a rotting soul. In the reflection, a tall, fat figure stalked up behind me. I turned on my heel away from the window and picked up my pace, hoping to create distance, but with each of my steps, two more hammered down quicker behind me. The thud of my heart in my ears now also joining the race.

Henrik's store was one more block down. I kept my gaze tunneled in on the faded green door and the shards of wood protruding from it.

A large hand collapsed over my shoulder and pushed me with such force that it was a miracle I stayed on my feet. Twisting enough to see which of the guard's it was, my heart ripped against my chest at the sight of the same man responsible for my freshest bruises.

"What do we have here?" He plucked the tied-together strap of my satchel off my shoulder.

"I don't want any trouble." I scrambled backwards. This guard in particular had hurt me before, many times. He'd beat me, taken parts of my womanhood I'm not sure I could ever have back, spat on me. Broke my collarbone, bit me. Someday, I hoped a version of him would visit me in my dreams where I could beat him once and for all.

Only five more steps. That's all I had left and I'd be under Henrik's watchful eye. They wouldn't hurt me in front of him.

The greasy man pushed me again, but this time it closed the distance between me and the splintered door to the shoe shop. I swung it open and tumbled inside.

"Amelie—what..." Henrik assessed the situation quickly and schooled his features to address the guard standing in the doorway with his eyes locked on my body. The guard's eyes were dark, sinister. Void of humanity.

"I'll take it from here, Rad. Thank you." Henrik's voice was stoic.

Rad narrowed his eyes at me but relented and closed the door behind him as he started toward the palace. My eyes couldn't stop watching him walk away. I needed to know he was gone for myself. I let the second tear of the day fall from my desperate soul and got to my feet, eyes still on him. Rad turned back toward the shop, a smile spread across his face, and my stomach folded in on itself. I tore my eyes away, praying to a God I knew never heard my pleas that Rad didn't take my stare as an invitation.

"Sorry," I said while sniffling back the ball in my throat. "Where should I start today?"

Henrik eyed the new bruises on my face and took a deep breath before letting us move on.

"Head to the back. Finish up those soles on Mr. Brandhuft's boots. Then shine up the orders going out tomorrow."

I nodded and went straight to my station in the back. The rest of the day, I took out my frustrations on the bottoms of the helpless boots and hoped these soles would tread lightly in this hell we lived in.

CHAPTER 2

Amelie

"Amelie, get yourself together. The guards are heading our way."

Lightning struck my spine, straightening painfully at the mention of the guards. I had already finished the last pair of shoes that needed shining, and I prayed Henrik had more for me to do so they couldn't take me.

The guards typically left Henrik's store alone. He lived as by the book as one could. While the guards were abusive and disgusting versions of men, Henrik, along with most of the non-Palace affiliated men in Holleberg, were just trying to survive like the rest of us.

We finish school at twelve and are expected to have a job immediately after. I walked into the shop battered and bruised the week before we graduated asking for a job. Henrik's looked after me ever since. When my father passed, he was the only one privy to my tears.

Henrik's shoe shop was nestled at the end of a three-way stop. If you walked straight down from the Palace, you'd walk right into it.

I pulled at the hem of my top in a nervous attempt to iron it out. The bottom of my tattered skirt was caked in wet mud from dragging on the ground. Tucking the stray hairs that had escaped my messy braid behind my ear, I started for the front of the shop. The soles of my boots were so worn that they flopped against the ground with each step, squishing cold rainwater and clumps of dirt into my socks, making my toes numb.

I stepped out from the backroom, Henrik was dead on the money. The guards were walking straight toward us. Three sets of eyes were locked on the door to the shop.

The guards' hands were resting on their daggers casually as they stepped through the threshold. Fear cowered in my veins, my heart thundered against my chest. Heat seemed to prick at my eyes as if a match had just missed the strike pad. The one to the left was the culprit behind my bruised face and broken satchel, Rad.

He was big and burly. His uniform looked like it would pop at the seams if he moved wrong. His hair was so greasy, it was hard to decide if it was brown or blonde.

The one on the right had bright blonde hair and looked just like the one in the middle, but younger. His muscles were on display through the navy tops they wore, and he held a stony expression on his face.

"Good afternoon." The guard in the middle spoke first. He was the one who never reported me for thieving. His blue eyes creased at the sides, showing his age, but he was otherwise a very fit man. I didn't know much about him, but I could see his rank on his lapel.

He was Lord Bosque's right-hand man and head guard.

"To what do we owe the pleasure, Arthur?" Henrik replied, keeping a pleasant expression on his face.

"We are collecting profits early this month," Arthur said. Rad was threatening me with his eyes—narrowed and fierce. His nose was twitching on one side and his jaw clenched tight. I couldn't peel my eyes away, afraid if I did he'd pounce.

"But there's still a week left to get them in order?" Henrik stuffed his hands in his pockets, trying to remain calm. The last time the Palace did this, they didn't report what they took, so when the real collectors came, none of the businesses could match their records for payment. Every shop on this block was still trying to recover from that.

"Lord's orders." Arthur puffed his chest out slightly, but not confidently. He'd always been kind to me, or as kind as a guard could be. Right now, though, it seemed like this wasn't something he was proud to be doing for Lord Bosque.

Henrik moved to the desk and started gathering each of the detailed logs he kept, along with the monies owed. All the money in Holleberg went through the Palace, and they conveniently failed to redistribute our wages fairly every month.

I kept a keen eye on the guards, specifically Rad. He'd been the man behind so many of my bruises before that I wouldn't put it past him to attack right here. But fuck, my eyes were on fire. I reminded myself to blink but it wasn't helping.

"Should be all there." Henrik handed over his records along with a canvas bag of jingling coins. "Will this be reported?" he asked Arthur in a hushed tone. Arthur didn't answer and instead gave Henrik and me an apologetic look instead. If this isn't reported, I'll have no wages to garnish. Henrik will fall even further behind on what he owed the Palace each month.

It's a trap, it always was.

Arthur and his quiet, blonde counterpart turned to leave, but Rad lingered long enough to send a fleet of spiders crawling over my skin. All of them settling in my stomach, making it churn. I swallowed the bile rising in my throat as he gave me another nasty smile before following his leader out the door.

I shook off the feeling that was settling deep in the marrow of my bones. Henrik bowed his head in his hands against the desk.

If I could burn the palace down, along with all the guard's in it, I would.

"You should be on your way home." Henrik's voice was muffled by his palms.

I grabbed my bag off the hook and gave Henrik a soothing touch to his shoulder. A shaky breath escaped him and I took that as my sign to leave. Nobody in Holleberg wanted to be caught crying. Tears were wasted water, life was miserable whether you cried about it or not.

I walked out of the store, feeling the humid August air on my face. Taking a good look around and making sure it was safe from any lurking guards, I started on my way home. There were usually two guards patrolling this street at all times and others that lingered just to prey on us but I didn't see anybody.

The bakery was one shop down so I discreetly looked over my shoulder, most women kept their heads down when they walked anywhere. At this point we knew the way home better than our own heartbeat.

A mother, father, and child were walking into the bakery and I sent a silent prayer up to God that there were a few more patrons inside. If it were even a few weeks later into the year, I would need my cloak and could hide under its hood but unfortunately my face would be on full display today.

Keeping my eyes trained on the toes of my boots, I walked into the bakery as another walked out. Good start. The child that walked in before was begging his mother for a sweet, the checker was talking with the father. I went straight for the shelf that had the spare ingredients and acted like I was browsing. When my eyes landed on the small glass jar I spotted earlier, I swiped it and tucked it into my bag with ease.

"Can I help you find anything?" The checker called from behind the counter. I took in a sharp breath, turning to give him a halfhearted smile.

"Just looking," I said, trying my hardest to not make eye

contact. It was horrible to steal, I knew that. Henrik let me take home shoes I'd made from spare materials for the boys and that felt icky enough. Stealing from someone who was under the same ruin as the rest of the shop owners and villagers in this town just felt wrong.

But it was for the birthday boy.

I spun on my heel to head back for the door when a haunting face in the window took the breath clean out of me. I couldn't move.

Rad's huge, greasy body was stealing any natural light from pouring into the bakery. My heart thudded in my ears.

His eyes were hungry, antagonizing. He stared at me but his lips were curled up in a way that made my gut roll in unease.

"Do you have a back door?" I called back to the checker. When I turned toward him, I noticed the pale coloring and fear etched across his face as he stared at the guard outside. He nodded subtly at me, the innocent family now caught in the crossfire.

I noted the door behind him that appeared to have sunlight poking through the cracks. In a dead sprint, I swung the door open and jumped down the three stairs, hitting ground and stumbling for a moment. I took a hard left, running parallel to the backs of the shops until the dilapidated homes came into view.

"You can run, but you can't hide," a breathless Rad shouted from behind me. My heart crashed wildly, my lungs were burning from the inside out, and my shoes were barely holding together.

I could see a large body in the spaces between the homes. My only hope was to cut through someone's yard and throw Rad off my trail.

Running between two houses, I took a sharp turn toward my own. Down the way, I could see Wren carrying Tildan inside. I tried to shout to them to get inside quickly but my winded lungs were void of sound.

Only a few more–

Ow. Fuck.

What was that?

My hair was yanked from behind me, picking me up from the ground I'd apparently collapsed onto. My head bobbed backward as the pain settled at the nape of my neck. The last few seconds came back to me, and I realized I had taken a blow to the side of my head. My body was being dragged in between my home and the neighbors.

"I love the chase, whore," a slimy voice whispered into my ear. I looked at my home, through the kitchen window, I saw Wren staring at me with glassy brown eyes. Hansel was bouncing behind him, trying to see, but Wren wasn't letting him watch as Rad dragged me away.

My brain was telling me to close my eyes, to concede. Let Holleberg win. I never wanted to kill myself, I had people depending on me. But that's not to say if Heaven opened its pearly gates and God himself came down and said, *"If you're ready, you may come now,"* that I wouldn't go.

Just before I could fully let go, I heard something I wasn't sure I'd ever hear again.

"Mama?" Hansel's voice was loud and full of excitement. It encouraged me to take one last look at my home before the guards finally took my life.

There she was, floating slowly toward the seat that was always hers at the kitchen table. The one that stayed vacant for the last year and a half.

As I closed my eyes, hopefully for good, I pictured that I was sitting at the table with them. The prickly grass pierced my cheek. My skirt pooled at the top of my upturned hips. I kept my eyes closed, though. I didn't want to live through this again. Tears fell from my eyes, watering the soil below me. Rad's body crashed into mine over and over again. I thought

I'd dried myself of tears by now, but a reserve that was saved for this very moment opened up.

His palm pressed between my shoulder blades, crushing me further into the ground. The smell of alcohol wafted off him.

A whimper escaped me as my already bruised cheek broke open against the grass. I wasn't sure what he was doing, I couldn't feel anymore. I couldn't let myself. Whatever was left of my soul was gone. I sent one more silent prayer up to God, but I knew it would fall on deaf ears.

His body moved against mine as my skirt grew heavier on my lower back. A force pushed against my body and for a moment it felt like no one was touching me. A release, maybe my mind tricking me into thinking I owned my body again. As the sound of the outdoors flowed back to my ears, there was a commotion behind me. I was lying by myself on the cool ground, my eyes barely opened but it was enough to see a set of boots approach me, scoop me up and carry me away.

PEELING MY EYES OPEN, a sky full of stars danced across my vision. It was much darker than I imagined Heaven might be. Cement blocks were piled high and closed me into a small box, the door had bars covering a tiny window at the top of it.

I laid on a tiny bed, even smaller than the one I had at home. Not daring to move I let the chilled draft tousle the stained sheets covering me.

My brain tried to regain its ability to think straight. I sat up with a groan, the pounding in my head sent a crushing pain through the side of my face that was now triply bruised. The pads of my fingers grazed that area with a feather-light touch, I shuddered at how fragile I felt. How many times can one's cheek break before it can never heal again? Furthering the pain as the pressure built in my cheek. Fire set off in my eyes, the tears that brimmed were fighting the flames.

"Fuck," I muttered to myself.

Footsteps at the door now had my heart matching the throb in my head. If this was Heaven, God needed a new decorator but I knew it wasn't. There was no pain or suffering in the supposed Heaven.

This was hell, which meant I was still in Holleberg.

"She's awake," the blonde guard from earlier said to someone approaching in the hallway.

Arthur slid past him, followed by Igor, Lord Bosque's son. He was said to be just as wicked as his father but those of us who dwelled at the bottom of their totem pole never saw him. He shared his father's brown eyes and sandy blonde hair. He was tall and well fed with toned muscles.

I looked down at my folded hands in my lap, not wanting to face whatever consequence I was about to endure. I breathed easier knowing that Rad wasn't in the room with us.

"We have some things to talk about." Arthur crouched at my side.

"I promise I won't steal again." It was an empty promise. The only way my family survived thus far was because of Wren only turning in half of what he'd foraged and my sleight of hand at merchant tables.

"Rad will never hurt you again." Arthur ignored my plea. My breathing picked up at the mere mention of his name, and the memories of what he'd done to me in the last few days tried to push to the forefront. I willed it back, along with the lump that was stuck in my throat.

Arthur positioned a curled finger under my chin and lifted it to force me to look at him.

"Did you hear me?" He tilted his head and I noticed how much he reminded me of my father at that moment, aside from his blue eyes. I nodded back to him, blinking back my tears. I didn't want to cry in front of any guard. "You are due in front of Lord Bosque now. Can you walk?"

I looked at Arthur, then Igor, wondering why I had to face the Lord right now.

"Rad's counterpart reported the theft. I can't get you out of this one."

My chest heaved. Surely I had at least one broken rib. Each breath felt like I was being stabbed.

It was not uncommon for women to be abused here. Being raped was just another form of it. I always preferred the blows from their fists to the violation of my soul. The last few days had been a proper test of faith. Faith I had little left of to test. Does God watch the abuse? Does he approve of the men that were created in his image?

The first time it happened, I was eleven. I had just left school and was walking home with my only friend, Prita. She lived closer to the school than I did so I walked the last bit alone, I still remember the goliath hands that wrapped around my neck like a scarf. He told me if I screamed for help or told anyone, he'd kill me. I walked in our front door with dark blue finger marks all over my neck, I didn't need to explain to my mother what had happened. She requested for me to be put on the birth control tea immediately, and the Palace granted the request.

It only took a few more times of being raped by the guards to know why birth control tea was so generously distributed. No one should ever have to say *a few more times of being raped* but it's been thirteen years since the first time, and it's never stopped.

"Is he going to take my hands?" The only punishment I knew of for a thief in Holleberg.

Arthur looked at the floor. The energy of the men in this room was not the evil kind I was used to. Igor and the blonde guard were standing shoulder to shoulder, almost leaning on each other. But I didn't know why they needed the comforting.

"I'm not sure. I'll do everything I can to help your case."

He stood and took my hand to help me do the same. I shuddered as we neared Igor. How he could watch someone be taken in front of his father to be punished so cruelly was beyond me.

I quickly realized we were in the cellars of the Palace. It was cold and the stone walls were shining like they were wet. Bile rose in my throat as the smell of rotting milk and mold from the water got stronger and stronger.

I stumbled as the pain that riddled my body pleaded for rest and recovery. Arthur caught me and threw my arm over his shoulder. My consciousness fading.

"Liam, grab the other side." Liam, the blonde guard, took my other arm over his shoulders and the two of them carried me to the common level of the Palace where villagers received their sentencing.

It was a large, open room with dark grey marbled floors. The Lord and Lady sat in their oversized chairs with stoic, arrogant faces. Large red and white banners hung from the walls, covering what looked like windows if the light that tried to shine through was any indication.

"Another thief in my village," Lord Bosque's poisonous voice boomed through the room as we approached.

Arthur and Liam dropped my shoulders, and without warning of it, I fell to my knees, giving our ruler the idea that I was bowing to him.

"I give enough rations to the villagers, and if you've used yours up, that is not the problem of the Palace, yet you made it our problem." He leaned on one elbow, entirely unconcerned with the punishment he was about to invoke. "You know the punishment for being a thief?"

I nodded.

"Use your words, peasant."

As I lifted my bruised face to meet his wicked eyes, my hair fell over my shoulders, the frayed ends scratched at my arms.

"I do, my Lord. I will repent however you deem fair." What I wanted to tell him was to go fuck himself the way his guards did me. Then maybe he'd have mercy on the souls he was stealing here.

Igor strutted up to his father, a confidence that he did not wear earlier surrounding him.

Lord Bosque leaned over the arm of the chair further to hear whatever Igor was whispering in his ear.

Standing at his father's side, I noticed him wink at Arthur, who was standing behind me now.

"Arthur, take her hands. The healer is unavailable this evening, so wrap the wounds. If she dies from the blood loss, she dies." Lord Bosque reached for his wife's hand. She smiled at him, pleased with her husband's viscous punishment. I stumbled to stand, barely able to fill my lungs with air.

"My Lord, may I suggest a better punishment? She's a thief. She will find other ways to steal." Arthur's words hit my heart like a bolt of lightning. He said he would try to help me. He'd always been kind to me, I never understood why, but now I wondered if it was him playing the long game to grant me an even worse fate than a one time offense.

"I'm listening," Lord Bosque drawled, tilting his head in wait.

CHAPTER 3

Amelie

"What if we sent her into the Whispering Forest? Let the monsters take care of her."

My skin covered in a gleam of cool sweat instantly at the mere mention of the Forest that haunted Holleberg's dreams, let alone the sentiment that I might find my end there.

"Arthur, you never fail in your service to the Palace. That is a fantastic idea." Lady Bosque's voice was joyous as she clapped her hands together and looked at the two-faced fucking guard standing next to me. "Dear, I think this would set a wonderful example of the zero tolerance we take to thievery," she drawled to her husband.

Lord Bosque ignored his wife, his eyes deadlocked on mine. Igor rested a hand on his father's shoulder and shared a look that I could only explain as agreement.

"Very well." Lord Bosque stood from his luxurious red velvet chair and started walking in my direction. I got to my feet. My body ached in all the familiar places but I wouldn't let my position on the floor be mistaken as obedience toward the piece of shit who ruled my village.

Arthur tugged at the back of my shirt, almost like he was trying to bring me closer to him.

"Arthur, prepare the girl to be released to the Forest," Lord Bosque said, keeping his eyes on mine before looking to his head guard. "Then take care of that family of hers. The Bloch's have caused enough trouble for this village."

I thought I might pass out. Not only would my soul be stolen from me by the evil that lurked in the Forest but my family would be punished for my offense too?

"If you touch my fam—"

"Silence!" Lord Bosque shouted as his palm struck the already bruised side of my face. Blood spewed from my mouth, painting the immaculate marbled floors crimson. Arthur's hold on my shirt kept me upright.

Igor and Arthur carried me away from Lord Bosque like a rag doll. He wore a sick smile on his face as he watched one of his villagers being dragged away to her death.

"Fight us," Arthur whispered. I hesitated, feeling like it was a taunt. But his slow nod told me it was a show. So I kicked my legs, and wrestled my arms in theirs the best I could through the pain.

"Keep fighting, sell it," Igor piped up now. I wasn't sure why they were encouraging me to fight until I heard a sinister laugh escape Lord Bosque's mouth as his head rolled back. We rounded the corner just in time for the evil view of laughter in the face of a death sentence to disappear.

Igor and Arthur let my feet find the floor, but Arthur kept a firm hold on the back of my arm. I noticed the guards that lined the hallways looking at us, their eyes were full of hunger as they studied my abused body. The pads of Arthur's fingers were absolutely going to leave a mark but it didn't feel like the evil touches I'd felt so many times before from the guards.

Not once had Arthur ever made me feel unsafe. Not until he offered my life up to the Forest that threatened my village daily with the stories passed down through generations.

A minimum of thirty sets of eyes took me in and watched as Lord Bosque's head guard and son escorted me to the last door in the hallway. Was this where we'd came from before? We stepped through to be greeted with a deep pit in the earth and spiral staircase.

"Where are you taking me?" I demanded from either of them.

"Just stay quiet a little longer." Arthur led us down the stairs, taking my hand to support me.

As we descended, I noticed the vision in my right eye narrowed to only a tiny slit. The swelling was setting in, along with the slow thump of blood rushing to the area. Maybe if I was lucky, a brain bleed would kill me before the Forest could.

"Only a few more stairs to go. Are you feeling okay?" Arthur's voice echoed through the damp smelling archway we were approaching. It was dark and cold ahead, a metaphor for what I imagine death felt like.

"No."

Arthur halted briefly, letting me rest against his back. I wrapped my arms around his neck and he bent to grab my legs and hoist me onto him. Nausea rolled through my stomach and threatened its way up my throat.

Arthur stepped into the hallway, small lanterns spread twenty feet apart from each other giving the already creepy dungeon a worse feeling. Iron doors lined either side and it hit me that this was where I woke up earlier. The putrid smell rushed a wave of adrenaline through my body.

"What's going on?" I choked out.

"You'll leave through here." Arthur opened one of the heavy cellar doors, setting my unsteady feet on the cold ground. I shook my head but Igor braced his hands on my shoulders and guided me forward.

"It's safe," he assured. "Come on."

Walking through the threshold, I noticed it was the same cell I was in before. This time, though, the bed had been lifted and Arthur was holding it up, exposing a human sized hole in the ground.

"What the hell is this? A tunnel?"

"When the palace was built, we tried over and over again to fill this hole with cement. Every time we'd come to check if it had dried, it would be wide open. Igor and Liam were playing when they were little and found it, they figured out it was a tunnel," Arthur explained, adjusting the bed against the wall so it stood on its own.

"Does Lord Bosque know?" I asked, trembling at the thought of going underground for my escape.

"No. He knows about the hole but he has no idea it's a way out of the palace."

"So, where will I end up?"

"At the tree line behind the palace. When you resurface, you will be shaded but you'll need to be quick or the moonlight might spot you."

Suddenly, this all started to feel like a quest from my dreams. Something my unconscious self would muster up, but awake Amelie would know better than to do. Survival 101 and all that.

The dreamer in me couldn't help but wonder what might find me on the other end. After all, this was a portal of sorts.

Arthur must've heard my heart beating as I focused in on the hole because my gaze was ripped from it as he cupped my cheeks in his hands.

"Amelie, this is important, okay? You need to listen to every word I say."

I nod the best I can in his hold.

My heart spun out of control. I wouldn't be surprised if it exploded in the next beat. To my surprise, it didn't.

"When you get to the trees, you are going to run. You aren't going to stop, sweetheart. Even when you feel like you couldn't possibly take another step, you take another and then take one hundred more." His tone was full of determination.

"Do you know of the ravine behind the palace?" I nod. "You are going to run through it, it will lead you to the other side of the mountain. Once you're on the other side, follow the river to the fork. Cross it, it will be deeper where it splits so be careful. Follow the stream as far as it will take you." He released my chin and allowed me to get my bearings.

"Do you understand Amelie? Can you do that?"

I tried to steady my breath and wondered how the fuck I was going to survive the night with broken ribs and a swollen eye. Not to mention all the evil things that lurked out there.

Nothing about this made any sense. Arthur had always looked out for me in his own way, but now he was sacrificing me to the Forest.

"Why would you send me to the Forest?" I was wasting precious time and finding it suspicious that I'm being led to the one place we've been told our entire lives to stay away from.

"Lord Bosque will want to see you away, so it's best to go now. You will be safe there."

I could tell Arthur's patience was wearing, but none of it made sense.

"How could you possibly know that I'll be safe there? You—" I pause to gesture toward all three of them. "All of you know what they say about the Forest…"

Arthur studied my eyes, seemingly following the flow of the gold rivers in them. He rolled his lips together and took a deep breath in then exhaled it slowly.

"You're a Bloch. Some things you'll need to learn on your own. Trust me, please." His please was a near whisper. Like it pained him to say.

"How could I trust you? I don't even know you." I searched his face for a lie, but I couldn't find one. Though Arthur never hurt me, he *was* Lord Bosque's head guard.

Arthur let out another long breath, his eyes laced with what looked like regret.

"Because I promised my brother I would take care of his

family, and I haven't done a good enough job thus far. I won't fail you or our family any further. There's too much at stake."

More confused than I was before, I asked one last question as I took a step down into the ground. "Your brother?"

"Alfred Bloch."

My father.

TO MY SURPRISE, the tunnel was short. It couldn't have taken longer than twenty minutes to get from the beginning to the end. I had to dig myself out where it opened into the tree line but so far it was manageable. So far, no danger. Adrenaline raced through my blood as I watched the moonlight creep closer and closer to the trees. I wiped my dirt caked hands on my satchel, trying to distract from the heavy feeling creeping in my gut.

Determination heated my skin, veiling my aching body and giving me a false sense of confidence that I might just survive this. I needed to believe Arthur, my uncle apparently, that it would be safe out here. If I spent too much time looking for a monster under the guise of night, my opportune escape would be meaningless. But I didn't need to look, I could *feel* it. The dark magic radiated from behind me, wrapping around my shoulders and curling itself down to the marrow of my bones. It was so fucking powerful.

I took one last fleeting look at my village, a soft glow shone in the window of the small, broken home I grew up in. Looking up to God's sky, I prayed they would be alright. Begged Him to have mercy on their souls should the Palace come for them. I needed them to be okay so this didn't feel so cruel. My heart was cracking at the thought of leaving them here. *Arthur wouldn't let it happen*, I soothed myself.

God and His angel's started a slow crescendo on their drums as thunder drew closer to Holleberg. Lightening struck, illuminating for a fleeting moment what I would leave behind. Save for the three little boys, a mother, and a headstone—it wasn't much.

So I turned my back on the only place I'd ever known and crossed the line I wasn't sure I'd ever come back from.

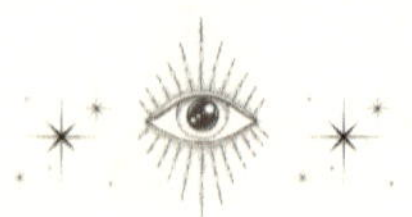

I MIGHT AS WELL HAVE BEEN a bird in the open summer air, not a cloud in sight. Just me and the open sky, soaring.

The ravine was easy to clear, just as Arthur said it would be. The moon was strung high in the sky now and my labored breath was taunting me as I came out the other side. In front of me, as far as the eye could see, which wasn't very far, was nothing but thick, fluffy trees. Doing as I was told, I followed the river, feeling clumsy as I hobbled over the brush that swept the Forest floor.

The river was calm, a stark contrast to my turbulence that flowed alongside it. If I had more time with my uncle, I would've at least asked how far to the fork. One, because I couldn't see shit and two, because I was already feeling like I couldn't keep this pace up for very long.

At least another twenty minutes passed before I heard it. The babbling sound of water moving over rocks, it had to be the fork. The sound grew louder and louder until it was right there beside me. Arthur wasn't kidding, this was going to be my first big hurdle.

He said it would be deeper here, the pressure of the flow changing the anatomy of the earth by the second. Assessing my safest path, I decided there wasn't one. I'm not sure how far I was from Holleberg but I knew there was no turning back. I had a better chance of finding sanctuary if I did as I was told, but I was never very good at doing what I was told.

Taking a hesitant step into the water, I *felt* the river. I took note of its strength and how deep it was. I had at least twenty feet to cross but only a foot off the embankment and the water was up to my knees. Taking as big a stride as I could, I slammed my foot down and went waist deep into the water. Calming my breathing, I continued until I reached the middle where the water soaked up to my chest.

The river was pulling and pushing like we're in line and they wanted to be first. My feet were unsteady on the rocks, slipping over the algae that's grown on them. My steps were no longer big and efficient. Shuffling along the river's bottom was the only way I kept upright.

I waited for my teeth to begin chattering, it was cold at night in Holleberg. The seasons had begun to change already. Even the leaves agreed it wasn't worth surviving through the winter. But here in the Forest, it was warm. The perfect temperature that only graced us at the beginning of summer.

My right foot slipped on an algae covered rock, causing me to stumble. The back of my head hit the water, but something caught me. *Someone.* I whipped around before I'd fully steadied myself, but I saw no one. Surely, I felt hands around my shoulders. I felt large, rough hands steady me, but it was gone.

I was alone.

Cool water dripped down my neck. My hair felt heavy on my back, sending a tingle up my spine. The river begging me to flow with it.

"Give me a break!" I screamed into the void, praying to God that the tales of the Forest silencing its victim's cries for help weren't true. My eyes pricked with heat. Anger. As the sound of my voice's echo faded through the trees. My heavy, wet hair was no longer weighing me down and the water flowing around me seemed to move in slow motion.

My brows furrowed as I watched the river that had just been racing for the finish line slow to a crawl. Using it to my advantage, I swam the rest of the way before walking out on the other side triumphant.

Knowing that the swim would cost me the rest of my clothes, I went to wring out my shirt but nothing dripped from it. I tried my skirt, same thing. My clothes were completely dry. I squeezed my braid, also dry. My body was warm and dry, as if I hadn't just been completely drenched. I looked behind me, trying to find the…magic. The essence that just helped me. But all I could see was a glow on the gentle breeze around me.

It was then that I realized Arthur didn't tell me where to go once I crossed. Maybe he thought I wouldn't make it this far. One deep breath later and I decided to continue straight. But with only one step, I was knocked to my left by a powerful gust. Little glowing flecks accompanied the wind as it floated in the direction it clearly wanted me to go.

Not wasting my time questioning the enchanted Forest, I started in another dead sprint.

Dense, thick Forest covered every square inch of the atmosphere around me but nothing was getting in my way. I mean, literally nothing. Through low hanging branches and ancient tree roots that sprawled the Forest floor cutting obstacles into what I assumed was a path, I evaporated through each one with ease. As if I wasn't solid for a moment and could just…move through solid things. My body felt light in the warm night air, my feet like blades on the ice.

I never once had a notion to enter this enchanted Forest. Tales from the elders reminded us of the witches, gremlins, and monsters that lurked at the edge of the woods. To always stay as far back as you could from the tree line to avoid being snatched.

It was easy enough to believe with all the encounters people had since settling in Holleberg. Kids had played on the low branches that wept down from the trunks and were sucked in, never to be seen again. Parents had seen it happen and rushed to warn the village. Or the couple who went to the woods for privacy and came back mangled to bits, living only long enough to tell the village that the trees were alive.

The one that stuck with me the most was the painter who sat in the same spot for months, painting the same section of the Forest day after day. Each painting showed a new creature. Gremlins that were small and had rows of long, sharp teeth. Witches casting spells straight toward the artist. Animals that looked like the ones we saw in the village but instead of cute and fluffy, they were ragged and evil. I saw those paintings and committed them to memory.

Those were the last pieces of art I had from my father.

Most of those tales were shared years before I was born but the threat still promised to act if we weren't careful.

Slowing my pace a bit and feeling as though I'd covered a good amount of ground, I took in my surroundings. Weeping willows cried, still as could be, save from the wind I created when I passed. The fir trees towered over the Forest floor. They spewed dominance, contributing to the density in a way that was bone-chilling.

The trees showed you what they wanted you to see. They were more powerful than the darkness of night in creating an illusion. A false sense of comfort when you'd see the gaps in the tree's form from where they allowed needles to fall. It made you feel like they weren't hiding things from you, but to the right or left of that gap could be something wicked waiting for you to take the bait.

A warm brush of air hit me, like a tap on the shoulder. A taunt. I wanted to stop to see what was lurking, but my feet wouldn't let me. I could feel it following me, creeping on me. There was no sound coming from the creature I'd finally encountered, though. It was silent, eerily quiet while its energy neared closer and closer.

When it reached my back, it slowly embraced my shoulders as if to steady me, comforting me then pushing me back to full speed. The touch was warm as it wrapped itself around my neck and up my face. Then my whole body was thrumming from the heat.

It was like a warm hug, carrying me through the woods. Making it almost effortless to continue through the thick without faltering.

It was unnatural, but safe. Unfamiliar, but home. As if it was changing my body's chemistry from the inside of my blood and bones. I became it. It became me.

My magical *friend* and I traveled like that for what felt like hours. The moon was still high in the sky and there was no answer for why I wasn't breathless and enervated yet. I felt the warmth pull back on me like I was in thicker air and couldn't move as swiftly. The surroundings were all the same as they had been but up ahead, the moonlight shone on what looked like a clearing. A small body of water with trickling sounds falling from it. Frogs croaked their midnight song, and crickets sang the harmony.

The thick of this Forest had been here for thousands of years, predating my village or any others. The effortless flow through my surroundings seemed to whisper…

Need not be afraid, for we know you will not bring harm to us.

You will not harm us, we will not harm you.

The hairs on the back of my neck stood at attention, that shadow was keeping my body warm, but my blood ran cold at the threat.

Then, out of thin air, a small cottage appeared in the middle of the clearing. Its stone structure showed its age and in the moonlight it appeared almost green as it reflected the Forest around it. Large vines covered the small cottage, over the windows and shutters, sealing the door with a wheel shape of overgrown branches. Smoke billowed from the chimney but there was no candlelight flickering to indicate someone being inside.

Coming to a complete stop and surveying my surroundings, I made sure I was alone and wasn't being baited into becoming something's midnight snack. There was a pond on my left. The river moved slower now, like a creek, to keep it full and safe for the creatures that lived in it. Lily pads with giant frogs floated across the top, and reeds sprouting around the perimeter swayed enough to make sounds of a lullaby.

To my right, nestled into the trees, were bushes and bushes of berries. Bright red ones, deep purple ones, and even some larger orange ones that I'd never seen before. I'd done enough foraging with the village school to know the difference between the poisonous red and purple ones. Confident that these were okay to eat, I plucked a handful from the bush. They were cool to the touch, as if they'd been chilling in an icebox. I folded my shirt up to use as a basket and picked just enough to snack on, but not so many that it would be rude.

Beyond the bushes, I saw a path. I was sure I wasn't on any specific trail on my way here, but there was one leading further into the Forest behind the cottage.

A fork in the road.

Stay in this cottage, or continue to wherever the trail would lead me.

As the question mulled in my mind, I caught the smell of warm pastries. I knew the smell well. It wafted through the village when the bakery made fresh bread for the Lord and his men. My curiosity piqued, looking into the dark cottage, the dimmest light flickered through the gaps in the vines that covered the window.

Then I saw it. The bread, the jam, even what looked like cubes of cheese. My mouth watered, and my stomach reminded me of its everlasting emptiness. The food was taunting me, but there was still no sign of life. I'd never been a thief because I enjoyed it. I'd learned how to take small rations of food in the village out of pure survival for my brothers and I.

I wanted the food so badly, but the thought of intruding on whoever lived in this cottage was daunting. I couldn't imagine they had many visitors, so what would they do if they had a disheveled, sweaty and no doubt rancid-smelling girl breaking and entering in the middle of the night?

I could bypass the temptation for food, take my berries, and continue on the trail. I was far enough from the village and so deep in the Forest that humans wouldn't dare enter. For now, I might have been safe.

I could continue on the path until morning. At dawn, maybe I would stumble on a castle. It would house selfless rulers, and the King would have a handsome, available son. He'd see me emerge from the brush and fall in love with me at first sight. He would approach me with an arrangement of my favorite colors of water lilies, tell me that the kitchen was already making a big breakfast of foods I'd never heard of but knew it would be better than days old meat and cheese.

I would play a little hard to get, be a little mysterious, so I was extra interesting to the Prince. By the end of breakfast, he would be so enthralled by me that he couldn't stand the idea of losing me. The King would absolve him of the arranged marriage he was set to enter into so he could be with me, the love of his life. His kingdom would accept me as their princess with open arms. I would spend the rest of my days teaching children how to paint, sing and dance.

The sun would never stop shining, and no tyrannical ruler would come in and take the kingdom. They wouldn't get the chance. They would be slain at the gates by good, kind guards and we would be safe and happy forever.

That was one outcome of thousands that could come from

following the path. The air felt darker that way, though. It didn't feel bright and hopeful. Neither did the cottage to my left, but there was *food* there. Potentially a bed, and if I was charming enough to the owner, maybe they wouldn't kill me for trespassing.

CHAPTER 4
Amelie

Food over fairy tale was the survivalist's choice. So I crept up to the door, careful of my feet and the branches cracking under them. As I approached the door, the vines disintegrated right before my eyes, as if they were never there. Before I connected my fist to the decrepit wood, the door creaked open. I waited to see if someone would poke their head out to peek at their visitor, but no one did. I pushed the door open a little further to see a small candle flickering, illuminating the small meal on the table.

"Hello?" Eerie silence crawled over my skin. The air in the Forest felt light and tingly, like finely milled glitter raining down. I first noticed it when I emerged from the river and magic soaked up the water right out of my clothes.

A warm breeze rushed in behind me, like my shadow friend from the journey here was following me inside. Not a breath to be heard, so I closed the door behind me and quietly stepped in to inspect. Rugs covered every inch of the floors. There was no particular theme. Hundreds of colors threaded through them. They were beautiful pieces that needed a loving touch of cleaning. If the owner didn't murder me in the morning, I'd offer to take the rugs to the creek and clean them in return for their hospitality.

The walls weren't in horrible shape, but they showed the cottage's age. Dust covered every surface besides the dining table. The sitting room had a lumpy couch in the dead center of it. It looked to be covered in empty potato sacks, soiled and filthy.

I called out again, "Hello? I promise I come meaning no harm. Your cottage is lovely but I don't want to intrude!"

I waited again for a response, but was quickly assured that I was, in fact, talking to myself and whatever magic roamed the Forest. Making my way to the table to inspect the food I saw in the window, I tore a small piece of bread from the loaf and pondered if eating magical food would be a bad way to die.

I decided it wasn't and popped it in my mouth.

The flavor exploded on my tongue, tasting better than any bread I'd ever had back home. Better than just fresh bread. It had a nutty, vanilla flavor, and it was so soft it was nearly dissolving on my tongue. Was fresh bread supposed to melt in your mouth? I was lucky to not crack a tooth on the leftovers we received in our rations.

No amount of willpower could keep me from devouring the rest of the loaf, jam, and cheese. I might have exploded at the unfamiliar quantity of food that was about to settle in my stomach, but I couldn't find a single part of my soul that cared. The food was incredible. Exhaustion crawled through my body. I was fading at the table, my eyes threatening to close right here. Then, my feet moved without command from my mind. Something was guiding me into a room with another smaller candle flickering on the bedside table.

The rest of the cottage was old and unkempt, but not this room. This room looked freshly cleaned, with a beautiful quilt splayed over the bed. It was warmer in here than it was in the first part of the house. Again, without my brain controlling my movement, something tucked me in under the quilt, and my head rested on a pillow so soft I wasn't sure any human was worthy of lying on it. I snuggled the quilt under my chin and breathed in the smell of cinnamon as I dipped into the pillow.

A small wisp of air breezed past my cheek. It took everything I had to pry my eyes open, but just a peek showed me a mug on the end table next to the bed. Steam floated around my nose, suggesting the smell of berries and caramel.

Tea.

The Lord and his guards were always drinking tea leading up to their nightly drunk-fests, but the village people were never allowed. Women were only given the birth control tea. We were told that our lesser bodies wouldn't be able to handle any other kind.

I sat up to take a sip, fully accepting the magic that was clearly watching and taking care of me. It was like drinking moonlight, soft and sleepy. I felt it course through each singular vein.

Only a few sips later, my eyes fluttered shut as I faded into a sleep filled with hopes and dreams. Just like usual. Except this time, I wasn't sure what the world would look like when I woke up in the morning.

It was the best night of sleep I'd ever had.

A WARM BLANKET of sunlight passed over my cheek, and for a moment I allowed it before I shot to a seated position. Unnervingly aware of waking up in someone's home, in a bed that some…thing made up for me. The mug of tea was nowhere in sight. I sat at attention, expecting the blood to rush to the wounds on my face, but it never came. I waited for a creak in the floor or the hum of a human in the home with me. It was so quiet you could hear a mouse and his family eating breakfast in the walls.

The room I slept in last night was spotless. There was a chest I didn't notice before sitting at the end of the bed, a desk with books stacked on it, paper with an ink pen in the center, and a new mug of tea steaming on the edge.

I was no fresh ear to the tales of this Forest, but this was just downright bizarre.

The dark magic I was told about often included the snatching and eating of children, gremlins that sucked your soul from you and leaving only your body in its wake, cursed Witches that were out for revenge and trees that told horror stories when you got too close to them.

So far, this *dark magic* had made me a delicious late night snack, two cups of aromatic tea, made up a bed for me, then cleaned the room and arranged furniture in it. The only thing it hasn't done for me was….

Nope, it did that, too.

A fresh change of clothes awaited me at the end of the bed. New, freshly shined boots sat on the floor.

Changing, and deciding to see if it was magic or just an extremely sneaky living thing in here, I sheepishly emerged from the bedroom, but I stopped dead in my tracks..

The dilapidated cottage was no longer the mess it had been when I arrived last night. Each of the rugs was now bright with their original colors of thread. The porcelain sink was glimmering under a fresh polish. There was no dust caking the walls or holes letting in a draft, and the couch had gone from being wrapped in literal potato sacks to a stunning cowhide. Blankets and quilts draped neatly over the back of it.

Twine laced through the rafters. Glowing orbs hung lazily above, washing the room with an airy morning light. Fresh plants hung in the corner, filling at least ten pots. The greenery inside no longer came from overgrown vines that invaded the cottage through the window. Instead, these plants seemed strategically placed, invited to live here. I felt invited too.

On the table, there was another smorgasbord of meats and cheeses, jams and sliced bread, pastries covered in white frosting, and so much fruit! Every fruit I'd tasted, and at least ten that I hadn't. Tildan would have gone feral for this. He loved when Wren brought home extra berries, his little cheeks always stained purple and red afterward.

I swallowed back my tears at the thought of my brothers. All I could hope was that they were safe.

Deciding to wait for another person to emerge before I ate their breakfast, I continued investigating.

Wanting to know if the interior facelift extended to the exterior, I strolled outside. The beauty of the Forest took my breath away, right before I lost my footing off the new porch of the cottage.

It was dark last night, sure, and I was likely delirious in some capacity, too, but I would've remembered this. This was new.

Off the porch was a short walkway lined with big, flat rocks. There was a small amount of grass surrounding the perimeter of the cottage. Beautiful arrangements of flowers grew wildly against the house in handcrafted flower beds. Some hung from the windows. Others grew straight from the ground. Large mushrooms protected the back of the cottage. Much like the ones from my dreams.

A few grew to my knees, others were as tall as me, and a few were competing with the fir trees in height. It was magnificent.

Further back behind the cottage was an endless abyss of dense Forest. In front, though, the small pond with the frogs from last night was now a large pond with more frogs, fish, and glowing wings on magical dragonflies. It started at the creek that flowed from the fork in the river all the way around the front of the cottage and back to a small, two-tiered waterfall.

A small, grassy bridge, laced with more of the twine and glowing orbs wrapped around the railing. The bridge allowed a person to cross from the Forest to the cottage. It was as if every fairy tale I'd ever dreamed up had become a reality right outside. I pinched myself to make sure it was real.

Well, that didn't feel great.

It was real, all of it. But my dreams often felt real too.

The brightest greens I'd ever seen surrounded the cottage—the trees, the grass, the bushes—paired with hazy, warm sunlight and trickling blue-green water. Words hardly did justice to the beauty and life that now breathed around the cottage. There was no other word than enchanting to describe it.

Need not be afraid, for we know you will not bring harm to us
You will not harm us, we will not harm you

The words from last night whispered in the wind again, but this time it sounded like less of a threat. How could someone hurt something so pristine? The Forest deserved to be known as enchanted, not evil like the villagers made it out to be.

It was late in the year. The winter chill would befall us soon, so the warm air was surprising to me. I chalked up feeling the warmth last night to the adrenaline.

When I saw the linen top and pants that were laid out for me, I thought the magic must be crazy, but now I realize that the sun shines differently here. The Forest protected its dwellers by staying at a comfortable temperature.

I craned my neck back to the cottage. I stood on the other side of the bridge to further inspect the change in scenery.

It looked almost sad that I was so far from it. The overgrown vines that covered the cottage last night were trimmed and now added to the charm rather than trapping it.

The roof was hiding beneath a thick layer of moss, tiny

flowers of all different colors poked out, speckling the greenery.

Deciding I didn't want to hurt the inanimate object's feelings, I went back to my new temporary home.

"I'm still here." I pressed my palm to the frame of the door. "I'm going to stay here for a little while if that's okay?" The door closed softly behind me. I took it as a yes. The air lightened, and it felt like the cottage was happy again, sunlight beamed through the windows.

I sat to devour the breakfast in front of me, feeling completely overwhelmed with happiness and guilt.

I've never had this amount of food in front of me to consume until my heart was content. I was afraid I'd wake up and have to stomach that this has all been a dream. That the hopes and dreams of a different life were only that and none of this was real.

I WATCHED the home closely today, trying to learn the ways of its magic. When I finished eating this morning, the food just disappeared. The table was spotless, like I hadn't just ravaged the delicious meal that was placed before me.

The same thing happened at noon, food appeared, I ate, and then it disappeared.

There were old games all over the house, it was hard to play by myself and the house noticed that almost immediately.

I had taken a checkerboard and its pieces out and set it up with my best guess. I studied the board and played by my own rules. The house quickly showed me the correct way to play, as if annoyed I played it any other way, and moved the pieces that it claimed. I think it won, but I didn't really care. It was fun to watch the house play with me.

I always took care of myself, so I was unfamiliar with the care it was taking of me. I felt like a princess of my own palace. It felt like I might have been taking advantage of its kindness, but a pastry I'd had in the morning was still on my tongue and I was greedily wanting more.

"Hi, uh, house? Actually, let's give you a name. Do you like Orla?" I always loved that name. It was my great grandmother's and though my grandmother Amelia had little to no memory of her mother, her name always stuck out to me. It meant the golden princess.

The house softly opened and closed its shutters. That was answer enough for me. "I like it too. Orla, do you have any more of those jam filled pastries? It was so good, I'll definitely need the recipe!"

I couldn't even finish laughing at my joke of needing a recipe for something I surely could never recreate before a fresh pastry appeared at the edge of the table. "I think I'm going to put some weight on the longer I stay here." Giggling to myself and trying to savor the pastry this time, the shutters on the windows softly opened and closed again, this time as if to laugh alongside me.

THREE DAYS SINCE I ARRIVED, and I was growing pretty attached to Orla.

She had a lot of personality for a house. She was perceptive and timed. Breakfast was always served within minutes of waking up. When the sun was high, lunch would be served, and in mid-afternoon a jam filled pastry would appear. During my dusk stroll, I would smell cuts of cooked meat and warm bread from the house, letting me know it was dinner time.

I'd never known a life this simple.

It was difficult to stomach and infuriating to think three days here had already been better than all twenty-four years in Holleberg.

My family was constantly on my mind.

Take care of that family of hers, too.

If I let myself think of them too long, I felt my heart pulling toward the door of the cottage. The guards would've shown them no mercy. If Heaven was real, I wanted to at least know they were okay. I fought with my mind whether to stay put or go back for them. I could go see for myself that they were gone. Maybe they got away. If they did, I'd find them and bring them back here. Orla might enjoy having more people to care for. Then again, I knew how it felt to care for too many with no time to care for myself.

I'm not sure I could do that to her, either. My best friend was now this house. My company was the magic in it, and the animals that roamed outside. I didn't feel alone here.

I wasn't afraid anymore, and I was just beginning to sit with that feeling. I couldn't remember a time when I wasn't scared.

Scared to ask for more water, or an extra ration for the baby when the milk ran out. Scared to steal so many berries that our puffy pockets would incriminate us, to be taken by one of the Lord's men and forced into yet another soul crushing act. Men hurt, they violate, they torture and use women.

As I looked around my safe, cozy new home, I was feeling very grateful that there were no men here. Just me and the magic.

CHAPTER 5

Kiaran

The girl living in my house was strange.

I knew mortals spent their time telling tales of the Forest. The fear that wafted from the girl when she showed up was proof of that. They had ideas of this Forest being evil. However, it was anything but.

If I were being honest, the most evil thing in this Forest was most likely me. There were certainly dangerous animals and creatures in the Forest but being as old as the Earth, they weren't interested in hunting mortals anymore.

It'd been five nights since I picked up the scent of the sapphire eyed girl sprinting through the thick Forest. She smelled delicious. Vanilla, strawberries, and an overwhelming sense of fear. I waited until she was slowing down to give her a second wind by chasing her with my shadows. I cast them out to take the shape of wolves, then they were to chase and bring her straight to me but those traitorous black wisps wrapped themselves around her shoulders, giving her a false sense of security.

She stole the berries from my bushes, even though I'd never been able to cross the clearing to get to them. Then welcomed herself in when the cottage opened right up for her.

The second the frizzy haired girl got close enough to the cottage, though, Fern bound me and my magic to the fucking attic. Clearly trying to take away the pleasure of scaring the girl off. The sentience in the cottage has been here as long as me, I think we're bound together by a centuries old curse. I assumed that she drew from my magic, bringing the cottage to life. Which made it so much more annoying that she used it against me.

I decided only two years into my sentence that the house was a woman. I liked to call her Fernweh, Fern for short, because I would have loved to be anywhere else. Home preferably.

When Fern released me the following morning, I made myself invisible to her.

I *planned* on scaring her ten ways out of hell but after I finally caught a good glimpse of her, there was no way I could do that. It would be foolish to waste such a pretty little sacrifice. As long as she had celestial blood, she was the closest thing I'd ever have to getting home. Though, if she did have celestial blood, she sure didn't use it.

Fern had laid the girl to rest in *my* bed, with *my* sleepy time tea, then this fucking house put a beautiful, handcrafted chest and desk in *my* room and filled it with books, journal paper, a bunch of new clothes, and a few pairs of boots.

I've been stuck in this unfortunately enchanting Forest for two centuries and all Fern has ever given me was a headache. To make matters worse, my perfectly dusted prison was spotless when I awoke, my couch was gone, and the appeal of the cottage became utterly charming.

Seriously, a half-moat with glowing lights and what smelled like thousands of flowers? Fern was pulling out all of her most impressive moves for our guest.

Last night, I got the chance to take the girl in completely. While she sat and ate like a barbarian at the table, I positioned myself across from her, entirely invisible but so consumed by every part of her. The yellow hue of the candlelight showed me fresh, blue bruises covering her beautiful face. One under each eye, another with the imprint of knuckles on her temple that would've been fatal if it had been a mere centimeter down, and many more faded ones on her cheeks that made her skin mimic someone about to hurl.

She'd pressed a light touch to her right eye and shuddered. My blood heated at the sight of her in pain at the hands of someone else. I wanted to know who the fuck hurt her. She didn't seem dangerous, so nothing would be a good enough reason to batter her stunning face.

I didn't know what she'd been through to get to me. All I knew was that she was here, and that was a beacon of hope toward my eventual return to my home in Avonya.

After dishonoring my Coven and failing the orders the High Priestess placed on me, my Coven sentenced me to spend eternity here. The High Priestess wrote my fate in the stars. I could earn my freedom by performing a sacrifice that would mirror the pain I caused nearly two hundred years ago. When the girl arrived, I swore it was my sacrifice being given to me on a silver platter. But it became obvious very quickly that the pretty girl living in my house bore no celestial blood. So, Winter Solstice would come and go, as it has two hundred times in a row.

I observed my surroundings here for a long time. Having been tethered to this fucking cottage for the better part of my entire life had given me the perfect opportunity to see it for how the mortals do. This Forest was said to be a purgatory for Lost Souls, and it was, but not in the sinister way the girl's kind thought. The Lost Souls walked among each other here, sharing stories and tales of times long forgotten by the living. Each night, they gathered around a campfire a good ways from the cottage and sang songs of times the living forgot.

If they were enemies when they were alive, you wouldn't

know it now. If I didn't know any better, they saw each gathering as a meeting of old friends.

I felt like an unwanted guest in their camaraderie and it bothered me for a long time that I never had a friend. Having spent so much of my early life not having any, I was jealous of the souls who laughed together, sharing the peace that didn't come until the afterlife.

While my cohorts in school were learning the fundamentals of our magic, like making a mess disappear or healing cuts and bruises; I was busy teaching myself how to summon portals to throw my sister through when she was getting on my nerves. She came back every time, so it obviously needed more work. After one hundred years of wreaking havoc on my realm, I made a seriously grave mistake.

Watching this stunning woman cozy up my dilapidated cottage for the last few days had been the most entertainment I had since being here, but it was starting to piss me off a little.

She spilled tea on the floor and ate food like a starved wolf. The rugs were taking the brunt of her mess, but Fern took care of it immediately every time. Truth be told, the ugly rugs that donned the rickety floors of the cottage weren't being ruined by the tea, but was she born in a fucking stable?

Who the fuck traipses in here looking like a complete and utter mess, then dines and sleeps in a home that was occupied?

I suppose she really didn't *know* it was occupied, since I hadn't exactly introduced myself yet.

Humans were different from what I remembered. This one, in particular, was much more striking than the ones that looked like the gremlins who lived down the trail. Behind the gnarly bruising to her face that had now turned to a faded green, she had a little button nose, full pouty lips, and her cheekbones, now that the swelling was gone, defined her face in sharp lines that the women back home would kill for. She had long, dark hair, always falling haphazardly out of her messy braid.

Her eyes were beacons. A sapphire blue that hypnotized me every time I stared too long. She was frail. I don't want to think of the cold shoulder Fern would've given me if I scared her off before she put some meat on her bones. Sadness reeked from her. Her entrancing eyes held little life when she first arrived, but they brightened a little more each day as she got more comfortable. I was never good at comforting people, or so my mother would say, so all I could do was absorb the pain that was emanating from her.

This evening, while the girl took her walk to talk to the frogs, Fern added a library onto the back of the cottage and filled it to the brim with books. I asked her for two hundred years to conjure up a book. Guess how many she's given me.f

From floor to ceiling, bookshelves lined the walls, and a ladder hinged on a track to roll around the perimeter of the room. It had a nook in the windowsill with more pillows than anyone should ever have. There was a large desk, even more exquisite than the one that she put in my old room. The raw edges of the oak were on display as a focal point, and Fern had already stocked it with books for her to start with.

"Orla!" The girl's voice called through the house as she shut the door. "I brought you flowers, I'm sure you can see that already, somehow. By the way, I've been meaning to ask you, how do you do that? Are you a ghost? I feel like I'm going crazy." She giggled to herself and it sent a tingle up my arms. Probably because I haven't heard laughter in two hundred years.

She was, clearly. Because who the fuck was Orla? She'd been saying the name for a few days but she was all by herself in here. Well, not entirely, but she didn't know that. And my name wasn't Orla.

"Anyways, is there a vase in here somewhere? Don't *magician* one in. These are for you, for everything." She scurried around the room like a mouse looking for crumbs. "Ah ha, found one. Okay, close your eyes." The shutters in the window closed on cue.

Was she talking to Fern?

She set the vase down on the table. Flowers in every color spilled over the edges. Fern had done a real number on renovating our home. It was lively and filled with decor that I had no inclination she had the ability to do. I couldn't lie, I was a little offended that she didn't think *I* was worth doing all this sprucing up for.

It looked truly magical in our home now, but with the girl's addition of flowers, life was not just existing here. It was breathing. As if the girl had given the structure a soul. One deeper than Fern.

"Oh, and Orla? My name is Amelie." She bowed her head to continue adjusting the already perfect arrangement, then she voiced a concern mostly to herself. "I hope someday someone says my name again."

And suddenly, I wanted to speak her name endlessly. Just to never see her so sad again.

Amelie.

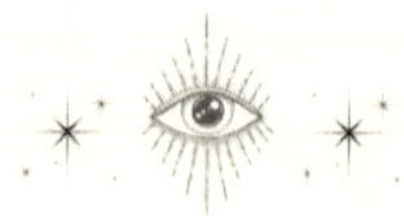

AMELIE ASKED ORLA, otherwise known as Fern, to hold off on dinner when she saw the new library. While she excused herself to the washroom to bathe after her walk, I took the liberty of replacing some of the boring books Fern picked out with romantic novels. Girls love romance. I lived in isolation for a long time, but some things never change. Girls in Avonya swooned at just a *wink* from me. So I was sure some of these books would set fire to Amelie's sad soul.

When she walked into the cozy new sanctuary of books,

she soaked it all in. Breathing in and out a few times, as if she was committing all of her senses in this room to memory. I hated to admit that Fern had impeccable taste, but she really did. The library was gorgeous. The laws of magic allowed it to be much bigger on the inside than it appeared from the outside.

Amelie floated over to the desk, running a palm over my hand-picked selection of books. Flipping the front cover open, she scoffed and slammed it shut. She *must* be going mad. I felt a jab in my side, as if Fern was ribbing me for having poor judgment.

She started touching each book on the middle shelf, running her finger over each spine. Stopping at a big green one, she tipped the spine out and decided that was the one to start with. She tucked herself into the nook and flipped to the first page. I took a seat beside her. She shuddered as if she knew something was invading her space. When I saw what was better than the books I picked out, I knew she had succumbed to complete and utter madness.

Philosophy of Alchemy.

I hadn't searched through the collection Fern brought in, but that was my book from home. My teachers were hellbent on us being well-rounded Witches and felt it was of the utmost importance to have a basic understanding of how dangerous alchemy was, but also how useful it was when performed safely.

I had all this magic, yet I couldn't figure out how to blend elements together without nearly setting the whole place on fire.

Amelie was reading it like it was the greatest work of literature she'd ever consumed, as if she understood every word. She stayed there for hours, long past Fern's promptly scheduled meal times. She called it quits with only a little left in the book and told Fern she would go to bed without dinner, completely unacceptable to our hostess.

Fern had the table set with an absurd amount of food before Amelie could even finish her request.

It's easy to go mad in isolation and your only company being an overbearing house of magic. I would know. I'd done it for about one hundred and ninety-nine years longer than she has.

The first few years I was here, I spent my time pissed off and sulking. Constantly racking my brain for a loophole in the magic, any lesson from fundamentals that would've been useful in breaking a tethering curse. Unfortunately, every attempt ended with singed eyebrows or a lightning bolt of energy thrashing down on me. Surely a message from the High Priestess.

My sentence, though, came with a way out. I decided long ago that it would've been better to not know that there was a way home, often wishing I was just exiled and sent to live among the other failures on the outskirts of Avonya.

Home wasn't far away at all from the Forest, but the realm hid behind enchantments and pools of magic that only the High Priestess could open.

I spent years trying to find something in this cottage to give up, but nothing in here was important to me. Nothing would hurt me to lose. I tried on every Winter Solstice, the longest night of the year. Fuck, I tried.

One year, I spent the better part of eight months trying to attach myself to a painting of a little family.

I spoke to the faces in the painting every day, sharing stories about my life back home. The family in the painting was bigger than mine. I had a mom, dad, and a little sister. These parents had four children, one girl, two boys, and a baby. The mother and father were smiling at each other with nothing but love in their eyes. The children played at the lake's shore. The baby was saddled on the little girl's hip. It looked ridiculous, this small girl holding such weight upon her small body.

It made sense that losing this family would teach me a lesson for what I had done. I understood at this point that the High Priestess needed me to feel the pain I'd caused.

When the Winter Solstice arrived that year, I placed the painting in the middle of the sacrificial circle. The oil paints bubbled, letting an acrid smell waft through the cottage. A puff of smoke swallowed the canvas, and I swore the window above the sink in the kitchen would've been the last thing I'd see in this Forest.

That was one hundred fifty years ago, and the only pain I had afterward was the sting in my nose from the burning oil.

I didn't like to admit to the lonely feelings I often felt here. Spending a lot of time wearing impenetrable armor became useless. The only person here to defend against was myself. But the only person I ever had was myself. No one could fill the empty parts of my heart, so I guarded it.

Like every other boy in my Coven, the girls held our main attention. Witches were notorious flirts. We are manipulative and talented in the art of romance. Willing into our lives the things we wanted grounded our entire existence. We were still honing our magic when we turned of age to potentially find our fated mate, and the only way to expel the power exuding from us was to fuck like the world might evaporate tomorrow.

When you found your counterpart, the one your soul was desperate to find, everything locked into place. Your magic balanced itself and would no longer search randomly for something to tether to. Those pulls of connection always ended in the physical form. I hadn't worshiped a woman in two centuries, it exhausted me at first, then the desires dwindled away.

Deciding after yet another reminder of how alone and desperate I'd become here, I figured maybe it was time to introduce myself.

I bathed while she strolled around the pond. Twisted my curls around my fingers and shaved my overgrown face down to a clean stubble. I threw on one of the three shirts Fern had given me in all my time here and my denim pants. Then, I waited. Like I'd been doing for two centuries.

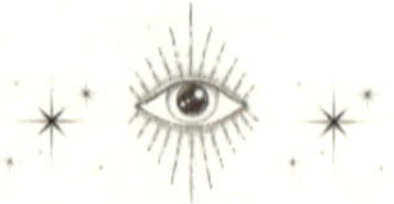

WHO KNEW WATCHING a beautiful woman shove two chicken wings into her mouth at once would be the most otherworldly thing I'd ever seen.

I cast myself here in less than a second. Having centuries of practice, I knew it would be silent. I thought that would be the right way to go about this meeting of cohabiters, but she hadn't even noticed me sitting across from her. My jaw parted in disbelief as I watched her huff down the food Fern had conjured for her.

I took her in. She was completely unabashed at her lack of table manners. Her fingers glistened with grease. There was something about a woman who didn't care to use a fork that baffled me.

Had she not realized by now that Fern would give her endless amounts of food at any given time? Clearly not, but I would be patient, not wanting to ruin this moment for myself. A girl this hungry seemed dangerous, and I didn't want to be caught in the cross of her being forced to slow down. She'd obviously been trying to be courteous to Fern by telling her she would skip dinner.

As she sucked the last drops of the grease from the wing with a pop of her lips and a moan, I realized this was putting me in an incredibly unsettling position. Apparently, it didn't take much these days. I shifted slightly in my seat, trying to make myself more comfortable.

She met my eyes as a squeak from her lost breath hitched in her throat. Not saying anything and seemingly not breathing either, she darted her eyes around the cottage behind me.

"Oh great. Now I'm seeing angels." She slid her chair back hard, screeching against the floorboards. Pacing behind the table, she pressed her palm to her forehead, as if checking for a fever. "For fuck's sake, Amelie, you've been here for less than a week, and you've already gone completely mad!"

She looked back to me, blinking so hard that I couldn't tell if she was trying to force herself to sleep or if she had something in her eyes.

I looked over my shoulder, she was seeing angels?

Hoping her hallucination would pass and we could continue our official meeting, I waited. She rounded the long oak table and stood beside me, breathing shakily down at me as I stayed seated.

I turned to look at her, fearful now that *I* was the one in danger. Me. A three hundred year old Witch in danger of a girl who just annihilated her chicken wings.

And I'd wager a bet that was probably the most damage she'd ever done to anything.

CHAPTER 6

Amelie

I was going to be sick.

This morning, I woke up to the same warm beam of sunlight I'd let be the tell to start my day for the last five days. Everything had been so perfect that the only reasonable explanation was that it was one of my dreams. That, or I was in some kind of purgatory.

Now, as I sat across from the gorgeous Angel of Death himself, I think it was safe to say it was the latter. The fatal end to this fairy tale story.

I suppose it made sense that God sent his best looking angels to pluck souls from their Earthly bodies. I was sure most people went with him willingly.

Not me though, at least not yet.

"I thought I'd have more time." I took steady breaths as I stood at the Angel's side hoping to intimidate him into letting me stay a little longer.

"Uh.. what?"

Not a very Godly response.

"I thought I would have more time here. I just.. I.. I want to stay a bit longer. Please?" I didn't know how it worked when the Angel of Death visited, if it was his decision when I went or if I got to decide, but I quickly gave up the intimidation act and went for the classic begging.

He looked enormously confused as he studied my face. For what, I'm not sure. "I mean, yeah. You can stay as long as you want. She obviously likes you better than she likes me." He popped a piece of bread in his mouth, locking his glittering blue eyes on mine.

His attention on me sent a wave of tingles up my arms. Each of the hairs on my arm stood straight up, like a magnet to him. Men normally put the fear of God in me, but that heavy feeling wasn't present right now. He looked like he inspired God's painting of the night sky, but I wasn't scared of the dark.

I looked around the cottage through narrowed eyes, searching for said *she*.

If there was another woman here, I couldn't see her, which sent a sharp slice of panic through my core.

"Who is *she*? God is a woman? Oh no. Is the *Devil* a woman? Am I going to hell for leaving home? If you only knew what I was running from. I promise I can plead my case!"

He let out a smug laugh, tilting his head to the side. "Human, I think you've really gone mad. I'm no angel. My name is Kiaran. This is my home."

Oh, Jesus Christ, was *she* his wife?

Surely I would've noticed a man living with me. A gorgeous one, at that. Had I been so exhausted from the life I'd been living that I waltzed around this man's house, made myself a bed, and had been eating all his food? Was he the one playing board games with me, and I was too delirious to see him? Were the berries I stole that first night actually of the poisonous variety and I was fading into a pure delusion?

I think I was breathing, I couldn't be sure. But a whirl started in the center of my forehead and I thought I was going to faint.

Resting my head on the table and breathing heavily, a strong hand covered my shoulder.

"Can we skip the melodramatics and talk about how this is going to work?"

I twisted my neck to look at him. His face was completely blank, emotionless.

Kiaran.

I'd never thought of a man as anything other than safe or dangerous. But Kiaran was *so* pretty. Perfectly tousled, midnight-black curls weaved around his ears. One ringlet fell out of place onto his forehead. A braver part of my soul was daring me to tuck it back into place so I could see every inch of his tanned skin clearly. His eyes were as crystalline blue as the sea outside my fairytale palace I so often dreamed of. But whether I was in danger with him, I wasn't sure yet.

Kiaran's calloused fingers picked my jaw up off the floor, shaking me back into the moment. "I am quite pretty, aren't I?"

My eyes went wide, his wife was going to kill me for gawking at him.

"I should probably tell you, I can hear any thoughts you have about me." He gave me a wink. "If I'm listening, that is."

Magic. A magical man.

I looked for my words again because they'd apparently completely escaped me. "I am so embarrassed. I promise I didn't know someone lived here. Food and blankets and books and warm tea all just kept showing up and…Oh, God is Orla your wife? Am I sick?" Sitting back to let the air fill every square inch of my lungs. "I'm sick aren't I? Five days ago, I escaped into the Forest. God! Only a sick person would do that."

I jumped from the bench, not allowing him to answer, and ran to the window. Orla, *Kiaran's wife apparently,* opened it already.

Why couldn't I see her?

Sucking in the fresh Forest air, I was left even more unnerved.

"Oh my god." I turned slowly to face Kiaran, pressing a hand to my chest. "I still see the Forest." I rushed toward the man at the table, grabbed hold of his elbow and tugged him to me. "Please, just tell me, am I too far gone? Is there a cure?"

He whipped his arm back into his personal space. One of his eyebrows was an inch higher than the other as he stared back at me.

"What. The Fuck. Are you talking about?" He straddled the bench, taking my face in his hands, giving my racing mind a gentle shake.

From this view, I saw him clearly. No longer hidden in the shadows of flickering candlelight. The moon washed his face, giving me a haunting view of him. His angular, stubbled jaw only added to his devastatingly handsome face.

"You're not sick. You showed up here five days ago after running for about four hours through the Forest. *Orla's* name is Fern, and she and I have been living in this cottage for two hundred years." He waited for my reaction to the news that he was, at minimum, two hundred years old, and I *was* actually in the enchanted Forest that held many evil creatures. One of which was sitting in front of me, holding my head in a way where he could snap my neck at any second.

"I'm not going to snap your neck. That's a terribly unsatisfying way to kill someone."

Oh, right. He could read my mind. Great!

"Again, I can if they are about me. However, you said that I was holding your head perfectly enough to snap your neck out loud."

Note to self: know when to hold my tongue.

"Anyways, Fern is extremely personable, as I'm sure you've figured out. I, however, usually am not. But you smelled of fear when you finally got here, and I didn't think you needed any more scares that night. By the way, who the fuck did that to your face?"

It took me a moment to realize he was asking about the bruising that was nearly gone now. That was not something I was going to discuss with someone I'd only just met. How does one even explain that? *Oh, those, ha ha, yeah. I come from a village where the men who are supposed to protect us, instead, beat and rape women for their own sick enjoyment. No big deal.*

Yeah, I don't think so. I'd hate for him to take that as an invitation to hurt me, just because I was used to it.

"I ran into some trees on my way here. Clumsy me." Shrugging my shoulders and getting to my feet slowly, I tried so hard to keep all thoughts of him or what happened to me out of my mind. I slapped my palms together and got to my feet, bobbing uncomfortably on my heels. "Well, it was nice to meet you, Kiaran. Thank you for allowing me to stay in your home." I used all my ladylike words and bowed before the immortal man.

That was weird. Why did I do that?

"Would it be okay for me to sleep here one more night? I'll leave before dawn. Promise." I swear I tried to keep my tone even, but I could see by his face that I failed.

"Scared, pretty girl?" A cheshire grin spread across his face. Suddenly, I prayed that I really had been dreaming this whole time.

Please don't hurt me. I didn't say it aloud, but it didn't matter.

"I won't hurt you. We've only just met. Go, sleep. The room you've been staying in was mine, I'll sleep in the attic."

Taking one more good look at the man who appeared out of thin air, I retreated to my new bedroom. Before I got to my door, a staircase to *the attic* appeared next to the washroom, the rail wrapped in vines and the steps shaped like halves of tree trunks. I shuttered at the idea of him watching me the last few days.

"Goodnight, Kiaran. Sleep tight." *Sleep tight?* Jesus fucking Christ, Amelie.

I took my knack at humiliating myself and closed the door behind me. Checking the handle, it was as tight as my chest right now. Orla sealed me in, or rather, sealed Kiaran out.

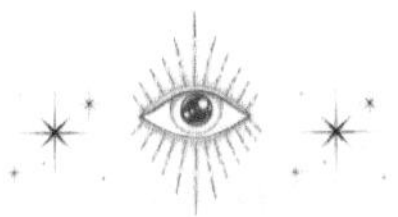

IT WAS NEARLY the middle of the night. I couldn't sleep knowing Kiaran was just upstairs, probably waiting for my guard to be lowered so he could attack.

I whispered to Fern in my restless state, "Your name is Fern? Do you like that? I like Orla better." One of the books flipped open, the wind taking the pages and settling them near the end, I tiptoed as quietly as possible over to it and read.

A dreadful sense of fernweh reaps my mind.
The idea of living another day in this life is unimaginable,
I want to see the stars up close, touch the sun while laying on
the sand the travelers speak about. I want to be anywhere but
here and as far away as can be.

Fernweh. Longing to be far, far away living a life you could only dream of. I understood that all too well.

"I hope you know that you're what I would dream of back home." A warm breeze lingered around my shoulders.

I had one chance to leave unnoticed. I prayed that the gift of immortality also came with the gift of at least sleeping like the dead and Kiaran wouldn't be waiting in the dark to live up to the tales of this Forest.

So far, the Forest had only showed me safety and kindness. Something about Kiaran didn't *exude* gentle.

I laced up my boots and stepped into a cream linen skirt

and a pale blue top I'd found in the trunk. Fern already learned my favorite color, I'm not even sure my mother knew that. I grabbed the thick cloak off the hook on the back of the door. Then I tore out the page Fern showed me and tucked into the waist of my pants. If I survived my second attempt at surviving dangerous men, I at least wanted a memory of the dreamy days I spent here.

Hoping Fern knew it wasn't her I was running from, I tried the doorknob and to my surprise, it twisted. "Thank you, Fern," I whispered.

My heart hurt at the thought of leaving the sentient home. I needed her to know I would've happily lived out the rest of my days here. Not considering how mad I might go by the end in solitude, at least I would've been happy in my delusion. I imagined that I'd think I was a princess by the time I was old and wrinkly. An almost happy ending.

The door typically creaked when it hit the halfway open point, but it was silent tonight. Checking for my housemate, I noticed the house was eerily still. No sounds of breath or life to ache the floorboards.

The front door was maybe twenty paces from the bedroom. Twenty paces and I would be alone again.

Taking meaningful, efficient steps to find my exit, the moonlight poured in through the window. Perfectly illuminating my path. I was only an arm's length away from safety when I turned to take one last look at Fern. Admiring the work she'd put in the last few days to make this once dirty, dilapidated cottage a nice, cozy home, my eyes pricked with tears that I had to leave it behind.

The couch already had an imprint from my butt having consumed so many books in the same spot. My book on alchemy I chose from the library was closed with my last read page dog-eared on the desk.

Each night, I rested in the sitting room and had a perfect view of the clearing outside. Right as day turned to dusk, fireflies would start flitting around as far as the eye could see. The petals on the wildflowers would start flowing and swaying to the music of the Forest.

Butterflies and strange looking dragonflies appeared out of nowhere and created the smallest breeze as they flapped their small wings. Pollen sparkled through the air, and the cottage brightened with candlelight. The Forest was no longer only the variety of bright greens and blues but every color God had added to Earth's pallet and then some. Shades of pinks and purples, reds and oranges. As if they were taking advantage of simply existing here.

It was the most magical thing I'd ever seen, and I felt so privileged to experience it. I would miss it terribly, but I kept a blind hope that where I ended up would be just as magical.

Hopefully, it wouldn't include an ancient Witch who was out for my blood either.

Turning back to the door, I ran into a wall. Fern must have sealed me in again.

She didn't have big, magical hands to grab my shoulders, though.

"You're leaving me already, pretty girl?"

Fuck.

"I'm not *ancient*, by the way. I'm somewhere around three hundred, I think. Birthday's don't matter when you'll have hundreds of them."

I scrunched my skirt in my hands, trying to keep them from trembling.

"I'm sorry if I woke you." My voice was shaky and terribly unconvincing. "I was hoping to see the lights again. I couldn't sleep."

"Oh?" he questioned. "Well, let's go see them, then. I wasn't aware that the creatures had a midnight showing, too." A knowing smirk appeared on his lips. He knew I was lying. It was hopeless. "Coming?" He stood in the doorway, waiting for me to follow.

"Uh…yeah."

His large body took up all the space in the doorway, not allowing me a way around him. Staring me down with a hungry expression on his face, he slowly turned to the side, leaving only enough space for my chest to graze his and my back to hitch on the door frame. Finally, on the front step of the cottage, I turned back to him standing an arm's length away.

I painted on my most convincing smile. "Okay, let's go, then."

He looked at his feet before moving his gaze up my body, drinking me in as he did. My stomach rolled, but not like it did when the guard's looked at me.

"I can't leave. But if you want to, all you have to do is run. I can't follow you." Kiaran leaned against the door frame lazily, tucking his hands into the pockets of his silky black pajama pants. "I can, however, send all the darkest parts of myself to chase you. Take that awful music the Forest sings for you and change it to the screams of the lives that have perished here. I'll make your departure as demoralizing as possible, only to drive you back here to me."

His words lingered in the air between us as my heart sank lower and lower into my stomach with each backward step.

"Is that a threat?"

Kiaran's head tilted slightly. One side of his mouth drew up in a smirk, then he fucking *winked* at me. "It's a promise."

Before I could respond, I fell straight on my ass. A large log tucked itself under my knees. A log that was *not* there before.

"See? So easy." He crossed his arms over his chest, looking all too impressed with himself.

"Ha! Good job, magic man. You put a log on the ground. Very scary," I taunted and put my hands up in a false surrender. Maybe not the smartest idea, but maybe it'd test if he was lying about not being able to leave the cottage. If I piss him off, he'd try to chase after me.

I wasn't thinking straight.

Why the fuck would I want him to chase me? Hadn't enough scary men chased me? I had to be dreaming, dream Amelie was so much braver.

"You want scary? I can do scary. Let's see…" He tapped his pointer finger against his chin, mocking me. Bringing his hand to shoulder height, he twirled his wrist around, creating a silhouette of something, then threw it toward me.

Though it looked terribly stupid, I felt it. The cool wisp cut through the air past my cheek so fast, I flinched. Trying to recover from the embarrassment of startling at literal air, I got back on my feet.

"Has it been boring being alive for, what was it? One thousand years? Scaring people by throwing air at them?"

He laughed now, forearms crossed over his stomach, like if he let go, his guts would fall out from laughing so hard. His head bobbed back as the sound of his laugh muffled, replaced by low, rumbling growls behind me.

Turning, I saw figures of wolves in the tree line past the cottage's clearing. They were snarling and stalking toward us. Realizing now that he wasn't throwing air at me, he was throwing magic out to the woods to summon *wolves*.

It would be safest to sprint inside, but that's exactly what he said he wanted. His laughter was softer now. He was studying me to see what my next move would be. A smarter human would accept their death now and concede, but I'm not sure anyone had ever accused me of being smart.

Spinning on my heels, I took off straight toward the path that called to me that first night. The one I should've taken. If I had just kept going, I would've only had to run for my life the first time.

I made it to the path, narrowly missing a rogue tree branch that appeared from thin air. The crackling of leaves warned me that the wolves were running in the trees beside me, barking at me as if calling for their dinner. My feet moved on their own accord, which made it hard to shift them when a large rock appeared in my path. I tried to hurdle it and almost cleared it, but my shin grazed the top, slowing me with a stumble.

A wolf slipped from the shadow of the large trees and was only a leap away from taking me down with it. I tried to pick up my speed, but the air was getting heavier. The air was thick like molasses. My feet stuck to the ground, I couldn't move. My upper body was fighting my legs. Exhaustion reaped my body at the push and pull. Fuck Kiaran.

"Give up yet?" His voiced boomed through the brush on either side of me.

"Nope," I shouted back.

I tumbled forward when he lifted the weight he'd place upon me. The wolves circled around me, dancing with each other, bringing me to a complete stop. I turned back to see the candlelight flickering in the cottage.

The oversized, magical wolf was only a few feet from me now, stalking me. It crept up to stand front and center. I held my breath as it panted into my face.

The wolf straightened his hind legs and lowered his head to hover over his massive paws, which were at least four times bigger than any dog I'd ever seen, then he pounced. Knocking me back on my ass with an oomph. I tried to defend myself, but before I could take a swing at the smelly creature, it was licking my face.

I couldn't help but laugh. I was sure this was not Kiaran's intention when he sent the predators after me. Even non-magical ones were incredibly dangerous. The hunters in the village, who were experts in tracking and killing them, did not show the animal disrespect by not fearing them.

But this wolf was basically an oversized dog. It took my shirt between its teeth and threw me up onto its back. I'd hoped it would be my ride on my journey away from the cottage, but to no avail, it was bringing me back to Kiaran and Fern. I couldn't help but laugh at the expression on Kiaran's face as he watched me approach atop his scary, magical wolf. His mouth popped open, and his arms uncrossed, falling flat against his sides.

He reversed the twirl of his hand that conjured the wolves initially, and before I could think, I was free-falling to the ground. My animal friend had disappeared into thin air, leaving me alone by the bushes of berries.

"How the fuck did you end up *riding* my wolf?" He didn't exactly seem mad, but he was definitely frustrated.

"My guess is as good as yours. I'm taking it as a compliment though that your bloodhounds didn't eat me when they had the chance."

"Well,"—he winked at me—"there's always next time."

That fucking wink.

CHAPTER 7

Kiaran

From the moment Amelie arrived, I could sense that she posed little threat to me. What I did *not* expect was for her to come back to me riding one of my wolves who I had spent the better part of three hundred years training to hunt and kill. She said he licked her, like a fucking dog?

As she approached the house, she was wearing a new cloak of confidence. She thought she bested me. I guess in a way she kind of had, but I'd be damned if I gave her the satisfaction of telling her that.

When I heard her trying to creep out of the house earlier, my gut rolled. I didn't want her to leave, and I felt… hurt? She'd been all too happy with just Fern. It was stupid to assume she wanted company. *My* company, anyway.

"Fern seems to have made you some tea. I can smell it from here."

She reached for the door frame and lingered on it for a minute. "Thank you, friend."

The way she endears this sentient, inanimate object was odd. Fern had a lot of personality, most of which, though, came in the form of a shitty attitude towards me. Even when I tried to charm her she'd been the bare minimum of cordial.

Or as cordial as a house could be. Watching Amelie treat the cottage with such kindness and gratitude had been humbling, to say the least. I wondered if I deserved Fern's cold shoulder this whole time.

"Can you just not torture me when you kill me? Just make it fast?" Amelie stunned me by blurting out. Mortals never ceased to amaze me with what they chose to say under duress, the few missions I'd completed with my father as a child told me that much.

But not once on those trips had any of those souls requested to pick their demise. "What a strange thing to ask. Who said I was going to kill you?"

She pondered the question, no doubt mulling over the tales I was sure she'd been told about the Whispering Forest and the *things* that live in it.

"I just assumed. Why else would you want me here?"

I'd been asking myself that same question since dinner when her dramatic performance had her in a pile on the floor asking how much time she had. She could've landed a lead role in the village play with that one.

Since I introduced myself earlier tonight, all notions of scaring her away had become blank puzzle pieces in my mind. All my time on Earth had been spent waiting. My first thought was surely this was the sacrifice I would have to make, but I could never love a mortal, nor could a mortal be crossed into my fate. The High Table made sure of that long ago, it was too messy.

It was pretty pathetic if you thought about it. I was well on my way to becoming a powerful High Priest. I would've ruled all of Avonya with my fated mate at my side. Whether I would've been a good ruler or not was no question. I wouldn't have been. That was why the High Priestess was so hard on me. She never let me forget that I was a disgrace to my family.

The darkness that followed me since I was a small child wasn't one that ever faded away. It was my shadow. I loathed it. Everywhere I went, it loomed over me. The boys who would be my friends were all bad, and not friendly at all. They were the sons of Witches who were exiled from the Coven. The High Priestess allowed them to go to fundamental school so they wouldn't run amok with their magic but it only fueled their fire.

They taught me things that a young Witch shouldn't know. The Black Magic that their families had to channel in order to have any magic at all was dangerous. I was plentiful with good magic. I came from a powerful family, but I ruined any chance at a normal life in Avonya. The Black Magic clung to me and everyone who saw *me*, saw *it*. They wanted nothing to do with me. All because I was a restless kid, hungry for something more.

Amelie hadn't mentioned the shadows that followed me. She either didn't see them because she's mortal, or she wasn't afraid of them. Either way, I thought I could enjoy having someone around who didn't see my darkness.

I thought I could enjoy simply having her around.

The way her perfect, pouty lips twisted together when she was deep in thought, or her obnoxious laugh that filled a room and made it feel like flowers might grow out of the pores of your skin, or watching her twirl knots into her chocolate curls, all of it. She had only known about me for a few hours, but I'd been watching her for days, and I wanted all of her to stay right here with me.

"It's been a long time since I've had company, pretty girl." I paused, not to show the desperate part of me that seemed drawn to her. "I don't mind you. You're kind of annoying, very messy, and have a bit of an attitude problem, but at least you're nice to look at." She turned away from me, but not before I caught a blush painting her pale cheeks.

"Right. Well, if you don't mind, I'm going to go to bed now. Same time tomorrow?" Her quick redirection to humor when she felt anything other than happy was endearing, but her sad eyes told me it was just a mask.

She strode across the kitchen to my old room. "One last thing, stop calling me *pretty girl*." She turned to look at me. "It's Amelie."

I laughed. "I know."

Then I added one more wink for good measure. She left me with pink cheeks and a bite of her lip to keep herself from smiling.

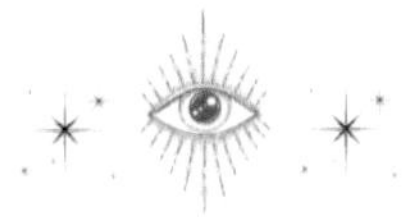

THE SUN THREATENED to climb over the Earth's edge and I hadn't so much as tried to close my eyes for five long nights now. The cot Fern conjured for me had to be stuffed with jagged pebbles from the pond. I swore she was keeping it freezing on purpose, but it didn't matter because the girl sleeping in my bed downstairs was all I could think about. It'd been almost a week of Amelie knowingly living with me, and I'd gathered a few things about her.

Number one, and the most prominent, she was very strange. She dances to music she sang herself. Not well, I might add. Unfortunately, I learned she was utterly tone deaf. She has absolutely no table manners, and I assumed she found herself to be very funny because when she told jokes to Fern, she laughed at herself every time.

For example, after her evening stroll, which, turns out, was just her putting her toes in the pond and talking to the frogs, she bounced into the house telling Fern that she had a question for her. She had a small stick with a pointy end on it, waving it around like a sword. A defenseless one, at that.

"What is the best way to carve a piece of wood, Fern?" she gleefully called out. "Come on, take a guess!" She was already laughing at herself

for asking the house to answer her. "Just kidding! The best way to carve a piece of wood is whittle by whittle."

It was such a stupid joke, but she landed in a pile on the floor, arms wrapped around her waist, as her laughter filled the cottage. Fern opened and closed her shutters softly. After having Amelie in the house for a few days, I learned that was Fern's way of showing that she was pleased.

Number two, she was resourceful. Fern supplied her with many more activities than I was ever gifted, but Amelie has been tinkering with all kinds of things that had been here since I arrived. There were some pictureless frames stacked together behind the couch in the sitting room that I'd never cared to look at. Amelie found that there were cracks all around the perimeter. She muttered to herself, *that simply won't do.*

She was gone for a while and came back with two of the frames tucked under her arm. Vines wrapped around the edges, and strategically placed flowers filled the empty spaces. The gold frame had pink and purple flowers, the silver one had flowers of three different shades of blue.

She asked Fern to pick the perfect paintings to fill the frames. Fern did just that, and at dusk, the flowers were glowing around the paintings.

"How'd you get those to stay alive after you cut them?" I asked Amelie, completely perplexed. The Forest was full of magic, but dead flowers were still dead flowers.

"I asked the Forest?" she replied, confused why I didn't know that already. She looked at the flowers like they were the most beautiful things she'd ever seen. I wondered how often she looked in a mirror.

And last, she was absolutely radiant. Pure fucking sunshine. Her eyes weren't that solid sapphire color I thought they were. They are less opaque. Rivers of gold flowed from her pupils, making her irises that of an enchanted pool.

Her hair was always a mess. The women in Avonya wore their hair in intricate styles at all times, it was a sign of power and class. Amelie would bathe and braid her hair but she never sat down for very long so she would always return with wild locks. Loose ends and the random spiral curls bounced over her shoulders.

She was slender but definitely adding a few needed pounds to her bones due to Fern's cooking. It looked amazing on her, she was looking less gaunt and frail and more like.... a woman. She had a round, perfect ass and perky breasts that weighed in on the smaller side. She was too perfect.

The first few days after she tried to escape, I taunted her relentlessly. From intimidation to playful humiliation, but her heart seemed to be made of bricks. Nothing bothered her. She laughed like I was joking when I told her she eats like a barbarian.

I learned to tune out the sounds of slurping and smacking at meal times. She hadn't said much to me, but when she was alone with Fern, she spoke like she was talking with a friend. As if Fern was answering her in their own secret language that I wasn't fluent in.

Tonight, I asked her to not track so much dirt in after her evening dip in the pond and she responded by asking me to come with her. I started to remind her that I am confined to the walls of this cottage, but before I could she called out, "Oh, that's right! You can't." Laughing her way to the water.

She was driving me insane.

But as I watched her waltz in for dinner, I noticed she left her boots on the porch.

I saw the tub in the bathroom steaming with candles lit around it. Fern had perfected the art of romanticizing everything.

Amelie floated in that direction. Deciding against my better judgment and with absolutely no plan in mind, I followed behind her. When my chest met her back, she spun and took in a sharp breath.

"I'm going to clean up before dinner. Did you need something in here?"

At a loss for words and knowing that I hadn't been able to piss her off yet, I went with being territorial. "That bath is for me. I asked Fern to run it just moments before you came inside."

She pinched her brows together and looked up at me through her dark, thick lashes. "You bathe?" Her tongue lingered on her lips as she taunted me.

Fucking hell. I'm going to kill her.

"I do, and this one is mine. Move, or I'll move you."

She'd cemented herself in the doorway so I picked her up by her shoulders and set her to the side, then walked into the bathroom.

"Can we share the bath?"

Coming to a complete stop, I replayed the last thirty seconds in my mind because I couldn't recall giving her any illusion that bathing together would be appropriate right now.

"Sorry?" That was the best I could come up with because this woman was unbelievable.

"I'm dirty. I don't want to show up for Fern's exquisite dinner in this filth. My brothers and I had to do it all the time when we were young so we could all have hot water." She was sure of herself, as if bathing together wasn't an extremely intimate act.

Trying to remain as cool and in control as possible, I let out a long breath. "Fine, but don't get any ideas about this. Keep your undergarments on, and I'll keep mine on." I hoped that would set a clear boundary between the two of us.

Then, I undressed for a bath that I didn't need.

She started back up again as I dropped my lounge pants on the floor hesitantly. "Duh, Kiaran. No funny ideas from me. I'm not sure losing my virginity to a Witch would earn me points in Heaven."

This time, she dropped what felt like an explosive in the

room and I considered grabbing the towel and throwing it over her body. "If you're a virgin, then we should definitely not bathe together."

She laughed, throwing her top on the floor and sank one leg into the tub. I stood at the sink, trying to gain any semblance of control.

"I thought we weren't getting any ideas, magic man." She tried to give me a wink, but failed miserably. So, she blinked, basically.

"Don't call me magic man."

Her body was on display to me, and it was taking everything in me to not wrap my arm around her waist and pull her leg up over my hip. What I would do with a fist full of her hair and my mouth on—

Oh fuck. *Get it together, man.* She's a virgin.

But—

Stop! I shouted at myself inside my own head. Thank her God she couldn't hear my thoughts like I could hers.

I'll chalk that up to being forcibly celibate for two centuries.

She plopped down on one end of the tub and rested her hands on the lip. "Get in Kiaran. Stop making this more than it is."

I did as I was told because, apparently, people could tell me what to do now. Or at least she could. But not before stretching the tub with a snap of my fingers so there was little chance of any stolen touches below the bubbles.

Sitting on the opposite end from Amelie, I stared at the outline of her jaw as she relaxed against the tub's edge. This woman was nothing like the ones I knew at home. She was celestial but in a way that held no magic at all.

Craning her neck back upright, she broke the silence. "Why were you cursed?" She lazily played with the bubbles floating across the top of the water.

"Story for another day. My turn, where did the bruises you

showed up with come from?" If she wanted to ask the questions she knew we both didn't want to answer, then fine.

Her shoulders tensed. Fear etched her face, making my skin heat, remembering her bruised face when she first arrived. She let it all roll off her shoulders and into the steam hovering over the bath, letting out a long breath, "Next question." Her voice was a broken whisper.

I reached through the bath water and took her trembling hands in mine. "You know you're safe with me, right?" If the answer was no, I wouldn't blame her. I haven't exactly been welcoming.

When she lifted her gaze, her eyes were full of unshed tears. I felt a crack form in my heart.

Her head nodded slowly, as if trying to convince herself it was true.

"Tell me about your family." Fuck, I hope her family didn't put those bruises on her face.

Amelie's watery smile appeared, endearing whatever thoughts flitted through her mind.

"I have three little brothers, Wren, Hansel and Tildan," she started. "Wren is a cranky old man in a thirteen year old's body, Hansel's a dreamer—happiest seven year old you'll ever..." She stopped. Swallowing thick and wiping a traitorous tear away.

"Hansel and I are the most alike. Then Tildan's the baby. They all have my dad's pretty brown eyes." She stared at her fingers beneath the suds.

"You have pretty eyes." I kind of blurted it, but I meant to say it. Her eyes were fucking gorgeous.

"Sorry." I cleared my throat. "What about your parents?"

Amelie chewed on her lip. "Next question."

Knowing that she used levity to break up her sad thoughts, I leaned back to my side of the tub. "I think it's strange that the books that pique your interest the most are about alchemy."

She smiled at that. "That's not a question, Kiaran."

"I know. But you seem like a girl who would much rather enjoy a steamy romance or fairy tale."

Her cheeks flattened her eyes, a sweet smile replacing the sad one. "I *do* love fairy tales, and a steamy romance story, but I don't need books for that." She had fire pulsing through her eyes. "Every night while I sleep, I dream—"

"Everyone has dreams, Amelie," I deadpanned.

She rolled her eyes. "But not everyone can remember them like I can. I used to ask the girls at school. Usually, they'd forget them when they woke up," she explained.

"Okay. Continue."

"So, I get to be all kinds of fairy tale characters. I've been a ballerina, a princess, a fairy, and even a huntress who protects the woods from bad guys. Then, at the end of the dream, my knight in shining armor comes and whisks me away. We always live happily ever after, and because of that, I've never wanted to read another romance. I just replay my own."

"Aren't you a little old to be wishing on knights in shining armor to come to your rescue?" I tried to relax into the unfamiliar situation a bit, but her eyes kept teasing me. Her gaze continued to trace the bounds of my face and every time she did, I felt my heart skip a little.

"Not when you grow up the way I did. You never stop dreaming of someone coming to save you."

CHAPTER 8
Amelie

It was true. Maybe I was too old to believe in fairy tales.

Then again, being here felt like a fairy tale. The warm feeling that always coursed through my veins when I'd meet my prince in my dreams was present in the room right now. All of the enchantments of the Forest were exact to the details of my dreams. My prince making butterflies set flight in my stomach at the lightest touch, all of it felt just like being here. With Fern and Kiaran.

Kiaran was trying so hard to keep his eyes off me while I soaped up my body. But he kept his eyes fixed on the blank walls of the washroom, studying each fleck of dust. I tested him by washing slowly over my décolleté and rolling my head back a bit. He shifted in response, and his jaw clenched so hard I thought he might crack his teeth in half.

I was still not convinced this wasn't all a dream, so my bravery was that of dream Amelie's when Kiaran was being a freak about the bath. But as I sat across from him, feeling confident in my body and its safety, I was beginning to believe this *was* real.

I figured when he made the bathtub double its normal size

that he wanted nothing to do with my body. I wasn't even sure I wanted him to do anything with my body. But there was something about him that made me feel safe. It often seemed like he didn't know what to do with me around, instead of the other way around. I'd never been sure of myself around men.

When I finished, I stood and let the excess water run down my body. Kiaran nearly broke his neck to avoid a glance. I cupped a handful of bubbles and blew them at him, coating his face and chest in the soapy liquid. He had no reaction other than to wipe a few of the bubbles from his eye.

I wrapped myself up in the fluffy robe that hung next to the tub and laughed at how much safer I felt testing an immortal Witch than the guards back home. Leaving the bathroom, I gave him a coy smile. "See you at dinner, *magic man.*"

Before I could shut the door to my room, I heard a sigh so loud from Kiaran I would venture to guess he'd been holding his breath the entire time we were in there. I spent the rest of the afternoon sending prayers into the void that my little brothers knew how much I missed them.

DINNER WENT as it usually did. Fern served great food, and I tried my best to eat like a lady. Kiaran was awkward, and I was chatty. Nothing new there. I'd seen the Forest's dusk performance every night since my first day here, and it was never short of spectacular. Even if Fern could summon the most vibrant, rare colors on the planet, nothing could do the light show justice. So each night, I committed it to memory.

The path of the butterflies, the direction of the wind as it encouraged the flowers to dance. I tried to count the sparkling pollen in the air to make sure each speck had a spot in the memory. I noted the shift in light as the sun fully set and differentiated in great detail how much brighter the Forest was when it first darkened.

I tried to explain to Kiaran how wonderful it was up close, but I caught myself before asking him to come with me next time. What it must feel like to not be able to leave. How many nights had he watched the show from the windows or the door frame and felt tortured by it? When I sat in the middle of it, I felt like I was one with the Forest. As if the plants, bugs, and trees were inviting me personally to their club. An exclusive member.

After spending most of dessert telling Kiaran about the wonders of tonight's show, he cut me off right as I was about to tell him about the deer that showed up to watch with me.

"Have you learned anything from your books? I noticed you've dusted off most of the ones on alchemy."

"Oh, it's fascinating! To be an alchemist and have the skills to blend properties together so precisely to make magic? I've started dreaming about it, actually," I admitted, he seemed curious about that, so I continued. "Like last night, I was out picking berries by the treeline, and a Dwarven man with facial hair down to his knees and a plump little nose came rushing up to me. He said his wife was terribly ill, and he needed a remedy as quickly as possible."

"Wait, can you think of your dream? You said you can replay them, but try to picture everything that happened." Kiaran leaned forward on the table like he was enacting a plan.

"Why?"

"Just do it."

I focused on the dreamy picture of helping the dwarf and his wife, the exact amount of berries on the bush, the color of the potion… but then the world went black.

"What the–" I shrieked. Someone was holding my hand when Kiaran's voice sounded into the void.

"Don't freak out."

Too late.

If this was death, then I'd be just fine with that. The world was bright again. Even though it was later in the evening, the birds were singing, and the sun was low in the sky. I took in the fresh, woodsy air, feeling the heat on my face. I turned to Kiaran. "What is this?"

He shrugged. "Look at the bushes."

Doing just that, my breath caught at the top of my throat.

It was me.

"What? What's going on?"

"Just watch, Amelie."

I was picking the berries from the bush and tossing them into a wicker basket on my arm when the little man from last night's dream ran up to me in a panic. Rattling off the same plea for help.

It was my dream.

Kiaran was still holding my hand, but his eyes were closed now.

I watched it play in front of me, just as it did in my sleep.

"Was that a real potion you learned?"

"No, but one thing that all of those books mention is that half of making potions and elixirs is about simply believing in what you're blending together." It made sense. Kiaran's magic was at least semi-limited, that much I understood. His wolves acted like domesticated dogs. But alchemists held the world at their fingertips. It was as if no matter what they put into their cauldron, whatever they manifested to happen, happened.

Kiaran's eyes remained closed, but I watched a dream version of myself and the Dwarven man scurry into the cottage. Just like a scene in a play, we were now watching from the kitchen inside. I was breathless from tirelessly stirring the thick elixir, so the dwarf ducked under my arms and took hold of the bottom of the ladle and helped me turn the mixture.

Finally, smoke billowed over from the cauldron. I scooped up a vial of the elixir, and the small magical creature gave me a sloppy kiss on the cheek, then hustled off to attend to his wife.

I turned to Kiaran, knowing the replay of my dream had finished. He never reopened his eyes, so I waggled our hands to get his attention, "All done?"

"Yeah," I replied, adoring the big scary Witch who somehow just showed me my own personal fairy tale. It was crystal clear, like it was happening in real time. I imagined that was how Hansel's imagination worked, and how he stayed so chipper.

Back to blackness. This time, not so jarring.

"If I'd known it was as easy as just winging it, I might've paid more attention in school," he scoffed at himself once we were back to our corporeal selves.

"Well, it's not *easy*," I explained, shaking away the dizziness from whatever magic Kiaran just used. "You have to learn how to control your mind and harbor the energy that thrums through you, then place your intention into that ball of energy and melt it into the cauldron as you mix. That's why it is crucial to mix counterclockwise. Stirring against the grain allows the manifestation to seep into the elements as they break down."

For some reason, that drew a smile from him. A wider one than I was usually granted, it was beautiful. Kiaran was beautiful. Even when he was hiding back in the shadows, brooding around or making things downright uncomfortable between us. There was no taking away from how striking he was.

Kiaran held my shoulders in his hands, studying me, checking my body over and then meeting my eyes again.

"Are you okay?"

"I'm fine, what the hell was that?" I asked.

He sighed in relief. "I went into your mind and drew from your memory."

"You *what?*"

What the hell did that even mean? If he could conjure up dreams like that, I wonder if he's done it for himself. Put himself somewhere that reminded him of being happy.

"It's Black Magic. It can be dangerous but I've only ever used it as a torture device when I was on orders from my High Priestess. I would find their deepest, darkest fears and play it for them up close and personal. It's really effective, actually."

Sometimes I thought he spoke before his brain gave him permission. "You've tortured people? When you were talking about how terrible you could be, you weren't kidding?"

His tanned skin paled briefly before schooling his features once again. "Next question?"

Not this time.

"I'm living in this house with you and trying to make myself believe you aren't going to kill me. I'd like to know who you hurt and why you hurt them."

"Wouldn't you rather watch your dream again?"

"*Kiaran.*"

"Fine."

He finally released my body from his grasp then sat back on the bench. Raking his hands through his hair before straightening to stare blankly ahead. "What tales were you told about the Whispering Forest?"

"Everything I was told growing up about this Forest has been the complete opposite of what I've experienced since being here. Aside from the immortal Witch who I'm now roommates with, that is. He seems to fit the mold of all the terrifying tales."

Kiaran bowed his head. He may have tortured people, and I'd get that story out of him at some point, but I thought maybe he was being tortured too. Whether by himself or by someone much more powerful than him, I wasn't sure. It was as if watching some kind of veil lift and then cover again when he admitted such things. It seemed like it hurt him to recount the memory.

"I shouldn't have done that, Amelie."

"Torture people? Ya don't say." I popped a hip and crossed my arms.

"No, draw from your memory. I shouldn't have gone into your mind like that. I've never done it for anything good, and I thought maybe I would try. Maybe it was time to do something good for once."

That was the first time I felt like I really *saw* him.

The overwhelming presence he carried with him was crumbling right before me. Broken and small. He seemed more like a boy right now. I didn't understand how he was able to do what he'd just done for me but I wasn't mad at him for that. In fact, I thought it was a lovely thing to do. The intention was clearly good.

I was mad that he'd done the same thing to other people, but used it to hurt them.

Taking a seat next to him, I removed his big hands from his temple and wrapped both of mine around them. "I'm not mad at you for showing me my dream. I'd love to tell you all of my dreams so I can see them again. All I've ever known is malice and hurt, it's just hard to hear that you've been that person to others."

He nodded in understanding, absentmindedly rubbing his thumb against my pointer finger. I didn't miss the tingle it sent down my spine at the delicate touch. All of his broken pieces were laid out in front of me, but he quickly scooped them back up and threw his mask back on.

"I'm sorry, nonetheless. I'd be happy to listen to your dreams anytime."

He walked a few paces toward the stairwell leading to the attic. I trained my gaze to my feet. Uncomfortable with the absence of him already.

"Hey Amelie?" He turned slightly before ascending the stairs. His arms were relaxed at his sides, but his fingers thrummed against his thigh.

"What?"

"There was no prince in your dream last night."

CHAPTER 9
Amelie

The Bloch family never owned a dog.

The boys and I always wanted one, but we could barely feed ourselves, let alone a dog too. My friend Prita from childhood had a dog and it would always chew up her things, then fold his ears back and tuck his tail between his legs when he got in trouble for it.

That's what Kiaran reminded me of today. A dog in trouble. Since the night he'd admitted to a dark part of his past, he'd been moping around the house with his theoretical tail tucked between his legs and his ears flopped back in submission. I could tell he was waiting for me to cut the tension, but it was evident to me that he had some penance to pay, and I was not God.

He could work that out with himself.

So, after three long days of shuffling around each other awkwardly, and a big lunch from Fern I decided I needed some fresh, non-Kiaran affected air.

"I'm going out for a walk. You can eat dinner without me if I'm not back by then." That perked up Kiaran's ears a little further than intended.

"Around the cottage? Why wouldn't you be back for dinner?" Kiaran began strumming his fingers against his thigh again.

"No, I thought I'd go into the Forest." I grabbed my satchel off the table.

"You can't go out there alone, Amelie." His tone was demanding, as if he could stop me if I walked out that door.

"Listen, you're sulking, and I can appreciate that you need to sort through whatever you're feeling, but I don't like to spend my days with people who feel bad for themselves. No time for that." Maybe he didn't deserve my snapping at him, but it was the truth. Spend too much time down on the ground feeling bad for yourself, and you leave yourself vulnerable to more attacks. Your only option was to get the hell up, dust yourself off, and brace for the next hit. That's life.

"I'm not *feeling bad for myself,*" he snapped back. "I just, I've never.. I–"

"No, Kiaran, you *are* feeling bad for yourself. The poor, lonely Witch who tortured people for his own sick reasons. *You* made those decisions. *You* hurt people. *You* made people live out their last moments on Earth living in their darkest fears, as if impending death wasn't terrifying enough." Apparently, there was a bit of fight left in me.

"Amelie, you don't know what or why I've done anything. You don't know the half of it. In fact–"

"Then tell me! I told you last night that the only fear I've felt since arriving here was of you. You want to explain yourself? The floor is yours." I dramatically swept my arms around the room, knowing he wouldn't take the opportunity. Kiaran broke my gaze with pinched brows and a tight line on his mouth. His stare was locked on whatever sat past the window in the kitchen.

"Didn't think so. What a privilege it is to feel bad for yourself instead of the souls who deserved your pity on Earth."

I turned on my heel, not allowing the chance for a rebuttal. Fern swung the door shut fiercely behind me, the period in my statement as if to say, *yeah, what she said.*

Floating over the bridge, feeling confident that he couldn't follow me, I approached the tree line at the edge of the clearing. I hadn't returned to the thick of the Forest since I arrived. I hadn't needed to. My confidence shook a little at the immensity of the wooded area before me. Kiaran wasn't exactly wrong about not knowing what could be out here.

I glanced back at my safe cottage. Kiaran was staring at me through the window, a look of concern and sadness laced his face. He wasn't masked right now, he knew I was looking back but he held the expression. Sending up a silent prayer that he'd keep that demeanor and not turn into the immortal torturer of souls and cast his wolves out, or any other lethal predators for that matter, I took off into the Forest, hoping I looked more confident than I felt.

The clearing was out of view within seconds. The massive, ancient trees and thick brush took the cottage out of sight. I was sure I'd get lost if I didn't mark my path, so I took a few pieces of journal paper out of my bag and stabbed a hole through the middle. Then I hung them on a branch every hundred paces as I walked and hoped they'd stay put.

The Forest was vast. The stories I'd been told growing up, and the fear it instilled in me seemed to be a far cry from what was in front of me right now. It looked like what I assumed any other Forest looked like. But it *felt* different. The churches detested magic and the danger of those who held it. The Priest said it was a malevolent force on Earth and all who possessed it were damned. At minimum, the light show was proof that it wasn't all so bad. I tried to decipher between my memories that were tainted by adrenaline during my life or death escape here and what was right in front of my eyes now as I trailed deeper and deeper.

The willows that cried that first night were singing beautiful melodies now. The oak trees chanted what you might hear when men were walking into battle. They were the leaders calling it out. The grass, fallen branches, flowing creek water and rocks were the men chanting it back.

I listened to the music and hummed along hoping my harmony wasn't imposing on their melody.

Coming to another clearing, I saw what looked like a campsite. It had a small fire pit in the middle of a large dirt circle and a glittering lake sat behind it. I hadn't seen one other person since staying at the cottage, well besides Kiaran. Only the creatures that showed up for the dusk show.

Taking another look around and feeling as if I was being watched. The campsite looked empty, but the fire pit still had smoldering ashes popping inside it.

Sitting with my back to a tree, I kept a keen eye on my surroundings as I pulled out my book, a pen, and the remainder of the paper I had. Fern had pulled another alchemist book out for me and it was the best one yet.

This one was older than Kiaran and talked about the origin of studying alchemy. How the first Witches who practiced were hardly magical at all. They'd been exiled from their Covens for being utterly horrible at magic actually. They'd failed every simple test that would've allowed them to keep learning their craft so they turned to trying to draw from the elements.

From the recounting of it, it sounded like many lives were lost in the process. Witches were extremely smart but lacked the ability to admit what they didn't know, the author's words, not mine. However, my time with Kiaran was proving that to be pretty accurate.

After the introduction, it talked all about how alchemy was a concept of magic and it didn't care if you had celestial bloodlines. It was just as I told Kiaran it was, a manifestation being blended with the elements to create what the maker willed it to be. I wasn't sure what drew me to these books but I was fascinated by the concept of being able to form something tangible by willing it alone.

With all my notes I'd accumulated from my days of reading and the free time I now had an abundance of, I wondered if Fern would help gather what I needed to try some of these recipes for myself. I didn't have any magic, but it sounded like maybe I didn't need to. Maybe it was the Forest, or the years of pent up rage that was slowly fading with each passing day in the Forest, but something deep inside of me was trying to crawl its way out. Every time I turned a page, tingles pricked the pads of my fingers and my eyes seared like hot coals. But in a good way, one that my soul seemed to welcome.

"Miss? Oh miss, you shouldn't be here." A quiet, grumbly voice shook me to my core. I figured if anything was going to attack me out here it would surely be something larger and much more terrifying than the small, plump woman hobbling toward me.

"I'm sorry!" Getting to my feet, I stuffed my things into my satchel. "Is this your campsite? Nobody was here. I just assumed it was free to anyone!"

The small woman played with her fingers like if she grabbed the right one it would tell her what to say next. "This is Frea's campsite. The men will be here soon, though, so you need to leave!" She darted her eyes around the area with furrowed brows, bobbing back and forth on her feet.

"Miss, did you hear me! You need to go!" Totally panicking now, the small woman grabbed my hand and started pulling me back to the treeline. I couldn't help but laugh. I'd dreamed of a Dwarven woman holding my hand and guiding me through the enchanted Forest so many nights, maybe I was dreaming of the one dragging me into the trees.

"Do you think this is funny? Frea does not like visitors, and those men will not take kindly to you."

I felt no fear with this woman. Even midst her panic, my heart felt calm with her hand wrapped around mine.

She didn't let up or let go as I ducked and weaved through the branches. I saw the first piece of paper and wondered if she was who I felt watching me. "What's your name?" I asked, trying to soothe this woman's anxiety.

Not stopping her little strides but turning back to me, she replied, "Ethel." Then continued to tug on my arm as I walked at a perfectly normal pace behind her near jog.

"Who's Frea?"

She stopped dead in her tracks then, looking up at the Forest's roof of limbs and leaves. Ethel slowly spun to me, motioning with her finger for me to bend down so she could whisper in my ear. "Frea is all around us." She stared back up at the towering trees, then back to me, arching a brow. "Do you see? Frea decides who lives, who dies, who comes, and who goes. So, you need to go back to where you came from."

"Does Frea live in the trees?" I asked, not understanding.

"No. Humans.." she scoffed. "Frea *is* the trees. The spirit that makes the Forest alive. Everything we are, is because of her."

A shiver ran down my spine, the voice I'd heard when I first got here. The one I thought was threatening me. All I'd known of the Forest and the things in it was far less scary than I'd been told it was all my life. Ethel seemed genuinely concerned for my being here, but we'd been far enough from the clearing now that she'd let my hand go and walked alongside me.

"You must respect Frea. She is *always* watching."

I nodded in understanding.

"Now tell me, girl, who are you and why are you here?" she asked.

I liked Ethel. It was strange seeing another person out

here, but I was glad to have a companion on my journey home. There was something about her that made me want to hold her hand and tell her all my secrets.

"My name is Amelie Bloch. I grew up just outside the Forest, miles away from here." As I spoke, Ethel's anxiety seemed to roll off her shoulders a bit. We walked more lazily now, enjoying the greenery. Passing another sheet of my journal paper, I plucked it off its branch and shoved it back in my satchel. It was unfamiliar to share my story with someone, but she was so nervous for me by the lake. I hoped it might continue to calm her.

"My next birthday will be my twenty-fifth. My home was…a hard place to call home. The men who guarded the village were evil. It was my brother's birthday the day the Palace banished me to the Forest." With tears now lining my eyes, I looked at Ethel. "He's seven now." Ethel looked at me the whole time I spoke, dodging branches and roots like it was a part of her routine.

"I knew the Blochs once upon a time. They were artists. A lot of the beauty you see around us was their dreams come to life." Taken aback by her words, I wondered if my family traveled through the Whispering Forest to arrive in Holleberg. It was maddening to think how different life might've been if they had settled here.

"There were Bloch's here?"

Ethel let out a big, hearty laugh. "Two of 'em. rowdy boys, but grew up to be fine gentlemen." A smile crept over her mouth, remembering the Blochs who preceded me.

I chewed on my lip. If I had an uncle living right under my nose, it shouldn't be a surprise to find out I had family from the Forest. From what I knew of my father's family, it was small. So, what are the chances Ethel's old friends were my family?

Stopping and turning toward me, Ethel stood on her tippy toes, reaching up and cupping my face with her palms. Overwhelmed at the proximity of another person after a lifetime of little to no affection, I tried my best to avoid eye contact.

Ethel's mouth slanted up on one side before saying, "You have the magic of gold in your eyes, girl." Then dropped our hands and continued our walk as if she hadn't just implied that I have a family that, in fact, wasn't human and that the streaks that bolted around in my irises were magical.

"So, you ran away to the Whispering Forest?" She wasn't believing that I left on my own free will. I explained to her the events that led to my new residency here. Ethel took my hand again. When she did this time, a wave of recognition hit me like a warm breath against my heart. Ethel *was* the dwarf I so often spoke to in my dreams. To my core, I knew that she'd been the one visiting me night after night, allowing me to pour out my darkest secrets to her.

She let me talk about the three little faces I'd been missing terribly. How Hansel would go nuts to find out I had a Witch for a roommate and a dwarf as a new acquaintance. Wren would spend every day by the river fishing, probably getting frustrated at Tildan for not staying quiet and scaring away the fish.

Ethel just listened, and when I finished talking and she squeezed my hand, I held back a smile—somehow my dearest friend from my dreams was standing at my side.

I knew it. I was so grateful for whatever magic allowed it.

Ethel knew right where my last piece of paper was hung. She turned to face me when we reached it, then took hold of my other hand, too.

A warm wind wrapped us in our own little bubble. Murmurings that I couldn't understand tickled up my arms, covering every inch of my being. Ethel's eyes widened as it got louder and louder. Like she understood every word that the wind was whispering.

She closed her eyes as her head bowed. "Of course, thank you for honoring me with this message." Pausing for a moment before continuing. "Thank you, Frea. Thank you for everything."

My heart fluttered. Ethel spoke with such admiration in her tone to the spirit in the trees. It was magical to see it happen right in front of me.

The warmth dissipated, the murmurs quieted. Save for the ever present song of the Forest. Ethel met my eyes, hers were watery as she curved her mouth into a smile. She looked completely overwhelmed with joy. "Frea would like you to know that you are welcome here, from all of us. She would also like your housemate to know that his heart will beat again."

She bowed her head into our hands and sobbed. To see someone so overcome with happiness that it came out in tears was overwhelming. I didn't cry often. Only when life boiled over my breaking point. But I always wiped the tears away as fast as they fell. Then raised the bar and carried on.

Still soaking our hands, she said, "Amelie, we are so fortunate for your company. Thank you."

Unsure of why she was thanking me, I replied, "No need to thank me, I didn't do anything."

"You will."

She kissed my knuckles, took one last good look, then walked back the way we came, just as the sun set. Right on cue, the Forest around the cottage's clearing lit up. Not wanting to miss my favorite show, I quickly made my way back home.

When I reached the glimmering clearing, I felt a small brush of skin against my arm. Ethel was standing next to me again. She was quiet as a mouse on her way back to me. I jumped when I saw her small frame staring at the cottage with even wider eyes than before.

"This is…" she whispered so quietly I could barely hear her before she trailed off.

"It happens every night at dusk. Isn't it beautiful?" I

replied, Ethel looked behind her, noting that it was, in fact, happening all around us but was the most alive here in this clearing.

"My family has lived here since the trees were little, Amelie. This has not been happening every night." She squeezed my hand before saying, "Go, your friend is waiting for you."

Through the glow and haze of fluttering creatures, I saw Kiaran standing in the doorway. His arms crossed over his chest, and he wore a small smile on his mouth. He was clearly trying to look friendly for our company. I went to make a joke to Ethel about Kiaran hardly being my friend, but she was gone again. I held my hand up, staring at my palm as it would show me evidence of my new little friend's presence. To no avail, I searched around the clearing and behind me until the thick took away my view. She was gone as fast as she came.

Shaking my head, hoping it would break up some of the pieces of crazy that were starting to form, I walked back to face Kiaran.

"Did you see that little woman standing beside me?"

Kiaran's brows pulled together. His blue eyes searching the clearing. "No?"

Pressing a hand to my forehead, checking for signs of illness, I took one more look at the tree line hoping to see her. I didn't.

I grabbed Kiaran's wrist to take a turn at checking my temperature, but a loud snap and a low, pained growl halted me.

His hand was snapping. I'd pulled his hand out of the doorway he'd been standing in.

"Amelie! Fuck, let go!" Doing as I was told, he cupped his hurt hand with his good one. "What the fuck were you thinking? You know I can't leave!"

"Oh my god. I'm so sorry! I wasn't trying to make you

leave, I swear!" He was already moving toward the stairs to the attic, so I followed. After all, this was my fault.

"What can I do? Oh my god, is it broken?" I ran my fingers through my hair and began pacing around Kiaran's room.

"Amelie, please. Shut the fuck up for a second."

Kiaran started splinting his wrist with a cast that looked like it'd been used one hundred too many times. He fastened buckles around it, covering his wrist and stabilizing his hand.

He closed his eyes and took a few steadying breaths before looking at me. With each of his heaving breaths, my eyes grew wider. I couldn't read how he felt about me right now.

Feels like this would be a great time for him to kill me.

"I won't lie, I considered killing you the second I felt it snap."

Oh yeah, he could read my mind.

"Kiaran, I'm so sorry. But why do you have a cast that looks like it's about to disintegrate to dust stashed in your bedroom?"

"You think that's the first time my hand has been out of the cottage? I've been here for two hundred years. I've tested the boundaries many times before, hoping the curse would fade over time. Fern gave me this one probably one hundred and fifty years ago, but she wouldn't give me a new one."

Well, that made perfect sense.

"You'd think after the first time you wouldn't try again," I said, trying to lighten the mood.

"You'd think. But you know I can't leave and you literally pulled my hand out and broke it. Guess our curiosity gets the best of us sometimes." He gave me a wink, tying nervous knots all through my stomach.

"I did not do that on purpose." He was going to hate me forever. This was a way better excuse for him to be a moody bitch.

"I'm not mad at you, pretty girl. You'll just have to make it up to me." He smirked.

Breaking his heated gaze, I looked up at the ceiling of the attic.

"Fern, can you please get the poor boy a new cast?" I sweetly asked our host. The old one became smoke on the wind as a new one perfectly splinted his broken wrist and fingers.

"Are you fucking kidding me?" Kiaran shouted up to the ceiling. She opened and closed her shutters in Kiaran's room. They were falling apart. Looking around finally, I noticed the attic was the only part of the house that hadn't been completely redone.

Holes riddled the floors, the walls were filthy and there were spots that opened to the outdoors, letting in a draft. Kiaran's bed was a tattered cot on the floor, and the chest that I assumed held his clothes had a lid that wasn't even connected at the hinges anymore.

"Fern, we're better than this. Would you please clean up Kiaran's room? I promise he'll be nicer to you if you do," I asked in a singsongy voice.

"She won't do it. I've been pleading with her for ages to fix up the place. My magic doesn't work on the structure. She's a prickly one."

Not allowing him to speak ill of her, Fern ripped the rug out from under Kiaran and he went falling right on his ass. Relenting, he laid all the way back on the dirty floor and covered his face.

"Sorry," he muttered.

I wasn't sure if he knew it, but he had more of an attitude problem than I did. I knew Fern thought so, too.

Moments later, the whole attic roared in a gust of wind. The small cot molted into a four poster king size frame with a new plush mattress and black silk sheets, topped with a puffy quilt laid over top. Two tables on either side. The chest was now a massive wardrobe with the doors spread open, exposing two racks of black, cream, and white tunics and pants.

The many rugs were now one large rug that covered the entire attic. This one was nicer than any of the ones on the main level. It had an intricate design and a thick border framing it in. Vibrant colors splashed around it, tying in the rest of the room. I knew Fern was nicer to me than she was to Kiaran, so I could only assume she pulled the most exquisite furniture out simply to show him what she could've done for him all this time.

Kiaran propped himself up on his forearms and scoffed. His eyes moved inch by inch through the room. If I didn't know any better, I'd say there were tears forming in his fierce eyes.

"Well, she really showed you, huh?"

Kiaran didn't say a word. He took in his new room with an intensity I hadn't yet seen.

"Kiaran?"

He peeled his eyes away from the bed and looked up at me. He was stunned, like he couldn't speak or even breath. Kneeling down, I pressed a palm to his cheek. He never left my gaze, but he pulled his knees in and rested his arms around them. Grabbing the other cheek to cup his face, I studied his watery, crystalline eyes. "Are you okay?"

"This was my room," he said in a pained voice. His breath was shaky as a lone tear betrayed him.

"It's still your room, Fern just made it nice for you." I brushed my thumb over his sharp cheek.

Kiaran stood and walked over to the bed. He ran his hand over the luxurious quilt, then opened the table sitting next to the bed. He pulled a small frame out. Not wanting to invade his space, I shuffled to the side to see what he was looking at.

"This was *my* room."

"What do you mean by that?"

Kiaran turned and showed me what was in the frame he'd taken out.

It was a painting of a little boy with dark, curly hair and mischief in his blue eyes, and a little girl with the same hair but sunshine written on her features, happy as could be. With them, two parents. The father held the little boy's shoulders proudly, showing the world his greatest creation. The mother was holding her daughter on her hip. She beamed for the artist. The mother watched her little girl, as if looking in a mirror.

I couldn't take my eyes off the matriarch of the family. She reminded me of the figure from my dreams. The one who'd take my hand and bring me to my prince.

"Back home. These are all things from my room." He took in his newly updated room, like it might vanish if he blinked. He looked so small again, the same way he did when he outed his mistakes a few nights ago.

I took my turn at a second glance around the room. This was so far from Fern's taste in clothes and furniture. Everything looked so expensive and fancy. My curiosity about his past grew by mountains now, especially since it looked a lot like the rooms in the Palace I often visited in my dreams.

Kiaran traced a finger over the little girl's smiling face. I understood now that it was a picture of his family. Of little him, his little sister, and his parents. The people he hadn't seen or spoken to in two centuries. My heart broke for him. I only knew a fraction of how it felt to no longer have family, but that little bit of understanding still made my heart ache for him.

Walking over to him, I laced my arm through the crook of his elbow and leaned into him. I wasn't short at 5'6, but Kiaran still felt like a tower. He had to be at least 6'3. I wasn't sure if my small presence would make a difference, but Ethel holding my hand today gave me comfort so I figured I'd try.

Without a second thought, he turned and wrapped both of his strong arms around me. Pressing one hand to the back of my head and bringing my cheek to his heart, the other secured around my lower back, the painting hanging on my hip in his hand.

He let out a shaky breath and let go of the embrace. As soon as his touch was gone, I missed it. I told myself it meant nothing, just a warm soul to hold in this moment, but my heart knew I was lying.

"I haven't been able to remember my sister's face. It's been so long." He sat on the edge of the bed, running a finger over the photo. "Every time I tried to remember them, they were faceless. Like melted clay. I…"—his voice cracked—"I miss them."

That did it.

Apparently, I'd been harboring my own tears and his words just set the sails.

"Are you okay?" he asked as I took a seat next to him. His face unreadable. Too many emotions for one to take a dominant place.

"Yeah, I'm fine. Are *you* okay?"

He took my hand in his good one. "I will be. This is just a lot to take in all at once. I accepted long ago that I might never see them again. This quilt?" He gestured back to the beautiful blanket covering his bed. "My grandmother gifted it to me when I finished fundamentals. She passed not long after that. I only had a few years with it before they sent me away."

I nodded, wanting to allow him the space to voice anything he needed to right now. He didn't take it but he squeezed my hand. I squeezed back in solidarity.

"I don't want to impose, I'm going to go freshen up. Do you want me to bring you up a plate for dinner?" I stood, unlacing our fingers that had apparently linked in a much more intimate way than intended.

"No, thank you." He smiled at me as I walked for the stairs.

"I'm sorry for breaking your hand. I swear I thought I was

going crazy, so I was going to have you check for a fever. I met a woman in the…" I cut myself off. This moment was not about me. "Never mind, I'll tell you about it later. You won't believe it." I laughed off the tension of the room and started down the stairs.

"Amelie," he called, "next time you want me to touch you, just ask. Preferably inside these walls." I blushed at the thought and then batted it away, knowing that was not how he meant it.

"That is how I meant it."

CHAPTER 10

Kiaran

In all my life, I was sure I'd never wanted to kill and kiss something as badly as I wanted to right now.

For two hundred years, Fern had the power to summon a piece of my home, and she'd made me sleep on a lumpy mattress with a quilt that was more holes than fabric. I'd worn the same few shirts and pants she'd given me every day, and never, not once, had she done anything this kind for me.

I was sure it was more for Amelie than anything. This was her first time up here, and I'm surprised it took her so long to notice the state of it. But it didn't surprise me that this was the one place in the house Fern just so happened to not redo, but still, it dug at me a bit that I wasn't good enough alone to live in the luxury Amelie was given.

A big difference in Fern's eyes might be that, according to Amelie's thoughts, I was a moody bitch, and Amelie was nothing but kind and pure with a touch of crazy. I felt imprisoned here, but for Amelie it was a sanctuary. Our reasons for taking up residence in the Forest alone was enough to know the difference between us. Amelie told Fern I'd be kinder to her in exchange for her sprucing up the attic, but this was too much. This was something I could never repay Fern for.

So I started with the one thing I'm not sure I'd ever said to her. "Thank you, Fern. This means the world to me."

She greeted me with a warm hug of wind, and it seemed as good a place as any to call a truce with the sentient cottage.

I sank all of my weight into my soft bed. My massive, perfectly comfortable bed. I wrapped myself in the blanket that still smelled just like my mother's incense she burned around the house to ward off negative energy. It smelled like home.

Winter Solstice was coming, less than a month and a half away. Amelie's arrival initially seemed like a gift from my Coven, my way home. But she was mortal. Falling for a mortal wasn't natural, the High Table wouldn't mingle the two worlds.

The High Priestesses words plagued my mind,

You are bound to the cottage in the mortal realm, in an enchanted Forest. In order to break your curse you will need to make an impossible sacrifice. You must offer your Coven something of value to you on Winter Solstice. You will have one chance, each year to be untethered. It must be of such value that handing it over to us will cause you unimaginable pain. If it does not mirror the pain you caused, it will not suffice.

Let the longest night approach and with it, the weight of your choice. Let your mind fill with every other option you think you have and may you find no reprieve. You will spend eternity there, Kiaran McCalmont. Until you feel the curse lock into place, you will be alone.

This would be my two-hundredth attempt and I came up empty once again on what they needed from me. It was impossible to know what I could sacrifice to them to atone for what I did. I'd already accepted that nothing would ever meet that level of pain. My one shot was Amelie, and after our short time together, I wasn't sure I could ever sacrifice that silly, ethereal woman. Thankfully, her blood didn't even make her an option.

Studying the painting, it felt like maybe the curse was only to drive me mad. To take me away from all that I knew and let the pain of that be my penance. I wondered what my sister looked like now. She was an adorable and annoying child. One that I tried to get rid of constantly. The Black Magic I'd learned came in handy when I wanted to cast a portal and toss her through it.

Knowing now that had she not come back every time, I would've missed her terribly. She was a shy kid. She giggled constantly but would try to stifle it, causing her to snort when she laughed. I hoped she still had that funny quirk. I imagined her as a radiant beacon in the Coven now. Someone everyone trusted and loved. Who used her magic to better Avonya. By now, I hoped that her fated mate had found her and treated her with respect. Would she be a mother now? She would be the best mom. She took such care of her dolls and the babies around the village.

My mother and father were still alive, at least. You knew when your parents passed. A tether to the world as you knew it snapped in your soul. It's said to be so painful that some people never recover. We were lucky to live so long that it didn't happen often, but I remember those whose parents had passed. They were never the same.

I heard Amelie's door close at least an hour ago, but I knew she stayed up late reading her books. She often paced back and forth from the desk to the bed in the middle of the night, creaking the floorboards as she did.

Setting the painting against the lantern on the nightstand, I dressed in my new, old pajamas and went downstairs.

I saw the faint flickering of a candle under the door and smelled the caramel from her sleepy time tea. Deciding that the moment we shared earlier was enough for me to impose on her space, I knocked on the door.

"Come in," she called.

Cracking the door open, I took in what she'd done with my old room. Amelie had the frame with blue water lilies hung on the wall, glowing in all its enchanted glory. The rug was a deep purple color with greens and golds laced in floral patterns around it.

Journals covered her desk, books with dog-eared pages piled one on top of the other sat in the corner. A mug of tea steamed on the nightstand.

She sat with crossed legs on the bed in a short, black sleep dress. It had tiny straps to hold it up, one side threatening to slip off her shoulder. Little slits on the sides showed some of her upper thigh. Much less than I saw of her in the bath, but all the more distracting.

A pen dangled from her lips as she finished reading her notes before those pretty eyes finally looked up at me.

I took a seat on the end of her bed, the farthest away I could be from the beautiful human sitting in her own perfect mess. Her puffy lips were swollen as if she'd been chewing on them and I couldn't help the fleeting thought at how they might taste. Her hair was let loose from her braid and it covered her shoulders like a blanket. Melted chocolate waves that I considered drowning in. Fucking hell, she was perfect.

"Everything okay?" She dropped the pen on the bed and focused on me. I realized my gaze had been locked on her lips and I didn't miss the slight twitch at the side of them when she noticed it too. I loved her attention being on me.

"Yeah, no, everything is fine. I just heard you pacing around down here."

"I'm sorry, I can be quieter," she replied shyly. I wasn't sure what my reason was for coming down here, but it wasn't to tell her to be quiet.

"You're fine. I just have really good ears. Had me wondering what was so exciting." I thumbed through the pages of the book closest to me. The girl should be an encyclopedia on all things alchemy at this point. I don't think she'd read anything else since the library was built.

"Actually, I've already read all of these. But, I was going back through my notes because I remembered something that

I wanted to try." Intrigued, I slid further back onto the bed and rested my back on the wall. My legs still hung off the bed, I couldn't believe I slept in this tiny thing for over half of my life. No wonder I was such a moody bitch, according to Amelie's thoughts.

"Yeah? What's that?"

"Veiling," she said, no humor in her voice at all, but I laughed anyway.

"Don't you want to try turning a frog into a bug or something first?"

She frowned at my suggestion. "I would never do that to my friends."

"Your friends with the frogs?"

"Actually, why don't you leave? I'm busy." She popped her brows at me.

"I'm sorry, please continue. What are you wanting to veil?"

"I thought I might try to veil your curse. Then I could make up for breaking your hand."

I stared at her, shocked. Veils of any kind were an incredibly difficult spell to perfect. So many things could go wrong, and with the amount she'd read, I knew she was aware of that.

"Professionals tried to teach us veiling in fundamentals school and I still never successfully made that elixir. While I appreciate the gesture, there's no need for that. Besides, it's against the law to interfere with my curse."

"Well that's too bad. I'm not under any orders and Fern already helped me gather almost everything I need. There's a few things in the clearing I need to grab and then I'll need some of your spit," she said it with no room to argue but I did anyway. "I really appreciate the idea, I do. But tampering with my curse will put a target on your back from my High Priestess. I won't do that to you."

"I have nowhere else to call home now, but you do. If it works, maybe you'd be able to figure out a way to go home."

She was impossibly stubborn, but her words made my heart jump a little. The High Priestess was the only one who could open the realms to travelers, but the sentiment alone was too pure for me to deserve.

"Make your potions, Amelie, but I won't be helping sign your death wish."

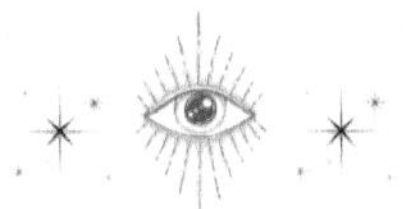

As PROMISED, Amelie was out the door first thing in the morning and back before I made my way downstairs for breakfast. Fern positioned a cauldron in a newly built cove off the kitchen. Amelie was bent over it, stirring like a mad scientist. Shelves were stacked high against the curved wall behind her, empty vials lining them along with an array of ingredients.

"Oh good! You're here. Come spit in this." Her tongue hooked around the corner of her mouth in pure determination.

"I told you I'm not helping you practice any sort of veiling and especially not for me." She rolled her eyes at me, never stopping the counterclockwise motion of the ladle.

"I'm not working on that. I'm making an elixir to boost endorphins. It's supposed to make you feel euphoric. If anyone in this house needs a mood booster, it's you."

"Ha, ha, very funny. You're lying." Giving her a displeased look, she nodded toward her journal. "Look. I swear I'm not lying. You were right, I should try some easier spells first."

Eyeing her warily, I walked over to her ridiculously unorganized notes. Sure enough, *Mood Booster was* scribbled in messy handwriting at the top of the page. "Fine. I'll do whatever you want so you stop calling me a moody bitch in your head." She blushed at my admission of listening in on her thoughts more than I replied aloud to.

Walking up to the bubbling cauldron, I spat in it. The worst part of alchemy was the bodily fluids infused in it to better bind it to someone. It wasn't a requirement, but its efficacy greatly increased with it.

As soon as it hit the mixture, Amelie stirred vigorously. Beads of sweat formed on her forehead, and she shrugged her hair off her shoulder to avoid adding it to the cauldron. She'd apparently left in such a hurry this morning that she didn't put in her typical messy style. Moving behind her, I started putting one long braid into her thick hair, and Fern summoned a tie around the end.

"How do you know how to braid?" Amelie asked, nearly out of breath.

"I used to braid my sister Mia's hair. She said I was more gentle than our mother was."

"Who knew you had such a soft side, magic man."

"There's a lot you don't know." I gave her a wink as I sat at the table to enjoy my breakfast. "And stop calling me that."

"Stop calling me pretty girl," she said in the worst impersonation of my voice.

"But you *are* a pretty girl."

Her cheeks pinked and her lips twisted to hide her smile. "And you're a man with magic."

I rolled my eyes and went back to my food. I wasn't sure what the tell was, but Amelie stopped stirring and took a few deep breaths in, straight over the smoke that was toppling over the cauldron.

"It's ready! You can take it after breakfast."

I wiped my mouth with my napkin. "I'm done. Give it to me." I felt happier than normal this morning, having had the best night of sleep in my cloud of a bed. But I didn't miss the intrigue trickling over me at the chance to feel euphoric for a short bit.

Amelie scooped a little glass vial through the thick mixture and strode over to me. "It shouldn't be hot, but it probably won't taste very good." She stretched her arm out to hand me the elixir. I grabbed it and tossed it back as if the last shot I took was yesterday and not two centuries ago. Amelie had already laid herself on the couch, not waiting for me to finish.

Back home, flowers bloomed when the clock struck midnight during the winter to spring season change. It happened in seconds. All around, gardens became bright with a variety of flowers in every color Avonya had ever seen. It was an explosion of florals, and the entire realm came to our estate to view the beguiling event.

That was what this felt like. My body thrummed with energy. It felt like my blood was moving faster than ever, looking for an escape. Feather light tingles trailed their way up my arms from my fingertips to the pit of my stomach. It felt like static all over the surface of my body. My brain was clear and full of light. My darkness washed away like old sand being sucked back into the Tala Sea.

"Amelie, it worked. You did it!" I yelled as I ran to her, hoping she might see the flowers blooming all over my soul.

She was lying on the couch, though, cold and unmoving. Her eyes were stuck on the ceiling directly above her. "Amelie?" She looked dead. As if her soul had—oh no.

No, no, no. She swore it wasn't a lie.

Running back to her journal, I looked at the page again. At the top it read *Mood Boosting Spell* but reading the summary and recipe closer, it was the same one she'd shown me last night when arguing about whether I'd allow her to work on veiling. If she veiled my curse, it would put her in a state between life and death. Because I was bound to the cottage, Amelie would be bound to her own inner consciousness.

To veil and unveil curses, memories, anything—it was

dangerous. Only members of the High Table could do it without repercussions. For a common Witch, it came with side effects. Their mind could turn to mush by taking on whatever was veiled, all magic needed a balance. Amelie wasn't a member of the High Table though, nor was she even a common Witch, so I prayed to her God she didn't just kill herself.

Amelie said that she wanted to do this so I could leave the cottage. It would've been the biggest piece of her manifestation. Fern had already opened the front door for me, a traitor if I'd ever seen one. She should not have been encouraging Amelie in her overzealous ideas. I wouldn't leave her side. As I pressed my ear over her heart, I heard the softest beat.

Suddenly, I became weightless. My body levitated over the couch, being pulled from Amelie's lifeless body. Fern was floating me toward the door. I fought and fought in fear of my entire body crumbling into a pile of broken bones. I definitely felt different, but Amelie's first try at alchemy could not have been perfect. The closer I got to the door, the faster my heart pounded in my chest.

The tips of my fingers searched for the door frame. My chest was tight and my soul pleaded for mercy. My head was through the doorway first. I braced for my skull to shatter, but it never came. Instead, my entire body crashed onto something plush and prickly. I peeked through one eye and saw bright green grass sprouting all around me.

The ground was soft compared to the wooden floors I'd padded around on for the better part of my life. I pressed my palms flat to the soil to stand. The fresh air filled my lungs with promises, hope. She did it. She got me out.

Unbelievable.

I was fully outside of the cottage for the first time in two centuries, and all I could think about was going back inside and waiting at the nearly dead girl's side for her to wake up.

Only those who sat at the High Table could veil perfectly.

Yet this anomaly of a woman who showed up battered and bruised a month ago did it seamlessly on her first try.

I marched back inside, and Fern slowly closed the door behind me. I swore I heard a whisper in the wind say *See? Don't doubt her.*

I lifted Amelie's head and sat down on the couch, resting her upper body in my lap. Checking her pulse again, a breath of relief escaped me when I noticed it was beating strong again. The veil should wear off quickly in our proximity, and when it did, I wouldn't hesitate to put her in her place.

She bested me, again. Just like she did the night she tried to escape. My walls with her were always down. Something in my soul wouldn't allow me to protect myself from her. She said jump, I asked how high. She said drink this elixir, I tossed it back like it was the water of life. Hell, if she said drop dead, I think my heart would stop on the beat.

Tracing my index finger around the curve of her delicate jaw, I admired her perfect face. Her cheeks had filled out, and it somehow contoured her high cheekbones even more. Her once pale, cracked lips were now smooth and blushed with a soft pink color. She was every bit as breathtaking as the day she arrived in complete disarray, but it was something more indescribable now. The golden rivers in her idle eyes were glowing like the air around fire.

And I was a moth to that flame.

The Morgenstern women had eyes like these. Murals of their blues and golds colored the walls of the business district in Avonya. They paid homage to the most powerful breed of Witches our realm had ever seen. Instead of holding soulful magic like the rest of Avonya, they had elemental magic. They drew from nature, making the sisters limitless. They were feared but respected, which drove our High Priestess mad. It was why their bloodline had to end.

If Amelie had celestial blood, I'd guess she was of the most powerful of families.

All celestial bloodlines were meticulously plotted out years before we were born. The High Priestess would choose to fate us based on our rank and looks. Vanity was important to immortals. My parents were likely fated to find each other when their great-grandparents were in their mother's womb.

You knew just by looking at someone if they were powerful or not. My mother, being a vital woman in the Coven, and my father being from a family that was riddled with high society Witches, it allowed my sister and I to have astounding genetics.

The girls in Avonya knew how fated mates worked. That if they were mine, it would secure a tether between us. It could never be broken. But it never stopped them from trying to weasel their way in. If the High Priestess could've fated me with someone like Amelie, she would've in a heartbeat.

McCalmont blood with the beauty of the woman laid across my lap would be unstoppable.

With Amelie, I imagined this was what those girls felt about me. Constantly wanting to be near me, smothering me with attention. Sometimes, it felt like she wanted that from me, but then sometimes it felt like she was still scared. I was a fish out of water here, this unfamiliar sense of longing for someone.

She came here seeking sanctuary, and I spent everyday wiping the drool from my mouth after panting for her like a dog.

Her face warmed under my touch, and the golden rivers in her eyes flowed crazily. The tingling in my skin faded and the bloomed flowers over my soul had gone back into hiding. As soon as I felt the emptiness, her eyes moved to mine.

"Did it work?" She shot to a sitting position.

"Are you okay? How do you feel?" I asked, not caring to answer her question.

"I'm fine. Great, actually. It didn't work, did it? My books said I would feel tired and weak after…" She checked over her body as if looking for missing pieces.

"That's true. I've never seen someone have an ounce of energy after an unveiling, either party."

She settled on her knees and faced me, resting her cheek on the back of the couch. "So it didn't work?" A pained look of defeat crossed her face, maybe even confusion. She was so sure it would work. I'm not sure I wanted her to know that it did. I didn't want her to do it again. It seemed she executed the enchantment perfectly, but I was chalking that up to beginner's luck. Although I wasn't sure luck played much of a part in a spell as powerful as this one.

Either way, I wouldn't let her do it again. So I lied. "No, it didn't work. It put you to sleep and made my skin tingle, but that was it." I didn't want her to lose complete faith in her natural ability.

She bowed her head to her hands and cursed. "Fuck."

"It's okay. I told you last night that I appreciated the gesture. You're forgiven for breaking my hand." I waved my cast at her. "You shouldn't have tricked me, Amelie. I trusted you."

She arched a brow at me. "You're kidding, right? You knew I was lying. You were just as excited to see if it would work as I was."

She was so wrong. I gave her a lot of unearned trust for reasons I didn't understand, and even though I'd spent two centuries looking for a way out, I meant what I said about not being worth the potential risks.

"What I don't understand is why I saw you lying on the ground outside. Like I was looking through your eyes when you did it. I felt scared for your bones but they didn't break."

What. The. Fuck.

That didn't happen under a veil.

"I don't know what to tell you. Maybe your mind made you see what you hoped would happen," I lied, hoping we could drop the issue before she realized she *somehow* saw exactly what happened.

"Maybe," she wondered, looking me over and stopping at my broken hand, "but then why is there dirt on your new cast?" Her brows popped, and I think she attempted to wink again.

I pursed my lips and interlocked the tips of my fingers. "Not sure. Guess it's dirty in here." I tried to keep my eyes on Amelie and off the immaculately kept cottage. She's too damn perceptive.

"Now who's lying to who?"

I rolled my eyes, turning my body away from hers.

"Oh my god! I did it." She hopped over to my side of the couch and grabbed my face, forcing me to look at her. She shuffled her hands down my arms, then my chest and legs. Then she crawled off the couch and picked up my feet, knocking on each boot. "No broken bones! This is fantastic. Where did you go?"

My idiotic mind wandered as she sat on her knees between my legs. I batted that fucking thought away, relented to the stubborn woman, and told her the truth. Because, like I said, if she told me to jump, I would immediately ask how high. "I didn't go anywhere. Honestly, I thought you killed yourself. Fern literally threw me outside, so I got up, and came right back in and waited for you to wake up so I could kick your ass for lying and putting your life on the line for me."

"Oh, don't be so dramatic. I told you I could do it." Amelie rolled her eyes. "You're so boring. You didn't even go to the pond to see the fish? Or the frogs? I almost died for you to touch grass? Bo-ring," she quipped in a singsongy tone. Then she tried, once again, to wink at me.

"Does that not hurt?" I asked. "You know you're not winking right?"

"*Whatever.*" She smacked my shoulder. The slight sting

from her palm quickly turned to a garden that I wanted her to keep watering with her touch.

"Promise you won't do that again. Please. It's not worth it, Amelie. *I'm* not worth it." Pleading with her, I hoped she knew I meant it.

The gold in her eyes sparked. Her gaze unbreakable. Shifting uncomfortably at the attention, I strummed my fingers against my thigh. "Promise me," I repeated, breaking the silence.

"No. I won't promise you that because I know how it feels to be trapped. To be so fucking sick of your life that you have to will yourself daily to keep going. I know how it feels to be alone with company, to hope that tomorrow will be different but knowing in your heart it won't be. We have potentially the rest of my life here together. I finally feel at peace. I feel happy here. I'm more at home with a magical house with the frogs, dragonflies, even the little woman I met in the woods and you, Kiaran, than I ever was in Holleberg."

Stopping only to breathe, she continued, "You can be a moody bitch all you want. You can refuse to do this with me but I'll just figure out a spell that will make you do what I want. But you *will* leave this cottage. You will find your little piece of heaven in this Forest. I'm going to make sure of it."

She rambled those words with such sincerity. No one had ever spoken to me with such affection. She only wanted me to find something to light me up, put life back in my soul. I wasn't sure how she didn't see that she did that for me. I'd felt more alive in the short time I've had with her than I had my entire life. She made me want to do better, be kinder, and do something with this half chance at life I was given.

From what I understood about mortal Heaven and Hell, that was what Heaven was for. The good, the better.

I'll never make it to Heaven, but Amelie might be the closest I'd ever get.

CHAPTER 11

Amelie

K iaran's heavy footsteps were lighter this morning as he came down the stairs to meet me for breakfast.

"Morning, pretty girl. Sleep well?" he asked as he grabbed a piece of toasted bread. I couldn't help the heat that flooded my cheeks every time he called me, *pretty girl*. It slipped off his tongue, sweet as honey, and I wasn't sure he knew how it affected me.

"I did. How 'bout you, magic man?"

He rolled his eyes and nodded in response, and to avoid talking with a mouth full of food.

"Any prince charmings come to your rescue in your dreams last night?"

I wasn't sure how to navigate friendship. Everyone in Holleberg was so focused on survival that no one had any real friends. Just a means to an escape. Even the ones my parents talked about from childhood were a distant memory to them.

The closest thing I ever had to a real friend was Wren. He was the only one of my brothers who remembered a time where I was just his sister. Hansel and Tildan knew me as a mother figure, the dependable one. Wren was who I could joke and play with. We shared secrets and had inside jokes, he asked for advice and didn't want it from his sister or stand-in mom. Being friends with Kiaran was nice. It felt natural and safe. A feeling I wasn't sure I'd ever had in a man's presence.

"There was a Prince, but he didn't come to my rescue." I tried to hide my smile at the memory of what the Prince and I had done last night. I could still feel his hands on my—

"On your what, Amelie?" Kiaran popped a piece of bacon into his mouth and raised his brows accusingly.

"Oh my god, get out of my mind." Blood rushed to my cheeks as I bowed my face into my hands.

Kiaran laughed it off and thankfully didn't try to embarrass me further.

Our relationship shifted the other day after I veiled his curse. I laid my heart out to him, allowed him to see why this place was so special to me and what his company meant to me. I knew my words sat well with him when he stopped fighting me on working on the veil further. We didn't know how far he could go so we planned to test the boundaries.

He'd been kinder and more talkative. We went back and forth in easy conversation, a stark difference from the unsynchronized dance we'd been doing since I got here nearly a month and a half ago.

He was also very funny. His wit was sharp and efficient. His snarky comments turned to fun banter. Everything was just easy with him.

It was nice having a friend. Especially one that was nice to look at. His curly black hair was messy from sleep and his bright blue eyes were nearly see-through in the morning glow that painted the cottage. His soul was lighter too, brighter. It looked amazing on him. Having his room from home did a number on him in the best way.

We hadn't tried the veil again since the first attempt. I didn't want to tell him that it gave me a terrible headache. The rest of me felt great, full of adrenaline, but my head, God, the pain. It was worse than when a guard dragged me by my hair behind Henrik's store, and that was a *bad* headache. If I told Kiaran, I knew he wouldn't do it again.

The past week, I worked on easier elixirs. One for headaches, stomach aches, and joint pains. Another for softer hair that made my frizzy locks melt into pretty waves. The elixir made it fall so perfectly, not a single hair out of place.

I made another elixir that made you sing your words rather than speak them. I wasn't sure what the point of that one was, but it made for great dinner entertainment after I'd poured it into Kiaran's drink. The last one was a pheromone elixir. My books said it was arguably the most dangerous elixir that was often used with malice.

I stashed it in my apothecary cabinet, far to the back. Maybe someday I'd be able to use it to play matchmaker.

We both agreed to try it again this afternoon, which allowed plenty of time for me to spend the rest of the day by the pond.

I'd been so busy playing alchemist that I hadn't visited my Forest friends in a few days. After we finished breakfast, Kiaran nestled into the nook of the library with one of the romance books he'd picked for me. I strolled out over the bridge, taking my spot near one of the large oak trees whose roots grew right into the pond. Dipping my toes into the water, I felt grounded.

It was rare to feel content back home. Even in the comfort of your own bed, in the room that belonged to you, that was built inside the walls of what you were supposed to call home, your edge to survive never dulled.

To sit outside the walls of my new home and feel as connected to the earth as the dirt that covered it, I was so grateful for it. Entirely unfamiliar, all while being the most comforting feeling I'd ever known. Those three little faces I missed so much popped back into my head every time happiness dared to fill my heart. I wished they were here. I hoped they were okay.

Knowing it would never be safe enough to return, I sent hopeless prayers up to God and asked him to relay the messages to my brothers.

I miss you, boys.

Be nice to the little ones, Wren.

I love you.

Tears pricked my eyes as I watched the frogs float around on the lily pads. The gentle breeze from the trees pulled and pushed them with no set direction and the creatures didn't protest. The strange dragonflies showed up today, normally only coming around for the light show, but in the light of day, I saw they weren't dragonflies at all.

As if the Forest couldn't come up with any more things to add to the madness, I saw Fairies. Little wings fluttering them through the Forest.

My breathing picked up as two of the braver ones landed on a rock in the pond to my right. Trying to avoid staring, I looked at my toes in the water and eavesdropped on their tiny voices talking amongst each other.

"She's so pretty," the black haired one said.

"Of course the gorgeous Witch found a girlfriend after two hundred years alone here."

That one got my attention.

"Sorry to interrupt, ladies, but he's not my boyfriend." Winking at the two small, magical creatures and enjoying the pink flush covering their cheeks. At least *they* didn't make fun of my wink.

The braver one of the two zipped my way hovering just in front of my face. Her hair mirrored the summer sun as it fell around her body in loose curls. She wore a baby blue top and matching skirt, and her wings were sparkling against the water behind her.

"Why? Have *you* ever seen a prettier man?" she swooned and I had to agree with her.

"No, I guess I haven't," I relented and gave her a small

smile, then glanced at her dark haired friend shyly approaching the conversation.

"I'm Poppy, this is Naida." Naida tucked a piece of her dark hair behind her ear as her friend introduced them.

"Nice to meet you girls. I'm Amelie." I instinctively went to shake her hand but stopped when I noticed that both of their bodies would fit in my palm.

"We know." Poppy came even closer, inspecting each pore on my face. Her hands, which couldn't be much bigger than a pea, tingled against my skin as she studied me.

"What's the Prince like?" Poppy asked, giggling back toward her friend.

"He's kind of grumpy, but funny."

"And those eyes…" Poppy crashed into her friend as if the thought of Kiaran's bright blue eyes was killing her. Naida laughed at her friend, snorting as she tried to catch her breath.

"He does have pretty eyes, huh?"

The brush behind me came to life and Poppy noticed our company first. Turning to greet whoever it was, I saw my friend.

"Ethel!" Poppy flew over to Ethel and Ethel greeted the Fairy happily. Naida stayed near me, still undecided on the human in front of her.

"You're close with Ethel?" I asked her quietly, hoping to earn her trust.

Naida nodded. "Everyone is." That sounded about right for my friend who seemed to have no enemies, only people who caused her a great deal of anxiety.

"Amelie, I see you've met Poppy and Naida." Ethel plopped down next to me, Poppy rested her behind on Ethel's shoulder, and leaned forward on her palms to smile at me.

"I have. Seems my new friends have a crush on my roommate."

Ethel threw her head back laughing, Naida's cheeks were beet red and Poppy joined Ethel in the humor of it all. "That makes three of ya then, right?" Ethel gave me a knowing look and now the flush filled my cheeks.

THE FAE WERE much like I'd dreamed of them many nights before. Poppy especially. The unshakable joy that exuded from her was contagious. I felt it nestling into the broken parts of my soul, like an immediate cure to an illness, reaping straight through my skin. Naida was different, though.

She held herself with such precariousness. As if she might crumble at any given moment. I was drawn to her. I wanted to protect her. The way I protected my brothers. Give her space to say what she wanted to say, unburdened by whatever weight was plaguing her. Poppy seemed to be what kept her spirit alive. Naida tried to keep her laughter in during Poppy's dramatics with each story, but she always broke. The pair were total opposites. But I already loved them.

Ethel sat with me by the pond once the girls left. Her white hair was perfectly styled with a curl at the ends framing her face. She always wore a patterned dress and little clogs, she was straight out of a storybook.

She was quick to explain the history of the Fae in the Forest. "Poppy is sunshine personified. Her entire family is. They're good people. Naida is terribly shy, but still as sweet as fresh jam. Fae are innately trusting creatures, they defy almost everything physical about them. Small, vulnerable creatures who would ride into battle in a second for anyone. Naida, though, carries a different love in her heart."

"What about Naida's family?"

Ethel straightened her tunic down her stomach and crossed one ankle over each other, leaning back on her palms.

"No one knows." My friend's nose crinkled, tears rimmed in her eyes but she swallowed them down.

"What do you mean?"

"She showed up a little over two hundred years ago. My husband found her near the creek. Couldn't remember anything, she couldn't even fly. Her poor wings needed so much care before they worked right. She's never said much. Luckily, she took to Poppy quickly, but she always seems to be preparing for a wicked storm. Always on edge, that girl."

Naida reminded me of parts of myself. The piece that used to live in fear and did what had to be done to keep moving forward. Between Naida and Poppy, it felt like there were two little pieces of my soul flitting around the Forest. The old Amelie, and the new one.

"Why was Poppy's touch on my skin so… tingly?"

Ethel let her head fall back, letting the sun soak her cheeks. "The Fae, for the most part, are very good. They are the secret movers of the Forest. If you watch closely, they're everywhere, all the time," Ethel explained.

I took a moment to look around the Forest, they *were* everywhere. The little floating things I had been seeing weren't all pollen or the sparkling essence of the wind, they were Fae.

Ethel righted herself and watched the frogs float by. "Most of their magic comes from the dark side. They are unnatural beings. They've never lived that way though, they defy the laws of magic by using Black Magic for good. However, their only means of protection is that little tingle. If Poppy wanted to, she could immobilize you completely with her touch alone. It is the only way they can protect themselves, so when they are in danger that tingle becomes lethal. It stops the blood flow of the person on the other end of it."

The hairs on the back of my neck stood straight up. "Jesus."

"Yeah. *Jesus*. But neither of those girls would ever do that. Especially to you."

"Why *especially to me*?" Ethel had a knack for giving enough information to pique my interest but never giving enough away to feel any resolution.

She eyed me with an endearing twinkle in her eye, the words she spoke when Frea sent her the message replayed in my mind.

"You're special to us. To the Forest. It hasn't always been safe here. I have two daughters somewhere out there that I haven't seen in years because it wasn't safe for them," Ethel finally said. My heart warmed at the sentiment but I still didn't understand *why*.

"And that's because…"

"Some things are better to learn for yourself, dear."

I mulled that over, feeling a pang of guilt that she hadn't mentioned having daughters before, but I also hadn't asked. "What were their names?"

Ethel's hazel eyes were glossy, she wouldn't look at me but she smiled as she said, "June and Delilah."

I put my arm around her small frame and pulled her into my side. She swallowed back the tears and cleared her throat as if they got stuck there.

"Would you like to come to dinner one of these evenings with your husband? Fern is an excellent host, and Kiaran is hard up for company these days," I asked, changing the subject.

Ethel gave me a smile, leaning into my body gently. "Edgar and I would enjoy that very much, Amelie. Thank you."

We enjoyed the silence for a moment. While Fern and Kiaran were my friends because they kind of had to be, I thought Ethel might be my friend because she wanted to be.

"How is it going with the boy? We've worried over him

since he's been here." Ethel's anxious tone that she had the day at the campsite was present in her question.

"He's okay. I'm hoping after tonight he'll be even better."

Ethel's head whipped to mine and she arched a disapproving brow.

"Oh my god, not like that! Sorry." Shaking off the embarrassment, I asked, "Why has no one ever visited him?"

Ethel laughed at the thought. "I believe the night you arrived in the Forest was only the second or third time we've ever been able to even *see* the cottage, let alone visit him."

"What do you mean?"

"That boy has had that cottage veiled in invisibility since he got here. Your home used to be the cutest in all the Forest. So homey and full of life, the woman who lived there was special."

I smiled at the thought of Fern taking pride in her structure, even when she was alone.

"Then, one day, it vanished. Myself and the rest of the dwarves take different parts of the Forest to clean up. Branches, algae, overgrown bushes and vines, and when we came here, my goodness, nearly two hundred years ago, it was gone."

"I would've thought I'd gone mad. How did you know it was just invisible then? That it was still here?"

Ethel's face fell suddenly. She chewed on her lip and leaned up to play with her fingers. "It was some time after it disappeared. I'd startled out of my sleep to pained screams and thought a human had scared themselves silly. I ran and ran until I was close enough to see. Through the trees, I saw the cottage again, overgrown and unkempt, with a man on all fours in the doorway. He was in agony, crying for his mother and shouting so loud I know *any* mother would've heard it. She never came though." Ethel's eyes rimmed with tears again, this time she let them fall. "I wanted to wrap him up and tell him it would be okay. We'd never been privy to his occupancy in the Forest. He didn't let us see him, let alone know the pain his heart was in." She took a quivering breath in and tried to shake away the memory from her mind.

"What happened after that?"

Ethel sighed and rested her hands in her lap.

"I watched him for a while. I asked Frea to bring his mother to him, tried to speak to him between our minds, but when he finally gathered himself, he stepped out of the cottage."

My breath hitched, knowing exactly what he was trying to do.

"His body contorted, the sound of his bones snapping bounced off the branches where I stood. He screamed so loud it rumbled through the sturdy trees."

Ethel and I were both rigid, her for reliving the memory and me for knowing that Kiaran was trying to end it all. "But then, something took him inside. I couldn't see anything physically doing it, but it dragged him by his boots back into the cottage and the soft cries he let out faded as the sun began to rise. It was years and years before we saw him again."

Sitting in silence once again, I looked to the cozy home Kiaran and I shared and felt a force pulling me to him. I noticed him crossing the small window in the attic, taking a glance at Ethel and I every time he did.

As I was palming the ground to stand, Ethel started again, asking about the past week.

"I learned how to make elixirs and potions," I told her excitedly, sitting back down and watching the attic window. "Kiaran says I'm a natural. That even the Witches who'd studied their whole lives weren't so quick to the craft as me." I couldn't explain it, but every time the smoke toppled over the lip of the cauldron, energy thrummed through me. The relentless sea that raged outside the castle in my dreams had menacing waves that took away the view of the sharp rocks that guarded the cliff's edge. That was how the spells made me feel. Like the sharp edges of my soul were being covered by something so much bigger than me.

"I told you that you have the magic of gold in your eyes, girl. I'm not sure why you're surprised," she replied off-hand-edly, as if successfully casting spells into elixirs was normal for someone like me.

"What does that mean?"

She mentioned that when we walked back from the camp-site and I hadn't stopped wondering what that meant.

"When you're working with the elixirs, can you feel the energy pouring out of you? Like a lit fire in your eyes trying to cover the world in embers?" Again, Ethel wasn't going to tell me. Only ask what I was already aware of. Though she was spot on with that description. It wasn't a wave, it was fire. A dangerous one.

"My eyes feel heavy over the cauldron, but I just assumed it was from the smoke."

I recalled the feeling that took over as the elixirs came to fruition. Like a match sparking on a strike pad.

"Amelie, do you know your mother's maiden name?" Hope danced gracefully through her hazel eyes.

"Morgenstern."

Ethel's lips rolled together, her eyes filling tears again.

"Do you have time for a story?"

"Always." I couldn't take my gaze off the piercing eyes staring at me from the attic window. Kiaran was standing in the frame like a painting. Without knowing what Ethel was about to tell me, I cleared my mind to keep it between only her and I.

"Long, long ago, a family of Witches was sent to the Forest on orders from their High Priestess. The Morgenstern sisters. Ophelia, Adella, and Evari—with your heart, I know that your lineage starts with Evari."

Evari.

"Anyway, Ophelia and Adella were hard at work, tainting the minds of those who dwelled in the Forest. It was easy to see that those two were under a delusion of some kind. The things they would spew made no sense. The reaping, the wicked stars, the almighty power of the High Priestess. They were completely mad. Evari, though, knew something was off about the orders the sisters were given. She and I became good friends, she was so incredibly kind. And brave, like you. Nothing was going to stop her from finding out the truth about why they were there."

That feeling was taking over my eyes, the fire began to roll through the rivers.

"Did she figure it out?" I gritted out through clenched teeth, my head feeling heavy and weightless all at once.

Ethel nodded. "This Forest was their final resting grounds. The Morgensterns were so powerful, their High Priestess wanted it rid from every realm, for good."

"What happened to Evari?"

Ethel's pursed her lips, battling with what to tell me. "She's safe. I cannot tell you more than that."

My attention was keen on my Dwarven friend. When she looked to me, though, I saw fear. She feared what she saw. Placing her hand over mine, she sent calming thoughts to me. Much like Kiaran does, but different. Like her words were only meant to caress the outer peaks and valleys of my mind.

Breathe.

Don't let it consume you.

Somewhere inside of me fought to contain the raging fire that was daring to escape. My chest heaved, my breath fanning the flames within. My skin tingled, and the knots in my stomach were twisting together haphazardly.

Ethel gave me an assuring nod. "Amelie, you're a Morgenstern *Witch*."

She proceeded to tell me what it meant, the magic, the

golden rivers that streaked my eyes. When she hugged me goodbye, I had a heavy, unsettled heart. Years of rage festering from the marrow of my bones. I wanted revenge.

CHAPTER 12

Kiaran

A melie was sitting by the pond with a dwarf. The little woman was just taller than Amelie's hip, and they were clearly fond of each other.

It wasn't like I put in much of an effort to have visitors since being here, but for fuck's sake, the girl made friends with a breed of creature who was historically afraid of everything but their own kind.

I tried to busy myself, but I just kept being drawn back to the window to watch my girl. Her hair fell like melted chocolate around her shoulders so intentionally that you'd think she styled it that way. I knew, though, that she would never go through the trouble.

I was sure she had no idea of how she shined. How even sitting among the bright colors of the Forest, the one she deemed the most beautiful thing she'd ever laid eyes on, she was all I could see. The focal point of a painting. There were thousands of details to admire but my eyes always landed back on her.

The Forest was drawn to her, just as I was.

As it neared dusk, Amelie folded herself around the lady dwarf giving her a hug. Amelie's back was to us and I couldn't break my gaze with the woman staring straight at me. I tried to smile at her, hoping she knew sending Amelie back inside was safe, but apparently I could only use those facial muscles in the presence of Amelie.

The dwarf closed her eyes tight and whispered something in Amelie's ear before pressing a kiss to the side of her face. Her mouth didn't move, but her eyes glazed and she held Amelie so tight that I wasn't sure she could take a deep breath if she needed to.

Then I heard it. *Felt* it.

She is your tether to life.

You've been suffocating for so long.

Breathe, sweet boy. She's here.

The woman told me to breathe, but there wasn't any air left in the room to do so. My eyes lined with tears, one after another, at the words of a fate that couldn't exist within my curse. My tether to life. A tether like that in my world meant only one thing.

My fate was chosen for me long before my mother or hers was even born. They were sealed with the High Priestess and the stars. When it locked into place, it changed life as you knew it. To tether your soul with your fated mate. It also couldn't be tampered with. It was the one thing I felt sure of under my curse. If my Fated Mate found me here, she couldn't be taken from me. It was against the Witch's Oath.

But fated mates could only be between the same kind of blood.

Mortal to mortal, celestial to celestial.

"Kiaran?" Amelie called out from downstairs. Still staring out the window, I saw now that the place Amelie and the woman were seated was empty. I blinked away the blur in my eyes and called back, "Be down in a second."

My voice cracked with more emotion than I thought I had.

Starting down the stairs, I saw Amelie in her cove, hard at

work already. Standing atop her footstool, sweat beaded on her forehead and her silky curls fell forward, threatening to add to the cauldron. I was beginning to think she did it on purpose so I would braid her hair. After all, my braids were far better than hers.

"Spit!" She hadn't even looked up from her madness before ordering me around. Her brows bunched together in frustration. She was upset and doing a terrible job at hiding it.

Ignoring her demand and moving behind her, I gently pulled her hair onto her back to lay between her shoulders. Grazing the bottom of her ear as I passed, she shuddered under my touch.

"You don't have to do that, ya know. My hair isn't messy anymore."

Ignoring her again, I started to weave three bundles of hair down her back and paused to let Fern secure my master-piece into place. "I told you if you wanted me to touch you all you had to do was ask." The bare skin on her arms broke out in goosebumps. I smirked to myself at her reaction.

"You aren't touching me, Kiaran. You're braiding my hair." Her words were breathy as she tired from her vigorous mixing.

"Do you want me to touch you, Amelie?" I rasped. The dwarf's words were on repeat in my mind, making me feel more possessive than I probably had permission to be. I let her braid fall down her back and slid my hands around her waist, holding her gently in place. Her core tightened under my fingers.

"Kiaran." Her voice was quiet. So quiet, I wasn't sure she wanted me to hear it.

Tracing her silhouette with my eyes and allowing my hands to follow, they landed on her hips.

"Yes?"

She didn't answer, but her breathing became ragged.

"What's got you upset?" It was radiating off of her like a

too hot sun. Something was bothering her. I didn't prefer intruding on her mind when she was upset. It felt like more of an invasion than a privilege then.

Letting go of the ladle, she laced her fingers through mine and squeezed. Her head rolled back, leaning into this moment. My heart thudded in slow, deep beats. The smell of strawberries and vanilla took over my senses and the need to spin her around and take her lips to mine was becoming hard to fight.

"It's nothing. I…um… I just…" She trailed off while I made lazy circles with my thumbs on her round ass, bunching her layered skirt the longer I did it. I'm not sure she realized it, but she arched her back slightly, pressing into me.

"Tell me."

"No need, it's not…"—she exhaled a shaky breath—"important."

"Whatever has you upset," I moved closer. Taking in the smell of her hair, I whispered against the shell of her ear, "is important to me."

She spun on the stool, the pads of my thumbs now adding pressure to the top of her hip bone. I pulled her closer to me, her eyes were locked on my lips, her chest unmoving.

Seeming to snap back into herself, she regained her composure and choked out, "It's done."

"What's done, pretty girl?" I asked, tipping my nose to touch hers.

She paused, the gold rivers in her eyes coursed with a raging fire.

"The um… elixir. It's done."

I tried to read her face, to see anything that gave me permission to force her to tell me what was bothering her. She gave nothing away, so I fanned off the flames and gave her hips a gentle squeeze before I lifted her up off the step stool and set her on the ground.

The second I released her, my soul longed to touch her again.

"Right, well…" Her eyes darted around the kitchen and locked on the clean vials. "Oh, there they are!" She hurried for the counter. Amelie grabbed one and lifted it to show me, throwing on the weirdest smile. Then she swept her hand through the cauldron and stretched her arm out as far as it could go with a small shot of the elixir in hand.

I walked toward her, forcing her arm to bend so the vial was tucked in tight between her chest and mine. Slipping it from her hand, I said, "Go, lie down."

She took the invitation and went for the couch. I grabbed a quilt to cover her. I knelt down as she turned her head to meet my eyes.

"Please tell me what's wrong."

One lonely tear fell from her eye.

"Later," she said, giving me a sweet smile.

Amelie joined my hand around the small vile, then lifted it to my lips and watched as the purple liquid slid into my mouth. Her gaze dropped to my throat as I swallowed heavily.

My skin covered again in the feeling of static just as the life in her eyes deadened and her body softened.

TRYING to avoid becoming a pile of broken bones, I tested each limb for good measure before stepping fully onto the porch. So far, so good. I did not want Fern's *help* this time. The clearing was a full blown habitat now, and it was breathtaking to see up close. I got to the bridge, the soft ground under my feet feeling unfamiliar in opposition to the hardwood floors I'd spent two hundred years on.

I noted any pull I felt to the cottage, hoping I'd have a

warning before the increasing proximity became too much. Amelie had been practicing so much with other elixirs, and she wanted so badly to veil my curse that I wouldn't be shocked if I could go all the way to the campsite where the Lost Souls gathered. Where I could put faces to the voices that kept me company in the darkest nights.

Crossing the bridge slowly, I said hello to Amelie's frog friends. Two more steps and I was on the other side, only a few more and I'd be in the thick of the Forest.

Bones intact, I glanced back to the cottage. It was as alive as it was the day I got here. A pang of guilt rolled through my gut at what I let Fern become.

Fern loved Amelie. I told myself that if something was wrong she would signal me.

Taking one more weary step, I entered the Forest for the very first time.

It was impossible to see out here, I was amazed that Amelie had pranced around with no problems. Normally, I could see miles and miles ahead of me, but not now.

I can *hear* where I was heading though. Amelie said that whether I went willingly or not, I was leaving the cottage. My first thought was to visit the men who kept me company every night without any knowledge of it. They were already singing the songs I'd become so fond of.

The walk would be long and deciding that wasting time wasn't an option, I summoned my wolves, hoping I could hitch a ride, since apparently they're Clydesdale's now. The power that usually pulsed through my fingers never came though. I tried to shift there, nothing. I might have been unpracticed in a lot of magic anymore, but I shifted around the house all the time. My magic wasn't working within Amelie's veil.

Relenting, I picked up a jog and went to find my friends who didn't yet know me.

The tree line sat at least fifty paces from the fire, and

hundreds of souls surrounded it. Up close, I saw the cave-dwelling gremlins, Fae, and dwarves. There were human looking people here too, many of them. They were all together as one, and not a single person looked out of place.

A small hand grabbed mine and tugged. Looking down, I saw the Dwarven woman from the pond.

"You shouldn't be here, boy. Amelie should not be trying such dangerous magic."

"I've learned that Amelie does what Amelie wants to do."

The little thing scoffed at me. "Clearly." She rolled her eyes. "But you should go, lively ones are not usually welcome here."

Looking back at the crowd, I couldn't agree less with her. These souls may roam freely from their physical bodies now, but I was lost too. This was maybe a perfect place for me. "I think I'll be okay. Thanks, though." Taking possession back of my hand, I walked toward the fire.

"Get back here, young man!" The dwarf shouted at me. The Lost Souls went deathly quiet, pun intended. When I turned to face her, her cheeks were void of color.

A tall, human looking man stepped between her and I, glancing between us. He didn't have a single hair on the top of his head, but grew an exceptional beard that made it hard to see his mouth. His eyes were dark and brows bushy. Familiarity was thick in the air around us, like we were old friends.

"Ethel, are you trying to ward away guests again?" He gave her a mischievous grin before he turned back to me. "What's your name, son?"

"Kiaran. Just wanted to come introduce myself, Sir." Striding toward the man, I reached out my hand to shake his. My father taught me a lot growing up. The few good parts of me were all him. One of those things was to always shake a man's hand before pissing him off.

I might have gotten those two things backward tonight judging by the look on the bearded man's face.

The man eyed my hand like it was diseased. "Kiaran," he repeated, puffing his chest out and crossing his tattooed arms over his chest, letting me know who was in charge here. "Friedrich, come over here. When's the last time we had a Witch at the camp?"

Feeling very vulnerable without my magic, I tried to side step the man to get back to Ethel, but he moved to stop me. His friend, Friedrich, now joining us.

"It's been a long while, we wondered when you'd relent and enter purgatory. Al, should I get the boy some ale?"

Al continued to burn holes through my skull with his eyes. I looked to Ethel, fear darkened her face as two more men stood behind her.

The static that had been tingling over my skin was fading.

"One, brother. Then he leaves." Al responded to Friedrich then looked to Ethel. "Josef, Niklaus, let her go."

I let out a satisfied breath.

"Do not come back here Ethel, I will not be so kind next time. This is your final warning to leave us be, we are not harming anything."

Ethel's fearful expression took over her whole face but her eyes held nothing but contempt. "You all used to be so kind," she said before locking eyes with me. Just as they had earlier when she was sitting with Amelie, her eyes seemed to glaze over and then I heard it.

You do not have long.

I didn't need to think about what that meant. I could feel it. The flowers on my skin were wilting and the static was nearly gone. Not wanting to piss off the dead guys any further, I gave her a wink and turned to follow Friedrich.

One drink and I'd be gone.

One was plenty.

It had been centuries since I'd felt the buzz of alcohol so one could assume my tolerance was shit now but I was pretty sure this ale was brewed to be stronger than the Forest itself. Chugging the last half of the drink, I listened to the men share their stories. Al seemed to be the leader of this specific posse.

So far, I'd gathered that Al and Friedrich were brothers, but their celestial blood was yet to be revealed. Niklaus and Josef were human, they explained their ties to celestial blood prior to their deaths which allowed them to enter purgatory in the Forest. They were allowed to wait here until their mates passed with them into the total afterlife. Neither of them was forthcoming with where their mates were though.

My skin was just skin now and the dirt the flowers grew in was getting cold.

"Thank you for the ale and the stories. I'll be on my way now." Getting to my feet from the log I'd sat on, Al studied my stature. "You'll come back then?" he asked inquisitively. They hadn't tried to kill me but I definitely didn't get the impression that they wanted me back.

"If you'll allow it, Sir," I replied, treading lightly. As vulnerable as I was without my magic, it was nice to feel kinship tonight. Walking to the edge of their circle and bidding the men a good night, Al came to stand at my side. He set a large, cold hand on my shoulder and said, "It will be your turn to tell your story."

I gave the leader a curt smile and entered the thick of the trees again. I didn't want them to see me sprint and believe I was afraid of them, but the lack of feeling in my bones made me feel uneasy.

Fuck not having magic.

I wasn't even sure I was that far from the cottage but the run was exhausting me nonetheless. Humans must have felt useless day in, and day out. No wonder they lived such short lives.

Trying to remember the way I came, and not having any vision, I sent a silent prayer to whoever might be listening to send a Forest guide out for me. Focusing in and watching for the candlelight in the windows, I felt it. The pull of my soul to hers. The wind picked up at my back, as if to help me get to her quicker. With the extra push behind me, I sailed. Not thinking of my direction, only feeling for Amelie.

I hadn't realized how thick the trees were just past the clearing but coming out of it and seeing my home and knowing my girl was waiting for me inside sent my stomach into an excited flurry of nerves. I couldn't wait to tell her everything.

Fern already had the door open for me as if to say, *about time!*

Amelie was lying exactly the same as when I left.

Doing the same thing I did the first time, I lifted her up and slid my body under her upper half to rest her head in my lap.

I'd left the cottage. My bones didn't break and the High Priestess didn't show up. The cottage was intact, and I had an invite to visit the men again. Now, I protected the head of the woman I'd come to adore and waited for her to wake. If I knew for sure that she would want me to, I would kiss her everywhere she'd let me for the gift she gave me today. With how much I cared for this woman, I thanked her God that she was mortal and I couldn't be ordered to give her up.

CHAPTER 13

Amelie

From Forest to black. Black, black, black. The darkest black the living world had never seen. I felt him return. I felt my mind fighting to come back. It felt like pounds of sand were being poured into my veins, starting at the tippy tops of my toes and up to my head.

Fuck, my head.

The pain was unbearable, but my heart's rhythm started keeping perfect time with the beat of life again and with every pump of my blood it knifed straight through my brain. Kiaran's breathing was slow and controlled, each exhale dissipating over my face.

"Amelie, please wake up…" he whispered and I felt the air fill my lungs. My chest rose tall and then sunk back down in steady motions, allowing for every inch of my body to be touched by precious air.

The darkness that pooled in my mind faded, leaving only the pounding of my blood pumping through my veins in its wake. The first time I woke with a headache, but this was splintering. It was uncomfortable, dizzying.

My eyes were dry as drought.

Blinking, the cottage's ceiling and Kiaran's face came into

view. His fingers were lightly tracing my cheek before tucking loose strands of hair behind my ear. Even through the pain, Kiaran's face made my heart skip a beat. The way he was holding my face was so intimate, butterflies took flight in my stomach. My body was feeling too many things at once.

"Amelie? Are you okay?" His voice was heavy with concern. My mouth was stuffed with cotton. I tried to swallow it, but my words were trapped in my throat. "Say something, please." He closed his eyes and laid a hand over my heart.

"Hi," I croaked.

A breath of relief escaped him as he folded himself over me, squeezing so tight that the little bit of life that returned threatened to leave again. His warm cinnamon and leather smell surrounded me, lightening the weight on my brain.

"Kiaran, I'm okay," I lied, my head was a tell tale sign that I was *not* okay. I needed to get the elixir for pain that I had prepared. If Kiaran saw me take it, though, he'd question me. He'd know something was wrong.

Finally releasing me, he helped me to sit up next to him. The shift in position sent the pounding into overdrive for a moment. The ringing in my ears was deafening, and my stomach threatened to project the contents of lunch.

"I hate this part. I hated it last time, but this time was worse, Amelie." His voice sounded like it was miles away, his mouth was moving but I barely heard him. I held on to my stomach and tried to focus on anything. The room spun around me. I found a piece of the checkered game on the floor. Fixating on its jagged edges, tracing each one with my eyes.

I needed that elixir, now.

"Can you give me a minute?" From my peripherals, I saw him staring at me. He was terrified and likely did not want to leave my side. But, doing as he was told, he reluctantly got to his feet and went to the washroom. Fighting through the pain, I went for my stash of elixirs. On my feet, I wobbled and stumbled. My mind felt like it was sloshing around in mush.

I pictured it looking like half melted snow mixed with mud on the ground in the Spring. Getting to the elixir, I struggled to screw the lid off the vial, nearly dropping it to the floor.

I barely got it open before tossing it back. The pain subsided immediately. Leaving only a bearable headache behind.

Note to self: prepare a lot more of this.

Bracing myself on the edge of the table, I took in the cottage. It was night time, candle lamps washed the room in a warm, golden hue.

"Kiaran?"

The bathroom door swung open as if he'd been standing behind it with his hand on the knob waiting for the go ahead.

"Fuck. Are you okay? This was so much worse than the first time." He ran his hands through his thick, black curls. He quickly got to me and he pulled the side of my body into him.

"Yes, I'm okay. You were gone for longer, that's all. Takes a bit more out of me. How long did it take after you returned?"

I couldn't see Kiaran's face from this position, but his breathing was unstable. He tried to remain calm, but it was radiating off him that he was anything but. "I got back about four hours ago. I was only gone for two."

Four hours. Last time, everything worked so well that my awakening took hardly any time at all. The books said the farther the tether went from the center of the veil, the longer it would take to undo itself. All of it was sound to the laws of magic but I'd be lying if it wasn't scary.

Mustering up a smile, I pulled back from Kiaran to look up at him. "I've been to the campsite you were at. That's where I met Ethel when I went into the Forest the other day."

Kiaran let me go and took his seat on the bench at the table. Fern had summoned food before our eyes. I sat next to him and tried to act like I had an appetite.

"So, you were able to see again?"

I nodded. "I was. It was blurry for a lot of it, but I heard voices and could make out the fire and the lake."

"Did you know I couldn't take my magic with me?"

"You didn't have your magic out there?" I didn't know that it wouldn't go with him. Nothing in the books said anything about that, but then again, I wasn't sure how often an unpracticed Witch tried to veil. I would assume none, because what I was doing was terribly stupid. After Ethel explained that my mother's side was full of powerful Witches, I decided that it was the only explanation for how I successfully veiled on my first try.

"No, I didn't. I've never not had my magic."

I could feel his fear through the veil, but I didn't know what he was afraid of.

"I'm sorry, I didn't know that would happen. Maybe I can adjust a few things in the recipe to avoid that happening next time," I said, taking a bite of the fresh slice of bread.

"Next time? Amelie, we cannot do this again. I didn't think you were ever going to wake up. Ethel agrees you shouldn't be doing such dangerous spells, and I've tried to tell you how dangerous it is."

I didn't really care what their opinion of it was. Kiaran's initial fear when he left the cottage subsided as he sat around the fire with the other men. I could *feel* it. He enjoyed himself for a moment, and that wasn't something I was willing to forget.

"Did you have fun?" I ignored his comment and reinforced that there were benefits to the veil. Kiaran picked at the cuts of meat that were beautifully folded into little flower shapes. He picked a piece of salami that was fashioned like a rose off the table and shoved it into his mouth in an attempt to hide his smile.

"Is that a yes?"

"I've listened to those men for years. It was surreal to see it up close."

"So you enjoyed yourself?"

Kiaran thought carefully about his next words, understanding that this was a trap. "Yes, I did." His eyes focused in on mine. "I will never forget what you gave me tonight, but I can't watch your body go through that again, pretty girl."

His care for me was not something I was used to. My father was affectionate, but he raised us to be independent, to not rely on anyone or anything, and to always assume that no one would be there to help you, so always be prepared to help yourself. Kiaran's need to watch out for me felt insulting and precious all at once.

"If I find something in my books to help with the unveiling, will you do it again?" Batting my eyes at him, I added, "For me?"

Kiaran rolled his pretty blue eyes, working so hard to fight his smile I thought his cheeks would freeze in place. "Nice try, but no."

I FOUND nothing about how to make the process easier. Everything that had been documented on veiling was painful, dangerous, and often times fatal. I'd learned a lot about the hierarchy of magical realms in these books. Alchemists were disgusted by those at the top of said hierarchy called the High Table, and often noted that it wasn't fair that they could do so much more with their magic. The more I read about it, the more I realized my initial study on the spell was distracted by my need to do something for Kiaran.

So many alchemists and Witches' brains had turned to pools

of darkness after a failed veiling. They weren't dead but their minds were as good as gone. Once the darkness took over, no light shone through the eyes of the tether. The nuances of veils defied the laws of balance between nature and magic. Therefore, it wasn't practiced by even the most skilled alchemists. Only those at the High Table were permitted, let alone dared, to try it.

The alternative to veiling was to bind your mind and soul to another. It was far less dangerous because, instead of a tether being anchored in place, both bodies remained alive. But the mind and soul could take residence in either body. Kiaran's soul could replace mine, and he could travel the woods in my body. The biggest risk was that switching back wasn't consistent.

I liked my new body, and I didn't want to be a man, so that was a no for me.

Frustrated by not finding the answers I so desperately needed, I chucked my pen across the room and tossed my journal to the floor. I slammed myself back into the pillows and covered my eyes.

The headache that followed my waking last night was pretty much gone and I prepared five more pain remedies after breakfast this morning, two of which were already gone because I couldn't bear the aftershocks that kept shaking my brain. Kiaran watched me closely all day, looking for signs of the side effects of the veil. It took all of my willpower to not let it show.

A soft knock on my door interrupted my pouting.

"Come in."

Kiaran came through the door holding two steaming mugs of tea. His hair was freshly washed and he smelled like the fresh breeze from the Forest mixed with cinnamon. He was dressed in a silk, long sleeve sleep shirt and loose pants. The room immediately swelled with heat, I told myself it was from his body having just been in hot water. But I was lying to myself.

"Ready to admit that veiling my curse a dumb way to spend our time and not worth risking your life over?" he taunted, positioning himself at the foot of the bed and stretching his arm to hand me my tea.

"Nope." Because tricking him the first time would be the only time. I wouldn't lie to him again, especially if it meant him coming back to find me unable to wake up. I wasn't sure he could live with himself for the rest of eternity if that happened because I lied.

"I enjoy spending time with you, Amelie. Meeting the men once was enough to get me through the rest of my time here, as long as that may be." He warily sipped his tea, peeling his eyes away from mine.

"Can I ask you something? And if you say yes then you have to actually tell me this time."

He thought on that for a moment, running his hands down his silk pajamas. "Anything."

"Will you tell me about your curse? Maybe if I understood the magic behind it I could focus harder on what exactly to veil."

"You don't tamper with the fates set by the High Priestess," he answered. If Ethel was right, my magic was elemental. The High Priestess may not know it was being tampered with.

"Fine. But tell me about it anyway, why were you sent here?"

He took a deep breath in and lifted himself to lean back on the wall, legs dangling off the small bed.

"I was a really bad kid. I come from one of the most coveted families in Avonya. My fate was to become a great High Priest and sit with the next High Priestess as my wife. From the day I was born, the Coven knew that. Fundamental school was easy for me, the teachers paid me no mind because of who my parents were, and my peers hated me for it. A few boys who were a little older than me were the only ones that would talk to me. They were the children of those who'd been exiled from the Coven for using Black Magic."

I listened intently, appreciating that he started from the beginning. "I've read a little about Black Magic, what makes someone choose to use that?" I asked.

"Witches don't hold equal power. For example, I was one of the most wealthy with it. My family has had so many advantageous bloodlines cross that our magic is one of the strongest Avonya's ever seen. Others have not been so lucky and their magic is weak. Mostly useless. So, they would conjure Black Magic to have more power.

"Anyway, those boys taught me a lot of what they knew. The Black Magic I'd learned alongside all of my other power was lethal. Once it was a part of me, it was hard to control. I was young and stupid and so fucking hungry for the position of power that was promised to me. My mother warned me over and over again to seek help from the healers to rid my body of the darkness, but I never listened."

"And you get on me for not doing as I'm told." Kiaran shot me a disapproving glance. "Sorry, continue."

"But my mother fell pregnant again and it was killing her. She exhausted the maternal power she had with us, and another would be her demise. The High Priestess ordered me to use the Black Magic I'd learned to interfere in the delivery, to save them both. My mother is extremely important to the Coven. Losing her would be detrimental to the hierarchy."

My stomach churned, fear rose in my throat as I wrote the end of this story myself. I pulled my knees to my chest, not knowing if I should go to him.

"I was to be at my mother's side to deliver the child. Her labor was agonizing to witness, not only was she in pain, but her power was fading. But I was too early with my intervention. I swore I heard the baby girl talking to me, that she said she was okay now. I *know* I heard her cry. I executed everything perfectly, but when the healers tended to my mother, I went to check on my baby sister, but she was gone. Her soul had vanished." A tear slipped out of the corner of Kiaran's eye. He wiped it away quickly as I crawled toward him. I grabbed his hand, pressing a kiss to his knuckles.

"You didn't mean to do that. Why would they punish you for something that was entirely accidental?"

I leaned my head on his shoulder, he responded by tilting his on top of mine. "I didn't follow through with my orders. They were so sure I would save them both that they'd placed a fate on my baby sister already. Because she didn't get the chance to fulfill that fate, at my hands, I had to stand in front of the High Table for sentencing. The only way back is to feel the pain and suffering that I'd caused my mother. She was devastated. She wouldn't look at me. I killed my baby sister and lost any grain of respect my mother had left for me. All in one fell swoop. If I'd listened to her and seen the healer, the High Priestess would've never placed those orders upon me."

My heart shattered for him. He was just a boy when the pressure to keep his sister and mother alive was set to crush him. I kept my brothers alive, fed and clothed, but their fate had never been so directly in my hands like Kiaran had been subjected to.

"How do you break your curse?"

Kiaran squeezed our now interlocked fingers tighter. "I am to perform a sacrifice every Winter Solstice. I have to give up something that causes me unimaginable pain. If it doesn't mirror the pain my mother has suffered, I remain here."

"What will you give up this year?" My throat closed in on itself, thinking of the impending Winter Solstice. The longest night of the year, and the night my mother birthed me nearly twenty-five years ago. This year, Solstice fell on my birthday. I told myself it was a coincidence, but the heat rising in my eyes told me it wasn't.

Kiaran turned to look at me, his eyes were fierce with defeat. "My curse has not locked in yet, so I'm not sure.

Someday, I'll feel the joy of loving something then have it ripped from me as my sister was from my mother."

Would he sacrifice me? No, he didn't love me. It wouldn't cause him an endless pool of pain to lose me, right?

"No. Please don't worry about that. The fates cannot cross between celestial and mortal blood."

The dam broke in my eyes, washing away my thoughts. I breathed in the smell of the room and focused on the cinnamon and leather coming from Kiaran. I closed him out of my mind. How could I tell him what I knew now about my blood?

"That's not fair." My already shattered heart doubled in broken pieces.

"It is the fate that was chosen for me. It's written in the stars. Wicked as it may be, it will happen. Winter Solstice is coming, I will fail another sacrifice and life will go on. If you're planning on staying here, which I hope you are, at least I will have company in my waiting."

I nodded, because words were escaping me as I listened to the man in front of me accept a fate that wasn't just. Fearful now that maybe I was his way home. A Morgenstern. It can't be a coincidence.

"Can I ask you something now?" he asked, a lighter tone in his voice now.

I nodded again, still keeping my thoughts to myself. Locked deep within where no one but me could find them. Where I kept all of my pain.

"Have you ever been in love?"

The answer was no, I hadn't. I couldn't give any insight on the feeling because I'd barely loved myself. I had no simple pleasures *to* love, and the love for my family was a given. I did not know how it felt to love someone because you wanted to.

"No, but I've dreamed of it. All my life, I've watched myself fall in love with a Prince who loves me back."

"Tell me about one of them," Kiaran asked.

"About what?"

"The dreams, tell me about one of them."

His arm wrapped around my shoulder and I nestled into his side. Tingles broke out over my skin at the intimate touch and the safety I felt with him.

"Don't laugh. This is my favorite one, so you can't make fun of me."

"I promise I won't laugh." He held up a pinky. I wasn't sure why, so I just looked at it. He must've realized I didn't know what to do with it, so he took my hand and linked my pinky to his.

"It's a pinky promise, now tell me."

I felt my cheeks heat and I curled back into his side so he wouldn't see the effect he had on me.

"Okay, so the first thing I saw was water. An ocean of it, I was standing on the balcony of a Palace that overlooked the massive waves and an empty beach of bright white sand." I stopped, he needed more background. "One thing about my dreams is that a lot of them are never ending stories, I've never seen the Prince's face but he's the same presence in every dream, this one started the night before and he'd rescued me from my room in Holleberg in the dead of night."

Kiaran laughed. "Okay, got it. Continue."

"So, I was watching the waves roll in and slide onto the beach. The balcony was off of a luxurious sitting room. Leather couches, beautiful paintings, large intricately threaded rugs, and an entire wall of ciders and ales. The sea breeze whipped my hair all around, it was a mess."

"I'm shocked." Kiaran interrupted with a mocking hand over his chest.

"Ha. Ha. Anyway," I drawled, "the Prince came up from behind and wrapped his arms around my waist. He kissed each side of my face over and over again, leaving no piece of it untouched by his lips. He told me when we were on our way to the palace the night before that he would need to be in important discussions the whole next day but he would cancel the rest of his schedule for the week after that. It was barely past breakfast, so I turned to face him and asked him why he wasn't in his meetings.

"He smiled and said that he had more important things to do. Then he picked me up and carried me through the sitting room, down a long hallway with dark stained wood floors and bright white walls. I was folded over his shoulder laughing, and he had nearly taken a sprint to get to where he was taking me. He carefully made it down the stairs and quietly opened a door that led outside. Then, he laid me down on the soft ground in a massive garden. the flowers were in full bloom. He positioned himself between my legs when he picked a water lily off its stem. He handed it to me and pressed a gentle kiss to my lips before making love to me."

Kiaran's breath had slowed to nearly nothing, and our bodies had heated in each other's hold. I looked up at him through my thick lashes, trying to hide my curiosity at his reaction to me having sex. I told him I was a virgin when we took that bath together, but I didn't tell him that I considered myself a virgin only to sex that I wanted. I knew too well what sex was, but I was sure I'd never felt it with anything other than malice.

I would never reduce myself to believing that what the guards did to me for years was sex.

Kiaran wasn't letting any emotion show though. His features were steeled.

"Let's go."

Then the world around us went dark.

CHAPTER 14

Kiaran

Surely it was just a coincidence that the palace Amelie described sounded exactly like my family's estate in Avonya. From the sitting room, to the bright, airy ambiance my mother created in the home along with the custom flooring my great grandfather's built for us, all the way to the garden where I'd taken many girls before.

But there we were. Her dreamself was positioned at the balcony that overlooked the Tala Sea and I was standing in the doorway watching her. Her white linen skirt curled and wisped in the breeze, rivaling the waves below. Her hair *was*, in fact, a mess. But those long chocolate waves were drawing a dream version of myself to her. Even my dreamself was drawn to her.

"Why are you in my dream?" Amelie asked, watching her dream version of me with intensity and confusion.

"I was going to ask you the same question," I replied.

We watched intently at what we both knew would unfold in front of us. My dreamself strode across the room and took Amelie's dreamself in my…his? arms, kissing every square inch of her face.

I looked at the corporeal version of Amelie standing next

to me, whose face was now beet red. Her shoulder brushed against my arm as she leaned forward toward the balcony.

"You said you've never seen the face of the Prince."

"I haven't, I just could feel it was the same one every time." She couldn't take her eyes off the scene in front of us.

Dream me picked dream Amelie up over my shoulder and carried her through the house and down to the garden. We followed our dream selves but instead of going downstairs, I opened the door to the room I remembered as mine. One with a perfect view of where our dream selves were going.

The room was a complete replica down to the smallest details of what Fern put in the attic per Amelie's request. Amelie's face was comical as she took in the sight.

"I swear I had no idea that I was dreaming of you."

I smiled at her.

"I believe you." And I did, she wouldn't have been able to keep it a secret this long that I was the Prince in her dreams. My only question now was how deep did Ethel's message to me run? The likelihood of Amelie ending up in *my* cottage.

I took Amelie's hand and stood in front of the window next to the wardrobe. We watched our dreamselves take each other. Dream Amelie's arms pulled me close to her, her eyes were rolling in her head. My dream self was rocking her world.

I was a little proud of how I looked in her dream, but I'd be lying if I said I wasn't a little jealous. Dream me had the girl standing next to me, all to himself.

Amelie couldn't peel her eyes away, as if seeing it in person now versus experiencing it first hand were two completely different experiences.

"You like what you see?" I winked at her, bringing her gaze from them to us.

Fat tears lined her eyes. "Is that really what it's like?"

Confused, I looked back to the garden, making passionate love to each other between the flowers. "Sex? I mean, I've never had sex like that." I point to our dream selves going at it below us. "That's passionate and raw. I've never had that."

Her tear filled eyes spilled onto her cheeks as she crushed into my chest.

"What's wrong?" Panic filled the hollow parts of my body. I could honestly say a woman had never cried at the thought of sex with me before. Maybe tears of happiness, but Amelie was in soul aching pain right now.

"I've never had sex that I've wanted before."

The choice of words she used straightened my spine and made my blood run hot. Grabbing her shoulders and stretching my arms out to make her look at me I asked, "What do you mean you've never had sex that you've *wanted* before?" Knowing the answer before she said it, I choked down the bile rising in my throat.

"The guards," she sobbed, "they took me so many times, I swear I didn't want it. They do it to all the women, they would call us whores and tell us no one would want us now that we are dirty."

I pulled her back to me, never wanting to let her go. My mind went dark, the dream we'd been in became a nightmare and when I opened my eyes we were back in her bedroom. Too far from her home, where the men whose blood will someday be on my hands were. Fuck those men, fuck anyone who'd hurt her.

"Amelie…" I whispered into her ear as she continued to sob over my heart. "Amelie, I'm so sorry. You are not dirty, that should've never happened to you. That should never happen to anyone." I held her close as her hands bunched in my shirt and twisted, as if my words were hurting her. "Listen to me, pretty girl. Sex should be just like your dream. It should make a woman feel strong and beautiful. No one will *ever* touch you like that again, I promise."

She leaned back only enough to meet my eyes. Her skin

was flushed and blotchy, eyes red and bright blue through the sheen of her tears.

She inhaled deeply.

"You are enchanting, Amelie. Radiant." I felt extremely protective of her in this moment. Her heart, her soul, her body. I meant it when I said no one would touch her like that again. I wasn't even sure I should be touching her now, trauma that horrific does unfathomable damage to a mind. To feel as if your body wasn't yours but rather that it was made to be used by another. Women were meant to be taken care of, in every way. Amelie was no different, any man who dared to look at her should be kissing the very ground she walked on.

Cupping my face with her delicate hands, she leaned in slowly, her eyes never leaving mine. Her breathing ragged, my heart hammered telling me to stop her. This wasn't how it should be, not the first time. The first time I kissed her it would be in worship, not in solidarity.

She stopped just short of my lips, grazing our noses together. Her sapphire eyes were full of need, sending a shiver down my neck. Goosebumps ruptured over my body and I trailed my hands to her hips on instinct, her arms crossed behind my neck as she crawled into my lap.

"Do you want to kiss the ground I walk on, Kiaran?" Had I said that out loud? I was sure I hadn't. She asked it so innocently. It sounded insane coming from the girl straddling me. Her pouty lips were parted slightly, her chocolate waves threatened to hide her face from me. I brushed them behind her ear so I could see all of her.

"I already do, pretty girl." I felt her core tighten as she arched her back, forcing her hips to move on me.

I couldn't help myself. I pressed soft kisses to her exposed neck, the taste of her skin like a sweet paradise on my lips. When she moaned I came undone. I stood with her legs wrapped around my waist and laid her on her back, kissing every piece of skin that was exposed by her little night dress.

Her hands found my hair, gently tugging at it as I worked my way around her body.

"Kiaran. Please," she panted.

I kissed my way up to her face but stopped short of her lips. She tilted her chin up, hoping to meet my mouth with hers. Thinking with my useful head and remembering that this wasn't the way it should happen, I did the one thing I knew I would regret later.

"I want to kiss you, Amelie. So bad, I swear I do. But not like this."

Her eyes opened and embarrassment blanketed her features. "What? No, please. Kiss me."

"Our first kiss isn't supposed to be like this. Our first kiss will be because we can't stand to not kiss each other. Not because you're sad." As soon as I said it, I wanted to slap myself.

I'd never been much of a romantic, but I wanted Amelie to have better than who I used to be. She deserved more than what I could ever give her.

"Fuck you, Kiaran. I don't need you to make me feel better."

"Amelie, I–"

"Get out," she demanded, adding a solid slap to my right cheek.

"I didn't mean it like that," I begged, rubbing away the sting.

"Poor, pathetic, Amelie. Guess the guards were right, huh, Kiaran? I am dirty now, right? No man could want me after that. You just proved it!" She was fuming, I was having a hard time understanding how trying to respect her led her to this impression of what I thought of her, but it was so far from the truth.

I took her wrists. She tried to wriggle them free but I didn't let her. She often got what she wanted from me. But not now.

"Look at me."

She twisted her neck in defiance.

"*Look* at me!" I snapped.

Reluctantly, she met my eyes. The gold in hers was billowing in flames and her unshed tears made her endless pools of blue ripple.

"I have wanted you since the day you fell into my life and I want you now. But I will not let the memory of our first time together be tainted with the night you trusted me with your past. If I kiss you right now, I'll have to keep kissing you forever. I'll never let you go and you need to be sure that's what you want before I try to make that decision for you."

She took deep, heavy breaths, in and out. Her eyes furiously danced between mine. "Get out."

She ripped her hands away and turned to climb back into her bed. It was already torture to leave her after this, so I didn't punish myself further by watching her cry. Leaving with the sound of soft sobs echoing behind me, I went to the attic and hoped that tomorrow I could make it better.

IT WASN'T BETTER.

Four fucking days. That's how long it had been since Amelie looked at me, much less talked to me. She was gone with the sun and returned with the moon everyday. I waited in the sitting room for her each evening, hoping she would come back to me but every time she walked in that door, she passed by like I was invisible. Completely unfazed at my presence and moved about her night as usual.

I knocked on her door, I left tea outside of it, I asked Fern to put flowers in her room, I even slept on the washroom floor the second night hoping she would need to use it and be forced to share space with me but to avail, four full days had passed.

Tonight, though, I had a plan that I was almost sure would work. I heard her say her goodnights to the frogs and fish and I was strumming my fingers on my thigh while I waited for her to come back inside. The door opened softly and the first thing she was forced to see was me.

"Hi, pretty girl," I started, she looked deep into my eyes and went to sidestep me. Moving with her, she crashed into my chest.

"Move, Kiaran." She tried to push my chest but I didn't budge. Best part of immortality was a mortal's touch felt like a butterfly's breath on my skin.

"That voice of yours is so damn sweet. I've missed it." I grabbed her chin and forced her to look at me.

"Move!" Her palms pushed at my chest again, but I was stone. Effortlessly using my strength to not waver from the force in the slightest. I often forgot in Amelie's presence that *I* was the powerful one.

"I want to try the veil tonight." The words felt like poison on my tongue. I didn't want to do that at all, but I knew the opportunity would entice my girl.

"Is that so?" she said as she popped a hip and crossed her arms.

"Yup. Let's do it, no time to waste. The guys invited me back the first time, it would be rude to not oblige."

She arched a brow at me, waiting for me to retreat from the one thing I told her I couldn't do again.

"Okay. I have one more vial ready from the last batch." Her tone had less bite and a lot more I-Don't-Give-A-Fuck-What-You-Do. Didn't love that but I'd take what I could get for now.

Following behind her as she beelined for the cabinet, I braced myself on the counter, closing her in. She remained unperturbed by the advance and held up a vial over her shoulder. "Take this first."

"What's this now?" I was suddenly reluctant to consume anything new from the woman who was irate with me.

"It should retain your magic while you're out." She may not have been speaking to me the last few days but she was still trying to perfect the spell. To work on something nice for me. Or maybe she just wanted me out of the house, either way she was thinking of me and I'm taking that as a win.

Tossing back the first vial, I felt nothing. A stark difference to the feeling I was about to have. She turned and held the second vial to my lips.

I stopped her, grabbing her hand. Her gaze flew to the touch. "Wait, go lie down first." She rolled her eyes but knew I was right. The elixir worked the instant the first drop hits my tongue, and I didn't need her to be mad for the bruises she'd acquire from a spill on the floor.

She ducked under my arms and went to lay in her respective position on the couch. I grabbed the quilt, covered her, then knelt down and leaned in close enough to share her air. Her eyes seemed sad, the rivers of gold were flowing but they weren't sparkling like they did when she was happy or raging fire when she was mad. Indifference. A pang shot through my heart.

"Everything okay?"

She studied my features, landing on my lips. They seemed to remind her that she was upset with me for not using them on her, and her eyes were back to fire. Good.

"Everything's great." She sucked in a shaky breath. "I hope you find a woman who *hasn't* been used up for you there."

"Amelie, for fuck's sak-" She shut me up by putting the vial to my mouth and tipping it back.

Before I could reply, the life in her eyes was gone entirely.

If she would've woken up that next morning and told

me to take her, I would have. It just didn't feel fated to write our first kiss in the story of her admitting to her fears of never being wanted by a good man. I wanted her so badly, every part of her from her crazy hair, barbaric table manners, and conversations with the frogs to her body and soul.

I wanted all of her, but until she told me that, she wasn't mine to take. Especially knowing now that she'd never had a say in who had her. The teary eyes she gave me when she told me made me want to tie each of those fucking guards up to a post and set them on fire.

I had no plans of actually leaving tonight but now I needed to clear my head. If the first elixir I took worked, I could be back within the hour. Then, after I returned, I'd resume with my original endeavor.

"Fern, I'll be back in an hour tops." The candlelight glowed brighter for a moment and then the door creaked opened for me.

As practiced, I tested the door frame before stepping fully onto the porch. If Amelie met the alchemists at home, they would put her brain in a glass case and study it. No one had ever perfected this spell as well as she had aside from the High Priestess herself. Even her books warned heavily against it because of the inconsistency. Amelie mixed elixirs as if she were making a family recipe for cake.

The next test was my magic. I decided to skip the wolves, it wasn't a sure thing that they would honor me with a ride as they did Amelie. So I focused on my intended destination, remembered the sound of crackling fire, laughter rumbling and the smell of ash in the air. The voices of many men filled my ears before I opened my eyes. *Damn, she was good.* I was sure the first elixir was filled with poison, but alas, my magic was intact beneath her veil.

Scanning for the group I'd met last time, my eyes caught on the hue of the flames bouncing off a bald head. Hearing the crunching under my boots on my approach, Al turned to meet me.

"You came back," he said in a flat, unaffected tone.

"You said it was my turn to tell my story."

Al almost smiled, I swore it. But he schooled his features quickly. He waved over Niklaus, Friedrich, and Josef. Josef grabbed a second large mug before joining us.

We circled around the fire, sitting on the hand crafted benches made from logs. Josef handed me the spare mug of ale, and I chugged every last drop as we reacquainted.

"Do you want to start with why you've only just started visiting us, or do you want to tell us about the girl?"

I brought the mug down from my lips slowly, feeling unmasked at the read from Al.

"You pick, I'm an open book right now."

"Let's hear about the girl," Niklaus affirmed, his brown eyes glowing against the crackling fire.

"Well, there's not much to say. That's my fault, I suppose. I've been alone in that cottage for two centuries. She showed up about two months ago, and she's been driving me crazy since." I took a deep breath and looked at Al. He was really smiling now. It was horrifying. Even when telling a story that had his comrades in shambles of laughter, he'd barely cracked a smile.

"My friend lived in that cottage for a long time, about as long as you, my boy. Her name was Orla." Al leaned forward, like I was supposed to know something about said Orla.

Orla… Orla. Why was that familiar? I couldn't place it.

"Is she here?" Assuming that all Lost Souls gathered here every night.

Al and Niklaus shared a sad, but fond look. "No, we haven't seen her since about the time you showed up. We assumed you drove her away, but that's obviously not the case."

Confused, I tried to remember those first days in the

cottage. It looked lived in. But I just assumed that was Fern's decorating.

"Hope she left you some food when you got here. She was a phenomenal cook. She'd feed everyone, all the souls that found her home. Didn't matter who or what ya' were, everyone was welcome in her house. Just don't piss her off, her bad side was a *bad* side."

The men shared a nostalgic laugh, remembering their friend for a moment. I thought of Fern, how her spirit definitely gave homage to the previous occupant.

"It's a lovely home, I haven't been very appreciative of it since I've been here but Amelie's changed that. The house is full of life again."

Al and Friedrich were both looking at me like I'd grown a second head. I was halfway through the second mug and wondered if the enchanted ale had a side effect I didn't know about.

"What?"

"What do you *mean* the house is full of life again?" Friedrich asked, Al leaned his elbows on his knees, anxiously awaiting my answer.

"The home is sentient, I call her Fern. You ask for anything and she'll deliver. She cleans, decorates, cooks. You name it, Fern does it," I told them matter-of-factly. We all lived in an enchanted Forest, so their confusion bled onto me.

"Houses can't have magic, boy. People have magic."

"Yeah, I'm a Witch. I know that."

"And where you're from, do a lot of houses cook and clean for you?"

I took a moment to search my brain, but they were right. Fern was the only house I'd ever known to be sentient. Not sure why it took me two hundred years to realize that, I always just assumed the cottage drew from my magic.

All four men were looking at one another, having a silent conversation that I wasn't privy to. Niklaus' eyes were twinkling under the moonlight. I couldn't tell if the unshed tears that had formed were of sadness or hope. Friedrich was resting a firm hand on his shoulder.

"Could you bring something back to your cottage for us Kiaran?" Niklaus asked.

"Uh… sure?" Niklaus dug in his pocket and pulled out a gold necklace. He held it out for me as I finished the second mug of ale. Magically, it was refilled and I went back in for the rest. I had the spinning feeling beginning to twist in the center of my head, but I wasn't drunk yet.

Al was watching me with mountains of curiosity in his eyes. Even though I wasn't making direct eye contact with him, I felt the weight of his gaze all the same. I polished off the third mug and set it down next to me, then held out my hand to let Niklaus drop the necklace in my palm.

Zaps of energy pricked my skin, competing with the static of the veil. I quickly tucked it into my pocket. "Who's necklace is this?" Feeling a little unnerved by the tension that had bubbled in our circle.

"It was my wife's. She gave it to our daughter before she disappeared."

I knew I wasn't the best at being social, but these guys were all a little off. I liked that about them, so I didn't really care why the necklace couldn't stay with Niklaus. "Yeah, I'll return it. No problem." I got to my feet and started for the treeline, feeling more wobbly than I thought I'd be.

Al accompanied me in silence until we reached the trees. Then he turned to me, mulling over the right words to leave me with and making it really awkward. I probably looked like I was waiting for him to give me a goodnight kiss as I bobbed on my feet.

"What's the girl's name?" he asked carefully.

"Amelie." My heart skipped a beat at the taste of her name on my tongue. I couldn't wait to get back to her. Hopefully, she would forgive me when she saw what I had planned.

"I thought so."

"What do you mean?" The territorial side of me was trying to push to the forefront.

"Would it be okay if we stopped by tomorrow night?" The dominant tone he normally took was gone with the November breeze. His question was sincere.

"Can you do that?"

"We can wander anywhere. We're lost. We just choose to call here our home." He motioned to the campsite. "Feels a little less tragic that way." His eyes were soft, a longing that ran deep in the veins of all the souls here, clear as day now.

"Sure, Al. That sounds nice."

The side of his mouth curved up into a half smile.

"We'd really like that."

CHAPTER 15
Amelie

The same pain, black void and weight ruled over my body. More than the first time, a little less than the last. I felt the gentle press of a hand against my cheek as the darkness was swallowed by candlelight. Kiaran's chiseled, stubbled jaw and clear blue eyes came into view. My head was resting in his lap.

There was no panic in his eyes or fear in his bones, he was calm. He was breathing evenly as he stared at something in the kitchen with a twinkle in his eyes.

I wasn't really mad at him anymore. I was only embarrassed by it all. The moment felt so special, I'd never voiced what had happened to me. It didn't feel necessary to do so back home because it was happening to all the women. None of us were special in that regard. If we shared the depravities of what the guards had done to us, it would be the saddest meeting of the minds the world had ever seen. So, we just kept our heads down, mouths shut, and went about our lives as if any of it was okay.

That dream had always stuck with me because it was the first time I felt like sex wasn't how it had been when it was forced upon me. The mornings I woke up from that dream, I always felt a little shimmer of hope that maybe someday I would experience love the way I dreamed of it.

Kiaran's initial reaction showed me he agreed, that he knew it was wrong. He comforted me, kissed my body, and made me feel safe. For the first time in my life, I'd asked for more instead of begging for it to stop. Him leaving me made me feel like I wasn't allowed to ask for it.

His gentle hand began drawing lazy circles around my temple, easing the pain in my head that he didn't know I had.

I sighed into his touch, surrendering my embarrassment to linger in his affection.

"Hi, pretty girl," he whispered as his lips stretched into a sloppy grin.

"Hi, magic man," I replied, leaning into his touch.

"Feeling okay?" His words slurred a bit, which piqued my attention.

A deep inhale sent me spiraling back to Holleberg for a moment. The smell of alcohol was heavy in Kiaran's hot breath.

My brows pinched together, realizing that Kiaran was drunk. "Yeah, are you?"

"I feel great. C'mon I wanna show you something."

Oh yeah. He was drunk.

He lifted my head so he could stand, then scooped me up like a baby to carry me to the kitchen.

Kiaran was smiling with pride as he walked us to the table, setting me down at a place setting that was surrounded by candles. Taking a look behind me, the cabinets were covered by huge arrangements of red roses and white water lilies, both of my favorites. Music played softly from somewhere in the house, but there was no music box in sight. It was a romantic tune that made my skin tingle to think of Kiaran choosing it for us.

Kiaran took the seat next to me at his own place setting,

and before us, a huge piece of steak along with creamy mashed potatoes appeared.

"What d'ya think?" Kiaran slurred. His midnight-black hair was mussed, like he'd been running his fingers through it. One curl fell onto his face contrasting against his glossy blue eyes.

"Are you drunk?" I blurted, already knowing the answer.

Kiaran let out a heavy breath and scrunched up his nose. "It turns out the ale the Souls make at their camp is really fucking strong."

My father drank sometimes. Lord Bosque kept alcohol mostly for his men, but some of the rowdier villagers would brew their own and get together in secret. When he did partake in the illegal activity, he was always so fun and full of life with the weight of our misfortune masked.

"Is this supposed to be a date?" I gestured to the romantic ambiance.

"Yeah?" He sounded unsure if that was the right answer.

"And you thought being drunk on our first date was a good idea?"

Kiaran's face was blank, likely trying to find words that would be easiest not to slur.

"I'm so fucking bad at this," was what he came up with.

I couldn't help but laugh. The gesture was so sweet, and if he wasn't drunk right now I would've already pounced on him, not caring if he rejected me again. I'd never been on a date, but it didn't take an experienced woman to know that you don't show up drunk.

"Ya' think?" I cut through my steak like it was butter and savored the taste of it in my mouth.

"If I wasn't drunk right now, would you be impressed?" Boyish, heavy eyes stared at me. He hadn't touched his food. His sole focus was on me and watching me pop the meat into my mouth.

God, Fern was an excellent cook.

Making him sweat it out a bit, I shoved some potatoes in with the last bite and took my time swallowing. His fingers began strumming the table, a tick I learned he does when he's nervous.

The man who introduced himself the first week I was here was so far from the one in front of me now. The one hoping he'd impressed me. Quickly after that first night, he shifted into a broody, awkward mess. I secretly hoped that was the effect I had on him, because he looked adorable as he tried to patiently wait for my answer.

"I'm impressed either way. Fern did an excellent job." I ribbed him. Finishing my food, I stood and wrapped the wooden pillar by the front door in a dramatic hug.

"Thank you for the flowers and dinner Fern. It was lovely. Maybe next time, you could add in sober company?"

Kiaran's face turned from sheepish to frustrated quickly as he rose his defenses. "This was my idea. Fern helped me arrange the flowers, but I picked them on my way back. Not to mention dinner and music, I chose those too."

I tried to hold back a laugh, it was too fun to antagonize hiim..

Letting go of Fern and starting for my bedroom, Kiaran stopped me at the end of the table.

He grabbed my wrist and spun me to face him. His gait was unsteady, but he was focused on my face. Looking back and forth from my eyes to my lips.

"Are you still mad at me?"

"Yup," I lied.

"Well, can you stop being mad at me?"

"Maybe."

He thought on that for a second before deciding that he should speak again.

"Should I kiss you right now?"

"No."

"No?"

"No."

Kiaran was taken aback by my proclamation. His brows bunched together and his bloodshot blue eyes were locked on mine.

"So, *don't* kiss you then?"

"That's right, don't kiss me."

"Is this a trick?"

The laugh that rippled out of me was so loud that the Forest was likely tuned in to it. My head fell forward into his chest as I tried to catch my breath. My laugh took all the air from my lungs.

"No, this isn't a trick." I leaned back just enough to look up at his beautifully drunken face. His cheeks were flushed and a few of his midnight-black curls were falling into his face. His lips twisted together in confusion, but an effortless smile still rested on his mouth.

"You rejected me because *it wasn't the right moment*," I mocked. "I'm sure sober you would agree that this isn't the right moment, either."

I reached for his hand that was still wrapped around my wrist and laced our fingers together. Bringing our hands to my heart and closing the space between us, I rested my head on his chest.

"I'm glad you had fun tonight."

Kiaran stroked a hand down to the small of my back, tangling the other in my long waves.

"And thank you for the *almost* date."

"I'm going to kiss you next time. I swear to your God, I won't fuck it up again."

Breaking the embrace, I finished the walk to my room but turned slightly when I got to my door. "Third time's the charm." I winked at him and got a drunken eye roll and lazy smile in return.

A soft beam of sunlight warmed my cheek in the same familiar way it had since my first morning in the cottage. The quiet, peaceful setting Fern always kept for us, however, did not accompany my usual princess like awakening.

Outside my bedroom door, it sounded like someone was practicing sprints across the wooden floors but instead of stopping when they reached a wall, they ran right into it. Oh, and the person was wearing clogs for sure because how the fuck else could someone make that much noise?

Peeling myself off the luxurious down pillow and forcing the warm quilt off my body, I staggered to my door to inspect who was ruining my ritualistic, dreamy morning.

Twisting the knob and pulling the door open, I was met with a scene that would forever stay in the part of my brain marked as *What the Fuck is Going On?*

Kiaran was racing around the kitchen like a chicken with his head cut off. He had a blue checkered apron hung around his neck, tied securely around his waist. Flour was caked across his forehead and some sort of batter was spilled over his mouth.

I stared at his back while his elbow worked furiously to stir whatever was in front of him. He was singing to himself, an upbeat song I'd never heard before.

The week is over, work is done
So now it's time to have some fun
The place is old and there's money owed
Tonight forget that heavy load

His voice was deep and raspy but beautiful. A siren if I'd ever heard one because I'd apparently walked to him and was now standing on his left.

"Amelie!" He startled at my presence.

"Mornin'." I rolled my lips together to contain my smile. "What's all this?"

"We have guests coming tonight, I wanted to make sure everything was perfect," Kiaran replied with a dash of shyness and a splash of anxiety in his voice.

"Trying to impress Ethel, huh?" I stuck my finger in the batter and took a taste.

Oh my fucking God. Vanilla buttercream frosting. I'd know the taste anywhere. It was on one of the pastries I'd swiped from the merchant cart for the boys. It was a lot sweeter now though, knowing I wouldn't be punished for taking some.

Kiaran had stopped stirring to watch me relish in the taste of his frosting, his gaze lingered long enough to break goosebumps out across my arms and send a tingle up my spine.

"Ethel? No. Al asked if he and the guys could join us for dinner tonight," he said, returning to his baking duties.

"Uh, noo. Ethel, and her husband are coming for dinner tonight."

Kiaran turned to look at me and something began racing in his eyes.

He looked panicked.

Staring around the kitchen, his gaze landed on the six pans that were already overflowing with puffy tops. He let out a sigh and hung his head over the bowl, letting go of his stirring stick and bracing himself on the table.

"We are going to need so many more muffins."

I looked at the pans and did quick mental math of dozens.

"Kiaran there are seventy two muffins over there. How many men is Al bringing?" Laughing, I laid a hand on his shoulder hoping to calm the adorably anxious man in our kitchen.

"Three? Plus him though!"

"You made seventy-two muffins for six total people?"

"Do I look like a man that has hosted before, Amelie?"

Taking the invitation to decide just exactly who Kiaran looked like, I noticed that he was wearing a lose, nearly see through short sleeved light blue shirt. He usually wore longer sleeves so I hadn't noticed before, but little tattoos separated by an inch or two between each of them covered his arms. All kinds of pictures that seemed to tell a story. The light material of his shirt suggested that tattoos covered his chest and back too.

His hair was disheveled with streaks of frosting coating random strands. His hands were pure white as if he'd measured the ingredients with them. He looked so fucking good. But to answer his question, "No, I don't think anyone has ever assumed six people would eat that many muffins. Is that supposed to be dinner too?"

"Amelie," He let out an exhausted breath, "either ask Fern for an apron or get out of my kitchen."

"Speaking of Fern, did you piss her off again? Why didn't you just ask her to help you?"

Kiaran dropped his stir stick so hard into the bowl then, it painted the table and the floors in sporadic stripes of precious frosting. Taking a step back from the table like I'd just lashed him with a whip, he landed his hands on his hips and took a slow, deep breath. His eyes closed and he shook his head slowly.

"You didn't ask her to help, did you?" It was becoming impossible to hold in my laughter.

"No, Amelie. I didn't ask her."

And I burst.

My body folded in half and a long winded laugh expelled from my lungs. I fell on my ass and tried to see Kiaran through my squinted eyes but all I could see was the colors of that girly blue apron, only making me laugh harder.

Footsteps approached my side and Kiaran crouched down next to me.

"You women are going to kill me, ya know that?" he

asked, leaving his anxiety and embarrassment back at the splattered bowl of frosting.

I finally steadied my breath and looked up at him. "You're a mess," was all I could come up with as my laughing fit started again.

"Right, well I'm going to go clean up. You and your partner in driving me insane can handle this out here." Straightening his legs, he turned toward the bathroom. Something in my bones felt compelled to follow him. So I did.

"It's not Fern's fault." I defended my friend.

"Who do you think gave me all the ingredients?" He arched a brow and his lips formed a flat line.

God, I loved Fern. I pictured her laughing in her spirit right now, she knew exactly what she was doing.

Kiaran walked into the bathroom, the tub full of steaming water already. I paused at the door, knowing how Kiaran felt the last time I invited myself into the bath with him.

Deciding to play it cool, I began undressing down to my undergarments.

"Why… what…" Kiaran cleared his throat trying to find a more masculine octave. "What are you doing?"

"Taking a bath with you. I'll help you clean up."

Kiaran looked over my nearly naked body, fingers strumming his thigh right on cue.

"It's only weird if you make it weird," I reminded him.

He chewed on his lip as he watched me dip my toe in the water, as if Fern would make it anything but the most perfect temperature. Sinking in fully, I tilted my head back and let my waves fall wherever they landed. Kiaran watched me reluctantly as if he hadn't kissed the body he was looking at all over the other night.

Giving in, he undressed, leaving his underwear on and joined me in the tub. This time, not making it two lengths longer than it needed to be.

"Turn around."

"Why?" He seriously looked like he was about to jump out of his skin.

"I told you I was going to help you clean up. Now turn around and come here."

His mind was going a million miles a minute. I might not be able to pluck thoughts from people's minds like him, but it read like an open book on his face.

Slowly, he turned his body and slid back between my legs. The tattoos that covered his back looked like pieces of a quilt. Perfectly placed but with no set pattern.

There was a little bunch of stars under his shoulder blade, a skull on the side of his spine at the nape of his neck almost covered by his hair, a crow mid-flight on the cap of his shoulder, and at least twenty more covering each arm.

The tiny mountain range caught my attention, I wondered what his home looked like. If it was dreadful like my home or full of hope and beauty. If his house in my dream was any insight, I'd say it was the latter. I chose not to ask most of the time, believing it would be too painful for him to talk about a place he may never see again.

"What do all of these tattoos mean?" I asked. I scooped out a dollop of soap from the jar, lathered it to a foam then slid my fingers into his hair and started to work it through his flour dusted curls. Kiaran's head leaned back a bit and his arms that were resting on the side of the tub finally relaxed.

"Fulfilled fates. When I cross the stars the High Priestess chose for me, another one appears."

"What does this one mean?" I traced the peaks of the mountains on the back of his left arm.

"It's for my sister. All the ones on my left arm are for the things that live in my heart." Looking closer at it, it wasn't a mountain range at all, it was a scribble of the name Mia.

"And the stars?" I asked while cupping water to rinse his hair. His arms slid down the side of the tub and rested on my legs. Suddenly aware of why Kiaran felt this was more intimate for us than the way I'd bathed with my brothers. I certainly did not think of him as a brother.

"It was for my first Winter Solstice," he replied, leaning his weight further into me.

"Why did you get a tattoo for your first try at breaking the curse?"

"It wasn't for the curse. I was sixteen, we completed fundamental school the day of Winter Solstice and that night a ritual for the Coven's newest graduates was performed to be initiated as official members."

Thinking of a young Kiaran made my heart hurt for the much older version of him. If that boy had any idea his life would turn out the way it had.

"I was obsessed with power back then. While I didn't expect to spend the rest of my life inside the walls of a cottage, I knew my downfall would be fast and hard."

"Sorry, I didn't mean to think that. I just… I wish it would've been different for you. You don't seem like someone who deserved to be punished the way you have."

There was no more soap in his hair, but I didn't want to stop touching him. I grabbed the bar of soap from the tray that hung from the side of the copper tub and began to explore his body under the guise of trying to be helpful.

"I deserved it. I still do. You see a side of me that I don't even really know."

I moved down his arms, letting my fingers linger on his skin. He melted into me and I felt my core tighten underneath the weight of his body.

"How do you mean?"

His chest was hard and strong, his heart was thudding in deep beats. I moved down a little lower, his abs could've cut me with how tightly they were wound. Kiaran's hips shifted involuntarily under my touch.

"You make me nervous. I've never not known how to handle something. You are literally impossible to *be handled*."

"I've never been good at being told what to do."

"Didn't your parents have rules?" His breath becoming ragged the more I explored.

"Not really. Lord Bosque had enough rules for us to follow that our parents didn't bother. Once my father died and my mother had my youngest brother, me and my siblings were essentially parentless and nothing changed. Well, other than not having parents."

Kiaran laced his fingers through mine when I got closer to what I was really interested in feeling. He stopped me though, bringing my arms around him. I might have been embracing him, but he held all the control here.

"Your dad died? You never said anything."

"Yeah, the guards said he killed himself at the tree line of the Forest nearly two years ago. I don't like talking about it."

"You don't believe that?"

"No, I don't believe that. I think they killed him. He was very valuable to our village. People adored him. Lord Bosque didn't take well to those who were loved."

Kiaran tilted his head to the side to look up at me. "If your mother was still around, why were you parentless?"

I let out a deep sigh, remembering the day my baby brother was born and the weight that was added onto my world when my mother's life escaped her eyes.

"The village doctor said the trauma from Tildan's birth along with the grief of losing my father plagued her with melancholia. She didn't leave the bed once after Tildie was born. My brothers and I picked up the slack."

Kiaran released my hands and turned to face me as he slid back to his side. He leaned forward and intertwined our fingers again in the water. He pulled me slowly through the water then spun me, ultimately flipping our previous position. His length was pressing into me. The butterflies in my stomach took flight at the size and hardness of it. It didn't seem to phase him though, he held me gently in his arms and lowered his voice to a near whisper against my ear.

"I'm sorry."

"For what?"

"For not being given the life you deserved. The love you deserved."

Tears pricked my eyes. "That's not your fault. It's barely my parent's fault, we were all just trying to survive."

"I'm still sorry."

Kiaran's forearms paralleled my chest in a firm, attentive hold. I leaned the side of my head on it like a pillow and let the tears fall in silent streams. I didn't want him to see me cry again. I'd shed more tears since being here in happiness than when I was at home in despair.

Instead of keeping my tears hidden, Kiaran begged to see them as he took my chin and tilted my face up to meet his.

"I really want to kiss you right now, but I know I shouldn't." His thumbs brushed my tears away. He pressed his lips to both of my eyelids, as if to kiss away my sadness.

I leaned forward slightly, waiting for him to finally give in to the inevitable. His length was pulsing against me.

"Why shouldn't you?"

He grazed his nose against mine, bringing his lips impossibly close. One tiny movement and they would lock together. The gold in my eyes was hot, heavy, and blinding as his crystal blue ones narrowed in on them.

Kiaran took my chin in his pointer finger and thumb, giving him better access. I moved a rogue black curl from his face as his eyes danced between mine.

"Fuck it." His voice gravely as—

Suddenly, a loud banging came from the front door. I jumped out of Kiaran's arms instinctively, like we'd been caught. My eyes lightened, and the steam in the bathroom was now the only thing obstructing my view.

"Are you expecting someone?" Kiaran whispered, pulling me back to him.

"Amelie, I have a dish to drop off for tonight!" Ethel's voice was loud and muffled through the front door.

Kiaran released an aggravated sigh and dropped his forehead to my shoulder.

"I'm so sorry." I blurted as I climbed out of the water. My robe hung right beside the tub so I shrugged it on but before I could leave, Kiaran grabbed my wrist.

"What are you apologizing for?" His tone was stern, a stark difference from the gentle one he used only a minute ago.

"For not being able to… ya know…?" Now that the heat of the moment chilled, it felt weird to address it. I didn't really know what I was apologizing for, but Kiaran was turned on and I didn't—

"No. Stop that thought right now, you are never under any obligation to me when it comes to that." His eyes burned through mine, as if he was trying to singe the message into my soul. "Ever."

Tears brimmed in my eyes, his words healed a tiny piece of me. The one that was conditioned into believing that my body was never fully mine. I gave him a tight smile and gulped back the emotion balling in my throat.

"Thank you." My voice cracked. I cleared my throat, shaking away the lifetime of pain.

I laughed to myself at the memory of Kiaran's manic episode earlier.

"What?" He asks curiously, still sitting in the tub.

"Seventy two muffins."

Kiaran scoffed but he was shaking his head with a smile on his face. I left him in the bathroom and went to get the dish Ethel felt necessary to drop off three hours early.

CHAPTER 16

Kiaran

I strummed my fingers obsessively against my thigh as I waited on the couch for our dinner party. Amelie was finishing up getting ready, the table was set for ten, appetizers covered the table around the place settings and the tea pot was hot and ready to serve. The same memory was playing on repeat in my mind, making me all the more anxious.

When I was ten, I invited my two friends to my home for a sleepover. Emmin and Leo were the only boys in fundamentals school who would be my friend. After going to their house countless times and my parents deciding that they needed to be the ones supervising us, they only allowed me to hang out with them at our house.

I supposed that was fair being that the first day I came home from Emmin's I had infested our house with rats. It took weeks to trap them all, my mother suspended all of my magic and told me to set literal traps. That wasn't interesting to me so I summoned the Black Magic and let birds loose thinking they'd just take care of it. So we ended up with a fuck ton of rats and bird shit.

Three weeks later, my mother, with only a snap of her

fingers, rid the house of all the vermin her ten-year-old put there.

Needless to say, McCalmont supervised visits were all I was allowed after that.

I told my mother I needed the afternoon to study for a test on Monday so she signed me out of school at noon on Friday. I spent the entire afternoon cleaning my room, the floorboards, I even took everything out from underneath the basement stairs and organized it. There was absolutely no reason they would have looked in there, but I was so nervous to have friends over for the first time.

My mother was supposed to bring them over when she finished her Coven duties. She always arrived home around five so I figured I'd still have a bit of time when the grand clock struck on the hour. But the door opened only a minute later.

Trying to keep my cool, I walked instead of skipped down the stairs to meet my friends. When I rounded the banister on the main level, I went straight for the kitchen where I figured my mother had brought them. I found her standing at the marbled counter bracing both hands on the edge.

My friends weren't there and when I asked her where they were, she gave me a pitiful look and asked how I felt about going out for sweets with her and Mia.

When I saw them at school the following week, they wouldn't talk to me anymore. I never knew what I did to make them upset with me.

I never had another friend after that.

All I could think about now was if the men from the campsite would come. The Forest lit up on cue as Amelie strode out of the bathroom, as if the show was just for her. I never told her that it only started after she got here. Everything she came in contact with loved her, lit up for her.

Including me.

Amelie floated on the air as she approached the table, not

a worry in the world if our guests would show. She was so used to people not showing up for her it probably wouldn't phase her if they didn't come.

Fern had given Amelie a dress fit for a princess. The pale blue fabric flowed and curved around her body like it was wind itself. Gold beading covered the seams and the delicate ruffles helped it bounce around the floor. The sleeves bunched at her wrists and if I didn't know any better I'd have said she was one of her God's most precious Angels.

Her hair was set in the natural curl pattern it had taken in her time here, her cheeks were blushed and her puffy lips were stained the most perfect shade of light spring pink. She was absolutely ethereal in the candle light.

I felt criminally underdressed now in my denim pants and black knit sweater.

The thunderstorm beating in my heart calmed at the thought of spending tonight with her. If the men didn't come, Amelie would be here. Much better company than my mother and Mia.

Amelie strode toward me, her smile sending me into a pathetic spiral. She was so fucking beautiful. I should go change.

"Why are you sitting like that?" she asked before plopping down very ungracefully next to me.

"Like what?"

"Like a string is tied to your spine and your hands are nailed to your legs?"

Taking inventory of my body, I relaxed and realized that I'd been sitting like some kind of gargoyle awaiting our visitors.

"Should I change?" I blurted, glancing down and noticing a speck of dirt on the hem of my jeans.

"No, I think you look *very* pretty."

I whipped my head to her, furrowing my brows and flattening my lips to try and hide my smile. Infuriating woman.

"I'm a man, Amelie. I'm very big and tough, don't call me pretty."

"You are *very* big and tough." She mocked my face and I wanted to kiss the broody look right off of it.

"I've never had guests here before," I admitted.

"Are you nervous?"

"No," I bit out too quickly.

Amelie bounced closer to me, the cushions dipping under the movement. Her arm slinked under mine as she leaned on my shoulder.

"Ethel will like you. Just be nice." She gently squeezed my bicep, I tried not to flex but who was I kidding, I wanted to impress her. "And your friends from the campsite wouldn't have asked to come if they didn't want to."

"I'm not sure they consider me their friend." My voice was pathetic as I admitted to caring about whether the Lost Souls liked me or not. They were lost and still found others to spend their afterlife with. I was more than alive and had no one.

No one at home, no one in the Forest. Until Amelie.

"You're easy to be friends with, Kiaran."

"I literally sent wolves after you the night you tried to run to keep you here."

Amelie laughed and squeezed my arm again before sliding her hand down to lace her fingers between mine.

"Yeah, you did do that."

"If I wouldn't have, you'd be long gone right now."

Amelie twisted our hands, inspecting every crack and callous and let out a sigh.

"Maybe. But even your wolves thought you deserved a friend and brought me right back to you."

The way she could turn my indiscretions into a compliment was fascinating.

My mother spent my entire childhood making me feel like my curiosity was a defect in my genetics. It was my fault that people didn't see me as a powerful member of the McCalmont family but rather a massive fuck up from the most influential family in Avonya.

"If you keep blasting your sunshine on my darkness, someone's going to be misled into thinking I'm not a bad guy."

Amelie shook her head against my arm before she grabbed the skirt of her dress and stood up on the couch. Her arms spread wide above her head, her fingers wiggling.

"What the hell are you doing?" I laughed as I took in the strange girl towering over me. Her hair cascading around her as her eyes danced playfully.

"Shining on you. Everyone should see how great you are."

I wrapped my arm around her waist and tugged her down to my lap. Her laugh erupted goosebumps all over my skin.

"You're amazing, do you know that? After everything you've been through, you're just so…amazing." I drank her in. She was stunning, the candlelight only making her shine brighter, somehow. My palm found her cheek and she tilted her head into the touch.

"This is Heaven compared to the Hell I grew up in."

As soon as she said it, her face fell. But only briefly, before she threw back on a smile and rested her head on my chest. She didn't like being vulnerable. It wasn't natural for her.

"I know this isn't Heaven to you. Seeing your home was surreal. I thought I dreamed of places that could never exist, people I'd never meet and scenarios that I'd never experience. Knowing you lived a life I could only dream of and now you're stuck here guts me. I'm sorry that this isn't more for you, but I hope you know that it is more than I could've ever hoped for."

My heart cracked under the weight of her words. The admission that she believed I wanted more than what I had right now was so fucking wrong. Maybe before her, but definitely not now.

I bunched the fabric of her dress in my hands and pulled her closer. She fit perfectly in my arms.

"It has been nothing short of an honor to have you here, Amelie. I've never opened my eyes in the morning and been excited for anything, but now? The idea of seeing you in the kitchen or playing mad alchemist over the cauldron has me waiting for the sun to rise every day."

I nudged her off my chest, forcing her to look at me. Her painted cheeks were even pinker now. My gaze dropped to her puffy lips as they parted slightly.

I closed the little amount of space between us.

"Kiss me," she whispered. My skin sizzled, the only sound in the room was her ragged breaths and the *thud, thud, thud* of my heart in my ears.

"I don't know if that's a good idea." I wasn't sure why anymore, but something in my bones trembled at the idea of finally kissing her.

"Please?" She batted her thick lashes, her tongue rolled slowly over her lips. *Fuck.*

"You need to be sure that's what you want, I won't be able to stop once I start."

Her golden rivers were ablaze, like lightning in a stormy, sapphire sky.

"Prove it."

Only a hairsbreadth away, the smell of vanilla and strawberries took over my senses, her long waves grazing my fingertips on her back

I shouldn't. *I want to.* I can't. *I have to.* I won't. *I need to.*

"Whatever you want, pretty girl." I whispered against her lips, my hand found the base of her neck, closing the tiny bit of space between us to ever so softly press my lips to hers.

Her soft lips welcomed mine and my stomach rolled with nerves. I knew she'd never had sex that she'd wanted before, but had she ever had a kiss she'd wanted before?

Because I hoped after this she'd never want to kiss anyone else. Selfish as that was.

My skin tingled as she explored, I matched her every move

and told her with my touch how much this meant to me. Amelie pressed her body into mine, wrapping her arms around my neck. My free one pulled her in close, holding on for dear life. Keeping the other tangled in her curls to deepen the kiss. She grew hungrier at the gesture so I teased her lips with my tongue. I didn't need to ask twice to be let in.

I committed the feeling of our lips locking together to memory. It felt like a promise, one that I would give up my life to keep.

Suddenly, without any warning, a weight so heavy settled over me. It was crippling. So substantial I wondered if my bones were turning to stone. I couldn't move. I didn't even think I could breathe.

No. It can't be.

"Did I do something wrong?" She pulled back, pleading with her eyes for the answer to be no.

No. I tried to say to her. I needed to say that to her. She did nothing wrong.

She's mortal. It can't be her.

My heart was thundering as I slowly regained feeling in my bones, but the weight was still there. My heart fought to keep beating through it.

Then, a knot in my soul tied so tight it strangled my lungs, throat, and stomach. *The* knot. The one every immortal waited their entire life to feel. And with it, the curse I'd been bound by two hundred years ago was set to end.

The feeling suffocated me for a fleeting moment. Long enough to be aware that it happened, but not long enough to plead for its undoing.

No.

No, no no.

It can't be. Not her, not now. *Not ever.*

"Kiaran, what's going on?" She placed both of her hands on my shoulders to balance herself as she leaned back to study me.

She was human, she couldn't be crossed into my fate. But somehow, at the same moment my curse was officially set to be broken, the most important tether between celestial souls settled between me and Amelie. *My fated mate.*

Before I could answer her or even move, a loud knock sounded at the door.

Our dinner guests had arrived.

ETHEL KNEW what we had been up to. I was sure of it. When Amelie scrambled off my lap to greet our guests, her face was flushed and the back of her head was mussed from my hands being tangled in it. She raised an eyebrow at Amelie and shot me a disapproving look.

Edgar, Ethel, and Amelie gathered at the table. I was sitting there too, but my mind was elsewhere. It was at home, thinking of the High Priestess guffawing with the members of the High Table. They made me wait two hundred years for this, for a woman to come along and change everything for me. To make waking up in the morning a blessing rather than a curse. But to pay for the things I had done, I wouldn't get to keep her.

The wooden door sounded again, alerting us to our newest arrivals. Opening the door, Al stood atop the porch, Friedrich, Niklaus, and Josef waited behind him.

"Bout' time, boy. Smells good in there." Al said, peeking around me.

"Sorry, come on in. Dinner is ready." My voice shook as I spoke. I hadn't said much since Ethel and Edgar settled in. I couldn't look at Amelie and I knew she'd already been in her head about the moments preceding our friends' arrival. She seemed to be paying attention to Ethel and Edgar, but her thoughts were louder than their voices.

What did I do wrong?

Why is he mad at me?

I wanted to run to her from across the room and take every questioning thought about that kiss out of her mind, but I couldn't. Touching her felt like a sin now. Taking from her felt evil. I just signed her death warrant and didn't read the fine print.

How did I not see this coming? I thought it was her when she arrived. But it was evident that she was human, so the thought evaporated and never returned. But it made so much sense otherwise. A girl showed up to *my* cottage of all places. I allowed her to see it even though I preferred being alone, I was completely mad for her and let her bring a version out in me that I actually liked.

Of course she was going to be the one who broke my curse.

Trying to find the will to continue with our night, I joined the Dwarves and Lost Souls at the table with my girl. My fate. My way home.

Ethel and Al were already at each other's throats. I wanted to know why they hated each other. Where the animosity came from in an otherwise synchronous Forest.

"Amelie invited us over last week, Al. Why would I choose to come and spend a night with you and your bunch of riffraff?" Ethel questioned.

"You seem to find your way into our riffraff more often than we'd like. Edgar, you should really keep a better handle on your wife. She pokes around the campsite and drives new guests away." Al responded.

"Now Al, you know as well as I do that Ethel does what she wants. Let's not talk as if she's not sitting right here."

Ethel crossed her arms, raised a brow and smirked at Al.

"Amelie, how are you enjoying the cottage?" Niklaus interjected, trying to alleviate the tension in the room.

"I love it here. I love Fern, the library, the frogs and Fae, the trees. It's infuriating that the people back home speak so harshly of the Forest. It has been nothing but lovely to me." Amelie explained, welcoming the change of subject.

Niklaus shared a look with Al that gave too much away. They knew something that we didn't. I had an overwhelming urge to protect Amelie and the way they were staring at each other tied knots all through my stomach.

"How long have you guys been here?" My fearless girl asked the men, giving all of them a solid amount of eye contact while she studied their faces.

Al looked back at her as if he was seeing an old friend before answering, "A long, long time." He gave her a fond smile, one that I got the sense that he expected her to reciprocate.

Ethel whispered something to Edgar and Edgar's face steeled. I gathered that his wife was the designated worrier and resolver of issues and he was the pillar that gave her the strength to do so. Him not arguing whatever she said to him was enough to ready her match just in case. I could see it written all over her face that she was in protect mode too.

"How about your families? Do they wander the Forest as well?" Amelie's voice cut through the sound of forks clinking against the plates.

Niklaus looked around the house, through the walls it seemed. Al continued to look at Amelie with tender eyes and Josef looked like he was ready to bolt. Friedrich was the one who answered, "You could say that."

Amelie wasn't the least bit perturbed by the vague answers the Lost Souls were giving her, she continued to stuff her face and smiled back with no worries in the world.

His friends are strange.

I heard it clear as day, no need to try and read her thoughts. They came to me as if they were my own.

Yeah, they are.

What the hell? Amelie's eyes were wide as her attention shifted to me, I didn't process it when I spoke back to her but she was hearing my thoughts as much as I was hearing hers.

The behavior of our dinner guests had distracted me from the new knot that tied itself onto my soul for a moment. It was well known that fated souls had a tether to one another that no one else could get in the way of, even the High Priestess herself. Fated souls were the highest power.

My parents could speak to each other by speaking their thoughts into the other's mind.

You can hear me? I asked.

Yeah? What the fuck?

I'll explain later. But I hated the impending conversation more than I hated the discomfort at the table right now.

Our guests continued to ignore each other while Amelie stared at me with a thousand questions floating behind her eyes. My head felt light and though my heart was beating slow and steady, it was so loud I couldn't hear myself think.

Finally finding a topic to address, I rummaged through my pocket and clamped onto the necklace that was again sending pulses through my hand and up my arm. I laid it out on the table and Amelie's eyes narrowed in confusion as she zeroed in on it.

"Niklaus was there somewhere you wanted this?" I asked, feeling far out of my comfort zone.

Al shot his eyes to Amelie, the fondness in his eyes gone as he searched her face for an answer to something. Or recognition for the necklace strewn on the table.

"I just wanted it back in its home. Amelie, did you look at my wife's necklace?" Niklaus prodded her.

"I haven't." She didn't break from her death glare on me. "Kiaran, may I see the necklace?" Her arm stretched across the table and her palm faced up, a stern and frustrated look etched her face.

I started to dangle it over her hand but before I could drop it, Ethel grasped it and tore it from me.

Al and Friedrich were on their feet before I could protest Ethel's thievery.

"Don't, Ethel. Let the girl see it." Al said, Friedrich slowly started to round the table. Niklaus had a longing expression on as he stared at Amelie. Josef's eyes closed before he bowed his head into his hands.

"Ethel why did you do that? What is that?" Amelie pleaded to her friend.

"Is this really your place, boys?" Ethel ignored Amelie's question and shot one right to the group of Souls. I could feel her trying to surround Amelie with a blanket of protection.

But Amelie did not take well to being taken care of.

Between me having a piece of jewelry I hadn't told her about, my friends being more awkward than I was most days and the woman she trusted keeping something from her, she was justified in having a shield around herself, much more of a force than Ethel or I could provide her.

Edgar was steel in his strength between the men and his overly confident wife.

"Do not do this tonight, this is not your place or ours." He spoke as Friedrich inched closer to Ethel. I started for Amelie but as I approached, she took an equal step back.

"Give me that, Ethel. Please. You promised." Amelie gave Ethel a knowing look. One that hinted to the conversation they'd had at the pond. Ethel battled with her options, folding it back and forth between her hands like it was hot to her touch.

She looked to Edgar for help in making her next move, "It's your choice. You know what she would want more than the rest of us." He assured her.

Ethel looked back to the necklace in her hands for a long

moment before stepping around her husband, then passing Friedrich and myself to get to Amelie.

She placed the necklace in Amelie's hands and covered them. She looked at Ethel in thanks and a little frustration but when she peered down at the necklace in her hands, her mouth gaped open.

"Who is this?" Amelie's voice was barely a whisper.

Confused, I closed the space between us and grabbed her hands to see that she was looking at the inside of the necklace where a little picture of what looked like a younger version of Amelie was placed. Much like the girl in the painting I once loved, but with hair in complete opposition to Amelie's.

"Who is this?" She repeated louder as she looked up and met the eyes of everyone in the room.

"Someone fucking answer me!" She cried. Her body trembling.

Al's eyes were full of tears, Niklaus was looking up at the kitchen ceiling. Josef was nearly under the table after how far he'd sunk in his chair. Friedrich was stone as he looked to his brother who was seconds from crumbling.

Giving my back to Amelie to hide her from the many eyes staring at her, I moved toward Al.

"Someone better start talking. Now."

CHAPTER 17

Amelie

I was feeling about one thousand different things right now. The butterflies from kissing Kiaran were still fluttering, the new advancement of being able to hear his thoughts back was unnerving, my dinner guests and Kiaran's having silent conversations across the table was frustrating me and now I was holding an old, gold locket with a picture of me in it.

Kiaran blocked my view of Al and it was the only thing keeping me from crumbling right now.

"Let's sit down. I'm happy to answer any of Amelie's questions." Al replied to Kiaran. Ethel came to my side and though I was not happy that she tried to keep something from me, she made me feel safe.

Kiaran's fists were balled at his side, trying to keep his composure. He turned slightly to look at me for permission to return to the table, I nodded.

We all reclaimed our seats while Kiaran's friends kept a very watchful eye on the necklace in my hands. Kiaran was on my left, resting a hand on my bouncing leg under the table. Ethel was on my right and wrapped her short arm as far as it could go around my shoulders.

"That's your great grandmother, Niklaus's wife."

Staring back at the photo, there were slight, barely noticeable differences between me and the girl's face, but her hair was lighter. Blonde I'd guess, but the black and white photo made it hair to tell exactly. It was blatantly obvious that she was family.

"Orla?"

"Orla." Niklaus affirmed, his voice trembling as he looked at me. A knife stabbed through my chest at the memory of my first few days here. Of the name that meant princess of gold and how it felt so fitting for Fern. How I'd always loved the name despite knowing nothing about my grandmother's mother.

"So you're my great grandfather?" I took slow, sharp breaths, trying to keep my heart calm.

"I am. Our daughter, Amelia, must have made it out of the Forest." A tear slipped from his eyes as his lip quivered. "She must've had a family," he choked out, heaving forward onto the table as the emotion spilled from him. Al rubbed his friends shoulders but he didn't look sad for him. He looked almost…thrilled? Too excited for somebody who was watching his friend break to pieces.

"Why isn't she with you in the Forest? Orla, I mean."

Niklaus looked to his friend and Al answered for him.

"I'm sure Ethel told you at least some of our family's history."

She had. But not that I had a grandfather wandering this Forest still.

I looked to Ethel, unsure of what I was supposed to know. She spoke very highly of Evari and Orla, even the Bloch family. But I knew nothing about Niklaus, or the other three Lost Souls at the table for that matter. Ethel and Al seemed to not get along in the slightest.

"Was this your plan? To come here and bombard the poor girl with her tragic lineage?" She scolded the men, Josef was the only one who looked apologetic. He hadn't said a word since they'd arrived and it looked like he wanted to jump out of his skin.

"We wanted to know if the prophecy..." Al cleared his throat. "If the stars were finally aligned."

"Prophecy?" I looked to Ethel. As far as anyone knew, Orla was the last of the Morgenstern bloodline. "Who's *they*?"

Kiaran was strumming his fingers against my leg now. He usually hid his worry on his own body but in his attempt to calm me down, he gave himself away.

"The Witches. I'm sure when Orla's star appeared, the boy's coven realized the Morgenstern's lived on. They have crossed stars hundreds of times over many, many years trying to satisfy their agenda," Niklaus explained with a determined tone shining through his shaking voice.

"My High Priestess took out the Morgensterns long, long ago. That's not possible," Kiaran interjected. His mind was racing.

Al gestured to me. "Clearly not."

"Amelie can't be a Morgenstern, she's human. Witches cannot cross the human fates," Kiaran argued. I knew I was a Morgenstern simply because I knew my mother's maiden name, it wasn't until arriving here that I learned how thick that blood ran. But why was Kiaran denying that?

"You're right, Kiaran. But Amelie has awoken her magic, she's no longer human. As she was before that is."

"But she's mortal..." He tried again, his voice a whisper.

"For now." Friedrich sounded bored at Kiaran's spiral.

My heartbeat picked up its pace, competing with my lungs at which could expand and contract faster.

"She can't be..." We all leaned in a bit closer to the Witch next to me who seemed to be having a conversation with himself.

"How did you leave the cottage?" Friedrich asked Kiaran.

"She...no..." Kiaran stumbled over his words, looking to me for an answer I didn't have. "It's not magic, she uses the elements. It's a cousin to baking a cake really. Right, Amelie? Tell them about how alchemy works." He was panicking. He absolutely knew something that I didn't, something changed in him when we kissed and I was fearful that it had something to do with the information we were being given right now.

"It's not magic in its purest form." I reassured Kiaran. "But after I told Ethel about it, she explained that I held the magic of gold. That any thought I manifested could become as valuable to the Earth as the precious metal itself." Kiaran stared at me with pleading eyes. Like he wanted me to take back my admission and make it untrue.

"You told me it was hardly magic." His voice was pained as it trailed off, but he held my leg in his hand like I might vanish underneath it.

"She doesn't have magic like yours, boy. She is half Morgenstern. Her magic, that she has unknowingly awoken, is one that can create mass chaos in any realm. Even yours. It doesn't require the balance and her will is enough to end bloodlines." Josef spoke. For the first time since being here, he spoke and it was with such conviction that the table went completely silent.

Kiaran shifted in his seat and burst into a fit of laughter.

"You mean to tell me that Amelie is a descendant of the most notoriously powerful Witches known to my realm?" He shook his head. "You're crazy."

Since Ethel told me what she knew about the Morgensterns, there was an ever present sting in my heart. That sting was present in Josef's deep blue eyes as he continued.

"That's exactly what I'm saying, son. Evari Morgenstern was the first to try to fight back against your High Priestess. She was bold and brave. She said the only chance her family had in breaking the orders was crossing their bloodlines with less powerful ones. Eventually finding more human blood than celestial." Josef continued, folding his hands together on the table and not taking his eyes away from them.

Al stared at his friend. He had something to add but I gathered that Josef speaking wasn't something you ever took away from him.

He looked up at me now. "I never got to meet her," utter despair was etched into his voice, "Orla, that is. My daughter." Josef straightened his wobbling voice, "I heard the stories about her years later when I came back after my death looking for Evari. She sent me away when we found out she was pregnant. Said it would be too dangerous for me here so I went home to farm with my family."

"Where did Evari go?" Ethel wouldn't tell me the first time I asked. My heart broke for both Josef and Niklaus who seemed to have lost more in the Forest than just their souls.

Ethel took over the story, adding more details to what she told me by the pond yesterday. "I heard Orla being born. Evari wanted to be alone so I listened to her manifestations as she gave her baby girl the elixirs, then herself. We were all so scared of the Witches coming to find out what Evari had done." Ethel was tugged back from her spot by me to meet Edgar. He held her close, giving her the strength to continue as her tears began to fall.

"I thought she was dead when I found her. Orla had been crying for much longer than a newborn should cry for, so I let myself in and Evari was laying on the couch with her baby girl in her arms. There was a note on the end table explaining what she did. She said she could live in that restful state under the veil forever, but if her heart stopped, so would Orla's."

Edgar held her tighter. I laced my fingers through Kiaran's. The men were listening to Ethel's admission with such fervor, needing to know what happened to their beloved Evari.

"So she's alive?" I asked.

"She is veiled. Frea helped me with the invisibility veil and she will remain that way until the Earth goes black."

Josef appeared to have replayed years of memories all to

end at the same fate every time. Lost in the Forest forever, looking for a woman who could never be found and a daughter he'd never know.

"So let me get this straight, You and Evari were expecting, she made you leave. She then had a baby girl, Orla, who lived here until she disappeared?" Josef nodded, "After delivery, Ethel, you somehow hid Evari's body and have kept her veiled for what, three hundred years?" Ethel twiddled her thumbs and concurred, "Niklaus, you and Orla had a baby girl, my grandma Amelia? How did Amelia end up in Holleberg? And where do you two fit into all of this?" I finished by asking Al and Friedrich.

Niklaus took the first answer, "Amelia would've been two or three when Orla disappeared. We didn't know where she went, the fact that you're here and have believed yourself to be human and come from the village outside of the Forest would suggest she somehow ended up there. I died only a few days after Orla disappeared. My heart was too broken to continue."

Al placed a hand on his friend's shoulder and answered the second half of my question. "I am your Father's grandfather." Al said with nothing but joy in his voice. Like he'd been waiting to shout from the rooftop that the great artist from Holleberg was of his blood.

"I am Alfred Bloch Senior. My son was Alfred Bloch Junior, his mother and I allowed him to leave for Holleberg to marry a human. Your father was Alfred Bloch III. As Ethel I'm sure has told you, we arrived to this Forest around the same time as your mother's family, though with a much less sinister agenda."

It was impossible now not to notice the uncanny resemblance between Al and my father. Friedrich looked like a replica of my Uncle Arthur.

The way he'd looked at me all night made sense. Who knows how long it had been since he'd seen someone from his family. Even though I looked like a dead ringer for the long lost spirit of Orla, I wondered if any part of me looked like the bright, creative creature that was my father. Maybe I only hoped for that so that I could look in the mirror and see past the magic of gold and the fates that had been at work in my blood long before I was born.

"And you?" I asked Friedrich.

"I am your father's great uncle." I already knew that, I could see it so clearly. That must be all there was to his story as he didn't have any notion to continue.

I took a moment to gaze around the room at my family, Kiaran was stone at my side. He had been crawling out of his skin since our guests arrived, but now, amongst my ancestors, he was strong, a pillar.

"And the Bloch's? They're celestial too?" I might have a stroke if the answer was yes. And the look of pride on Al's face was enough of an answer. My stomach rolled. Why didn't Ethel tell me that?

"We are in a way, celestial. But not in the way of the Morgensterns nor like your boy over here."

The similarity between him and Ethel only giving me *just enough* of an answer was incredible.

"So in what way are you…we…celestial?" I prodded, not letting him get away with half an answer.

Friedrich adjusted in his chair, leaning forward on the table with laced fingers. "The only way for a Bloch to find true enlightenment as to what we are, is to figure it out for yourself."

The gold in my eyes lit on fire. This time, it was obvious. Before, it was a heaviness. A weight that felt like a wave was taking me under, but now the rage coursing through my blood made the magic that I held in my eyes an inferno.

"And how do I do that?"

Al and Friedrich laughed to each other, "It is a right of passage for every Bloch child to ask that. But don't worry, with all that is happening, I'm sure it will come to you soon." Al said, reaching across the table to hold my hand in his. I wanted to take it back from him but it was in that moment that I felt a thrumming sensation expelling from my skin. No one else at the table seemed to notice it but when I looked at Kiaran, I saw the reason for it.

Whatever happened during our kiss was *alive* between us now. I could see the connection flowing between us in every color under the sun. Reds tied our hearts, yellows tied our bodies, blues tied our souls, greens to our feet and the rest of the colors blending it all together seamlessly into a perfect rainbow.

It's said that you could never find the end of a rainbow, you could search forever but never find it. However, in front of me, the beginning and the end was Kiaran and me.

This kitchen was filled with those who shared my blood, originated it, created the very essence of my existence with years of crossed stars. Ethel, she knew every one of them. The day we met she looked at me like she was dreaming of days past. Old friends she'd never see again, stories she'd never be able to tell, all on display in front of her.

"Why are you lost here?" I asked to no one in particular.

Josef answered, "We are not with our soulmates. Until we can cross into the eternal afterlife together, we will wait here for them."

His eyes sparkled like it wasn't sad to be waiting for an unknown frame of time to be released from purgatory. He said it as if it was a privilege to wait here for the love of his life.

Niklaus was next to speak, "I may not have been Orla's soul mate, but she was mine. That girl didn't need anyone, so damn independent. I loved her more than my heart could stand to feel. On my way to death, I only hoped I could stay in this Forest and wait for her."

Celestial love sounded so powerful. Apparently so shattering it made you pray to remain in purgatory just to wait for your person to enter into eternal darkness together. I might never feel that kind of love, by the looks of it my fate was as fucked up as my life in Holleberg was, but at least I knew now that a love like that existed in this world.

That kind of love was real.

CHAPTER 18

Kiaran

Amelie learned more about her family tonight than most people did in an entire lifetime. Her brain was muddled by the outpouring of honesty. She deserved all of the answers she wanted and I hoped she got them. I felt her mind haze over as Josef and Niklaus cracked everyone's hearts wide open with how devastating love truly was.

I assumed with everything that happened, she missed the tiny comment that Al made about the prophecy. Weird word to use for a curse but after all was revealed, it made everything that I'd felt before they walked through our front door feel so much heavier.

Witches were known for doing good, benefiting the enchanted world and making life better. When droughts took over, we brought rain. When famine hit, we sent crops and animals. When babies got sick, we sent souls of the past to strengthen them. When a Witch broke the rules, they were exiled.

Our current High Priestess was great at showing the celestial world how great we could be, but she had a bad habit of twisting fates that should've never even been close to each other. She had a sinister side that everyone feared.

Long before I was born, she took charge. Everyone in the Coven knew her, she was extremely well respected but you did not call her by her name. Only her family was allowed to do that and even they had a hard time doing so. She was a ruthless leader, just as the women before her but she had insidious ulterior motives that she'd been playing at for years.

As the Lost Souls continued to memorialize their lost Morgenstern women, their history in Avonya was coming back to me. The only other family that rivaled the family in power was the Morgensterns. Their power was unbound by any laws of magic and completely tied to the elements. Water, air, earth, fire. Four different places to siphon magic from and at any given time, those elements were available. It was limitless.

It wasn't power that could be learned, only passed on through bloodlines. They held their magic in their eyes, I can't believe I didn't remember that when I first noticed the gold in Amelie's.

The High Priestess wanted that power so badly, she created a fucking mess to get it. When she learned that it wasn't a power she could order them to give or teach her, she sent them to the enchanted Forest to *practice*, to become so powerful they could take over an entire realm. I didn't remember much about their send off, being only four or five at the time, but the sisters were determined, unaware of what the High Priestesses really had in store for them.

The Lost Souls still believed they were here on less harmful orders, another Witch trait was knowing how to keep a secret.

Evari ruined the Coven's plan by tampering with the fates. She started crossing bloodlines, passing the magic down.

I wasn't sure how far the High Priestess knew it had gone, surely she didn't know that there was now a Morgenstern heir back in the Forest. She would've sent someone already to take care of that if she did.

Our guests left a few hours ago. Amelie gave Ethel a tight hug and then slipped a vial of something into Edgar's hand. It occurred to me that Ethel's husband might've been the Dwarven man who Amelie helped in her dreams. Her dreams were so fucking real.

I had been sitting on the couch trying to respect her space but who was I kidding? Being in separate rooms was crushing me.

Without thinking, my feet padded across the hardwood floors. I swung her door open, ignoring the knocking part because that would just waste time.

"Kiaran, please. Not tonight." I heard exactly what she said but I didn't really care.

She was strewn across her bed in that fucking slip dress. Her hair was perfectly mussed, her arm laid flat across her face pushing her breasts together. One leg was bent and tilting to one side giving me even less of a reason to stay on this side of the room.

"Too bad," I replied as I took my place on the bed next to her. She tried to make room but I grabbed her and held her so close we only took up space for one person.

"You okay?" I asked, but the new bond between us was already telling me more than her words would. She wasn't okay.

"I'm fine, just a lot happened tonight," she said in a flat tone but what her soul said, *How did I end up here?*

"Why did you stop kissing me?" Amelie's voice was sprinkled with dread. After everything that she learned tonight, the fact that I abruptly ended our kiss was what was torturing her.

And now that was going to torture me.

"Our guests arrived, it would've been rude to continue." I lied, and she knew because she could read my soul as well as I could read hers now.

"Stop lying to me." She peeked back from my hold to

catch my eyes. Every inch of her face was begging me to be honest, to tell her everything. "I'm a bad kisser aren't I?"

I scoffed. "The worst."

She hit my chest, I took that stupid fucking sweater off and wore my silk pajamas now. Though the fabric was cool, Amelie's playful touch heated my skin.

"No, pretty girl. You're not a bad kisser at all."

Winter Solstice was only a few weeks away at this point. Knowing now what it felt like to have Amelie for myself and having less than a month to spend with her before I had to make the most painful decision someone could make was gutting me. If I told her everything, then every second would become precious.

The pressure would be crushing. Would it break us before we could stop it? Would she accept me as her fated mate and try to die for me? Sacrifice herself?

If I didn't perform the sacrifice, the consequence would be fatal. If I did complete it, Amelie would die. Either way the curse ended in death. There was no fucking way to win here and the High Priestess made sure of that. Making my fated mate the thing I lost was against every law of the Coven, and there weren't any loopholes in that law. They were clear, the High Table could not, under any circumstance, *ever*, tamper with mates.

"You better not be lying to me. What is this between us?" Very direct question, most girls waited at least a few dates before asking.

"Well, I really like you. Don't humans, or whatever you are I guess, kiss the people they like?" I asked.

She popped an annoyed brow at me and her nostrils flared slightly.

"No, this?" She waggles a finger between the small amount of space between us.

"I'm not sure what you mean. This is… space between

us?" I was desperately trying to find the answer she was looking for.

"God, you are infuriating." She rolled her eyes at me. "The colors, Kiaran. The rainbow that's literally whirling between our bodies." She looked back down between us and I followed her lead, I didn't see what she was talking about. Pressing my hand against her forehead, I checked for a fever. Maybe she was officially going mad.

When she realized what I was doing she whacked my hand away and fought my hold on her body.

"I'm not mad you idiot! How can you not see this? Just look!"

And as if it was willed from her power alone, her alleged madness appeared right before my eyes. Vibrant shades of every color you could imagine created a celestial tie between our two souls.

Fated mates were not a mystery to me. We were told about them our entire lives. Women flocked to me constantly prior to my exile to the Forest. Everybody wanted to be a McCalmont. But we were also warned about how dangerous it was to find that person. The way your soul would fight to shrivel up before it allowed you to see the loss of them. They are the most important link to the world as you know it.

However, no one had ever talked about the colors that matched our souls and bound one to the other.

I unwrapped my arms from her body and stood from the bed, watching the colors stretch further as I walked around the room. Where I went, they went. No set beginning or end between us, it just flowed as if it was a part of nature itself.

"I don't know what this is." I told her honestly.

"It has to do with the kiss, doesn't it?" she asked, and I knew that it had to. I just didn't know what it meant.

Staring at the colors in awe, I wondered if she felt the curse lock into place too. "Did you feel anything when we kissed?"

Her cheeks turned bright red and she averted her eyes to anywhere but mine.

"You did, didn't you?" I panicked.

"No. It was just a kiss." She was shying away.

I tilted my head and arched my brow. She was lying and we both knew it. No kiss like that was just a kiss.

"Fine. I had butterflies." Her cheeks heated as she tried to cover her body with the nonexistent fabric of her slip dress. "Is your ego stroked? You're a good kisser. But you're an asshole for teasing me." She hid behind her chocolate locks.

I smiled at her, she obviously didn't feel the curse lock into place but her admission was adorable.

"Come here." I said, rejoining her on the bed blending the colors together. I held her tight to my chest before rolling her to her back to hang over the top of her.

She was still avoiding eye contact with me so I held her chin with my thumb and pointer finger to force her to look at me.

"I had butterflies, too. I promise I wasn't trying to tease you." I pressed a light kiss to the corner of her mouth. Her mind might have still been upset with me but her body's response to my touch was quite the opposite.

"Pinky promise?" She held her pinky up between us.

"Pinky promise." I linked my pinky with hers, kissing her knuckles.

"I'd like to keep kissing you. If you'll let me." I pressed another featherweight kiss to the other corner of her mouth, then leaned around her to press another to the space under her ear. She quivered and slowly wrapped her arms around my neck.

"I already told you to prove that you wouldn't stop. Then you stopped." She tried to wink.

"Well, we'll have to stop to breathe at some point." I leaned close and whispered against her ear before taking her lobe into my mouth and sucking gently.

"I'm good." Her voice was rushed, her body moving under me, begging for more. "I don't need air."

She arched her back and exposed her neck to me, I took the opportunity to trail kisses up and down her throat. My hands were exploring her soft, toned legs. Amelie bent her knee and gravity helped me move toward a place that she'd never wanted a man before.

Moving back to her mouth, I stopped just short of our lips touching entirely. Her breath was shaky as she writhed under my wandering hands.

"I lied again." I whispered against her lips, her eyes shot open looking utterly pissed.

"I'm going to tease you, but you'll like it." I traced a finger up the inside of her thigh, drawing light circles just an inch from where I wanted to be.

Her sapphire eyes and the golden rivers within them were twinkling, I could feel in our bond that she wanted it. But her thoughts were racing.

"Tell me what you want. I'll give it to you, anything."

"Kiss me. Then show me how it feels to want and be wanted back."

I crushed my lips to hers.

Our kiss earlier was slow, gentle and agonizing. It drove the hunger that this one was filled with. She met every movement with as much fervor. I slid my tongue through her lips and she welcomed it, tangling hers with mine.

She was right, I didn't need air.

Her mouth on mine was enough to satiate me for life.

I moved in long strokes with my fingers along her upper thigh, inching closer to her center each time. She moaned into my mouth and I came undone. I had to touch her but I wanted her to know how safe she was with me. I wanted her to feel everything. I wanted my hands to erase every unwanted touch that came before mine.

"Tell me to keep going. If you want this, I need you to tell me." I blurted in a quick breath.

"Don't stop."

So I didn't. I moved my finger through her slit. She was ready for me, her want evident from how soaked she was. A growl escaped me as it coated my touch.

"Is this all for me, pretty girl?"

She arched her back again and I sucked on her neck, moving my mouth down to her breasts that were begging to fall from her slip dress.

Moving the strap down her shoulder, I took her nipple into my mouth and grazed the swollen nub with my teeth. She whimpered and tangled her fingers through my hair.

Learning what she liked was the most exciting part about this for me. I did exactly as I was told and showed her what wanting and being wanted back felt like. I gave each of her breasts equal amounts of attention and kept a steady pace as I teased her entrance with my fingers.

I found her clit and moved in slow circles around it. My touch was light on the second most sacred part of her.

She moved her hips, aching for more friction but I wouldn't give that to her yet. I wanted to see her build up so high that the fall when she came on me would be a story she told for years. *The free fall of ecstasy*, she'd call it.

"Please, Kiaran."

"Please what, pretty girl?"

She moaned again, unable to form words as I melted her into my hands.

"Talk to me, Amelie. Ask for what you want and I'll give it to you."

"Please..." She breathed out. "Keep doing that..." She didn't need to say please but it was a nice touch. If she asked me to burn the world down simply so she could keep warm I would do it without hesitation.

I traced the middle of her abdomen with my lips before meeting her pussy. Taking each of her legs and placing them over my shoulders, she let out a long breath when I parted her with my tongue. She might be the air in my lungs but this was my water.

This was sustenance, I could drown here and die a happy man.

"Kiaran." Amelie panted, only encouraging me to continue working her clit with expert precision. I wanted to tease her, hold her up so high as she waited for the drop. I felt myself rising with her though, we'd both fall with no one to catch us. I slid a finger into her, curling it to press rhythmically against the spot I knew would crumble her.

"Something's hap-"

"Not yet." I cut her off. "Look at me, baby." I slowed my pace. Her disappointment evident in the fall of her body.

"Don't stop. Please don't stop." She panted, covering her face with her hands.

"Look at me," I demanded.

She lifted herself onto her elbows and looked deep into my eyes.

"I want to see you when you come for me. I want you to see how crazy you drive me."

She moaned and threw her head back when I crushed my mouth back on her clit. Doing as she was told, she forced herself to look at me. I slid my finger out only enough to add another and worked in and out of her, keeping a perfect harmony to the melody my mouth was singing for her.

Amelie dropped to the bed, eyes closing as she climbed higher and higher. Slowing down again, she got the hint and propped herself to watch me, watch her. Her pupils were blown, making her sapphire eyes darken.

Fuck.

"You are radiant," I reminded her before diving back in for the grand finale.

Her pussy tightened around my fingers as a moan escaped

her mouth, her legs crossed behind my neck taking my air away as I drew out every second of her release. Her body shook, her breathing became ragged and her hands found my hair again. Tugging at the strands, she used me like a puppet to ride out her high.

Amelie's body softened and her legs untangled behind me allowing me the best view of the girl splayed out in a heap of bliss. Her face was glistening with a light sheen as she tried to steady her breathing. I kissed my way up her body.

"That was…" She trailed off, rolling her face into my chest.

"No. Let me see you. Don't hide from me." I grabbed her chin and forced her eyes to mine.

We spoke without words, two souls connected in a way that only the Earth could understand. The way the trees were rooted in this Forest, fated to remain that way forever.

That's never happened to me before.

Her voice was sweet and timid along the ridges of my mind.

I'm the first man to taste you?

Beaming with pride, I made sure I understood her correctly. What an honor that would be if it were true.

Yes, but also the first man to make me feel like that.

Of course. If the only way a man had her was by force, they never would've taken care of her. I wanted them all dead, but I thanked her heavens for allowing me to be the man to change that for her.

I will drop to my knees anytime you want to feel like that, Amelie.

She moaned into my mouth before pressing her lips to mine. I rolled to my back allowing her to settle under my arm and rest her head on my chest. Her delicate fingers drew lazy circles over my core, tracing the toned abs under my shirt.

"Have you been with a lot of women?" Amelie broke the silence with a question I knew better than to answer.

"Why do you ask?"

"You're really good at… that."

I couldn't help but smile, she peeked and saw the smug expression I held.

"So you have been with a lot of women?" She tried to hide the jealousy in her tone but failed miserably. I loved a possessive woman. Well, I haven't always. When girls from home tried to claim me it turned me off. But that changed as of right now, because Amelie owned me.

"None that I've ever cared about." In my head, that sounded like it would be the right answer but out loud I sounded like a fucking idiot.

She propped herself up, looking at me disapprovingly.

"That's horrible!" She squealed.

Humans were so strange. As dumb as it was that I admitted to not caring about the girls I'd been with in the past, how could Amelie be upset about that?

"You wish that I'd care about other girls the way I care about you?" I asked, genuinely confused and unsure of how to not ruin the moment we were sharing.

"Well… no. But that's so mean. Those poor women!"

"Amelie, it's all in the past. I'm sure they have long since forgotten about me."

"If you did to them what you just did to me, they didn't forget," she said before laying back down on my chest.

I smiled at the compliment. "You're so strange."

She scoffed, but I felt her cheeks get fuller telling me that her beautiful smile was on display and she wasn't offended.

"Will you show me how I can do that to you?" she asked, sending my heart into an unsteady rhythm.

"You don't need to do anything for me, pretty girl. Holding you in my arms right now is plenty."

"But I want to."

I felt my dick strain against my pants, begging me to let her explore.

Against my second head's better judgment, I replied, "Tonight is about you."

"Are you telling me no?"

Well fuck. I literally couldn't say no to her.

"Um.. no?" My words were full of uncertainty. "I just don't want you to feel like you owe me anything. It's okay to have things just be about you sometimes."

"What if I said it was more about me than it would be about you?"

If any of the girls back home said that to me, I would've laughed in their face. Making a man come was always about him. Girls don't get turned on by that. Hearing it from Amelie's sweet mouth though? That had me in shambles, breaking apart at the thought of her on her knees in front of me, using me.

She wanted to enjoy touching a man, not be forced to do so.

Before I could reply, her hand was trailing over my core and landing at the waistband of my pants. She played with it expertly, as if she'd teased a man plenty of times before. The thought pissed me off, but I knew it wasn't true. This was all for me, all of her curiosity. Her comfort in being bold, it was for me to see and no one else and it only made it harder to stand my ground with her.

She slipped her hand underneath the fabric and found my dick hard, cum already beaded at the top.

"Oh, my god." She gasped as she took it in her hand. I tried to keep my breathing steady but her sentiment was sending me.

"What can I say?"

"I don't know, sorry in advance?"

I almost laughed but she started stroking me, her attention focused on my face.

"You don't… have.. to do anything." I choked out. She smiled at me, leaning up on her elbow to give her leverage.

"Am I doing it right?"

My eyes rolled back in my head. "Yeah.. yeah that's good. You're doing a great job, baby."

She smiled at me, then leaned down to suck my bottom lip into her mouth.

Stopping only to pull me free from my pants, my dick sprung up. Ready to meet the girl who now controlled it face to face. She kissed me with the synchronized pace of her hand.

"Amelie…" I breathed into her mouth. She moaned while pulling back and crawling down between my legs.

I lifted my head up to stop her. "What are you doing? Just take your time. You don't need to do that."

"I won't, but you got to watch me come up close. Now it's my turn."

"Fuck…" I moaned, resting my head back on the pillow.

She stopped completely, her hand still wrapped around the base but no longer moving it.

"Are you okay? Fuck. I'm sorry I should've stop–"

"You made me watch you. Watch me now." Her voice was sin itself. Low and sultry.

Fucking hell, she was going to kill me.

She started again, I felt the pulsing start at the base and move its way to my tip. Amelie watched as her hand moved up and down, I saw her brain working before she leaned over top and spit onto my dick. I groaned in approval. She made each movement effortless.

Her smile was triumphant as my eyes struggled to stay open, the pulsing became a full blown beat as she moved faster and faster, gripping tighter and adding a twist on the way up. I watched as I came, cum spilled over the top and just when I thought Amelie had pulled out all the stops, she stuck her tongue out and pressed it to my shaft to clean up the mess I'd made.

My jaw dropped in awe as this tornado of a woman blew my mind. Never letting me see what she had in store next.

She swallowed thickly then smiled at me like she'd just won a great war.

"That was so worth it," she said as she wiped her mouth and crawled back up to the crook in my arm. I pressed a kiss to her forehead and rolled toward her to hold her close.

"You are everything to me," I admitted to her.

She leaned up to greet my mouth with hers.

Then she settled into my chest and fell asleep.

She brought me into her dreams as she fell deeper into rest, and it was the first night I'd ever slept in complete peace. Alone in a version of the world that was all our own. She dreamed of us, back in my home in Avonya. She allowed me to take her again in the garden, in my room, on the beach. I watched as I bowed before my girl. I gave her the power to ruin me, she was in control of my brain, body and soul.

I'd never be able to give her the dreams she had. She'd never come to Avonya, and seeing it first hand what life could look like with her if we were free from this cottage together was going to kill me.

CHAPTER 19

Amelie

A beam of warm sunlight shone over my cheeks, my daily wake up call. My back was to Kiaran's chest as he held me tight to him, one of his hands laid over my collarbone and the other was lazily feeling around my waist then over my stomach.

"Good morning," I croaked, my voice still sleepy. The dream I had of us played in my mind, urging me to close the thread of space between us.

"Shh," he whispered against my ear. Moving his hand lower while his arm locked me in place.

Pulling up my night dress to rest over my hip, he slid a finger through my slit and added pressure exactly where I needed him to.

I arched into him, feeling his length harden against me. Hungry to feel him inside of me, starving to bring my dreams to reality.

"So greedy." He pressed a kiss to my neck and started to circle my sensitive nerves painstakingly slow.

"I dreamed of you last night," I admitted.

"I know."

My heart pounded.

"I was there, I saw everything."

"Oh."

"Yeah, oh." I felt him smile against my ear as he teased my entrance. "Touch yourself."

His strong hand covered mine, guiding it between my legs. He pressed my fingers through the slit before bringing them back up my body. My fingers glistened as he held them in front of me.

"Do you see this?"

I nodded.

"This is want."

He took my earlobe between his teeth, grazing it just enough to send a sizzle of energy down my spine. His hand traced my body, running a featherlight finger down and back up my inner thigh. I sucked in a sharp breath as he slid a finger in and started to press against that spot he'd found last night. His thumb circled my clit and I was already climbing.

"Kiar—"

"And this is being wanted back." He cut me off, gently covering my mouth with his free hand.

The control he had over me right now would've scared me if it were anyone else. When the guards covered my mouth it was to keep me from screaming for help. I moaned into his hand and decided he could take me however he wanted.

I was safe with him. If I screamed right now it would be out of sheer pleasure and nothing else.

He held me tight. I tilted my head to give him access to my neck.

"You had very dirty dreams about me last night."

"Mh-hm," I murmured against his hand.

"Tell me, do you want me to fill you like I did in the garden?"

"Mhhh." The memory made me pulse around his fingers.

"Do you want to ride me like you did on the beach?"

I nodded. He added another finger, curling them slowly. I gripped his wrist tight, holding on to this feeling for dear life.

"Is this okay?" he whispered in my ear and pulled his hand back from my mouth. "I'm so sorry, I didn't even think—"

I covered my mouth with his palm. My eyes pricked with tears as I trusted him not to hurt me.

My release was so fucking close. His words were sending me into a spiral more than his fingers, he saw everything and woke up needing me. I wasn't embarrassed or ashamed. I was so fucking turned on by how dominant he was right now. But most of all, I was *safe*.

I reached back, needing to feel him.

"Hey, pretty girl." Kiaran turned my face just enough to look me in my eyes. His crystal blues were washed in the morning's hazy sun. "There's no rush. We can take it slow."

"I'm ready," I breathed, pressing a kiss to the side of his mouth. I meant it too, I wanted it all with him.

"Are you sure? Because when I fuck you, Amelie, it will be better than your dreams. You will see the stars up close and never want to come back to Earth. But I'll bring you back down here to me, just to fuck you again."

That did it.

I dove clear over the edge trusting that he would catch me. I writhed in his strong arms, thankful that he could see what he does to me.

I wanted him.

Now.

I rode out every shake and tremble as he continued to work every last second out of my release.

He finally loosened his hold, and I rolled my body into his. Hunger danced in his eyes, matching the heat coursing in my own. Desire was raging through our veins.

I climbed on top of him, straddling his hips. Kiaran ran his fingers through his messy black curls as he watched me settle on him. My arousal dripping out of me onto his body.

He wanted to stop me, I could see his hesitation in wanting me to want this.

I want this. I told him, mind to mind.

His chest rose and fell hard under my palms. I could feel the want, *the need*, radiating from him. The whispers of our darkest desires were telling secrets to each other along the rainbow between us. Finally, Kiaran grabbed my hips and put me where he wanted me. He was letting me explore before completely taking me.

"Amelie...fuck." He lifted his hips slightly, the pressure against my already sensitive nerves made me quiver. His lips parted as he watched. He wasn't even inside of me yet and he was going crazy. It felt so unfamiliar to *want* this back.

I adjusted to grab his length and position it at my entrance.

"We don't have to do this right now. I can wait," he pleaded genuinely.

"I can't."

I started to press him into me, he was so big. Last night, I understood that much but feeling how I stretched around him now was enough to send me climbing again. Inch by inch, we went together into the abyss. He held on to my hips, guiding me down to fit all of him.

"Fuck. You're so tight, baby."

I dropped my head back, feeling him fill me.

When I found his hips and there was no more of him to go, I wasn't sure what to do next. The pain quickly turned to pleasure, I didn't want to move and ruin it.

"You're doing so good, pretty girl. So fucking good," he said in a whisper as he raised his hips again. My heart fluttered.

Pretty girl.

When he called me that last night I felt like a princess, completely at his will to do anything he wanted to get him to call me that again. He's called me pretty girl since the night we met, but it was different now. Now I was *his* pretty girl. Now it wasn't a playful name that I met with *magic man*.

"This feels *so* good," I panted.

His big hands took my hips, moving me, teaching me. I folded over on his chest, the pressure too much and too good to bear. Pleasure spilled out of me. Every inch of my body was on fire for him.

Kiaran rolled his hips up and down, in perfect rhythm with how he was moving me, my legs trembled.

I laid on his chest and he started to work me harder. His hips moving up and down. His arm wrapped around my back and the other moved to my ass. He was so deep inside of me I felt it at the base of my stomach, another release rolling in like a strong wave begging to release its tension on the beach.

He paused only for a moment to flip me onto my back so he was on top.

"Eyes on me," he commanded. I wrapped my arms around his neck and watched his crystal blue eyes burn through me. He was holding himself back and that just wouldn't do.

"Make me see the stars."

He came undone.

Kiaran thrusted his hips forward, driving himself deeper with each entry. He dropped his head to watch himself move in and out of me.

"Look at us, Amelie. Do you see how perfect you are? How I fit inside of you? I was fucking *made* for you."

I couldn't look. All I could see was that heaven sent the man above me. A few damp curls hung in his face, I wanted to move them away just so I could see every inch of him. He took care of me the way I'd always dreamed someone would. He let me be in control but took dominance when I allowed it. He was everything I'd always wanted and now I got to have all of him. For the first time, I wanted it.

He was closing in on his own release, his pace slowed and

he braced his forearms on either side of my head. Pressing hungry kisses to my lips.

"More," I panted.

He moved faster.

"No, I want to *feel* more."

"Amelie…" he moaned.

I pushed him back and flipped on to my stomach.

This position was important to me. It was the one I'd been put in nearly every time by the guards. They'd taken everything from me then, but I was stealing it back. With a man I trusted to never take anything away from me again.

I climbed onto my knees and moved backwards to meet his length. Glancing back, I saw Kiaran staring at my ass with hesitancy.

"Please. Reclaim this. Claim me."

Kiaran reluctantly grabbed my hips. "Amelie…"

"Please." I bowed my head into the pillow, praying he wouldn't reject me. Reject what I needed from him in this moment.

"Your body is yours. It always will be. This is *you*, claiming it back." He pressed a gentle kiss to the lumbar of my back as he repositioned himself.

A tear slipped from the corner of my eye. I chewed on my lip to keep from fully letting myself go right now. I'd never felt like I owned my body, that anything that was done with it was my choice.

Kiaran took care of me, worshiped me. He controlled my body, but that was my choice. *My choice.* I wanted him to do this to me and that was something I wasn't sure I'd ever have.

He pulled back, straightening himself while using my hips for balance as he pressed into me again. I wept when my body let him in.

It had never done that before. It had always hurt so much. My body fought with every ounce to make it hard for them to rape me, but it only made it hurt worse.

He moved slowly. Pushing himself deeper with every stroke. I started to move with him, tears free falling as I regained ownership of my body.

"You look so fucking good," he panted. "You're doing so good."

One hand left my hip, reaching around to circle the already sensitive nerves.

My release shattered me, I didn't even feel it coming but it was there and Kiaran came with me.

He braced himself over my head, pressing kisses to my cheek.

"Are you okay?"

The pillow beneath me was soaked and I was terrified of showing him that I'd been crying.

He pulled himself out of me, scrambling to the side of the bed and dropping to his knees.

"Fuck! What's going on? Did I hurt you?" He stroked the back of my head. I turned to the side and his face drained of color.

Climbing onto the bed, he scooped me up and held me in his lap. The embrace was so full of love.

"You.. didn't.." I steadied my breath. "hurt me."

"Then why are those pretty eyes filled with tears?"

He'd done everything right. He respected what I wanted, he showed me what sex was meant to feel like, he took care of me and didn't force anything.

I cupped his cheeks in my hands and kissed him, he grasped the back of my neck and kissed me back.

"The guards. That was how they would hurt me, almost always from behind. Crushing my face into whatever surface they had me folded over. They would take turns on me, never making sure I was ready or caring if I asked them to stop. I just wanted to know if it would've felt good had it been the right person."

"Did it?" Kiaran asked, searching my eyes for a lie I might tell.

But it was no lie. Not in the slightest.

My watery smile and slow nod was all the answer I could muster without falling apart.

Kiaran pulled me in close, his heartbeat against my ear thudding hard.

"I'm falling for you, Amelie. I'm completely mad for you."

My breath hitched.

I melted into him, never wanting to leave this room again. I wanted to hear him tell me that one million times over, to call me pretty girl and continue to make love to me forever.

I think it, I don't say it. But I know I'd fallen recklessly for him too.

KIARAN and I spent the next two days tangled up in each other. Our own little bubble of connection that no one could burst. Fern was virtually non-existent, only showing herself at meal times which we'd accidentally missed every time. I learned that Kiaran telling me how good I was doing was becoming an insatiable craving of mine so I tried to spend as much of my time as I could earning his praise.

I hadn't seen Ethel since the calamitous dinner though and I wanted to talk to my friend. I wanted to sort out what it all meant and ask her about the prophecy my family had mentioned. Kiaran hadn't brought it up and I was so enthralled by the rest of the information I was being drowned in that I forgot to bring it back up.

"Where are you going, pretty girl?" Kiaran asked from his perch in the library as I exited the bathroom. His black curls were messy, tangled in wild knots from my fingers constantly being lost in it. His crystal blue eyes hadn't stopped dancing since yesterday morning and he had been so sweet with me. Every time he called me his pretty girl it sent butterflies awry in my stomach.

It was embarrassing to be so mad for him yet he was meeting my every move so we could be embarrassing together.

"I'm going to go find Ethel. I still have some questions from the other night and I'm hoping she'll give them to me."

Kiaran closed his book and strode over to me. Taking my face in his hands, he tilted my head up and kissed me like it would be the last time he'd have the chance. I twisted my hands in his cream sweater to keep him close.

"Okay, be safe. Can you be home for dinner? I have something planned for you."

My heart skipped a beat in anticipation, a fleeting thought crossed my mind to just simply stay here with him. I kissed his cheek. "Yes, I'll be back before dinner."

"Pinky promise?"

I linked my pinky with his. "Pinky promise." I pressed another kiss to his cheek and floated out the front door.

Leaving the cottage for the first time in two days, I took in the fresh Forest air. Stepping down from the porch, the gentle breeze from the trees floated me across the clearing. Everything from the past few days had been nothing short of spectacular. Even the truth about my family, all of it made me feel closer to finding *me*. As upset as I was that Al didn't give me the answers I wanted, I understood it. Further, I was used to the idea of *if you want something done, you have to do it yourself.* So that's what I was going to do. I wanted to learn the full extent of my celestial blood.

I still hadn't told Kiaran everything I knew. Mostly because I could hardly explain it myself.

I wasn't sure where Ethel lived but she always seemed to find me when I wandered, so I left my paper trail behind me and continued to walk to nowhere in particular.

Amelie…

I heard the call coming from somewhere. It wasn't a voice I felt afraid of but it was one that held power. There was something familiar about it.

Amelie…

"Yes?" I tried to sound confident but my voice trembled slightly. The wind picked up, swirling around me.

It brings us much joy that you continue to visit us, Princess. Come, we have a story we think you're ready to hear. Are you listening?

"Yes…" I trailed off as I continued to walk aimlessly. The voice hung from the trees.

It was Frea.

Long ago, when my fellow trees were no bigger than you, the stars watched over us and the sun helped us grow. It was scary at first. The night, that is. When we were little, we couldn't hold each other. With at least ten feet between each of our trunks, all we could do was share our cries with the howling of the night's wind.

We had no sense of time, every night felt like a lifetime of dread and waiting. Then the sun would come out and all would be well again. We could see each other clearly in the light, tear stained grooves shaped our growing bodies. As our trunks grew wider and our leaves became stronger, the grooves became so deep that the evidence of our fear as we grew was not only visible but tangible.

Some were humiliated by it while others wore them as a badge of bravery.

When we were big enough to wrap our branches through each other, the darkness of night was less intimidating with our brothers and sisters to hold on to. When we were all grown up, the creatures of the Forest were protected from the night by our big arms and leafy blankets. The sun smiled at us every day and reminded us that we were doing a good job. Like they'd passed on their jobs of helping us grow and keeping us healthy. Now we were responsible for helping the Forest thrive.

My eyes pricked with tears as Frea laid her heart out for me. I never thought of baby trees as scared children. How terrifying it had to be to stand alone amongst the elements. I guess I related to that in some small way. Feeling small and alone against the ruthless ways of the world.

Travelers told tales of Kings and Queens, Princes and Princesses. They said that they were good and took care of their people. There were so many of them who claimed lands and kingdoms that we always wondered when one would want us. One to protect us and let us sleep at night. We took our job very seriously in protecting the creatures of the Forest.

Then you came to us. Our murmuring turned to music, we were singing the same songs and speaking the same language. All of us, the grass and the dirt. The Fae and Dwarves, the butterflies, and the pollen that lifted from flowers. Every single one of us could sing together. For the first time in thousands and thousands of years, the Forest was harmonious.

You take precious care of us, you ask permission to take what is already yours and because of your kindness, we wanted to gift you something. We know the nights are scary, we know better than anyone, but something spoke to us that you knew that too. That the darkness might've been what created the grooves in your soul as it did ours.

Tears flowed in steady streams down my cheeks. Poetic, beautiful words all for me, I hoped no one else could hear them.

So we sang our song loud enough for all the creatures to hear, to tell them the good news. The next night at dusk, just when the scary part of every day was about to begin, everything lit up. We'd never seen anything so magnificent. We all agreed to come together every night after in solidarity, not only had our brothers and sisters been afraid of the dark, so had every other creature of the Forest.

Oh my god, the light show. It was for me?

All that time we'd spent in fear, we needed each other. It wasn't until the missing piece was positioned at our core that we'd finally found peace. It was always known to Frea that a Morgenstern girl would save us, we are so happy it is you.

The harmony you enjoy so much here is because of you, Princess Amelie.

You are the reason we are no longer afraid.

Just as the Forest was mine.

The wind that had been whipping around me stopped dead and the Forest was calm again.

Doing something Kiaran would have surely called strange, I found the nearest tree and ran my fingers down the deep grooves. Then I wrapped my arms around its sturdy trunk and I swore it melted into my hug. The way I would when my father held me. The feeling that for just a moment, I didn't need to be the pillar of strength.

Undoing my embrace, I backed into a brick wall. However, there were no brick walls in this Forest so when I whipped around to see a tall, broad man standing in front of me, my stomach sank.

He looked a lot like Kiaran but his eyes weren't as kind, his hair wasn't as black and his energy was enormously more sinister.

"Hello there." His voice was a haunt. Something conjured in a nightmare. The hair on my neck stood at attention. I peeked around him hoping to see my paper trail but I couldn't see the small white flecks anywhere. I had no idea how far I'd walked since Frea started talking to me, but the Forest all looked the same.

Help. I tried to speak to Kiaran.

The man's lips tipped upward and my heart dropped to my stomach. It was evil. Everything about him was evil.

"Won't work out here, darling. Not with me here. Call to him all you want but he can't come. He won't hear you."

"Who are you?"

The man's smile grew wider.

"My baby brother didn't tell you about me?"

My heart was gone now. I felt its thudding presence but it wasn't in my chest anymore. Kiaran didn't have a brother. Only a sister, Mia. He never mentioned a brother.

"Our mother sent for you. You're coming with me."

"The hell I am!" I shouted at him and spun on my heel to

run. I made it a total of three steps before I ran into him again.

"Oh, this will be fun," he said, reaching for me.

Trying again, I ran the opposite direction only making it a little further.

This time, he clasped the back of my neck in his strong hands and my legs flew out from under me. He had me in a chokehold and was laughing at me. "Remind me to thank Mom when we get back. You're going to love her!" he quipped. "No really. She's been waiting for you for years."

"Why are you doing this?" I screamed, my skin crawling under his touch.

"She wants to meet her beloved son's newest toy. See if she approves. You've made quite the impression back home with Mommy."

"Let me go!" I choked out, losing air quickly the tighter he squeezed on my throat.

"Kiaran always preferred the bitchy ones."

"Do not…" I panted, "say his name!"

"Tsk tsk tsk," he sounded. "Protective over a man who has such a tragic fate? Stupid, worthless girl." His breath reeked of alcohol.

Kiaran had only just gave me ownership of my body back. We wrote into the stars together that no one would touch me without permission again. This nasty fucking man restraining me was fucking with that.

I would not let him take me without a fight.

Kicking my legs and clawing his arms, he dragged me through the Forest. My heels finally connected with the dirt and propelled me upward. The back of my head connected with his nose. He stumbled, weakening his hold around my neck enough for me to break away.

He cradled his nose in his hands. Good, I hope I broke it. I wanted him in pieces. I wanted him broken and ripped apart on the ground for Frea to do with him as she pleased.

A sacrifice of sorts.

Kiaran!

I tried to call to him again. No answer.

My eyes stung but not with tears. Rage burned through me, fire flared in the rivers of gold around my irises. Through the flames, I saw the man holding his nose start to scream in agony.

I kept my eyes tunneled in on him.

Kiaran showed me how it felt to be in control and what it felt like to embrace a wanted touch. The man in front of me didn't. He was forcing me and he was going to pay for that.

I heard tree branches crunching all around me.

No.

It was his bones. His hand bent unnaturally first, then his upper leg, then his lower leg.

His screams were summoning the creatures of the Forest. Dwarves lined up on my left, I could feel their passion thrumming as they watched this outsider crumble at my hands.

Fae were floating in the air, their tiny voices buzzing in solidarity. What I could only describe as gremlins hobbled to hide behind trees, peeking out at the horror in front of them, chanting in support for me. The Lost Souls filled in the spaces, Al, Friedrich, Niklaus and Josef stood a few feet behind the man writhing in pain on the ground. My family watched with pride as I took Kiaran's brother to the ground, no hesitation in the pain I inflicted on the man who dared to touch me.

The camaraderie that surrounded me in this Forest could only be described as an army. Ready for battle if I just said so.

"You bitch! Stop! She'll come for you!"

I burned, energy vibrating through me uncontrollably.

"Good. I'll be waiting for her."

Walking up to stand over him, I bent down in front of the heap of broken bones he'd collapsed into so he could look me in the eyes. "Do not *ever* lay your hands on another woman again. Enough men have come to the garden of my soul and plucked flowers that I did not give permission to take. If you ever take what is not yours again, I will know and the pain you feel now?" A sinister laugh escaped me, one of years of torture and rage. "It won't compare. You will beg for mercy but it will be far too late."

He looked at me with fearful eyes. A feeling I'd never incited in a man and one I will revel in forever.

Then I snapped what was left of his wrist. Wind swept around me, aiding me. As if it was a snake tightening where I wanted him to break.

"You'll never touch me again."

His bicep bent in half.

"I swore someday I would take you down, Rad"

Each one of his fingers became a zig-zag. Someone pulled at my side, saying something, but I couldn't hear them.

I pulled up the sleeve on my right arm. "Remember this?" A deep laugh, layered by more voices than just mine, escaped me. "Remember when you tore a piece of my skin off with your teeth?"

His jaw cracked and hung unhinged to the side, his screams threatening to drown out my voice but he wouldn't prevail.

"Or this one?" I pulled at the neckline of my sweater, exposing the slightly crooked bone. "Do you remember when you shoved me into the back of the shoe shop and broke my collarbone before *raping* me?"

I knew it wasn't Rad in front of me, or any of the other guards, and Kiaran's brother hadn't done a fraction of the damage the guards back home had, but he was going to pay for it. The magic that was siphoning out of me didn't know the difference and frankly, I didn't care. I wanted him to pay, as a message to his fucking mother, at minimum.

Taking a broader view of the crumpled up man before me, I saw eyes that looked a lot like Kiaran's. Eyes that said maybe he did have a soul tucked somewhere inside of him.

But they don't get to break Kiaran's bones for merely leaving the confines of his home. No, they don't get to hurt people anymore. Men, nor the McCalmonts, would never hurt another one of my people for as long as I could help it.

I was to protect this Forest and I would do so with my life. No one will hurt me, the creatures here, or the ground that gave us foundation under my watch. Ever.

Fire burned through my eyes as the weight of the moment settled in. I felt the Earth shake beneath my feet as those who watched the massacre rushed toward me.

The last thing I remembered was Ethel's warm hand pressing into my cheek as my limp body slumped into Friedrich's arms.

CHAPTER 20

Kiaran

The door flew up so hard I thought a torrential wind had taken through the Forest.

My girl was needy to get back to me and my heart skipped a beat at the thought. I lazily strode out of the library with the hope of my tall, dark haired, sapphire eyed girl to be waiting for me in the kitchen.

But instead, a small, Dwarven woman and two small Fae stood where Amelie should've been.

"Ethel? Amelie isn't–"

"No time! Amelie isn't well."

My stomach sank, my head whirled and my heart was shooting out of my chest trying to find the other half of it.

"Where is she?" I panicked. Steadying my erratic breath, I locked my eyes on the doorway and waited.

"She's coming, but Kiaran, it's not good. Your brother showed up when she was wandering. He tried to take her."

What the fuck. Why the fuck was Adan here? The family fuck up, the family disappointment until I came of age. My mother hated him, despised his existence, and used me to make up for her eldest's shortcomings. He'd been estranged for most of my life, exiled from the Coven before he reached the age of ten. No one mistook him as a true McCalmont, people rarely even knew he existed.

"Where is he now?"

"He vanished. Amelie.. Amelie did things to him that I'm not sure she's processed yet."

"What do you mean?"

Just then, a cloud of despair stumbled in through the front door, an arm slung around Friedrich's neck. It was Amelie but her eyes were on fire, the gold in her eyes were lit up so bright they were covering the sapphire blue I loved so much. It would be a breathtaking sight if it weren't for her unorganized movements and dead expression on the rest of her face.

Rushing to her, Friedrich grasped a crumbling Ethel as I grabbed Amelie's cheeks. "Amelie?" I searched for a sign of life, any notion that her soul was in there.

"Hey, pretty girl. Please talk to me, it's Kiaran," I pleaded with her as the fire danced chaotically through her beautiful blue eyes.

The mention of my name brought life back to her but it was malevolent. It was dark, my hands on her face felt like they were being crushed under the weight of a thousand bulls. My arms went rigid and my legs became weak under me.

"Amelie stop! It's Kiaran, honey! Don't hurt him!" Ethel cried out. The black haired Fairy was over Amelie's shoulder, the blonde one was rapt watching from her perch on Friedrich's shoulder..

I tried to speak but my voice was muted by my throat closing in on itself. The air being sucked out of my lungs, inch by inch. Amelie's eyes were burning into me like seeing me on fire was her life's purpose.

Amelie please stop, it's me.

The hot white flicker turned to a deep red, the blaze steadying for a moment. She could hear me.

That's right, baby. It's Kiaran. Come on.

I could see the blue in her eyes coming forward through the flames.

You're safe. Please.

My body softened, I could move again. The fire was gone leaving only ashes in its wake against the sapphire banks of her gold rivers.

She stared at me in terror, looking at my hands, then my eyes, then to those who were watching behind her. She let out a sob and I pulled her tight to my chest.

What the hell was going on? Adan being here was the furthest from what I could've guessed would happen today. Or any day for the rest of my life.

Amelie and I woke up this morning and made love over and over again. We spent the entire morning wrapped up in each other, falling deeper into a dangerous kind of love. We ate breakfast together, I fed her bits of the pastry she loved and she laughed at how cliche it was. I didn't care, being blissfully happy with her was a dream and I didn't consider that anyone could take it from me. Or try to anyway.

I supposed if the High Priestess knew that my punishment had made a turn for the better, it was only a matter of time before they sent someone to ruin that. I'd spent two centuries in pure agony waiting for my sentence to be over, now I found a reason to wish I would never break the curse at all. That wouldn't suit the evil woman who ruled our Coven. The High Priestess must've believed that my selfish streak would continue with Amelie, but it wouldn't. I wouldn't give her up.

Amelie continued to sob into my chest, twisting my shirt like she was in pain. I scooped her up and held her in my lap on the couch. Ethel took residence in the chair in the corner of the room, both Fae sat on either side of her and Friedrich leaned against the pillar by the door.

"What happened, Ethel?"

She bowed her head and closed her eyes tightly, like reliving the memory was painful to her.

"We heard her screaming."

"Who's we?"

"All of us, everyone from the Forest. The gremlins even came out of the cave. We thought she needed help."

"Of course she did! You have never met my brother. Adan is evil! He is who haunts the nightmares of children!"

Ethel's lips curved into a proud smile through her tears. "Well, your girl will now be the one who haunts his."

Chills broke out over my skin.

"What happened, pretty girl? Are you okay?"

Amelie lifted her head and through her sobs said to Ethel, "Is he dead? Did I kill him?"

Ethel joined us on the couch then, smoothing Amelie's hair behind her ear. But Friedrich answered.

"You didn't kill him, but nobody would've blamed you if you did. Fucking Witches."

I was taken aback at the dwarf's profanity. But it was fair. Totally fucking fair, my kind has done nothing good for this forest.

"What did you do to him?" I asked Amelie.

Her sobs turned into quick breaths. "Please don't be mad at me."

"I could never be mad at you."

"She broke every single bone in his body. Then told him if he ever laid a hand on another girl she'd finish what she started," Ethel said with pride for my girl, it bloomed out of her.

Amelie bested him. My girl.

"He touched you?"

"He said he was taking me to your mother. That she sent for me, wanted to meet her son's newest toy." The pain in her voice cracked my heart open. *Newest toy.* My mother knew exactly what Amelie was, and she sure as fuck wasn't something to play with.

Beyond confused, my mind reeled for an explanation. Amelie was my curse breaker, my fated mate. They couldn't tamper with that tether unless they changed the fates, if they did I was entitled to know about it.

I held my girl close and thought about all the reasons why Adan would've showed up here today. Why he would've found her in the woods instead of clipping her right from the cottage. He'd known where to find her, he knew if he would've come in here I would've killed him myself in an instant.

They didn't come for me, they came to take her away.

"You were so brave today Amelie," Ethel started. "Your grandfather's were so proud of you. You should've heard Al bragging to his friends. He told everyone you were a Bloch and that it was an honor to bear the same name as you."

Amelie's eyes softened. I wanted her to be proud of herself. Proud of what she did today. She fought back. He threatened her safety and she took it back tenfold. I wanted to be the one to protect her from the horrors that could occur in the enchanted world but she proved today that she could do that on her own.

"I'm so proud of you," I whispered only to her.

"We all are," Friedrich said, the Fae nodded in agreement. They turned to leave, but the black haired, winged creature let her eyes linger on Amelie, something like rage stirred as she watched my girl cry.

Ethel gave me a knowing smile and rubbed my shoulder before tucking more strands of hair behind Amelie's ear.

"You call for me whenever you need to. Both of you. I will have everyone here to help however we can." Ethel's message was clear. She'd been here a long time and knew when there was trouble in the distance. She was an anxious woman, fidgety and worrying constantly but her offer said this isn't over. When it was time to fight back again, we didn't have to be alone.

I'd been alone for two hundred years, and in the face of danger right now, I felt more protected and thankful to be here with the creatures of the Forest outside and me and my girl in here.

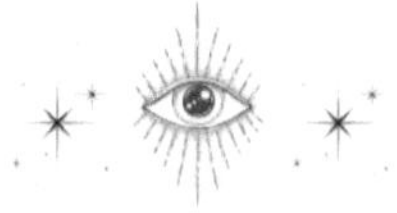

AFTER EVERYONE LEFT, I grabbed food from the table for Amelie. Fern laid out all of her favorites, lit candles that smelled like comfort and ran a bath. I helped Amelie eat as she stared into nothingness and then picked her up and set her between my legs in the bath.

We'd been sitting in this position for at least an hour when her voice finally cut the silence I'd been trying not to drown in.

"Why didn't you tell me you had a brother?"

I never admitted to anyone that Adan was my brother. In more ways than one, he wasn't. He was fated to be the next High Priest but was so outwardly sinister that he was exiled before he even made it halfway through fundamental school. I wasn't privy to where he was exiled to though.

Since being here, I hadn't thought of him once. His existence was better off not being remembered. Mia's memory was the only one I cared to keep.

"It's been a long time since Adan's mattered in any way to me or my family. It never crossed my mind to mention someone who was dead to me," I replied.

"He said your mother sent him."

That was what threw me more than his appearance today. My mother despised him. If she had control of his demise she would've placed it already but mother's couldn't kill their children. For some reason that was a part of our Witches Oath.

"Apparently a lot has changed since I left home." A shake trembled through my throat. It could be assumed that if I ever made it back there life would be drastically different, it was just never so obvious as it was today.

I started untangling Amelie's hair with the wooden comb Fern placed next to the tub, raking gentle lines through the tendrils of curls. Her head tilted back to give me better access, allowing me the honor of taking care of her.

She let out a soft giggle, one she was clearly trying to muffle.

"What's so funny?"

"It's nothing," she said, shaking the thought out of her head. I watched to see if I could catch it.

"Not much about your day is funny to me, I'd like to know what's lightening your mood." I was trying to say it nicely, but truly it felt wrong to be laughing right now.

"I.." She thought about her words and then leaned all the way back to my chest, my arms naturally folded around her. "I was sure I'd never meet your mother but I guess I hoped maybe she would like me."

The admission hurt. Amelie spent most of her life feeling like no one could love her properly. The people who were supposed to fill her with love forgot to do that, lost in their own survival. She spoke highly of her father but her mother was a touchy subject.

"My mother is complicated. There is a reason the Coven holds her as high as they do."

"What does she do for them?"

Thinking carefully about revealing things that were held to the highest standard of secrecy within the Coven, I explained as cautiously as I could.

"My mother is the adjudicator. She makes all final decisions about fates, punishments, magic used in the mortal realms, exiles, you name it. It goes through my mother to be finalized."

"Mhhh." Amelie sighed in thought. "You made it sound like the High Priestess was the most important position in your

Coven? What is the difference between your mother and the High Priestess?"

"There isn't much of one, they work very closely together to make things happen."

Something clicked with Amelie in that moment and she pulled herself away from my hold to look at me, the warm water trickling off of her.

"Your mother chose for you to be sentenced here?" White hot heat flamed her voice, hostility toward the woman who birthed me at an all time high. As if sending my big brother after her wasn't the worst thing in Amelie's eyes that my mother could have done.

"She was," I admitted. The memory of that day too painful to let it take up space in my mind. I gently shake it away as Amelie turned completely to face me, sitting with her knees scrunched to her chest, she ran an arm down my tattooed bicep.

"How could she do that?" She bit down hard on each word as she choked them out. Rage emanated from her, the gold in her eyes ignited as her brain worked.

"She was heartbroken, Amelie. I killed her baby."

Her lips pursed and the fire exploded in her eyes, though she had more control of it now than she did earlier. She was channeling it differently, letting it fester in her heart right where the notion of my mother sending me away sat.

You did not deserve this. Her voice in my mind was soft and loving, a far cry from the expression on her face.

Tucking her wild hair behind her ear, I smiled at her. "Maybe not, but here I am. I don't deserve this either but here *you* are." A tear slipped from my eye, my soul reminding me of the imminent fate we were coming close to crossing.

Her fire dwindled, the water pouring from my soul killing it.

"Why are you crying?" she whispered to me.

It could have been the fact that we had very little time left before I lost my life. I would take my own before they could force me to take Amelie's. Or maybe it was the fact that I only got a few months out of all my years to experience love. It was potentially because I knew that soon, a war would break out. The Witches would come to the Forest when I didn't sacrifice Amelie on Winter Solstice and peace on Earth would be forever changed.

At least in this corner of it.

But ultimately, I thought it was maybe that the woman in front of me had barely lived. She survived daily, but she was mortal. As far as I knew, her ancestry didn't change that fact. Her lifespan was so short that in the eyes of the world it would hardly matter, but in that short time she'd barely experienced love, freedom, protection and overall happiness. I had three hundred years to do something meaningful with my life and I didn't. I gave that up, I had every opportunity in the world but was careless with each one.

Amelie didn't have those opportunities. Even now, she was here because she had to be. She left her family behind out of survival, I left my family behind because I was forced to as a consequence of my own actions.

Amelie deserved so much better than what the fates gave her.

AFTER OUR BATH, I helped Amelie get ready for bed and held her as she dozed in and out of sleep as I read to her from the book I'd started.

"Can we sleep in your bed?" she asked sleepily when I finished the last chapter. The thought hadn't occurred to me but my bed was far more comfortable and had a lot more space for the two of us.

"Of course, pretty girl." I scooped her up and carried her bridal style up the stairs before laying her across my black silk sheets and tucking her under my grandmother's quilt. She settled into the down pillow and fell asleep instantly. Her chest slowly rising and falling.

I pressed a kiss to her forehead and crammed myself into the pillowy nook Fern built for me at some point since the remodel of the attic. Opening up another book, I began reading about the history of the Forest.

Jolting like lightning struck me, I checked the surroundings of the room. It was dark, so dark that the moonlight couldn't even cut through it. As if a thick, black cloud of smoke was hovering. I could hear Amelie breathing in and out shakily on the bed. The book I'd opened was folded with my hand between the pages.

I must've dozed off at some point between the birth of the trees and where the gremlins lived.

Feeling my way through the haze, I found the bed and crawled to get to Amelie. She was restless, not awake, and sweating uncontrollably. I grabbed her face and called to her, "Amelie, wake up."

Nothing.

"Baby, it's just a bad dream, wake up," I said a little more frantically but she had no reaction.

Not knowing what else to do, I laid down next to her and tried to will myself to sleep hoping that she would take me into her dreams again.

My brain was on overdrive and I couldn't find the sweet spot to fall into a slumber. Replaying the moments of Amelie and I spending days in pure bliss, I slowly felt my body relax. I thought of her lips on mine, her sweet voice and the blanket of her hair that covered me when we made love.

The world went dark before I was standing at the balcony of my sitting room at home. The sky was a dark cloud of grey, ominous air whispering around me.

Try to find her.

It taunted.

I could feel her here, but there was no sign of life. The beach was empty and the sand was black, as opposed to its normal alabaster color. The smell of smoke filled my nose and I leaned over the balcony to see something ablaze in the direction of the garden. Stepping back into the room, I took a moment to listen.

Nothing but the faint sound of crackles and pops from the flames.

I took off in a full sprint down the hall and swung the door open to my bedroom.

A large man with ratty black hair was on his knees, legs kicking underneath him but I couldn't see who it was.

I didn't need to. Red and orange flames blazed outside the window, giving the already eerie ambiance of the room an even more dreadful feeling. Moving for the bed, I grabbed the man's shoulder. Startling him, he turned and gave me a smile that was identical to mine but an insidious threat was laced between his teeth. Then I saw the woman lying beneath him.

Amelie was screaming but no sound was coming from her. Her face was a stark white as she began to realize what was happening. As if she came here in some kind of trance. She locked in on me with eyes full of unshed tears.

"Hello, brother," Adan drawled. All too pleased with himself. I lunged at him with the force of one thousand men.

We tumbled off the bed to the floor, Adan held a nasty smile the entire time. Reveling in the reaction he'd elicited from me. I glanced back to the bed for a moment so brief, nothing should've happened. But in the second that I took to myself, I saw Amelie no longer on it and the fire from the garden ripping through the window and crawling up the wall.

I grabbed Adan's shirt and hooked my fist into his jaw. His head thudded against the floor. My brother looked as evil as the day he was sent away.

"Where is she?" I demanded.

His eyes were rolling and his body was limp but he was still able to whisper through the pain. "She came to me, brother. Fair game."

My blood reached its boiling point, partially due to the fire that was burning through my room.

Where are you?

Holding my brother's shirt and placing my knees on each side of him to pin his arms into the floor, I waited to hear her voice.

Adan's smile crept across his face, seemingly finding a second wind as he struggled against the restraint. I hated him. We all did, none of this made sense. The idea of him being back in Avonya made this all feel so much more sinister.

Expertly placing another blow to his nose. Successfully wiping that fucking grin off his mouth, Adan collapsed. No longer struggling to free himself. I stood, taking in the room and finding the only safe way out.

Stepping over embers on the hardwood floor, I focused on where I knew the door was and tried to will away the blaze as it threatened to engulf me.

I closed my eyes and started toward the exit. Where I should've felt the heat melting through my skin, there was a cool, wet air circling me. Peeling an eye open, there was a clear path to the door. Behind me and all the way to my brother's limp body was ablaze. So I knew who parted this sea of fire.

Amelie.

I took the opportunity and finished the distance, swinging the door open.

The hallway was still free of flames, but the window that held the perfect view of the garden showed a tragic scene of our estate's most treasured amenity.

Deciding to mourn that later, I took off toward the Grand Sitting room. Bracing myself on the antique trim of the archway, I slipped on the rug as I swung myself around the corner and into the room.

Amelie was perched like a stone statue on the couch, staring in the direction of the bar. Her eyes were glowing, the sapphire blue only a memory as the golds blazed. I followed her gaze to see my mother pouring herself a drink. She looked exactly the same as the day I left.

Her alabaster face was cut with her fierce cheek and jaw bones, lips painted the soft pink she wore every day. Her long black hair that matched mine grew to her lower back and was stick straight. Not a single strand out of place as half of it fell behind her, the other half over her shoulder.

She was even wearing the same dress she donned the day my curse was officially fated. It was the ceremony dress that each of the women at the High Table of the Coven wore for adjudication days. All aside from the headdress that affirmed her position at said table.

The floor length, high neck, cape sleeved gown was a deep blue, as close to the color of Amelie's eyes as I'd ever seen. Silver diamonds shaped our family crest, holding the cape together in the center of her collarbone.

She stirred the drink, no notion of Amelie's presence in the room.

A familiar presence gingerly slipped into the room around me, paying me no mind.

"Mom, please don't do this." A smaller voice came from the mouth of a much younger me.

"The decision has been made, Kiaran." Steel gripped my mother's tone.

"You finalize those decisions!"

"Are you raising your voice at me?" she taunted.

"No…I'm sorry." Little me bowed his head in defeat.

This memory was of the hours leading up to my sentencing before the Coven. Why was Amelie dreaming of this? *How* was she dreaming of this? How was this the past but Adan was in the present?

"You made a grave mistake. You tampered with the fates the Coven set forth for you and your baby sister and you know what happens to those who fail to complete High Priestess orders."

"I didn't have a choice, Mom. I didn't mean to kill her…" My dream self's voice shook. I didn't remember ever being this weak in front of my mother.

"Yet, you did. Do you not believe murderers should be punished? You're very lucky that you weren't sentenced to death," she said as she floated to the couch without a care in the world. She tossed her hair over her shoulder with a dramatic motion of her head. "A life for a life, and all that. Right?"

A sinister smile etched her face.

Little dream me shied away from the look. I remembered it well. The rolling feeling in my gut when she'd give it to me was present now, seeing it again after two hundred years. He turned and sulked out of the room and I watched him descend the stairs, shoulders sunk low and head bowed.

That kid had no idea what was to come. He hadn't watched his mother sign off on his potential life sentence. He hadn't yet been dropped in the middle of a Forest in a desolate cottage, scared and pissed off. It took everything in me not to follow him, to force him to look at me so I could tell him to run. To just fucking listen for once.

A hand tugged at my attention, where I turned to find Amelie back in her true form. The fear that I'd found in her eyes when I got here was gone, as was the fire that was present just minutes prior, the injuries she should've had from Adan were nonexistent, she was just Amelie.

"I burned down the garden."

"I know."

"I didn't mean to come here."

Somehow, Amelie had managed to find a present version of Adan and a past version of my mother. She melded time together and was now standing in front of me like a perfectly normal human, completely unscathed by a magic that should've made the most powerful Witch crumble when they came down.

Before we could get ourselves into any more trouble in the dream version of Avonya, Amelie fell into a new dream. One where she and I were happily, and freely exploring the Forest together. We visited Ethel, stopped by the campsite to mingle with the Lost Souls, and enjoyed being out of the cottage, hand in hand.

Freedom with Amelie in our own personal version of her Heaven was everything to me. Every dream she took me along with was a promise I couldn't keep, so I tried not to make it. But nonetheless, it was a really good dream.

CHAPTER 21

Amelie

I woke up before the sun could even peek through the trees at the horrors of what happened while the world slept. Kiaran was holding me tight to his body so I sneakily escaped his arms and went downstairs to drink my hot tea and try to make sense of the last twenty four hours. Fern kept me company while Kiaran hopefully slept off the memory I replayed for him last night.

I wasn't sure how I even did it. When Kiaran carried me up to his bed, I finally felt my body relax and it took no time at all to finally let the day vaporize in my mind. The darkness that proceeded when my eyes closed felt comfortable, but only for a moment. Then I was ripped from the blissful nothingness so effortlessly it was as if I was a ripe apple picked to be swallowed whole.

Adan's face was a haunted version of Kiaran's. Up close I noticed almost every feature was the same save for the unholy threats that engulfed his soul.

His large hand wrapped around my throat and chucked me onto the bed I recognized as Kiaran's. Adan stole my voice and my ability to move. Even the involuntary motion of breathing, though I didn't think that was his magic.

I'd never been more afraid of a man than I had been in that moment. Mostly because I was doing this. It was *my* dream, and my dreams were never so nightmarish. My dreams were my sanctuary. Men like Adan didn't belong in my sanctuary.

The heat in my eyes blazed and I knew the fear was turning to rage and manifestation of the destruction my awakened power was capable of. Unfocused, I tried to burn it into him. Melt his skin and use his bones as firewood to continue to scorch his soul until it was rid of him forever.

"My brother couldn't satisfy you could he?" he drawled, his breath hot on my face as he shoved himself between my legs. *"I'll show you a much better time, then we'll go see mom."*

Threats.

I tried to scream, hoping Kiaran's mother would appear and have mercy on me. Maybe punish her truly evil son in ways that wouldn't compare to Kiaran's punishment.

The pain I tried to inflict on him missed, I thought it was hopeless since my dreams were always so out of my control. But an orange glow was creeping higher and higher up the walls around us. Adan searched for where it was coming from and then turned his attention back to me.

"Horrible first impression on your future family," he hissed.

All I could do was wait for the fire to consume me.

When the door flew open and Kiaran came in, my heart calmed and with Adan and him now in a tangle on the floor, I escaped.

"Hi, pretty girl." Kiaran's sleepy voice broke me free from the memory of last night's events. He looked so tired, so haunted, and I knew it was my fault.

"Hi." I gave him an apologetic smile which he erased with a kiss. Fern summoned a cup of tea for him as he joined me at the table.

"How did you sleep?" he asked, taking a sip from the steaming clay mug.

"Not well. I was scared we'd go back there again," I admitted.

Kiaran seemed to read his tea, looking for the words I knew he wanted to say.

There was no way he wasn't upset with me. Even though it was a dream, I'd set fire to his home. I gave his brother an opportunity to hurt me again, I summoned the memory of him and his mother before his sentencing. I pressed on each of the triggers that he'd built over the years and fucking *dreamed* of them.

"Has that ever happened before?" he asked.

"I've never seen your brother in my dreams, no. But I have seen your mother."

His eyes slowly moved from his mug to me.

"What do you mean?"

"She's visited me in my dreams before. Not often, but it's her. I'm sure of it." The second she appeared last night, I knew she was the woman who waited in the willows to bring me to my prince in my dreams.

Kiaran's head tilted slightly and he squinted his eyes in confusion. "Does she talk to you?"

"No," I said, "she just leads me to my prince." I chewed on my lip. "To you."

Kiaran's silence was deafening and uncomfortable.

"It's not a big deal. Remember the dwarf from my dreams? The one who needed medicine for his wife?"

Kiaran nodded slowly.

"Didn't you recognize Edgar when they came for dinner?"

It was surprising, but I took it as a sign to slip Edgar the remedy from my apothecary cabinet just in case when they left our dinner party. I also knew that Ethel was the dwarf I often walked with and told my deepest secrets to.

"Does that happen often?" He leaned forward, anxiously awaiting my answer.

"Kind of. Only since being here though. A lot of my

favorite dreams from the past have happened almost exactly since being here."

Kiaran's brows pinched together. His eyes searched around the table for something that I couldn't see.

"What's the big deal?"

"Do you have control over it?"

"Over what?"

"What you're dreaming of, who you see, where you go?"

I thought about that for a moment. When I was little I went to sleep every night with thoughts of all the beautiful, enchanted things I hoped existed. I only had nightmares on days when we went hungry or the guards had visited. In a way, I supposed I had controlled it. On good days, I dreamed of good things. The opposite for bad days.

"Not always."

"Huh," was all he said before he sipped his tea and wandered back inside the walls of his haunted mind.

"I'm going to try and find Ethel again today," I said, hoping to move on from the trials of our nighttime escapade.

Upon the words leaving my mouth, I realized that it only added another thick layer of tension to the room.

"The fuck you are," he scoffed before finishing off his tea.

"Okay… so I don't know what this," I waggled a finger between us, "all means but it is not going to be you telling me when and what I can do." I smiled lovingly but kept my tone firm.

"Amelie," he sighed, "I'm not trying to control you. It would simply be a waste of breath. But you could've been killed yesterday, you almost burned yourself alive in your dreams, your track record in the last twenty four hours hasn't been great," he explained as he mockingly returned a smile. There we stood at a crossroad.

I spent my entire life being controlled. As well intentioned as Kiaran was, it made me feel heavy.

"Thank you for the concern, but your creepy as fuck

brother left this Forest with not one single bone intact. I think I'll be fine," I said then stood to go to my room to change.

Kiaran was on my trail too quickly. "Please, just take one day. If only for my sanity, I can't help you out there."

"Did I need your help yesterday?" I bit back.

Kiaran rubbed his temples with the pads of his fingers, indicating I was giving him a headache. He could rest all he wanted when I was gone.

I stuffed a book into my satchel and tore of my pajama shirt. Kiaran drank in my body, his eyes softening momentarily.

"Don't distract me."

"Don't be so easily distracted," I replied while tugging my new shirt on.

I reached my door frame that Kiaran was effectively blocking. Moving my weight to the tips of my toes, I leaned up and caught his lips with mine. Surrendering the anxiety he'd built up in the last few minutes, he wrapped his arms around my waist and pulled me closer, deepening the kiss.

I pulled back slightly and he tried to follow me, like my lips were a siren song. "I'll see you in a bit." Then I smiled and reveled in the fact that my kiss distracted him from the half turn I made, allowing me to leave.

Kiaran groaned. "You're going to be the death of me." A playful tone took in his voice.

"Well let's pray it's a long, slow death then," I sang back at him as I skipped out of Fern's loving arms, otherwise known as the front door, and back toward potential danger.

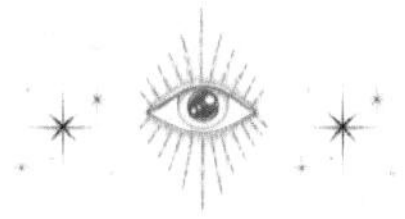

Taking a different approach than yesterday, I asked Frea for help finding Ethel's home.

Wandering was a sure way to increase the chances of finding another attack.

The spirit delivered and I saw a few tiny wings bouncing on the air toward me.

Poppy and Naida approached, Poppy was radiating energy. "You were so brave yesterday! He crumbled like a leaf!" she shrieked and punched her fist into her palm.

I smiled at my tiny friend, not wanting to start the day reliving the previous one. "I'm just looking for Ethel. Can you girls help me?"

Poppy and Naida banded together at the elbow. "Of course! We'd love to help you." Poppy gave me a warm smile before waving me to follow.

"Ethel is usually at home right now. It's not far from here." Poppy took her Forest guide duties very seriously. She led at the perfect pace and didn't skip any stories about historic landmarks we were passing on the way.

We'd just passed the riverbed that Naida was found on. Poppy recounted the story again for me, but she held Naida's hand the entire time.

Poppy went ahead and Naida stayed to float right next to me. "What you did yesterday was spectacular, Amelie." Her tiny voice was quiet. If you didn't listen closely, you wouldn't hear her at all.

"Thank you. I don't really know how I did it," I admitted.

"That's okay, we don't have to know everything about why things are the way there are," she said with a watery voice. The poor girl had no family, no recollection of her life prior.

"I suppose so."

I walked quietly as she inched closer and closer to me, finally mustering up enough courage to rest on my shoulder.

"I love your name." I told her.

Out of my peripherals, I saw her cheeks flush of color and her body try to close in on herself.

"I picked it myself."

"How do you mean?"

She chewed on her lip then turned her body and leaned back on the half moon shaped crook between my neck and shoulder. Her little fingers tapped against the lavender colored fabric of her dress.

"When Edgar found me by the creek, the first thing they asked was my name. I couldn't remember it, all I could remember in the moment was that flowing water meant Naida. It just seemed to fit."

Every time someone called her by her name, she would have to remember that it was simply a word she remembered. "And you have no idea how you ended up here?"

She sighed, all too comfortable with using my body as a carrier to our destination.

"None." I suppose if there wasn't a memory to be told, that was likely all she had to say about that. Her fingers began strumming again, this time on my shoulder. It was such a light touch but I felt the tingle all the same. I thought of Kiaran and how I would definitely need to make up for tricking him before I left.

With perfect timing, Poppy called back, "It's right over here!"

Rounding one of the trees, a quaint little cottage appeared, tucked into the side of the hill. From the other side, you wouldn't see it at all. It was built with beige stones and worn black shutters to accent the two windows that framed the door. There was a colorful garden with an assortment of flowers to the left in a spot that seemed to have the most sunlight through the breaks in the leaves of the forest above us.

Knocking on the door, Naida and Poppy bounced past my ear. Their wings made the most adorable puffs of air around me. "Frea will lead you home. We have to go help my brother," Poppy said.

"Of course, thank you." Then they both popped the

tiniest kiss to either of my cheeks and fluttered off in a fit of shy laughter into the thick brush behind us.

"Amelie? Is everything alright?" Turning back toward Ethel anxiously checking both ways out of the door of her cottage, I smiled at my friend.

"Everything's fine. No evil McCalmont brothers today. Can I come in?"

"Of course. Let me get you some tea."

Ducking to enter Ethel's home, I noticed Edgar lounging on their couch to my right. He was nearly asleep and paid no attention to my arrival.

Ethel rummaged around her kitchen that was directly opposite from the front door, a kettle was being brought to a boil on the stove.

"Sit," she said over her shoulder as she crawled onto her wooden countertop to find a couple of mugs. "What on earth are you doing in my neck of the woods?"

Taking in the adorable miniature cottage with standard sized cabinetry, I wondered why I hadn't come sooner. This was no home of Fern's making but seeing a real kettle and dishes around the kitchen was unfamiliar after getting used to my sentient home's tendencies.

"You come to my neck of the woods all the time," I quipped, earning a hearty laugh from Ethel.

"Fair enough."

Deciding to make good use of my height, I rounded the table, "May I?"

She arched a brow at me disapprovingly. "Hundreds of years in this cottage and I've never needed a hand with the top shelf." Bringing both of my palms up in submission I went back to my seat at the table.

Ethel finally hooked her fingers around two different handles and pulled them down. Crawling off the counter, she held both mugs up in victory.

Joining me at the table finally with fresh tea in hand, she

started, "Now really, I appreciate the visit but to what do I owe then pleasure?"

Taking a sip of tea, I noted its flaming hot temperature and took a second to appreciate Fern's ability to keep all the water, whether for bathing or drinking, at a perfect temperature.

"I have some questions that I didn't get to ask at dinner. I hoped you would have the answers."

She nodded in agreement. Knowing Ethel, she probably already anticipated the questions I had.

"The prophecy my grandfather's mentioned," I paused to gauge her interest in answering.

"Go on.." She rolled her hand in front of her impatiently.

"Well…what is it?"

She smiled to herself, "I wondered if you caught that part."

"I did, but somehow it was the last thing I remembered to follow up on." I laughed, hoping it wasn't as serious as it sounded.

Any time I heard the word prophecy mentioned, it was always some set-in-stone fate that people waited their whole lives to see play out. Even so, very few were actually given the privilege of being alive when it happened.

"Well, we all agreed after we left that night that it was, in fact, happening right before our eyes. I suppose it's been slowly beginning since that boy of yours arrived, but it's a lot more unmistakable since you've joined him."

"Kiaran and I are a part of some kind of celestial prophecy?"

Ethel's smile grew so wide I thought it might have grown beyond the bounds of her face.

"You and Kiaran *are* the prophecy."

CHAPTER 22
Kiaran

It was taking her too long to return.

She left only an hour before lunch and now was about to miss dinner. Our nightly show of lights was about to begin so I propped a chair in the door frame, back far enough to not earn myself any broken bones, and waited for any sign of my girl.

I told myself over and over again that if something had happened, Ethel would've been by already. But what if whoever took Amelie took Ethel too? Who else would be so kind to come tell the strange Witch that couldn't leave his home the news of his two friends' peril?

Ethel said Amelie broke so many bones in Adan's body that he'd be laid up for a long while. However, last night in her dream, he was fine. No broken bones. Aside from his nose, a result of my fist and not Amelie's fury. What if the healer back home had mercy on my evil brother and was perfectly fine now to finish what he started?

My heart was pounding in a calamitous beat, my palms were sweaty and the knots in my stomach were loosening and tightening with every one of my breaths.

Where are you? I pleaded to her but was met with no response.

Visions of her with her insides splayed out on the forest floor poisoned my mind, her crimson blood muddying the dirt. The gremlins coming out of their caves to feast on her remains. Adan sitting back and watching the Forest reclaim her body.

Knowing that death between a bond like ours would sever a tie so deep in my soul I would be feeling more than just anxiety, a different scenario played out in the previous one's place. Amelie, sitting in front of the High Table in Avonya, my mother sinking her claws through each untainted ridge of Amelie's mind.

Making a deal with her to save her life over mine. Telling her all of the ugly parts of my soul that no woman should be bound to.

Soon, my heart would stop. Amelie would go on and my mother would get the ultimate revenge for me taking her daughter's life. A life for a life, she'd said that afternoon before the Adjudication Ceremony. I hadn't known what it meant then, but I believe I understood it now. The torture of spending two hundred years in a prison, only to find the meaning of life in my fated mate, all to have it taken away.

Sitting in my own dark cloud of work, I caught a glimpse of swishing skirts in the distance. Narrowing my eyes to tunnel my vision through the thick of the Forest, Amelie and Ethel were slowly moving along their path back to our home. No rush, no danger, just two friends enjoying their evening stroll.

"Where have you been?" I shouted, Amelie's head snapped up to the cottage and she and Ethel shared a knowing grin.

They made their way to the clearing and kept their slow paces, somehow making my heart do the opposite. It was infuriating being forced to just stand here and wait. It would be a really good time for her to veil my curse right now. Then she'd be locked away safe in the cottage. Nearly dead, but safe.

I couldn't have gone after her had she not returned. Being tethered to this cottage had never bothered me as much as it did now.

The women crossed the bridge and finally, Amelie spoke, "I went to visit Ethel. I told you that." Her voice like sweet honey.

"You've been gone all day and you didn't answer me when I called to you."

Amelie narrowed her eyes at me and popped an eyebrow, seemingly looking for a hint of sarcasm in my controlling words that she absolutely would not find.

"You're not her keeper, boy. I live a good distance from here and we had a lot to talk about," Ethel explained, but my eyes were trained on Amelie.

She'd stopped where Ethel had continued to the front door. Showing the amount of power she had to not reenter the cottage since I couldn't leave it. She could stay there all night and not fully return to me.

"I didn't hear you calling for me. I would've responded if I had." She popped a hip, her hands landed on her waist.

"Bullshit. You left earlier out of spite and you kept your whereabouts from me with the same intention."

Ethel began twiddling her thumbs, clearly uncomfortable between the tension I was creating between me and Amelie.

"No, I left earlier because I planned on visiting my friend yesterday but your *family* had other plans, so I went today. I tried to call to you during the attack yesterday but Adan said it wouldn't work out here."

My mouth popped open, threatening to tell her she was lying yet again but I hadn't heard her calling to me at all yesterday.

"It's true. She was calling for you the whole time. Out loud and between that little bond you two share."

I wasn't aware that the Dwarves held magic, but I knew that Ethel could speak to my thoughts. We called them Whispers back home, they were rare, but Amelie's friend seemed to be one.

The bond between fated mates was the strongest bond that could be created. It was unable to be snapped unless death fell upon one or the other and no one, not even the High Priestess, could veil it. Especially the part that allowed us to speak without words, it was the most organic part of the bond. The first thing that sprouted when it took root and the last thing to go when it was severed.

"Maybe it's just the distance, I'm not sure. But I didn't ignore you and I chose to believe you didn't ignore me yesterday either." Amelie's voice begged for a truce between us and I wanted to lower my walls to shake her figurative hand but the rolling in my stomach from the strange happenings was too chaotic.

"Yeah. Maybe."

Ethel clapped her hands together and spun toward the bridge again. "I'd better get going," she called over her shoulder, then pulled Amelie down so she could whisper in her ear. "Remember what we talked about." Then like a breeze through the trees, she was gone.

When I looked back to Amelie, she was still standing on the little patch of grass that grew before the bridge to the other side, hip still popped and a massive attitude growing across her features.

"Apologize," she demanded.

"Excuse me?"

"Apologize."

"For what?"

"For being an asshole."

I tilted my head, stunned at the bold words coming from her perfect mouth.

"You first," I taunted.

"What would *I* need to apologize for?"

"Well, for starters, your tricky little move of kissing me in order to leave earlier."

A playful smile stretched across her face.

"Then, for making me sick with worry over your late return."

Her brows raised and she nodded slowly in a condescending spirit.

"Last, for calling me an asshole."

She pursed her lips and chewed on her cheek to tamp down a smile.

"I don't think I'm interested in apologizing for any of those things," she purred as she sauntered toward the door.

When she got to the steps she took each step carefully,

One

"I think,"

Two

"I'd rather,"

Three

"You *show* me how mad you are at me," she whispered into my ear as she topped the stairs and pressed herself flush to my body.

My skin heated and static rippled through each pore sprouting goosebumps all over my arms. My traitorous dick grew in an instant and Amelie's hand traced the imprint, effectively killing me.

"Oh?" Was the only thing I could choke out.

"You think you're so big and tough?" she nipped at the lobe of my ear, then flicked her tongue out to trace up the side of my neck.

"I am very big and tough," I replied, willing myself to believe it before I melted into her.

"Then punish me."

Then, just as she did earlier, she distracted me with her

onslaught of seduction and had already spun us so she could enter the cottage.

She walked backward toward the stairs to the attic, looking at me with playful, hungry eyes. Her soul was summoning mine.

I took long quick strides toward her, she squealed and sprinted for the stairs, taking two at a time before she reached the top floor. I caught her around the waist before she got two steps into the attic and hoisted her over my shoulder then threw her on the bed.

Hungry eyes stared back at me and the mischief in her smile was enough to make my dick pulse.

"You are nothing but trouble," I said, leaning down to press light kisses around her jaw. Wrapping my hand around her throat and adding the slightest amount of pressure.

She tilted her head back and moaned, sending vibrations through my palm.

Crushing my lips to hers, she wasted no time exploring my mouth with her tongue. Her arms locked around my neck as she pulled me closer, deepening the kiss. With her, it was never enough. She always wanted more and I'd search every corner of my soul to give it to her.

However, if she wanted to feel like a bad girl, then letting her have control simply wouldn't do.

Breaking our lips apart, I grabbed her wrists from my neck and held them above her head with one hand, using the other to palm her full breasts.

"Keep your hands up here," I commanded.

"Make me." A dare hung in her voice. Her magic fingers laced through my curls.

Bringing her arms back to where I wanted them, I snapped my fingers, casting two pieces of rope to the far posters of the bed and tied her wrists together.

"What—"

"Keep your hands up here." I told her again, cutting her off. Desire raged behind her eyes.

Another snap of my fingers and her clothes disappeared. Out of instinct, she tried to shy away from her sudden nudity.

"Kiaran!" she shouted.

"Shh." I kissed my way down the toned center line of her stomach, stopping right before one of my favorite parts of her body.

Amelie's legs were hanging off the bed so I put both of them over my shoulders and gave myself perfect access to her most sensitive spot.

Running my tongue over her slit, she quivered and fought the restraints on her wrists.

Using my middle finger, I teased at her entrance.

"Kiaran…" she breathily choked out.

"Yes, pretty girl?" I whispered, letting only an inch of my finger slip inside before removing it and continuing that tease.

"Please…" she cried to me.

"So fucking needy."

I slid my entire finger in, curling it to caress the spot that drove her crazy. Her heels dug into my back as I started to work her slowly. She was already climbing towards release but it wouldn't be that easy this time.

"I'm going to come…"

Removing my fingers and leaving her empty, her head shot up at me. "Asshole!" she shouted, earning a deep laugh from me.

"Good girls get to come when they want. Bad girls get to come when *I* want."

She let out a frustrated breath. "I'll be good, I swear."

"Apologize."

She hesitated, weighing her options but she was stubborn as fuck so I should've expected her answer.

"I'm good."

I flicked my tongue out and circled her clit, sending a shiver down her body. The restraints pulled and rattled the posts as she fought the restraints, begging them to free her wrists.

Using two fingers, I stretched her while working my tongue. I kept a slow, steady pace. One that she'd have to concentrate really hard on to find her release.

"More," she moaned.

"Apologize." I blew a cool breath over her, she shuttered.

"No." It came out in barely a breath. She was hanging on by a thread.

I removed my fingers only to add a third, her legs wrapped around my neck begging for me to let her finish.

Yeah, not happening yet.

Pausing only to shorten the rope that held her wrists, she was pulled further onto the bed, her head almost to the edge of the other side. I cast more restraints on the two free posters and let each one wrap around her ankles, spreading her open for me.

"Kiaran!" she shouted, but desire still fired in her eyes. Positioning a knee between her legs, I leaned over to kiss her lips gently.

"Apologize," I whispered against them.

"No! I have nothing to apologize for."

"Very well, then. I'll gladly spend the rest of my days between your legs."

Returning my mouth to her clit, I sucked and nipped, earning a shriek from Amelie's mouth.

"Fuck!" she hissed, her body fighting the compromising position I put her in. Using my fingers again, I brought her as close to the finish line as I could, her eyes fluttered and her breathing became unsteady.

Then I stopped.

Again.

"Are you fucking kidding me?" She was irate. But it only

fueled my game as her eyes filled with rage, though her pussy dripped with need.

"You look so fucking good right now." I leaned back to admire her, taking in her helpless body on my bed. Her toned legs flexed in her useless fight, her arms begging to punch me, probably.

"Let me come. Now. Or I'll do it myself."

That was an intriguing idea. "Yeah? I'd love to see you try."

Her eyes looked up toward her tied wrists, she groaned in frustration.

I snapped my fingers and released the knot holding her hands hostage, leaving her legs still spread.

"What are you doing?" she questioned.

"Do it yourself."

She eyed me curiously, taken aback by the permission I gave her.

Using one of her unsteady hands, she started circling her clit, keeping her eyes on me the whole time. Her free hand caressed her breast, rolling her nipple between her thumb and index finger.

I wasn't even mad at her anymore, I really didn't even care if she apologized, but watching her hands do what mine should have been doing made my blood heat. The tension between us growing too thick to withstand and my willpower to hold back was crumbling.

Her eyes closed as she continued to work herself. I watched in awe, she was pure sunshine. Some people, like myself, were darkness personified. My mother lived to remind me of that. But others were light, and for some reason, those who had the light sometimes decided to shine on those of us who couldn't break out of the shadows.

Amelie was the light. A break in my stormy clouds. She was radiant. She was…*everything*.

"Mhhh." A moan escaped her swollen lips and jealousy

seeped through my walls, the walls that were never stable around Amelie. Her pulse was fluttering in her neck, her pupils blown.

I thought telling her to do it herself would make her feel shy, embarrassed to be so intimate with herself in front of me, but I should've known better.

She was a master at besting me. I was only ever allowed to *think* I was a few steps ahead of her. But her comfort with me was one I knew she never had with anyone else, and I wanted, rather, needed, to show her how much I appreciated that.

She was closing in on her release and I decided right then and there that no one but me would ever bring her that ecstasy again.

I took a firm hold of her hand, and brought them to my lips to taste her. Her eyes rolled in her head so I released the remaining restraints and closed my mouth over her sensitive nerves, ravaging her.

"I love the way you taste, pretty girl." I slid my middle finger into her and curled it to caress the spot I knew made her crazy.

"Baby…" she breathed out.

And fucking hell, that had me climbing with her.

Amelie wasn't a very affectionate person. Her touches were intentional, not natural. Her sweet words were always meant for truths and never used for anything but. She was sunshine, but that also meant she didn't want you to be too close.

I added another finger. Circling her clit with my tongue, and grazing it with my teeth.

"Look at me," I demanded.

She propped herself up on her elbows, eyes on fire for me. Her chocolate waves turning to spirals around her beautiful face as sweat beaded at her hairline.

"Come for me, Amelie." I blew a cool wisp of air over her, her legs trembled on either side of my head. I crushed my mouth to her and used my tongue to coax exactly what I wanted from her.

She toppled over the edge with a guttural moan, her legs wrapped tightly around my neck.

"Kiaran!" Her shriek was muffled by her heaving breaths as I continued to suck gently. A tremble shot up her spine and her legs shook, but I didn't stop.

But Amelie found a moment to gather herself enough to twist her palms in my shirt, pull me up her body, then flip onto her stomach, bending her knees and giving me a perfect view.

Her body had changed so much in her time here. One of my favorite changes being how her ass had rounded and was perfect to take a handful of.

Snapping my clothes off now, I grabbed her hips and positioned myself at her entrance. Her cheek pressed into the bed as she slid back onto me, I watched as I filled her. Her pussy willingly stretching to fit all of me.

I was always so struck by her boldness. She was so comfortable with me, I just wanted a moment to appreciate her. To worship her how she deserved, but she didn't allow that. She rocked her body back and forth, moaning and arching her back to allow me to fill her completely.

"Amelie.." I moaned, tilting my head back.

"Can you…" she panted, "the dream."

"The dream?" I repeated, confused at what she meant.

"The dream, when we did it this way…" she explained, barely audible as she continued to move back and forth. "It's the last thing I need to take back."

The dream. *Holy fucking shit.* I already knew I was beyond undeserving of this woman but not only had I somehow shown her she could trust me, she wanted to experiment with me. Go further with me than most women would ever choose to go in a lifetime.

I'd be damned if I didn't give her everything she wanted.

To give her what she needed to heal from the trauma those fucking guards placed upon her heart?

It was my honor.

I gripped her hips tight, forcing her to wait and take this next step slowly. "Let me."

Starting my own rhythm, I rolled my hips into her, lifting hers at the hilt to sink as deep as I could.

"Please…" she whispered, as if she thought I wouldn't give her what she asked for.

"You tell me if it's too much okay? You say stop, and we stop." I assured her, wanting her to know that she was still in control.

I kept a steady pace as I teased her ass with my thumb. She moaned at the pressure. "More…"

I pulled out, using her arousal to lubricate the tight spot before I pressed back into the tight hole with my thumb. "Oh." She sighed.

Oh. I couldn't help but smile at her thought.

"Is this okay?"

"Fuck, baby.." If she keeps calling me baby, I'm going to have to put one in her. That word on her lips for me was unleashing a feral part of my soul that had been waiting specifically for her.

"Kiaran." Her voice was sweet like honey but sharp like a blade. She was so close.

"You're doing so good, baby." I assured her as I watched our bodies move completely in sync with the other. "You look fucking incredible."

"You *feel* so good," she replied.

Watching her take me and knowing that she finally understood what it felt like to want and be wanted, I felt an overwhelming weight lift from my shoulders. I needed her to know that she would *always* be safe with me. I'd decided it was my sole purpose to protect her.

I was proud of her for asking for what she wanted, and felt

a warmth in my heart to be the one that gave it to her. To help her take the shame the guards placed on her and turn it into power and control over every inch of her body.

I found the top of my climb as the base of my dick began to throb and I released myself inside of her. Amelie came with me as her body went limp. I pulled out slowly, my thumb following, watching the evidence of our arousal drip from her.

Crawling onto the bed, I took her body and lifted it to become flush with mine.

"I'm sorry." Was the first thing she said. I laughed at her timing. "But I'm probably going to keep pissing you off if it means doing *that* again."

A guttural laugh escaped me, my chest shook as I struggled to catch my breath. Amelie leaned up to kiss my cheek, then rested her head over my heart.

The heart that now only beat for her.

"I love you," I blurted, not realizing what the fuck my mouth was about to say before I said it. Amelie's body tensed in my arms. *Fuck.*

"I—" I cut myself off. I wasn't going to take it back because I knew it was true, but surely my free-for-all mouth was about to fuck it up.

Amelie rested her chin on my chest, searching my eyes. Her golden rivers were ablaze, on the precipice of setting the world on fire.

She rolled her lips together to hide her pretty smile, which pissed me off more than the fact that she hadn't said anything back to me, then rested her head back in the crook of my arm. Her dark hair threatening to suffocate me as it tangled up over my face.

I wasn't sure if death by hair strangulation or word vomiting the L word would be more embarrassing.

"Thank you, *baby*," she teased.

Always bringing her light into my darkness.

WINTER SOLSTICE WAS one week away. I hadn't told Amelie yet that the curse was secured during our first kiss and I was terrified I'd waited too long to beg for forgiveness when I did.

However, I knew she was hiding something from me too. I'd been pressing for two days to learn what she spoke with Ethel about. Amelie returned to the cottage that evening with tenacity, hunger, desire, fight, and submission. Different from the girl who was a little unsteady in herself that I was familiar with. Wasn't a bad look on her in the slightest, but a little unnerving nonetheless. Whatever answers she found sparked something in her.

Descending the stairs, I went straight for my girl who I knew would still be curled up in the nook of the library.

Lost in a book I'd never seen on these shelves before, I squeezed in beside her, wrapping her up in my arms as she leaned into my chest. Her layered cream skirt hung from the bench and her feet were tucked under her. She leaned into the embrace.

"Hi, pretty girl," I said, pressing a kiss to her temple.

"Hi," she said, hiding her giddy tone horribly.

"Where did this book come from?" I asked, trying to flip the cover to see the title. She fought me, pressing it back against her legs.

"Ethel brought it by earlier." Amelie painted a fake smile across her puffy lips.

"Oh? Well what is it?" I pressed harder.

"Just a lot of history about the Forest." She closed the book and wriggled out of my arms to stand. From what I could see, the pages were filled with scribbles. It was a journal, not a book.

"And you're being secretive about that, why?" My palms

began to sweat under the strumming of my fingers on my thigh. It took everything I had not to tackle that fucking book out of her hands.

"I'm not, I just want to be careful with it. It's not mine." She lied through her teeth. Amelie was nothing if not the least careful person I'd ever met.

"If you say so," I relented, studying the tiny white half circles on my nails. There was nothing interesting to learn there but it was that or cast a truth spell and deplete any trust I held between Amelie and me.

Deciding to push the anxiety to the side for now, I got to my feet and pursued the rest of my plans for the night.

"Can you put the very delicate, secret book down and come with me?" My tone had more bite than I intended.

Amelie nodded, setting the book inside one of the drawers on the desk. A drawer I was sure she'd never once used being that most of her active reads were lying wide open around the house at any given moment.

Setting that on a shelf in my mind along with her irritating behavior, I grabbed her hand and led her up the stairs to the attic. We walked awkwardly, hand in hand, as the secrets we were holding from each other weighed down the colorful bond that glowed between us.

"Kiaran, dinner will be ready soon."

"Yeah, well Fern and I made other plans."

She nodded and I regretted for a brief moment continuing my plan for our evening. That was until I helped her through the window of my room and onto the roof that faced the pond and saw Amelie's beautiful face light up and her perfect lips curl into a watery smile.

Fern helped me with the food but I set out the warm blankets strewn about, the candles strategically placed at each corner and two canvases with at least fifty different colors of paint in front of them and a few brushes.

"What is all this?" she asked with awe in her voice.

"Your dad passed two years ago next week, right?" Praying I was right.

"Yeah," she replied in a ragged breath.

A pool of tears filled her eyes and through the blur, the golden rivers were glowing.

"So I thought we could paint something together. To honor him." Suddenly feeling bashful at the intimate gesture, I hoped I hadn't brought up bad memories. I knew she loved her father by the way she spoke of him, but I'd only ever lost my grandmother so I wasn't sure how the human world celebrated life after death. Witches memorialized their lost loved ones. Usually placing something on their body when they died to remember the living in their afterlife.

Turning her gaze back to the supplies in front of us she trembled as she spoke, "This is…" She shook her head slowly, her eyes closed and fat tears spilled at the tension.

"I'm sorry, I–"

"No." She locked our fingers together and leaned into me. "This is the most thoughtful thing anyone has ever done for me."

I let out a sigh of relief and felt a pang of despair split my heart open. With only a few days left together before the world turned upside down, I longed so desperately for more time.

For the ability to give her one million more kind gestures.

CHAPTER 23

Amelie

The Forest was alive with all of my favorite colors and washed a romantic hue of light across the top of the cottage. Kiaran looked so fucking good in the oranges and pinks that flickered over his face. His blue eyes were twinkling, competing with the sparkling of the Fae and enchantments happening below.

It was killing me to not tell him about the Prophecy. Ethel said that I would know in my bones when the moment was right to tell him but until then, take the time to understand it for myself.

To understand that God himself once created a love so great that the world wasn't ready for it. That he separated it and wrote it into the stars that one day those two halves would find themselves whole again.

He'd asked me no less than one hundred times about it since I returned and I could feel in our bond how anxious he was becoming. His fingers were constantly tapping along his thigh, his curls were always mussed from running his hands through it. He'd shut himself in his room every time I dodged his questions and would return after pacing back and forth in the attic.

Now, while we sat here under the magical light of the Forest painting in memory of my father, I wondered how there could ever be another moment to absolve his anxiety and be honest with him.

"I think I'm doing your father a disservice by holding a paintbrush," Kiaran admitted before sticking the tip of his tongue out again in concentration.

I laughed at him, my father would've been so proud to see two people painting, being creative.

"You aren't, he used to say that there is no such thing as a bad painting. No matter what, somebody will be proud to hang it on their wall." I smiled at the memory of my father's words, I knew that Fern would be happy to have our artwork on her walls.

Kiaran and I decided to turn our canvases away from each other so whatever was displeasing him was still a mystery to me. I was working on my dream come true. Painting the cottage was easy, then I added the pond and made sure to count each flower so they all had a home on this still frame. The bridge was executed perfectly and in the doorway, Kiaran and I stood hand in hand. Fern's warm light shone all throughout the house.

"What do you miss the most about him?" he asked, leaning to the side of his painting to look at me.

There was a long list of things that I missed about my father. His voice, his jokes, the way he could ground our family and make it all not seem so bad for a minute. I missed when he would check on me before I went to sleep, especially on the days I came home black and blue at the guard's hands. He would sit on my bed and smooth my frizzy hair while telling me a fairy tale to let my mind drift into a dream.

But what I missed the most was, "His hugs."

Kiaran bowed his head and reached his hand to take mine. "I'm sorry."

"A lot of people have said that but I'm not sure why. As

much as I miss him, he's not suffering anymore. He doesn't have to live in Holleberg, being driven mad and hollowing his soul out any further." A tear slipped from my eye and one from Kiaran's joined it. "Really, dying is a much better fate than living a long life back home."

"I'm still sorry. I always dreaded the thought of losing my father, even though immortality makes those losses few and far between, I could never stomach the idea."

"Not your mother?" I asked, already knowing the answer.

Kiaran laughed but it was humorless. "My mother can't die unless she is killed, no one is brave nor stupid enough to try that, so I never gave her passing much thought."

"How is that possible?"

"It's a perk of her position at the High Table," he replied.

"The Adjudicator?"

"Yeah."

Returning to putting the finishing touches on my painting, I decided now was as good of a time as any. "My turn to ask a question?"

"Shoot," he replied by also picking his brush back up.

"Do you feel anything special when you think of me?" I chewed on my lip, knowing that question sounded fucking weird.

Kiaran chewed on his lip, tamping down his smile. "I already told you I loved you, pretty girl."

He had told me that, and I froze. Never having said it to anyone outside my family, barely understanding the feeling. My heart had only just created a pocket of space to feel it, and I'm sure Kiaran was filling it up tenfold. I fiddled with the paint brush in my hand, uncomfortable with how to continue.

"What are you hiding from me?" he didn't have to be perceptive to know my question had ulterior motives.

"I'm not hi—"

"Don't. Please. I'm going to stop my own heart if we spend one more day teetering around the secrets between us."

I knew he was right but now I wasn't sure if this was the moment Ethel was talking about.

"Wait, what secret are you keeping from me?" I replied defensively.

"I'll tell you. I won't skip any details, but you need to go first."

I conceded only because I was especially irritated now and I wanted to hear what he'd been hiding. "At our dinner with Ethel's family and my grandfather's, Al mentioned something about a prophecy. With everything else I learned that night, I couldn't round back to that one so I went to ask Ethel about it."

Kiaran held a stone expression, nodding but not giving anything away.

"She told me all about it, what they meant by if the stars had finally aligned." I trailed off while Kiaran's eyes dug deeper into my mind. I tried to clear my thoughts so he couldn't read them. "And that's all."

Kiaran wasn't believing it. Moving from his painting completely now and squatting on his knees before me, he took my hands and kissed my knuckles. My lying soul was being given too much love in this moment and if it was a way to guilt me, it was working.

"Okay, fine. That's not all," I blurted.

"You don't say," he quipped, pressing another kiss to my wrists.

"It's us, we're a part of a prophecy, or *are* the prophecy, I'm not sure. I'm still trying to understand it myself."

"Us?" he reaffirmed and continued placing kisses all the way up my arms, making my skin break out in goosebumps. "About us being fated mates?"

His woodsy scent distracted me as I melted into him. I didn't hear him correctly, so I questioned the words he'd just said. "What did you just say?"

Kiaran tilted his head, the colors between us moving so

fast it was a blur of color rather than its usual segmented blend of a rainbow.

"Fated mates?" he asked but it wasn't a question, what he knew was not what I knew.

"We're fated mates?"

Both of us stared at the other waiting for someone to fill in the missing pieces of our secret puzzle we apparently had both been working on.

"Yeah?" He watched me cautiously for my reaction. Hoping to not fully give myself away, I steeled my features and took a deep breath before continuing.

"When did you decide this?" I asked first.

Kiaran squinted his eyes, seeing through my defense. "After dinner with Ethel and the Souls. Well right before that actually, when we kissed, but it was confirmed when we learned about your ancestry, I realized that was why we could speak to each other without words."

He was holding me tight. I couldn't move if I wanted to, if I made a sudden movement to escape, I could fall off the roof. I was trapped.

My heart began to race and anger flooded my bones. He had been sulking that I was keeping secrets from him but he started it.

"You've known for weeks?" I shouted at him, removing his arms from around me and turning to face him. He grabbed my hands before I could create too much distance between us.

"Because I didn't know how to tell you."

I scoffed at him, trying to regain possession of my arms but I lost that fight.

"Terrible fucking excuse." I bit out, my lips flattened and I felt my nostrils flaring. A trait I remember my mother having but never until now knew I inherited.

"That was the *first* night we kissed," he started.

"I remember. Something changed when we kissed but you never fully explained what that was."

"We changed, our fate," he explained, "because our kiss locked everything into place. I felt it and it made my entire body lock up."

"The prophecy locked into place?"

Kiaran hung his head like this was bothering him, but our fate was supposed to be beautiful. A miracle that it was written just for us, so his reaction was unnerving.

"Prophecy, curse, same thing," he said in a near whisper as he studied our hands.

"No, Ethel didn't say a thing about your curse."

Kiaran's eyes snapped back to mine, genuine confusion painted more boldly across his face than the pictures on our canvases.

"What did Ethel say?" he questioned.

I cleared my throat, now feeling like maybe this wasn't the right time. That I'd already fucked up fulfilling said prophecy.

"Just that we have been fated to be together for a very long time," I summarized, leaving out the romantic details.

Kiaran mulled over my words for longer than anyone should have to sit in silence for. He bounced his eyes back and forth between our hands and his lap, then to the Forest and back to our hands again. His jaw kept twitching and honestly I wished he'd come right out and say what he was thinking, because for some reason the bond that we had before was weak now.

It didn't work when Adan was here, or when I was with Ethel and now I was sitting mere inches from him and I couldn't hear a thing he was thinking. It was really nice being able to hear his thoughts so when he got all broody I didn't have to guess why.

"It's okay if you don't want that. I understand."

As if he forgot I was sitting here, he shook his brain back to the present and stared straight through my soul.

"No, it's not that. It's just…" His mouth gaped open like he'd just discovered a new kind of creature. "Fuck."

"What?"

"Amelie, you are my way home." I smiled at that, he felt like home to me too.

"No, you are how I break my curse." My smile escaped as fast as it came. "That's what locked into place during our kiss alongside the mating bond."

It was my turn to sit in silence. That couldn't be right, the prophecy was so clear. It had been told for many, many years that the Prince and the Princess would save each other. The dreams I had for so long, Ethel explained them. She told me that my mother's bloodline held an abundance of magic, unable to be learned, only awakened. My dreams though, that was a Bloch trait.

The way God watched over us and the Witches fated us, Bloch bloodlines could dream of a new world, live there if they wanted to. They could let people in, chase people out, things that happened in their dreams happened in the real world. A lot of the strange happenings in the Forest were a direct result of *my* dreams. I'd spent the entire time since leaving Ethel trying to remember every dream I'd had and wondered if I created Kiaran somehow.

I told her about the fire in Kiaran's garden, she said it was likely to have really burned down. Adan could've perished in that fire.

She also told me that she no longer got along with Al because he'd been trying to find Evari since she disappeared. Using his dreams to try and change what was done. It caused a riff, Ethel swore to protect Evari's whereabouts, Al wanted to find her.

The prophecy, though, never changed. It was a tragic romance of hardship and two broken hearts meeting each other and turning the world upside down. But it had a happily ever after, it wasn't the breaking of a curse. I wasn't a means to an end in that story.

Reality washed over my body like a thick mud, coating my skin and weighing me down. Winter Solstice was only a week away. We hadn't talked about it and I wasn't sure what would happen but Kiaran had known what he had to do and it was to give me up.

"So what," I started, voice cracking as a tear slid down my face, "you were just going to lie to me for the next seven days? Kiss me, tell me you love me, fuck me? Then what Kiaran?" I paused and he almost got a word in but I didn't let him. "What was your plan?" I let out an aggravated breath. "I can't believe you!"

My chest heaved as I took in the date he'd planned for us tonight. "My father's anniversary is *next* week." I realized.

He nodded.

"I won't be here next week."

"Amel–"

"I returned from Ethel's thinking we had forever. That it was a cruel joke God had played my entire life making me live the way I did, then to bring me to you and show me the life I wanted. Now after only months of reprieve, I'll be gone in a week."

Kiaran's eyes close tight as his shoulders shrugged in defeat. I got to my feet and moved for the window.

"Amelie, please. It's none of those things."

"I'm having the girls over tonight." I blurted out. God, I hoped they didn't have plans.

I scrambled through the window, wanting to get out of the cottage as fast as possible. Apparently dreaming of it alone was enough to get me there because in an instant, I was standing on the front porch of the cottage. With little time to think, I bunched up my skirt and ran to find Ethel, Naida, and Poppy.

I DIDN'T EVEN LET Ethel fully open her front door before my anxiety, fear, and rage poured out of me like vomit. Ending the story with something like, *so I need you, Poppy, and Naida to sleepover, so I can avoid him.*

I didn't have to ask my friend twice.

Before we were halfway back, our winged counterparts found us and now we all sat cross legged in a very lopsided circle on the plush rug in the sitting room of the cottage.

Kiaran banished himself to the attic.

Good.

Within the walls of the cottage, our bond worked and he'd been pleading to me from the moment I got back.

I'm sorry.

Please talk to me.

I love you.

None of which I replied to. If I did, I was sure I'd poison him with my words. No nice things were coming to mind at the moment and I prayed that feeling would pass.

The events from earlier were on repeat in my mind and each time I thought of the reaping that was our fate, my stomach somersaulted over my heart, tangling my vital organs and making it hard to fucking breathe.

Sprinkle in that he'd told me he loved me, I was a mess. An absolute fucking mess. Because even though I was pretty sure I loved him too, I'd never said that to anyone outside my brothers and parents. I wasn't sure love even existed outside the obligatory kind. Until now. But of course I fell in love with the man who was going to kill me. Sorry, *sacrifice* me.

"Amelie, I think you should invite the boy down here," Ethel interrupted my inner thoughts.

"Absolutely not." I took a bite of the warm cornbread Fern had set out for us.

Poppy and Naida giggled to themselves and Ethel popped a brow at me.

I just shrugged back. Even if I wasn't mad at him, what would he do down here? Join in on a hair braiding train?

Actually, he'd be great at that.

But still. No.

"What does your magic feel like?" Poppy inquired, sliding on to her tummy and resting her face in her palms, her blonde hair fanning over her shoulders. She and Naida were perched on the tea table so they could be eye level with Ethel and I.

"Like my eyes are lighting on fire."

Naida audibly gasped, shocked and scared at the admission. She covered her mouth with her hand and her eyes went completely round. "That sounds horrible," Naida choked out, tugging her knees to her chest.

"It sounds worse than it is," I assured, setting another couple cubes of cheese on the table for the Fae.

"You and Orla are so similar. You even look just like each other, except her hair was white as that cold stuff the humans get." Poppy looked at Ethel, they nodded in agreement.

"Snow?" I laughed, realizing they'd never had to bear a cold winter and feeling thankful my friends called the Forest home.

"Did you just slur your words?" Poppy snickered.

I shook my head and furrowed my brows in confusion—Sno—oh.

"No, s-n-o-w. That's what the white stuff is called." I covered my mouth with my hand while another giggle escaped me.

"I bet you like the white stuff here better," Poppy said while repeatedly popping her brows. Naida's mouth gaped open and I burst at the seams with laughter, Ethel rolled her eyes.

"Enough of that talk, girl," she chided the dirty minded Fae.

I took Ethel's redirection seriously.

"What was she like? Orla, I mean." We were still suppressing our laughs when the energy in the room shifted.

Ethel's eyes immediately pricked with tears, I knew she loved my great grandmother. Ethel and Evari were good friends, I often wondered if Ethel's endearment for Orla was that of a mother's.

"She was a force to be reckoned with, no doubt about that. I remember Niklaus being head over heels for her, half the time I think that was because the girl moved so fast he couldn't keep up. She was constantly honing her magic. Evari left me with that journal I gave to you, she had generations of notes in it all about Morgenstern magic. Orla took it further though, pushing herself endlessly and learning how everyone's magic worked. I think it bothered her that she didn't have the fundamentals they learned back in Avonya."

Poppy took over then. "And she was *beautiful*." She drew out the last word.

"Absolutely radiant," Ethel agreed.

"And very kind. She'd do anything for anyone, no matter their kind. All of us Fae live within twenty hollowed out oaks and a few of them were struck down by travelers. Orla heard the awful news and put it all back together. We'd been working tirelessly for days to clean up the mess those men made, but Orla came and her eyes did the thing yours do and poof, our homes were rebuilt and better than ever."

I put my hand over my heart, feeling so connected right now to my strong maternal genes. So much of the Morgenstern history felt so devastating, but so far, all I knew of those women was that they deserved so much fucking more than they were given.

"Oh, and I think she killed the men," Poppy added, biting down on a piece of cheese.

A smile crept across my face. I tried to roll my lips together to hide the fact that I was smiling at the men's demise. They crossed a Morgenstern woman and the people she loved, I understood that rage completely.

"Ack," Ethel sounded, "nobody missed 'em. Good riddance."

We all broke out into a laughing fit. Even Naida. She rolled onto her back, holding her stomach as she wheezed. Poppy ribbed her, encouraging her shy friend and it sent Naida laughing even harder.

Soft snorts came from her as she tried to catch her breath which made the rest of us nearly die from how hard it made us laugh. Naida's cheeks blushed but she couldn't stop the fit.

Unsure footsteps creaked the stairs, stalling the joy that filled the room. Everyone went silent, save for Poppy, who was stifling a giggle at the awkward shift.

Kiaran's bobbed on his feet at the bottom of the stairs, his fingers twiddling with a vine wrapped on the rail.

"Ladies." He nodded to us with a tight smile.

Poppy was literally about to explode from how hard she was trying not to laugh.

Naida was prodding her to stop, but that made Naida laugh again.

I loved seeing the two of them together, it was so obvious that Poppy was Naida's home. It didn't matter where she came from, the pair of them were sisters regardless.

Kiaran walked to the kitchen, acting like there was anything in there that he could just grab. He was rummaging through the cabinets and the girls all looked at me. I shook my head at them, hiding my own smile then rolled my eyes.

Poppy stood up on her perch, put her knuckles to her hips and cleared her throat.

"Ladies," she said in a low, mocking voice as she gestured her hand forward like she was bowing to a queen.

We all burst at the seams again, clearly having a case of

the unstoppable giggles. Kiaran was standing with his back to us, but I could feel that he was in tune with whatever was happening over here with us. His shoulders began shaking, and I swore I heard him take a sharp breath, the one he took when he was stifling a laugh.

"Come over here, boy. You're being strange," Ethel called through her own laughter.

When he turned to us, his smile was on full display. His eyes found mine immediately.

I love seeing you enjoy yourself.

A warmth settled over me and the butterflies in my stomach took flight.

"What's so funny over here?" he prodded as he plopped himself down on the couch.

Poppy, being Poppy, cleared her throat and mocked him again. "Ladies."

He looked at me with narrowed, twinkling eyes. A smile crept over his face as he realized they were making fun of him. I felt kind of bad for not letting him enjoy our company. But I hadn't forgotten the tension that could cut the laughter in the room in a heartbeat if it was brought up.

Poppy and Naida were laughing again, which bled onto Kiaran. The harder they laughed, he laughed.

Ethel and I watched the three of them crack each other up, Poppy kept puffing out her chest and mimicking Kiaran's awkward walk to the kitchen.

I swore there was never a room more filled with joy. I'd never seen Kiaran laugh so hard, he even started snorting like Naida.

If I could, I would sit in this moment forever.

It was a lot lighter to be here than in my head. My dreams always took me to this Forest. I'd defeated so many monsters and villains here before, and I was beginning to think those weren't great adventures but rather preparation. Because in less than a week, I would have to defeat the greatest villain of them all, and I think I knew exactly who could help me with that.

The last few nights, my father had been visiting me in my dreams. He'd walk in the background, give me a fond smile, then disappear. I wasn't sure what it meant, but something told me that it might be the key.

CHAPTER 24

Kiaran

There really was no good time to tell the love of your life that you had to sacrifice her.

She was dead on the money about me being an idiot because I went up to the rooftop tonight upset with her and she left it ten times more upset with me. For good reason too.

We were fated, that much was clear. I felt it. We had the bond of mind, body, and soul. Ethel confirmed it. It was all I needed to know to understand that the High Priestess planned this long ago.

The curse was only to be broken by giving up something that would cause as much pain as my mistake caused. Though losing a fated mate would be exponentially more painful. It was your strongest tether to Earth. I'd seen people die mere hours after their mate passed because the pain was so unbearable.

But she didn't give me a chance to tell her that I had no plans of following through with the sacrifice, and that the reason I hadn't told her about the curse locking in was because my heart would fail to beat by the time the sun rose on Solstice. If I tampered with the laws of the curse, it would be my life that was taken. Knowing Amelie, she'd try to inter-fere somehow and get us both killed.

A life for a life.

But Amelie's would not be that life. I only hoped that since she was not a *true* Witch that the pain wouldn't kill her like it would me. Morgenstern women lived by their own set of laws since their magic was tied to the elements. The were limitless. The rest of Avonya's was a blood magic. We only had as much of it as we did crimson blood in our bodies. Limited. If she died, if I was forced to give her up, there would be no more purpose for me. The four months we spent together would be the only time in my long life that felt meaningful.

No, I wouldn't live without her but she didn't fucking wait for me to tell her that.

Amelie was getting stronger though, more powerful. When she was desperately trying to run from our conversation earlier, she vanished into thin air. I was sure she didn't know how to do that, nor did she mean to because I heard her panicked heaves down on the porch before I saw her skirt swish over the river and into the thick brush.

I immediately panicked.

My first thought was that if Adan came back, she'd prob-ably go willingly this time. Plead to my mother to save her life. If she would've just let me fucking speak before freaking out, I could've assured her one million times over that she had nothing to worry about. I would never jeopardize her life. Even if it meant giving up mine.

The second thought was that she was running back to that evil place she called home prior to finding sanctuary at the cottage. If she did that, there was a good chance I'd never see her again.

Before I could fully descend into a pit of despair, I heard chirpy voices carried by the light breeze. When I peered out the window I saw two sets of glowing wings, the Dwarven woman I'd grown fond of, and the love of my life all approaching the cottage.

I busied myself in the kitchen, which was really stupid because there was nothing in this kitchen unless Fern, or Orla, put it there. Amelie walked in first, not sparing me even a pity glance, before heading straight to the sitting room and plopping down on the floor. Ethel said hello and gave me a tight smile, surely already aware of what happened tonight. The blonde Fae, Poppy, giggled as she zipped past, but her black haired friend, Naida, if I remembered correctly, lingered for a moment.

She looked so familiar, but in a way only my soul knew. Not my memory. She didn't say anything though, and as soon as she realized she'd been staring, she anxiously buzzed off to rejoin the others.

I took the hint from my girl that she didn't want me there so I went to the attic, pleading to Amelie to talk with me. We didn't have much time left together and I wasn't going to spend it not by her side, whether she liked it or not. I'd waited two hundred years for her, she couldn't get rid of me now. So I tried to enter the den of laughing women with a false cloak of confidence and Ethel was my saving grace for asking me to join.

I wasn't bothered in the slightest that Poppy was mocking me. Seeing Amelie's shy Fae friend completely lose it every time Poppy said 'ladies' in that casanova voice she must've thought I had, Naida would fall to the table laughing. It reminded me of Mia and her friends. One word and the group would lose their breath from giggling so hard.

The familiar memory shook a laugh so deep out of me I started snorting right along Naida. Amelie's cheeks flushed bright pink as she desperately tried to swallow the laugh I knew was festering in her. Though she was still upset with me, I gave her a wink anyway and let my eyes linger on hers for a moment.

I couldn't stand that she thought for even a moment that I would consider letting her go.

I told the girls after their giggle fest died down that they could stay in the attic. The bed could accommodate them all and it gave me the freedom to go for the book Amelie tried to hide from me earlier. It was a book of spells, elemental magic that were all endorsed by a Morgenstern woman. Orla's signature was written all over it, it seemed she spent most of her time here trying to veil the magic and release the tether her mother was bound by.

The last page detailed a spell of sentience. She journaled her plans to bind herself to her home and continue working in her own version of purgatory on the solution. Orla was afraid the Witches would come for her, she felt something coming. The date was only a day before I arrived here. Her life's work was in this book. She hoped one day her family would come back to her. And they had.

I had a creeping suspicion after our dinner party that Orla was really Fern, but I hadn't told Amelie and I figured the Lost Souls already knew. It was their reason for wanting to visit in the first place. The way Niklaus endeared the structure told me as much.

Why was this book such a secret to Amelie?

What answers was Amelie seeking that I couldn't give her? The laws of which a curse can and cannot be broken were clear. The High Priestess wanted the Morgenstern women to be rid from the past, present, and future. She fated the last one to be mine, then to be sacrificed.

Witches were as wicked as they were efficient.

I FELL asleep on the couch with the bible of Morgenstern magic resting on my chest.

I was sure the girls weren't awake yet. Amelie's soft snores were still adding dissonance to the bird's morning chirps outside. So I asked Orla to help me prepare breakfast for them. Before my eyes, four spreads on serving trays appeared on the table.

High stacks of pancakes, a personal serving of fruits and cheeses—complete with a steaming cup of tea for each of them.

I carried the trays up to the attic, taking every step carefully so I wouldn't creak the floorboards. Orla placed a square table by the window, she set it with a deep blue table runner and pale blue place mats. There were vines wrapped and twisted together in the middle, leaving a perfect amount of space for the food.

"I see we are not above brown nosing in this house."

I jumped at the sudden company.

"Oh for fuck's sake, Ethel. You scared the shit out of me." My hand braced against my chest, my heart rate trying to find a steady rhythm again.

"Would you accompany me home? Edgar will be lost with his morning tea."

Ethel was already heading toward the stairs. I looked back to the table and noticed there were only three settings now. Orla had already taken Ethel's away.

"I can't leave the cottage without Amelie's veil…" I whisper-yelled, following behind the dwarf. For such a small woman, she moves fucking fast.

Ethel didn't respond and instead walked through the already open front door, then looked back to the cottage lovingly. She flicked her wrist toward herself, motioning for me to follow.

My free will was stolen from me as I stood a good three feet from the threshold. My feet started walking straight toward the portal to broken-bones land and the anticipation had my heart thrashing against my chest.

"Fuck," I sputtered, spit flying through my clenched teeth as the cool morning air whooshed around my body.

I braced on the door frame trying to hold myself upright but Orla was too fucking strong. I toppled over onto the porch as the breeze swept my legs out from under me. I waited for the agony of hundreds of breaking bones to set it but it never did.

I looked up to Ethel, she wore a content smile on her face as she endeared the spirit of her old friend.

A relieved breath escaped me as I got to my feet.

"See? You're fine." She turned to walk over the bridge and I spun toward the cottage.

"Are you fucking kidding me?" I called to Orla, wherever she was.

No magic. No veils. No broken bones.

I felt utterly betrayed that she, in fact, did have the ability to veil the curse and I could've been free this entire fucking time. Amelie also didn't need to be veiling, traitor. Orla's soft morning candlelight dimmed and brightened. I took it as her apology for aiding in my imprisonment. I'm still pissed, but I didn't have time to hold grudges.

I had to pick up a light jog to catch up to the quick, tiny strides Ethel was taking.

"We have a few things to discuss, so listen up," Ethel began. I took her words as an order and kept my mouth shut.

"First, I'm not sure what all transpired last night, but when Amelie showed up at my door, she was a wreck. You'll fix that at once. Neither of you have time to spend upset at the other. Got it?"

Another order. I nodded.

"Second, she awakened her Bloch…*magic*…" She cringed to herself, like she was afraid of it. Which was interesting because as far as I knew, her Morgenstern side was the lethal one. "Amelie is a perceptive girl, but you seem to jumble that brain of hers. I'm not sure she realized she did it. But when she dreams, or hopes, she can change reality."

Like wanting so badly to get away from me last night that she cast herself for the first time and executed it perfectly. A pang struck my heart at the thought.

"What does it mean?" I asked Ethel, doing what she told me not to do.

"Bloch's are Originators."

"Originators of what?" I'd never heard of such a thing.

She shrugged, as if it was simple. "Of everything. They are the original Angels from their God. I'm not entirely keen on the whole story, but they have more power in their pinky nails," she wiggled her stubby fifth finger, "than you or I could hone in a thousand years."

"So Amelie has the most powerful magic known to the Witches *and* a magic that dates back to the beginning of time?" A chill spread through my body as goosebumps erupted and I felt a dizziness spiral around my brain.

Ethel only nodded in confirmation.

"Fuck."

"Yes, that," she replied waving her hand as if to swat away my expletive. "She said that she is your cursebreaker."

"She is. I learned it just before you arrived for the dinner party. When I kissed her…" I trailed off, reliving the moment I knew I would lose her. "But I won't sacrifice her. I refuse."

Ethel held her hand up to my increasingly anxious tone. "No need to panic. I know you fear that High Priestess of yours, but she likely does not know how deep Amelie's blood runs."

The High Priestess knew everything. Each celestial thing gets a star long before they're born and I was sure that Amelie's star showed she was the most powerful creature that would someday come into existence. I was also sure that it was exactly why she was fated to be mine.

Efficient. Take out any power that might rival the High Priestess. It made perfect, horrible, wicked sense.

"I can't interfere with the curse, Ethel."

"You won't have to. You just need to trust our girl."

We stepped into a clearing that was a bit smaller than the one at the cottage, but just as charming. Ethel clearly took pride in her home and the Forest that surrounded it. She even had a garden I knew Amelie probably loves. It bathed in the sunlight and had all the colors of the Morgenstern eyes in them.

"Amelie has the entire Forest behind her. She's incredibly stubborn, and as mad as she is at you right now, I wouldn't be surprised if she doesn't tell you what she's up to. But that girl had fury coursing through those golden rivers last night when she spoke of your High Priestess. Do not mistake her anger as anything but pure love for you. The prophecy will prevail, whether that vapid leader of yours likes it or not."

CHAPTER 25
Amelie

I had no idea why I came here.

My entire life had been a tragic pit of nowhere to go but up, but every time I felt like maybe I was getting somewhere, the ladder was kicked out from under me.

When Arthur, Igor, and Liam helped me escape, I had no notions of a fairy tale to come. If I was being totally honest with myself, I didn't think I'd make it through the night in the Forest alone.

Finding the cottage was a safe haven. I let myself fall into the dream of freedom, of happiness, and I was proven foolish again. Such a stupid girl to believe life was meant to be full of the finer things. Not material things, but things like friendship, a safe home, love.

But for a brief moment, I found myself wishing Kiaran would've stayed hidden. He should've continued to be an asshole, he shouldn't have made me feel like I was worth something. I wish I hadn't felt kindred with him, that this gravitational pull between us wasn't such an entrancing array of colors that I wanted to continue to paint.

I felt it in my bones to the tips of my fingers that the prophecy was correct. That he was who I'd dreamed of my entire life, potentially created specially for me. But I supposed that the tragedy I was surrounded by manifested a tragic end to fit the narrative that was Amelie Bloch's legacy. It wasn't until a figure in my dreams started to make me think there was hope.

My friend's staying with me last night was everything I needed to feel reset. To let my rage find the purpose I really felt it for. The High Priestess of Avonya. After the lovely breakfast that was set for us and reading Ethel's note about leaving at dawn, I went to look for Kiaran but he was nowhere to be found. I assumed he'd hidden himself in shame, the way he hid himself from me when I'd first arrived.

It felt nasty to leave him in the cottage alone. I knew he couldn't follow me and it would kill him to know I was alone out here without our bond to communicate. I had half a mind to turn around and go to him, kick his ass for keeping things from me then spend the last few days we had together, together.

But as I stood on the line between enchanted Forest and ruin, before the gaping hole in the Earth that I used to escape in the Forest mere months ago, I knew I needed answers and this time I would not be afraid. My father was trying to talk to me, but I couldn't get close enough to him in my dreams to find him.

The ground was colder now, being the dead of winter. As I took a step into the tunnel, I turned back to adore the Forest in case I didn't make it back out. The Forest that protected me, warmed my cheeks every morning, showed me how powerful I could be. Brought me a type of love that the story tellers passed down through generations.

My vision blurred as I thought about the man I left behind, regret churned through my stomach at the thought of him waiting for me to return.

"If you never see me again," I whispered to the wind,

"please find a way to tell him I love him." I sunk down an inch and added, "And that I'm sorry."

The underground path was colder than before, it felt darker and more foreboding and I feared what I might find at the other end. Holleberg seemed unreal to me now, a lifetime shadowed by a few months of freedom.

I heard chatter as I came to the tiny bit of light shining down from the opening. The voices were quiet and owned by men, of course. The underside of the bed was all that stood between me and the palace now. I held my breath hoping to identify the voices and one in particular gave me the courage to show myself.

I lifted the bed slightly, the cell was lit up with a few lanterns as three sets of boots stood facing each other, bobbing back and forth.

"We act tonight. This is the last opportunity we will have, Igor." Arthur's tone was demanding, yet defeated.

"He'll be surrounded all night, it's too dangerous," Igor added.

"If it's not tonight, everyone in Holleberg will be dead by morning."

A long, pained sigh left all three men and I took my opportunity to crawl out from under the mattress completely.

"Fuck!"

"Amelie!"

"What the fuck!"

All three exclaimed, to be expected.

Arthur got to me first, his palms covered my shoulders completely as he checked to see if I was real.

"What the hell are you doing here?"

Igor found me next, grabbing my hand in his and giving a second set of eyes to my well being.

"I want answers," I started with. Arthur took a deep breath and released me, Igor followed. Liam already retreated to the door to stand watch.

The two men in front of me shared a look, they had plans for tonight and that was fine. What I needed was only a few moments of honesty.

"We don't have time," Igor told Arthur. I hadn't noticed it before but he looked to his father's second in command with the eyes of a son. Arthur was his guide, as Ethel was mine. Not a parent by blood but someone to trust as such. I held my friend with such fondness, with so much respect and it made me feel better about Igor's situation knowing he had someone like that too.

The fact that he helped me escape told me that maybe he wasn't anything like his father.

"What is going on?" I asked. Realizing that prior to scaring them, they said Holleberg wasn't going to survive the night.

"We are executing my parents tonight. My father is planning on burning the city down at midnight, we are taking Holleberg back."

My breath caught in my throat and I had to will myself to let air pass again. So much had changed, yet being here still paralyzed me with fear.

"What? Why? Is my family…" I choked out, realizing I hadn't had time to remember them the last few weeks. Guilt rolled through my bones.

"Well…" Arthur looked to Igor, they were deciding with unspoken words how to explain in the least amount of words. "After you left, Lord Bosque fired most of his men. No one would admit to letting you escape. We said that after your sentencing, you fled and we couldn't find you. Lady Marilla was on a warpath to find you, mortified at the indignity of a *peasant* besting the royals." All three men scoffed, they knew as well as I did that the only indignity here was centered between Lord Bosque and his wife.

"He's spinning out of control," Igor added, "Arthur and I have been trying to redesign the laws and each time he enforces the old ones tenfold, changing them for the worse. People are worse off now than ever before."

"We don't have much time," Liam spoke, one of very few times he'd done so. That fact made it all the more troublesome to the energy in the room that they were going to need to act now.

"What do you need from us? It's too dangerous for you here."

No part of me felt safe here, nor did I think coming back would be as easy as getting in and out unscathed. I just had one question for my uncle. One that had been haunting me since I started to realize how much power I held within my dreams. Ethel confirmed what I thought was happening, explaining just how far the Bloch blood could bleed into the world.

I was awake all night chewing on every word Kiaran and I shared. The same answer kept coming to me; where was my father and why has he been visiting me in my dreams?

"I know my father is alive." I gauged all three of their reactions. Arthur rolled his shoulders back and let out a long breath. "And I need to know where he is."

Arthur rolled his lips together and narrowed his dark brown eyes at me.

"Who told you?"

And my heart dropped to my stomach. I knew it. I felt it but I had no confirmation of it.

"He started appearing in my dreams, every night. Always in the background though, like he was waiting for me to come find him." I gestured around the room. "So here I am."

Arthur nodded slowly as I spoke. Unshed tears pooled in his eyes and I could see a figurative weight lift from his shoulders. His lips curled up slightly at the corners.

"He, your mother, and brothers are all safe."

My entire family?

"We relocated them to the outskirts of the Kirny Hills."

The room spun for a moment, or maybe it was just my head. I wasn't sure, but my family was together, without me, while my life was fated for sacrifice.

"I need to see them." The tears that poured cut my voice up, making it shake and tremble.

Igor stepped forward, taking my hand. Liam walked up behind him and wrapped his arms around Igor's chest, I looked between the two of them. Realizing now why they were the only two men besides Arthur who worked for the Palace and had never hurt me.

Igor's voice shook as he spoke. "After we complete tonight's mission, you will be safe to return, as will your family. I promise." He kissed my knuckles, Liam pressed his lips to Igor's shoulder.

A partner, comforting his person in the face of his fathers impending execution.

I missed Kiaran in this moment. A strong pillar to lean on.

I endeared the two men in front of me with a smile, then looked to Arthur. "Did you know?"

He knew what I was talking about, as did the other two men. Their sidelong glances told me as much.

"I did. So does your father. It's how I've been able to keep them safe."

"You knew our dreams could change reality?" I pointedly replied.

He nodded.

"Why didn't my father tell me? Why didn't *you?* You sent me into the Forest blind."

"You've met Grandfather Al?"

My neck jutted suddenly in surprise, my brows bunching. How the hell did he know Al?

"I assumed so. He came to me and your father in a dream long, long ago. We were on a great adventure, when we conquered, he said that Bloch's would always conquer and that someday, a Bloch woman would save us all."

Chills rippled down my spine.

"Me?" I whispered, feeling arrogant for assuming.

He nodded at the same time as a loud crash sounded from the hallway outside the cell.

Arthur gave me a firm look, Liam and Igor took off in the direction of the echo.

"I wish we had more time, but we need to go. I have faith in you." With an affirming squeeze to my shoulder, my uncle took off toward his son and the heir of Holleberg toward whatever peril laid ahead of my village tonight.

Faith.

Something I never had much of, but now it seemed everyone had so much of it in me. But why? Faith was just blind hope. It was wishing on a star because it made you believe it was attached to something greater than yourself, that the wish would actually go somewhere. Faith was praying, voicing your wants and needs out loud just to say you tried. It's fake and powerless. And the more I learned about who I was and what I was capable of, I felt the same way. Fake and powerless.

I shook my shoulders, loosening the grip desperation still held on my soul. Then I turned to leave but before I could, whispers haunted the cool, moist air around me in the absence of the three men. It wasn't as gentle as Frea's and was less frightening than Valla McCalmont's from my dream.

She's here…

She's here…

It got louder and louder until it was a breath against my ear. Spinning on my heel so fast I stumbled backward as the heel of my boot caught the edge of the drain. A woman with long, white, wiry hair and white irises with golden rivers around them stood in front of me. She was frail, just bone and sagged skin.

"Come with me," she hissed, her voice was layered and enchanting.

I took a frightened step backward.

She met it with an equal one toward me.

"Who are you?" My stomach was in knots, my mind began to whirl as she got closer.

"You know who I am."

"Who are you!" I bit out each shaky word, hoping the syllables hit her in three separate blows. My bravery was wearing thin, tears pooled in my eyes. I prayed Kiaran got my message through Frea. Whatever this creature in front of me was, it had parts of my soul cowering in fear.

"You've known me your whole life," she said, but this time she reached for my hand.

With no input from my brain, my soul reached back and held the bony hand in front of me. Static crackled over my skin, beginning at my fingertips and traveling like a wave up my arms and through my chest. My shaky breaths turned to desperate heaves, the air in the room seemed to dissipate. The gold in the eyes I was staring into began to spark, the way Kiaran said mine had with Adan, like they did in the dream, like I'd realize they did when my magic came to life.

A crushing wave covered my soul as my eyes widened in fear, submission, and then freedom.

"Orla."

The woman took one last step toward me and I instinctively tried to take an equal one back, but I was stuck. The air in the room was gone, none left for my lungs to breathe. She didn't stop as she seemed to walk straight through me, but instead of crossing to the other side, she planted herself straight into the center of my soul.

Then the world went black.

CHAPTER 26

Kiaran

"Amelie?" The dead silence of the cottage caused immediate panic in my heart.

There was no response, not even a flicker of light from Orla. The only sound that pulsed a sign of life was my heart beating through my ears. I tested the waters carefully, I'd left under no specific veil. If the High Priestess was keen to that, surely she came to finish what she'd started before with Orla.

The normally wild ribbons of color between Amelie and I were stretched so thin it was like seeing through fine crystal. I could only guess this specific tether had to do with Amelie's Bloch side. It wasn't something that happened between Fated Mates.

What I could feel and see in the cottage told me no one was here, no High Table member or spirit in the walls. I sprinted up the stairs, hoping to Amelie's God that she at least left a fucking note. On my nightstand was a piece of paper that read…

Left early.

It wasn't Amelie's handwriting though, it was loopy with unnecessary swirls. My heart sank into my stomach at the whiplash I gave my body as I descended the stairs and rushed out the front door.

The pull between our bond was tugging me toward the Forest, into the brush and in a direction I'd never wandered before.

"Everything alright, boy?" My already panicked heart skipped another beat at the scare from Al who had seemingly, out of nowhere, appeared on the other side of the bridge.

"I can't find Amelie, and I think…" I stumbled over my words, pressing a clammy hand to my equally clammy forehead. "Orla. They're both gone." My voice cracked at the last second. Because there it was, the secret inside the walls of our cottage. The daughter of the beloved Evari Morgenstern. I hadn't realized how furiously I wanted to protect the Morgenstern women in my life. I gauged Al, hoping this wasn't news to him.

I got to Al who seemed unfazed by my admission, his cold palms landed on my shoulder. The touch alone seemed to calm my worries and send a numbness to the hollows of my bones.

"Are your colors still intact?"

Well, that confirmed my earlier assumption. It was, indeed, a Bloch trait.

"Yes."

"Good. Follow them. They'll always lead you back to her," he answered, studying my face intently.

The air around us lightened, making it a little easier to breathe.

"What are they… the colors?" I asked, as I tried to feel for the other end of the rainbow. Al and I started to take quick steps in the direction I felt a pull to.

"It's your fated mate bond. It's the tether that will snap should either of you find your death."

"I've never heard of anyone being able to *see* the tether." I could feel it now, the tug her soul had on mine.

"You're fated with a Bloch. Comes with different privileges," he replied matter-of-factly.

We'd made just a little ways into the brush, now standing near the babbling waters of the river that flowed to the pond in our clearing. Al's presence was grounding. Much like Amelie's was, which was funny because Amelie's head was always in the clouds.

I needed to get to her now, wherever she was made my soul ache.

"Do you have any idea where she went?" I asked in a near whisper.

"My guess is she went to find her father."

I shot my eyes up to the leader of the Lost Souls, panic was carving up my bones again. "Her father is dead?" It was a statement but it came out in a plea.

"No."

I waited for him to say more, but he didn't.

"How did she know that?"

Al's lips turned upward to a proud smile. He endeared his family with pride as he spoke.

"Told ya boy, Bloch's have special privileges." He pointed in the direction I now remembered led toward Amelie's village. "She's only just learning what it all means, but I'd go find her before she accidentally sets the world on fire."

Funny thing about his warning was she'd had mine ablaze since the moment I met her.

The Forest being an alliance to Amelie was the second best thing about tonight's search. The first being that I didn't need a map to find her, I just followed where my soul led.

I knew nothing about Amelie's world as far as its geography and as I stepped into the hole in the ground that the Forest assured me was the way back to my girl, my heart broke for the journey she'd taken to get to me. Her chance at getting away from it, only to run back because she was scared of her fate with me.

My girl was nothing if not a runner. Every time things got hard, Amelie tucked it away into the darkest parts of her. That way she could never find it again, she could just keep moving and leave it in the past, but not this time. Not now.

I'd moved on from Fern's indiscretion toward aiding and abetting my curse by not allowing me to leave the cottage for two hundred years. I supposed as much as she was my only *friend,* I was hers. Maybe the person I was prior to Amelie wouldn't have returned to her, I didn't think Fern would've cared. But Orla would've.

Seemed to me I was nothing but a pest in her home for the last two centuries, but now I was looking for both of them. To return with the good parts of my cottage. Amelie brought the good. She *was* the good.

The tunnel was presumably taking me to the small palace in the distance. A dim light came into view and when I reached it, I noticed it was covered by fabric. Muffled cries and the sound of Amelie's name on another man's mouth had my skin tingling with rage. Well, actually it was a lot worse than a tingle. I was going to kill whoever was muttering her name. I tried to move whatever was covering the opening and quickly realized it was a bed and laying on the ground before it was Amelie, eyes wide open but seemingly not breathing. A blonde man sat on his knees with her head in his lap as he wept over her.

"What the fuck did you do to her?" I demanded as I grasped the back of the blubbering man's neck.

"Nothing…" he sobbed. "I would never hurt her."

Not allowing Amelie to crash to the floor, I held the man in my clutch searching his face for the lie. His body had no defense wounds, his bones seemed to all be intact, and he didn't seem like the fear of Amelie's power was forever stained on his soul so I guessed it would be safe to believe him.

I released the pressure on the man's neck slightly and it was only then that he realized he didn't know me.

"I won't let you hurt her either," he said, hiding her face from me and trying to school his features and steady his shaky voice. I laughed at the idea of this guy protecting Amelie from me. "Who are you?" He demanded from me now, bolder.

"I'm hers," I replied honestly, because who the fuck else would have me risking my bones, trekking for hours through the Forest, walking hunchback through an underground tunnel, crawling out of the Earth and not blowing the man holding my girl to shreds. "And who the fuck are you?"

"Igor," he replied instantly, as if finally understanding that he was not the alpha male in the room. It struck me that Amelie mentioned along with her Uncle Arthur, the heir of Holleberg, Igor, helped her escape. So for that, I guess I could give him an iota of respect.

"Well, Igor, I'm going to need you to hand over my girl." I told him with a smile. "Now." Adding that last part with much less of a smile.

"Something in my bones told me to come back. To check on her, and she was just…" he sobbed into her again.

From what Amelie told me about her time in Holleberg, it was less than ideal. However, Igor seemed to care for her.

She wasn't dead though, I'd feel it in my connection between life and death. Al said I'd see it in our tether, it would've snapped and my will to continue fighting would have been long gone. I knew I'd be one of the unfortunate souls who wouldn't survive the loss. I'd lie down next to her cold body and cross into purgatory with her.

I pressed a hand to her heart. A mortal wouldn't know it, but the beat was there. It's faint, but she was alive. Her open, empty eyes were enough to tell me exactly what was happening.

"I need to take her back, Igor. She's not dead but whatever veiled her isn't here and the further it gets, the closer to death she will be."

Igor furrowed his brows in confusion, his chest heaved in and out slowly as he steadied his emotional heart.

"How did you find her?" he asked, curiosity in his voice, as if now was a good time for explanations.

"Followed my heart." Igor didn't wince in the slightest at my poetic words, finding her was easy aside from how long it took. I definitely thought once or twice that the Forest would purposefully keep me from her. It had always protected her and the insecure part of me told me that I was something it would need to protect her against. The fact that it brought me right to her reinstilled that I had to fix this. I had to get her home.

"I'm going to take her now." I changed the grasp I'd had on his neck to something friendlier.

"Yeah," he said, as he shook his head back to the moment. "Yeah, I need to go too."

I took the opportunity to scoop Amelie up into my arms. Her body wasn't that of a warm, alive person but it absolutely wasn't cold and full of rigor yet. Cradling her in my arms, I stood and started back for the way I came.

"Is she happy?" Igor questioned, now standing in the door of this dungeon.

It stunned me a bit. Aside from her family, Amelie didn't say much about her village. Whenever it was brought up or something would trigger a memory, I felt her mind go dark and fearful. It wasn't something she liked to remember. But I hoped she knew there was someone who clearly cared about her here.

"I hope so."

"She deserves that. I hope the rest of us get the same luxury come tomorrow." He shrugged. He lingered for a moment, I'm not sure for what, but his heart was bleeding right now.

I gave him a narrow smile and tried my best to wear my kindest eyes as I descended back into the tunnel.

CHAPTER 27

Amelie

'How Long Will I Love You' by The Cairn String Quartet on repeat for this chapter

Green grass, blue skies, and a few expertly fluffed clouds by God himself floated above me.

The light pink, lavender and pastel blue flowers grew in perfect arrangements on either side of an aisle that nature created. My father's closed fist pressed into his stomach. He was dressed in a sharp black suit, perfectly tailored to fit his tall, lean body. His hair wasn't as gray as I remembered. Instead it was more the mousy brown color that I remembered from childhood.

His eyes had life in them again, the deep chocolates and caramels were in full light. My entire life everyone complimented my eyes, said they'd kill for eyes like mine, but I was always jealous of my father's. They were more unique, aside from the golden rivers in mine. A few unshed tears gathered and he took a few sharp breaths as he stared down at me.

Letting a single tear fall, he wrapped his arms around me. As if he'd heard my conversation with Kiaran and knew this was what I'd missed the most since he'd been gone.

"I've missed you, my special girl. I've been looking for you."

Tears spilled onto my blushing cheeks and over my bare décolleté.

"Hi, papa." He pulled me in closer and the acrylic smell of paint filled my nose, making me sink further into this precious moment. This was home.

He pushed me back by my shoulders and used his finger to make a spinning motion at me. I grabbed the top layer of white tulle at my sides and twirled like a little girl in a field of daisies under the summer sun. My sheer sleeves let in a warm breeze. I came to a stop and my father took my hands to notice each intricate detail on the boning of the dress. Small, shiny pearls contoured the slight curve my waist had settled into these last few months. The skirt of the dress flowed at the tiniest movement, heavy enough to be elegant but light enough that I felt absolutely ethereal. Like an Angel.

"You are the most stunning bride I've ever seen," my father said as tears fell down his slightly wrinkled cheeks. I was a *bride*.

"You have to say that." I smiled through a blurry vision of the first man who ever loved me. My father took the top half of my veil that was pooled around my shoulders and covered my face with it.

Faceless people filled in the seats before us. A row of people with black hair sat in a row at the front, all wearing similar dresses and distinct headdresses. The one on the aisle seat turned and found my eyes through my veil immediately. A face I would never forget again. Kiaran's mother had been leading me through my dreams my entire life, popping in here or there to guide me to this moment. If only she could dissuade the High Priestess from tearing Kiaran and I apart.

I knew this was a dream. The awareness made me feel dizzy but Orla was showing me this for a reason. The core of my soul was changing as the seconds of it drew on. I always wondered how long a dream truly lasted.

Unmoving, Valla McCalmont held my gaze and I didn't dare break it first.

"Are you ready?" my father asked, but I paused.

When I watched Kiaran and his mother's last interaction before he was sent away, there was something sinister about her. Something untouchable, yet I wanted to break it. Destroy it. I wasn't afraid to try.

"Yes." I tucked my arm under his and held my oversized bouquet of pale blue water lilies and baby's breath.

A full set of strings began playing a traditional melody, signaling for the guests to stand for the bride's walk down the aisle. We approached the first set of chairs. Ethel and Edgar were facing me with smiles on their faces and tears in their eyes. Ethel leaned back into her husband as she sobbed into a small handkerchief. Magda and Henrik sat with pride on the other side of my Dwarven friends. I gave the four of them a soft smile as we passed.

The next row of people faced me and I saw the men who gave me a second chance. My quiet cousin Liam, my uncle Arthur, and the heir of Holleberg, Igor, all giving me victorious smiles. I hoped it meant two things Holleberg survived and Lord and Lady Bosque didn't. I returned the smile just in time for my father and his brother to share a fond look.

Half way down the aisle, I saw four Lost Souls. My grandfathers. All broken hearted men who waited in purgatory for their fated mates to join them. My father choked on his tears at the sight of the men who looked just like him, his grandfathers too. Al smiled proudly at us, Niklaus was a mess of tears while Friedrich consoled him in the most manly way a friend could. Josef gave an approving look and nodded to me and my father.

Finally standing at the end of the aisle, a small hand tugged on my dress. I looked down to see my youngest brother with chubby, fed cheeks, and the brightest smile I'd ever seen. Behind him, my second youngest brother sobbed like the empathetic hearted boy he was, then I saw Wren.

He shared the brown eyes my father had and just like our dad's, his were full of life again. He smiled at me. Really, really smiled and I thought I would die right there. I'd held it together so far, but Wren was my first friend in this world. Seeing him look like a young boy rather than a tired, hungry man, I couldn't hold it in any longer. I realized I couldn't remember the last time I saw my little brother smile and knowing he was happy in this moment cracked my heart wide open.

My mother though, she was a vision. Her magic of gold was on full display as it danced through her eyes and met the gold in mine. They somehow shined brighter with the flow of tears that was staining her cheeks. Her hair wasn't the matted mess it was for the year and a half prior to my leaving. Instead, it was waved like mine. Long and silky. Deep browns and hues of a dark red melted seamlessly throughout.

I took each of them in, committing their beautiful, bright faces to memory because this might've been the first time I'd ever seen them in this light.

I couldn't let it be the last. My brothers were apparently unaware of wedding etiquette so they took my pause as an invitation to bury me in their arms. Six tiny arms surrounded me and I hoped for a moment that they'd never let me go.

My mom found my father and he wrapped her in a hug so tight I thought she might burst at the seams. The Bloch family together, once again. This time, happy. Healthy and safe. No rumbling bellies, no bruised faces, no dead fathers or melancholy mothers. There were still tears, but this time, every single one of them was filled with joy rather than despair.

When our parents joined us, I could hear Ethel's sobs

growing louder and louder. I chuckled at my funny friend and the unabashed emotions she showed all the time. Niklaus was asking his friends if they should join us, to which Friedrich told him to read the room. I smiled at the people around me and wondered if all of this love was around me the entire time. If maybe we'd all just been too jaded to allow ourselves to feel it. My mother cupped the back of my head and nestled my face into the crook of her neck.

"I love you so much, Amelie. My fearless, selfless, special girl," she started as she stroked my perfectly styled hair down my back. "You were created with a heavy fate and without knowing, fulfilled every obstacle set for you. You fought even when you thought you didn't. Without being asked, you took on every responsibility and never once complained about it. You are and forever will be the light in this world." She moved her hand to my chin and tipped it up to look at her, her tears laying to rest at the base of her eyes. "Thank you, Amelie."

As I stared at my mother, I realized that all eyes were on us. My brothers and father stood in their row and over my mother's shoulder, Valla was burning holes through me with her eyes.

Each person who sat on my side of the aisle was someone who played a key role in getting me to this day. Like the trees in the Forest, they were pillars that allowed me to lean on them or provided comfort, safety. It was a life that I would leave behind the second I said I do. This was to show me what would come next. That there *was* something that came next.

I stood back from my family and patted my dress back to its flowing glory, the train faded into the dreamy haze beyond my feet. I rolled my shoulders back and finally came eye to eye with the love of my life.

Hi, pretty girl.

He whispered through to me, our colorful souls spun in circles as it tried to find where one began and the other ended.

All at once, I knew why Orla was showing me this. What this was changing for and within me.

Kiaran wore a crisp black suit, much like my father's. He had a pastel blue tie tucked into his suit jacket, playing perfectly off the colorful flowers and decor that covered the Earth around us. His black curls were tousled and styled back perfectly to show off his gorgeous face.

The man I loved stood in front of me, his bottom lip was bit between his teeth in attempt to keep his smile within the bounds of his cheeks. His eyes matched the rest of the guests, filled with tears of joy. To be at the receiving end of those joyous tears was a dream come true.

In this dream, I got to marry my soul mate. My fated one. The one who was created specially for me.

My father shook Kiaran's hand, giving my mortality away.

This dream was an awakening.

My immortal awakening.

But most of all, it was a promise from the world and all its makers that Morgenstern blood will prevail.

CHAPTER 28
Kiaran

Amelie bobbed lifelessly in my arms as I trudged back toward the cottage. I'd sent silent prayers up to Frea hoping she could somehow help make her weightless because this was more physical activity than I had done my entire life. I felt my bones growing tired and my lungs burned as I tried to suck in enough air to sustain myself. The colors that swirled between Amelie and I were fading and I couldn't tell if it was because of me or her.

Pain seared through the muscles in my arms, my thighs burned with each step, and the arches of my feet stung as I continued to find each jagged rock on the path.

I'd tried right away to use my magic, but I was too far from the cottage's veil to muster enough for the both of us.

If I was my old self, I'd have given up right here and now. I'd set Amelie down and leave her on the Forest floor and move on with my life. Take the consequences of not fulfilling the ritual on Winter Solstice, because this life really never mattered much anyways. When I was young, I listened to stories of good and evil. I wanted so badly to have a story told about me that would make children want to be better, do better. Strive for greatness and hone their magic so they could make a positive impact on the world.

Where the fuck I went wrong was beyond me.

But I wasn't myself anymore, I was new. A version I didn't know was resting beneath all the darkness. I'd wondered a lot over the last few months though if I was ever really bad. I made mistakes, of course, but when I went to sleep at night I wasn't dreaming of setting the world on fire just to watch it burn. The High Priestess took every chance she had to punish me, to berate me in front of my peers, tell me that I was disgracing the powerful McCalmont name.

She forced my hand then punished me for failing. The same magic she told me I was too stupid to use correctly, she ordered me to use then sent me away for it.

So no, I wasn't my old self anymore.

I wouldn't leave Amelie here and serve only myself. The woman cradled in my arms called me out the moment she met me. She thought I was an Angel. Of death, of course, but that was neither here nor there.

When I first met her eyes, she didn't see darkness or evil. It was the first thing I loved about her. She shined on the thick exterior I'd built to protect myself from people telling me I wasn't good enough, powerful enough. Amelie made me soft and though anatomically my heart had always been beating, I was sure it didn't beat for any good reason until it met her. It only thumped along because it had to, much like I did with living. It was just what I was meant to do, though it served no purpose, until her.

I felt the tether to Orla pulling me closer and closer to our home. Something that wasn't there earlier. Wherever, however, Orla left—she was back. Warm light bled from the tiny openings through the Forest and it was all I needed to pick up my pace.

The buzzing around the pond grew louder and louder, its

usual welcoming melody felt more like a warning tonight. Amelie's frog friends croaked long, low sounds from their throats. The bugs could be heard all over but were nowhere in sight. I felt thousands of eyes on me and Amelie as we stepped into the clearing. Thunder boomed through my chest. Something wasn't right.

Whatever Amelie was tethered to right now couldn't be here or was hiding. Otherwise she'd be showing some kind of life. Her breathing should've picked up by now, the gold in her eyes should have been glaring already, but there was nothing. I paused before the bridge and stared down at my girl. Our colors were the lightest pastel I'd ever seen them, they were holding on to every particle of color they still had but it wasn't near as breathtaking.

Her tether to life was coming dangerously close to taking her from me all together. The thought of it alone made me consider ending it for both of us now. What if she enacted some kind of veil like Evari had and she'd never come to life again? I couldn't wander the Forest like Niklaus and Josef for the rest of time without her.

I took in a deep breath and started over the bridge, laughter filled the inside of the cottage but it wasn't the kind that I shared with Amelie's grandfathers or the kind Amelie shared with Ethel. It was malevolent. A cackle into the wind that would've sent a shiver down the spine of anyone unfortunate enough to hear it.

At the door, I felt a tremble in the walls. An innately human characteristic of fear, Orla was scared. I'd be lying if I said I wasn't frightened too. She knew Amelie and I were home, so she melted into us, searching for protection. Orla had protected me, cared for me in her own way, veiled the High Priestess' magic so I could find our girl. I would protect both of the women before me until the very last beat of my heart.

Orla cracked the door for me. I took a reluctant step in

and the laughter turned to short breaths, then silence. The High Priestess of Avonya sat at the head of the long oak table, two others sat with their backs to us, faces covered in their High Table garb.

The woman who ruled my realm rolled her shoulders back, straightened her spine and tipped her chin up to me in a domineering fashion. My breath shook at the vision of the woman who sent me away and fated me with a curse that was far worse than the pain I'd caused. My nostrils flared and my eyes blinked unevenly, it felt as though I might pass out but I couldn't do that safely with Amelie in my arms.

I gave my Coven's leader a curt nod before going to the sitting room with Amelie and laying her across the couch. Pressing my ear to her heart, I could still hear a faint beat but it was softer than it had been during any dangerous magic she'd done before.

I couldn't do anything for her with our guests in this home so I stroked her cheek gently, checking once more for any trace of light in her eyes. But they were empty. I hesitated before getting to my feet to meet the Coven members at the table.

Three long strides and I stood before the woman who cursed me, then I took a bow of respect. She was clad in her traditional gown and Coven cloak, the headdress that indicated her place in the hierarchy of the Coven sat atop her head like a badge of honor.

Standing back to full attention, my chest heaved in and out with deep breaths but I managed to take one good one, letting out a steadying exhale before addressing her.

"What are you doing here?"

"Hello, dear," she replied with a sinister grin. "It's been a long time. How are you?"

She was steady as a rock, eyes of determination and a ferocity that had me feeling the opposite.

"What the fuck are you doing here?"

"We won't be here long." She stood from the table and relaxed her hip against it. "There are just a few things to remember as your final ritual approaches. One, you will perform it exactly as you were taught. Two, if your little Morgenstern girl interferes with the fates we have set and succeeds, you both will be punished. She was never supposed to awaken that unnatural magic."

"Probably shouldn't have sent her to the very Forest it idled in then," I bit back. My shaky breath could be heard around the room. "If you believe for a second that I would hurt her, you are sorely mistaken."

Taking a step to close the distance between us, she reached up and ran her knuckles down my cheek. I tried to shake her touch off but she won by grabbing the sides of my chin between her thumb and fingers and holding on tight.

"It was all in the fates, my dear. A life for a life."

I felt my cheeks heat and my stomach roll, I wanted to kill her. I wanted to end her.

"Then you'll take mine. But you will not use my curse as a way to fulfill a centuries old agenda toward the Morgenstern women."

Finally letting me go, I stepped back from her and it took everything I had not to fight back. The High Priestess cackled at my assertion.

"Oh…" She tried to catch her breath, the louder she laughed the more my blood raged. "Dear, you are too humorous. This was all in the stars, you've never had a say in what I destined for the two of you."

I stared at the back of one of the heads I knew was sitting at the table, praying to Amelie's God that she would fucking say something.

"I love her. More than I've ever loved anything." I dangerously admitted. It was leverage but I was out of options.

"No, she's just the only person who's ever cared about you."

A gross smile spread across the High Priestess' face. "She'll never *truly* love you. She's grown up in ruin, I made sure of it. Each unholy touch was meant to make yours feel sweeter, each hungry day, her father passing, the constant pleas to her God to let her die, all of it was written in the stars. I wanted her to believe that finding you was the best thing that ever happened to her. But do not be mistaken, my dear, no one could love *you*."

I swore I could feel my heart stop for a moment.

Amelie's upbringing being a wicked game to the High Priestess, to steer her to me and believe that a cursed Witch was the best it would ever be for her, it sickened me. Because it was true. I knew I didn't deserve her, but the woman who cursed me just confirmed all the things I tried not to believe about myself. The fact that Amelie had never told me she loved me back, all of it was too much.

The room spun as the High Table started for the door.

Then, in the window above the sink, a little winged creature landed so softly that no one but me knew she was there. Naida was eavesdropping. A terribly bold thing for the anxious little Fae to do. Her bright blue eyes were piercing into the High Priestess, and for a moment I believed that the feeling I had the other night when she smiled at me was more than just a feeling. But it was impossible, right?

"We will see you in four days." One of the Coven members said under their veil. It was a voice I recognized all too well.

"What?"

"You didn't think we'd trust you to complete your ritual honorably, did you?" The High Priestess laughed as she gave me her back and strode out the front door.

I followed after them, "I—" but when I stepped out of the door, they were gone. A force pushed me back inside and the door slammed shut, the lights flickered rapidly. Orla was scared.

How did they get in here? Orla would've veiled herself, kept the doors locked.

"Are you okay?" I asked the spirit in the home.

Her warm lights that surrounded the cottage slowly dimmed and brightened.

"Don't let them in here without me again."

There was no response this time.

CHAPTER 29

Amelie

THREE NIGHTS UNTIL WINTER SOLSTICE...

"Amelie, please..." Kiaran choked out as he continued dripping water on me.

I tried to speak but the pain that consumed my mind didn't allow for the connection to my voice. The world was black, the darkness was swallowing me, but I wasn't afraid. Somehow I knew that if I never woke up, I'd be okay falling asleep here in Kiaran's lap forever.

I understood the tether now. In my soul, I knew how it worked, where it started, where it had been and where it led. When Evari passed the point of ever coming back to life, Orla would've needed to find a center. Somewhere to come back to, she came to the only home she knew and she stayed there.

She was Fern.

She found me in Holleberg, she showed me what was to come.

Orla made sure I knew we could beat the High Priestess. Generations of Morgenstern magic had been brewing behind veils for hundreds of years in wait for *me*.

Kiaran was tucking my hair behind my ear, breathing slow

and controlled. I wanted to stay like this. Relive the feeling of my soul's awakening.

Before that blissful dream ended, something eternal changed in me. Orla guided me, telling me about her life and relaying what she'd read about Evari's childhood in Avonya. The history between the High Priestess and Evari Morgenstern dating back so far that it was more than just their exiling to the Forest that doomed our family.

"My mother kept very detailed journals about her life, it feels like I actually know her." Orla gazed deep into the white abyss we were walking through, a fondness toward the mother she never got to know welling in her waterline.

"Before my mother veiled herself, the step before she gave me the elixir, she placed a spell upon our bloodline. One that only allowed for our awakening to come after we understood what it meant to be a Morgenstern and the fury held for Avonya's High Priestsess. Once that is recognized, you're allowed to see where your life will go should you choose to cross into immortality." She brushed away a tear that betrayed her. Her snow white hair waved and curled like a breeze was passing through, but there wasn't one.

She was absolutely radiant.

"So, dear child, should you choose to see what lies beyond, know that it means your star will become permanent in the night sky. Forever and eternity. You cannot look back at what life could've been like otherwise."

I didn't need to think twice, I knew I needed more time. Orla's hand took mine and I nodded to her. My heart thudding in my ears in wait of what would come next.

I hoped God was watching over me now and that my pleas to him weren't falling on deaf ears as they had for most of my life. I hoped he and Frea were working together to clear the pool of black settling in my brain.

"Amelie…" Kiaran pressed soft kisses to my forehead, then my cheek, then the other, the last one landing on the tip of my nose.

Drop, drop, drop, rippling through my mind and clearing the blackness that blanketed it.

Kiaran was crying over me.

His tears were pouring out so rapidly I felt as though I might drown as they wet my lips. The darkness began to fade, the tears were washing it away. My body felt heavy and tired but I knew my soul was fighting. It was trying to smother the darkness and allow light to shine through.

Kiaran's distraught, panicked face came into view, a memory I wanted gone as fast as it came.

He was folded over me, squeezing my shoulders tight to his stomach as I laid over his lap. "Kiaran?" I managed to say. His body stiffened, still holding me close.

"Say it again."

"Kiaran." My voice rasped.

Peeling himself back to look at me, he studied my face for a moment before collapsing into my chest. "Don't scare me like that again, pretty girl."

My head was aching from coming back from the near dead but the sense of fear I'd felt when I saw Orla in the cellar was gone. My bones felt strong, my eyes burned as the gold began to dance, an all knowing power flooded over me and if it weren't for the pounding in my brain, I'd jump up to tell Kiaran everything right now. But Orla said this awakening would be exhausting before it surged.

Kiaran began pressing kisses all over my face. Every inch of my cheeks, my nose, over both of my eyes and finally my tear stained lips.

"I was so worried," he admitted against my mouth. Wrapping my hand behind his neck, I pulled him back into me.

"Amelie…" He tried again as I found the muscle on the side of his neck, trailing my tongue along it.

"Can we talk about it later, please?" I whispered. Energy started pumping in my veins, bursting out and looking for something to satiate the new found hunger in my body.

Take me upstairs.

As if I willed by my words, hopes and dreams alone—Kiaran did as he was told.

He slipped his arm under my back and tightened his hold around my waist, lifting me up and turning me toward him. Gripping my thigh, he pulled me over his lap to straddle him.

"Are you sure you're okay?" His voice was coarse.

"I'm fine." I thought. "But I need you, *now*."

I wasn't sure what he saw in my face as he searched it, but it was enough for him to give me what I wanted in this moment.

He buried his face into my neck, hungrily kissing and sucking as he stood with me wrapped around him. Kiaran walked to the stairs and up to the attic, his lips never leaving my neck. At the top, he pressed my back into the wall and took my mouth with his. I matched his need and slipped my tongue through his lips which he welcomed with a groan.

His length hardened between us and I slipped a hand down to grip him, earning me another rumble in his chest.

"Promise me that you're okay…" he whispered in a breath.

I cupped his cheeks, forcing him to look at me. "I have *never* felt better."

It was mostly the truth. Aside from the headache that was slowly being clouded by arousal, I felt stronger now than I'd ever been before. I saw more clearly, felt things deeper. The answer to everything was placed at the center of my soul and the light of my life was positioned between my legs.

We have a lifetime ahead of us and Orla blessed me by showing me that.

I looked deep into his eyes, passed the crystalline blues and into the soul that gave him life, and let my heart bleed for him.

"I love you."

He came undone at the confession. I could finally say it. I deserved this. I deserved to be happy. So did he.

He got on his knees for me then propped my legs over his shoulders. Pausing, he looked up at me. Blue eyes piercing through the moon washed room.

"You love me?"

I tangled my fingers in his thick, curls. "I *love* you."

I swore I saw tears pool in his eyes but he hid them away from me as he bunched my skirt around my hips. Kiaran wasted no time pressing his skillful tongue against my sensitive nerves. He loved to be gentle with me, tease me. Make me wait for it.

But not right now.

What he must've felt while I was veiled. The worry.

It was all laid out in this room as he ravaged me.

Two of his fingers entered me while his other hand was splayed firmly across my stomach keeping me in place against the wall. Kiaran curled his fingers and pressed the spot I craved his touch on over and over again as he expertly sucked and nipped at my center.

My fingers were tangled in his hair, I needed more. I tugged, hoping to send that message but he was busy. Rolling my hips forward, Kiaran's eyes flitted to mine, dark and hungry for me.

He stood and slid my legs back down around his waist and walked us over to the bed. He threw me down on it, spreading my legs with his knees and beginning to undo his pants. As he slid them down and moved to meet me, I grabbed his hand and gave him my most devilish eyes. The gold sparked. I felt it telling him how badly I wanted him inside of me but with what I knew now I wanted to give him everything.

"Can I?" I asked, tilting my chin down then looking back up at him through my lashes.

A tight smile met his lips as he backed himself off the bed.

"Lay down. Head over here."

I popped my head to the side in intrigue. Following his

orders, I turned to lay on my back, my hair falling off the edge of his plush bed.

"Come closer to me," he directed, lightly caressing my shoulders toward him.

"Like this?"

He smiled at me, confirming I was in the right spot. The nape of my neck curved over the edge.

"Open." He caressed my cheek before pressing his thumb through my lips. I did as I was told and sucked gently. A preview.

Kiaran held his thick length in his hand, stroking it. His eyes fluttered and a deep groan escaped him as he watched.

"Stick out your tongue." His voice was gravely.

I had never done this before. But I wanted to submit to him. I needed him to know he had me forever. All of me.

Stroking himself slowly as he watched me serve his desire, he bent down and pressed a kiss to my forehead. Then he slipped the straps of my dress down my shoulders and moved the top of my dress down to my waist, giving him a perfect view of my breasts.

Good girl, he praised as he slid the tip into my mouth. I didn't understand why my tongue needed to be out until he continued to slide further in and reached the back of my throat with ease.

"Fuck. You are taking it so well, baby," he reassured me like always.

I felt him throbbing in my mouth, he pulled out and rounded the other side of the bed, crawling up and fitting himself once again between my legs. Pulling my body back up on to the bed, he pressed a light kiss to my lips and whispered, "I love you."

"I love *you*."

Kiaran paused, like he didn't believe it the first time I said it, but did now. Unshed tears pricked his eyes again, disbelief etched across his face as if only now realizing that this *was* love.

"Say it again." Hope flitted through his gorgeous eyes. The colors between us beaming.

"I." I kissed his stubbled jaw. "Love." Another kiss to his neck. "You," I said against his lips before pressing into them. He kissed me back for only a moment before leaning back, just enough to see me.

He let a single tear to fall as a shaky smile spread across his face. Positioning himself at my entrance, I felt my arousal coat him. My body welcomed him as he slowly entered me. Inch by inch. Arching my neck on the bed, I cried out his name in need.

Kiaran allowed me to ask for what I wanted out of sex. He never made me feel shy or embarrassed for wanting to try things, put my body in positions that I'd only known to be hateful ones. He owned my body but still let me be in control.

His hips rocked agonizingly slow, each one harder and deeper somehow than the last. Keeping his loving eyes glued to mine, he brushed stray hairs from my face then pressed feather light kisses to the sides of my mouth.

"I thought I lost you," he whispered.

In.

"I know."

Out.

"I was so worried."

In.

"I know."

Out.

"Don't ever leave me like that again."

In.

"I won't," I promised, holding up a pinky which earned a small smile from Kiaran. He twisted his with mine and met my mouth with another kiss. His tongue swept in, dancing with mine.

Continuing his rhythmic movements, he pulled away and eyed me cautiously.

What needed to be done wouldn't be an easy sell to him. Not with how inexperienced I was. Kiaran was an anxious person, he worried so deeply for me. Nobody had ever taken much interest in my well being and as uncomfortable as it was, I needed it. He grounded me. When my dreams took me to the clouds and showed me a world view, Kiaran showed me the details down below I was missing.

I would give anything to allow Kiaran a better life. Of course, I'd love to be by his side as he earned his second chance but there was no guarantee. I knew when he told me I was his way home that I would give myself up for him without hesitation. What bothered me so much was that he kept it from me.

I couldn't help but wish he'd told me from the beginning, from the moment he introduced himself to me. We could've had months to prepare, to practice, rather than mere weeks.

Most days back home, I'd pray to God that it would be my last day. That he'd open the gates and let me go to my eternal home. I wished every time the guards attacked that the true Angel of Death would come for me, take my hands and lead me to the pearly gates.

It was a plea I sent up to the skies every night when I bowed against my bed with folded hands. Having never lived for anything, it was such an easy decision at the time. I'd never been scared of death, I welcomed it.

Now it was a plea to save the man I loved. A life for a life, as Valla committed to word. Risk mine to save his. It wasn't something I needed to question. Even if it didn't work, I would rest peacefully knowing he had a second chance.

"Yes, baby..." I moaned, feeling the newfound energy in my body revel in this.

Kiaran's hips rolled expertly into me as he neared his climax, my word of endearment only encouraging him. He slid his hand between us and expertly circled my sensitive nerves bringing me with him on his climb.

Nestling his face against my neck, we shared a euphoric release. *Always* together.

Heavy breathing was all that was left in our high's wake. Kiaran's entire body covered mine, I wrapped my arms around his neck and squeezed him tight.

"You have to promise never to leave me again," he rasped against my ear as he connected his big arms around me, rolling me into his side. I'd already promised him I wouldn't, I wouldn't need to. I realized now how cruel it was to leave earlier.

"Kiaran.."

"No. This isn't up for debate. You will not leave my side again until Solstice is passed." His tone was stern. I knew he meant every word.

"Kiaran…" I tried again.

"Amelie, my High Priestess was here tonight."

My body stilled, rigid as a body in frozen water.

"Why?" I choked out, barely audible.

"It was a warning. She knew you went to Holleberg, she knows you are a Morgenstern. She knows everything."

Ah, nothing about being a Bloch. *Good.* Using Morgenstern and Bloch magic together might go undetected.

"So?" I asked, confused why those two things mattered to her.

"So she knows what you are capable of."

"Maybe she shouldn't have fucked with the Morgensterns. *Again.*"

Every spell had a loophole. Every magical thing could be altered with different manifestations. The difference between me and Valla McCalmont was that my magic was more powerful. I might have a reckless handle on it at the moment, but that's neither here nor there.

Orla showed me that.

"Don't, Amelie. You don't know who you are dealing with."

"I met Orla tonight, Kiaran." The energy in the room shifted. My great grandmother's spirit in the house was alive again, and the tight smile that appeared on Kiaran's face told me he already knew. We both endeared the room for a moment, my cheeks heated as I found myself hoping that her sentience came with privacy.

I took a quiet pride in knowing that a part of my family had been here all along. I'd fallen recklessly for Kiaran, into this all-consuming dream, so much so that I wouldn't let the fear of not knowing whether my family was safe pierce through the illusion. I missed them constantly – but the thought that a part of me had always been here brought a bittersweet comfort.

"She was there tonight. In the cellar, she veiled me, brought me into a different world. Everyone was there, even your family. It was our wedding day. We are *supposed* to get married. I–"

"No more. Orla should not have shown you that. She shouldn't have given you false hope. From what we know about her, she knows not to tamper with my curse." Kiaran cut me off before I could tell him that my soul was no longer mortal, a fact that should surely make it hard to sacrifice me.

My lips curled up into a triumphant smile. She didn't tamper with the curse, she just showed me that there was a way around it. "Her reveal tonight was an awakening, Kiaran. Everything I didn't know about the magic I held and the long history of scorned women at the hands of *your* Coven. I am more sure than ever that I know how to beat your High Priestess."

"I can't, I won't do it. I'm sorry," he whispered, taking my hands and pressing a kiss to the tips of my fingers.

"Recite the curse to me again." Kiaran was silent for a long moment. "Please." I pleaded. He let out a heavy sigh before reciting the words I was sure had been burned into his mind since the day he was sentenced.

"You are bound to the cottage in the mortal realm, in an enchanted Forest. In order to break your curse you will need to make an impossible sacrifice. You must offer your Coven something of value to you on Winter Solstice. You will have one chance, each year to be untethered. It must be of such value that handing it over to us will cause you unimaginable pain. If it does not mirror the pain that you caused, it will not suffice.

Let the longest night approach and with it, the weight of your choice. Let your mind fill with every other option you think you have and may you find no reprieve. You will spend eternity there, Kiaran McCalmont. Until you feel the curse lock into place, you will be alone."

"*Mirror* the pain." It was what I hoped I'd heard right the first time I heard it.

"Yes, it's crystal clear. There isn't a way around it, she ordered as much."

I turned to rest my chin on his chest. "Oh, my sweet Kiaran. Have you not been listening to the stories of my family?" I tsk'd at him. Then, as not to chance the High Priestess continuing her all-knowing streak, I tried to speak to Kiaran through our bond. I could see each of my words melt into the threads of colors between us. Whatever veil they used against Kiaran and my ability to speak within our minds wasn't present inside these walls.

They made a grave mistake crossing your star with a Morgenstern.

Then I sent a silent thank you to Orla for showing me just how much I'm capable of.

CHAPTER 30
Kiaran

Amelie was a force. Since she woke up from whatever the fuck happened to her, she'd been speaking in riddles, plastering an everlasting, calculating smile on her face, and working furiously over her cauldron. She'd made at least fifty vials of a bright red elixir, stashing them deep in her apothecary cabinet. It was nearing the front and if she tried to stuff any more, I thought the shelf might collapse.

With the new found knowledge that Orla had the power to veil the curse and allow me to leave the cottage, I took to exploring the grounds around my home for the last two hundred years.

I felt useless to Amelie's dreaming mind. Listening to her plan felt like a blip in the void I'd been in for two hundred years. Watching her have the same hope I had over and over again over the years was too much. There was also no telling her it wouldn't work.

Amelie had studied magic over the last four months and absolutely knew more than I ever did in my hundreds of years of actually honing it. But loopholes were strategically avoided, even when you thought you found one, it would be a dead end. Witches were smart and cunning, they could manipulate fates to fit their perfect ideals and trick anyone into doing exactly what they wanted.

No mortal, even with Morgenstern and Bloch blood, would be able to best them.

Ethel had once told Amelie that her father's blood was God sent. Angels even. But I thought it was just her way of building up the good that was brought to the Forest by the Bloch's. Amelie went looking for answers, once again proving that she didn't need my help. But I hoped tonight she would humor me and go looking for more answers together.

I didn't hold it against her that she'd made a pattern of leaving me in the cottage to worry for her. When she was upset, she ran. She didn't like talking to me about what was bothering her. Maybe she felt like I wouldn't care to hear her out, but I would listen to anything she had to say. But recently, all she wanted to talk about was Solstice, and it was the one thing I couldn't entertain.

We only had a few days left together and spending them on pointless tries would be wasteful. I also didn't want to spend it on the outs, she was different last night. Every morsel of her body exuded power in a way I only knew of the High Priestess holding. A confidence rippled from her that could bring a grown man to his knees. And it did.

After inspecting the ninth frog that floated around the pond today, I went back to the cottage to find Amelie still working away at the boiling pot in front of her. At some point, you'd think my girl would learn to tie her hair back but as usual, it was falling into the cauldron in lush waves. A few strands were stuck to her forehead from the sheen of sweat.

"Good! You're back," she exclaimed as I closed the door behind me. "So, as you know," she looked up at me through thick, dark lashes, "because you're snoopy. Orla's journal had all kinds of spells in it."

"And?" I motioned for her to continue because she loved to pause to make sure I was listening.

"And there's one in here about making your dreams a portal. How to escape by dreaming, you don't even have to fall asleep! It's essentially day dreaming, and if you do it right, you can bring people with. She has all kinds of stuff documented on the Bloch…*magic*." She was so excited I worried she might fall straight into the goo she was stirring.

I took my place behind her and began to cross the strands as she continued.

"We can make it look just like what the sacrifice is supposed to look like. Then your curse will unlock."

I got to the thin part of the braid and motioned for our Orla to tie it together.

"Amelie…" I rolled my eyes, wanting to never speak of trying to trick the curse again.

She spun around, swiping my masterpiece of a braid through the cauldron. I reached behind her, pulling it out and crossed it over her shoulder. Amelie smiled but was completely unfazed by her hair dripping with a thick red liquid.

"It'll work, I swear!"

Her golden rivers were portals all by themselves, completely wild and full of hope. She had to be as unsure of it working as I was that it wouldn't. She wasn't practiced enough to even attempt it. Since I told her the exact words the High Priestess used to curse me, she hadn't let it go that there was a way to work around it. A mirror, whatever the hell that meant. It was almost insulting that she assumed I hadn't thought of any other way.

"Kiaran you have magic too. You are capable and—" I cut her off with a soft kiss to her lips. "Amelie, I won't listen to any more of this."

Her face fell, betrayed that my kiss wasn't done with romantic intent but rather a way to stop her from finishing her sentence. The gold that I treasured in her eyes dimmed, nearly to a bronze color as if I alone deflated her excitement.

"I can't just not try to save us," she admitted, bowing her head and letting out a quiet whimper. I cupped her cheeks and forced her teary eyes to look at mine. Every time she cried, my heart cracked open. The sapphire color emulated the deepest part of the sea in Avonya. The tears began to fall looking like gentle waves rolling onto her sand colored cheeks.

"I won't help you get yourself killed."

"So you're just giving up?"

No. I wasn't. But I couldn't tell her that. She'd never let me sacrifice myself for her.

And I didn't need her to save me. My girl was always dreaming of someone saving her but if given the chance, I knew she'd never let anyone take her burden and bear the weight. If I tried to lift it off of her shoulders, she'd wrap herself back up in it like it was a precious childhood blanket.

I never wanted to be needed. I wanted to be left alone, no responsibilities, no one to depend on me. Then I couldn't disappoint someone I cared about. The one time I took on a burden I was cursed to a cottage so far from home that even my loudest cries into the night for my mother didn't reach her. Or at least she never reached back.

The High Priestess' wicked words kept reminding me of how little I meant to this world, *no one could love you.*

But I loved Amelie, she swore she loved me back. She was everything to me. She broke up my dark clouds with her sunlight. Her presence alone could assure that if only for a moment, everything could be okay.

"I'm still here, pretty girl. You're acting like you've already lost me." My heart thudded slow at the false reassurance I gave her. Her eyes softened as she laid her hands over mine on her cheeks. Stroking my fingers gently, she took a deep breath before steeling her features and retreating behind the iron shield she used to ward off anyone from getting too close to her.

"You won't be in a matter of days if you don't start helping me." Then she peeled my hold on her face away and turned back to her boiling pot of spells. She was pushing me away. Again.

THE LAST NIGHT before the Winter Solstice…

Dinner tonight might as well have been in an underground pit of snakes. I sighed earlier, more or less just breathed a bit louder than normal, and Amelie asked me if I could not do that, not *breathe.* I shifted on the bench and it made a tiny creak and she rolled her eyes.

I hadn't even spoke a true sentence but I was sure if I did she'd take her fangs out and sink the venom straight into my blood.

The gold in her eyes was on fire and I decided it was a nice feature for her emotions to be on such clear display through her eyes. Even if it was petrifying to be on the other end of those emotions.

With my new found ability to leave the cottage, I hoped Orla might let us go for a night out in the Forest together.

"Finish eating and grab your cloak." I wiped the sides of my mouth with my napkin and stood from the table.

"Can't. I have things to do," she replied immediately without looking up from her plate.

"Wasn't a question. I'll be back down in a minute."

Amelie was stubborn. More stubborn than my mother, which was hard to beat. But I knew she liked me telling her what to do, even if she protested it. She was too curious to not follow along.

I took the stairs to the attic quickly and paced around my room for a moment to make it seem like I was doing something important. I wasn't.

Silverware clanged against the plate entirely too hard and I smiled to myself when I heard her push back from the table with a grunt and stomp to her room.

Her footsteps slowly entered the kitchen again and the creaks back and forth told me she was waiting. Descending the stairs, I pulled my cloak around my shoulders and gave her a half grin, trying to keep my excitement for our outing tied up beneath my features.

I grabbed her hand and pulled her out the door with me.

"Absolutely despicable that Orla has apparently been able to do that the whole time." I told her as we left the cottage together for the first time.

Amelie giggled to herself but when I looked back hoping to catch a glimpse of her smile, she shut it down.

I had a surplus of magic to use without the effects of Amelie's veil or the added elixirs and I wanted to make our last night together something special.

"Do you trust me?" I asked, stopping her at the edge of the clearing.

"No," she lied.

I tilted my head at her and shot an annoyed glance at her.

"Say yes."

"Fine. I trust you."

"Good girl."

Taking her arms and placing them over my shoulders, I pulled out a move that would hopefully impress my girl.

Melting our bodies into one another, Amelie's eyes widened as we disappeared and reappeared above the trees.

It'd been a long time since I'd flown, and never had I done it with someone wrapped around me. I had to find my balance in the air, unlike the Fae or the clumsy butterflies who had wings, my flight was completely based on my own balance and focus. Amelie had a habit of making me lose my focus. So I had to try extra hard to not be distracted by her soft hair gently breezing across my face or the smell of vanilla and strawberry that surrounded me.

"Kiaran!" she shrieked as she took notice of our proximity to the ground below us.

"Just hold on." I reassured with a kiss on her cheek and then took a smooth glide through the cool, winter air. The tops of the trees danced for us, their leaves and branches moving together in complete synchronicity.

Amelie sunk into my chest, squeezing her arms around my neck tight as she twisted her head to see the view below us.

"Oh my god…" she muttered. I smiled to myself. I knew my dreamy girl would love this. The view from the top of the world was always better than seeing what was right in front of you. It's harder to notice mistakes, crying sounded like laughter, faces were masses of people, dead leaves were blended in with the bright greens so they seem less significant against the brush.

She preferred her dreams to reality because she designed them to be better. She curated a fantastical world to live in while she slept and found a way to make them a portal so they felt real enough to continue to matter when she woke up.

From up here, the cottage was small. The curse that tied me to it was a piece of thread rather than a tether between the curse and freedom. Even I could understand why she so often dreamed of worlds so different than our own, but eventually, we would land. The worries that walked with us on the ground would surround us again and escape would be only that.

The faint orange glow I was en route to grew brighter as we approached. The sounds of many men laughing and playful music sounded from below us as we hovered over top of the Lost Souls.

"Ready?" I asked her as I idled above the group of friends

and family below. Amelie turned her head back to me with a shy smile on her face and nodded.

I landed us safely on the edge of the clearing, ahead of us all of Amelie's grandfathers sat around the same fire tossing back mugs of ale and laughing together.

Her shy smile grew with joy as I placed a hand to her lower back and led her toward her family.

CHAPTER 31

Amelie

Sitting around the fire with my family and Kiaran, I took in each detail of their faces. The orange and red hues danced across their faces, illuminating different details of each of them. Al was clean shaven now with a structured jaw and eyes like my father's. Niklaus and Josef were a perfect combination of my mother under the guise of night. All of them held themselves as if they were once soldiers, protectors, always on guard, but soft enough to pay attention to you when you were speaking.

My father was the glue, but my mother was the paper my family was written on. She created me and my brothers within her own body, nearing death in Tildan's delivery and still had enough left in her to love us until she couldn't anymore. So with each piece of herself that grew into a child, my father kept us together.

Just as I needed my father's hug, I wondered if she needed hers when she was melancholy. If one big embrace from her dad would've made it all better.

Friedrich was a replica of my dad. While my uncle Arthur looked just like Al, funny how that worked. At dinner, it was overwhelming seeing them all around the table like we were a real family. Bright faces under Orla's light on full display but here, sitting in their element, halfway hidden by the blend of moonlight and fire glow, they were just the Lost Souls who found each other.

Kiaran was kindred with them. He was lost too. His shoulders relaxed as we approached my grandfathers hand in hand. They welcomed us with warm smiles.

He was constantly searching for something else, something more. Never satisfied and always choosing the wrong path simply because he had the privilege of turning around and changing direction if he so pleased. Kiaran's life wasn't based on survival, as deep rooted as his insecurities and restlessness was, he'd been just a boy.

His mother berated him for not focusing on his studies and honing his magic. Shamed him for not living up to his family name. But he was just a boy. His mother and sister's lives were put on his shoulders and he failed. But he was *just* a boy. He'd spent the better part of two hundred years feeling like he failed, but you could not fail in something you did not know the extent of.

My failures came from knowing my brothers were hungry, our mother bedridden, my consequence for stealing from the palace. I knew the end result for me would be my life. But I was mortal then. I woke up every morning knowing I would die one day and my life would be a long list of missteps that I had to recover from until one day I didn't.

He was born knowing the end was nowhere in sight. How could he possibly have the full understanding of a consequence? This wasn't fair.

He was just a *boy*.

The man sitting next to me now understood what a consequence was. He understood that not fulfilling the sacrifice tomorrow night would end his life, potentially mine. It allowed him to think about his decisions and the High Priestess knew that when she enacted his curse. Telling him that every resolve he tried to find would be of no use. She put it into an order that he must mirror the pain he caused. Not that he had to feel it, it just had to mirror it.

Why did he not understand that? It was as simple as the illusion of a disappearing house. If he didn't want it to be seen, it was hidden. When he did, he unveiled it. I had less than twenty four hours to convince him to walk with me into the last attempt at breaking his curse. If he wouldn't, then I would lie to him for the very last time.

Kiaran squeezed my knee, leaning in to press a kiss to my temple. I blushed at the public display of affection in front of the origins of my blood. Al gave us a soft, approving smile and I wondered if they knew how this would end.

The music around us grew louder, a song made for bouncing around the fire until you were begging for air. Kiaran must've felt the shift too and stood from the log with an outstretched hand. He smiled at me, no embarrassment in his expression whatsoever. I took his hand and he pulled me into his body before placing his other hand on the lumbar of my back.

He danced like a maniac, leading me no which way and I went right along with it. Singing every word, I realized it was the same song he serenaded himself with when he was baking the absurd amount of muffins for our dinner.

Now it's time to stop a while

Forget your worries everyone

Kiaran was an anxious, nervous person. Shy and reserved usually but in front of all his kindred Lost Souls, he sang loudly. His voice attracting stares from everyone while my family around us looked at us with so much affection it made my heart hurt.

Like hand and glove, could this be love?

Is there magic in the air?

As beautiful as his voice was, his dancing was just the opposite. He swung me around to no specific beat, he was marching to his own. This free version of him made my heart ache further.

With the one who sends me in a trance
If not, at least, you'll get to dance
Down at the ballroom of romance

He leaned in as the song quieted, the end was near and the metaphor made my heart fully break open. Pressing the lightest kiss to my brow, he rested his forehead on mine. "I love you."

I love you more.

I leaned into him, linking my pinky finger with his.

Pinky promise.

He pressed a gentle kiss to my lips. My skin heated and visions of our future flashed in my eyes. The wedding, a little girl running around with Kiaran's curly, black hair and my eyes, and two rocking chairs positioned on the balcony overlooking the sea I'd always visited my prince at.

Tears pricked my eyes, but before they could fall, I swallowed them. Keeping them stashed away for when there was something to cry about.

"I'm going to go sit with Al for a bit."

He nodded into the top of my head, placing a kiss at the crown of it for good measure. Breaking his hold, I rounded the fire and sat next to my great-great-grandfather and he greeted me with an arm around my shoulder.

"What's going on in that mind of yours, girl?" he asked in a gentle voice.

"Can I ask you a few questions about tomorrow?" Al tensed, as if I was bringing forward a forbidden subject, but agreed anyway to my inquisition.

"Is there a loophole in Kiaran's curse?" I whispered, not wanting the man in question to hear.

Al nodded slowly.

"Okay. Do you know what it is?"

His head moved back and forth.

"If I told you what I think it is, would you know?"

Al took a deep breath in and exhaled, rolling his shoulder back and giving the slightest nod.

"My dreams…" I started, searching his face to see if it was the right direction. He gave away nothing. "I can use them like portals. Travel places."

Another nod from Al. My heart rate picked up and my blood heated. I could *feel* how close I was.

"I think I can alter things here, in the real world. I think what happens in my dreams appears to the naked eye to be happening right in front of them."

"You are a wise one, girl," he replied after a moment of silence. A smile spread across my face and my eyes sparked to life.

I relaxed into my seat with grandpa Al's arm lovingly hung around me now. "Now I just need to find my father before tomorrow."

Al turned slightly. "He's been visiting you has he?"

I nodded.

"Good man."

"I'm not sure how yet. I saw his casket be lowered to the ground, we mourned his death–"

"Do you understand the Bloch blood yet, Amelie?" Al inquired, making the hair on my neck stand at attention. From what I read in Orla's journals and the little that Ethel knew, we were called Originators. But I didn't know what that meant, I only knew that our minds were a powerful place.

"Can you tell me how it works now?" I leaned in close, like I might miss the answer if I wasn't close enough.

"We are Originators. Without us, the world wouldn't exist. So we get to make changes to it as we see fit."

I flattened my lips in a thin line and shrugged at him, still not totally aware of what it all meant.

"Aren't you a Christian?"

Ha! I nearly fell off the log we are sitting on in a laughing fit. To ask the girl who came from a poverty ridden village, beaten and raped more times than she was told she was loved, and less food than most insects ever having been in my belly was insanity.

Who could believe in a God that watched his people suffer that way?

"Amelie?" he asked, more concern this time in his tone. Kiaran and Niklaus' conversation was stopped as they looked over to see what all the fuss was about.

"What does believing in God's hyper masculine teachings have to do with our blood?" It was a rhetorical question because honestly fuck my grandfather for asking. We were in a magical Forest, Christians believed magic was derived from Hell itself.

"You haven't learned anything of it yet?" He was confused, clearly under the impression that I'd found the true book of answers somewhere and was coming to him with an all knowing knowledge.

Kiaran sat down next to me, sensing the change in energy between me and Al.

"Learned what? I am so sick of everyone asking me what I know instead of just telling me what I'm missing!"

I laughed at the ridiculous statement. Kiaran had done it too, inquired about the knowledge I already had, keeping key details in his pocket for when he felt I was ready for them.

"I have ten brothers and sisters, they are placed all throughout the world to watch over the mortals. Take care of them, place miracles on the sick, those kinds of things. We are the original Angel's God took in, then he sent us here."

"Yeah, yeah, we are all the son's and daughter's of Christ. That doesn't give you magical powers." I waggled my fingers in front of his face like Kiaran did when he cast a spell. Kiaran bowed his head into his palms to stifle the laugh falling from him at my outburst.

"Sure it does," Al responded without a second thought.

"That's what faith is. It's magical, powerful. Not in the same way Kiaran's or your maternal magic is but it's magical nonetheless." Al spoke so nonchalantly like explaining this wasn't a ridiculous piece of my history.

"So what? If I'm a good little Christian, say my prayers and thank God for the horrific life I and so many others have I'll be able to snap my fingers and all will be right in the world? Get on my knees and praise the almighty?" I scoffed at him. Horrified that I had family that believed so heavily in God being good.

"Do not take that tone with me." His voice was stern. Much like my father's was the few times he disciplined me or my brothers.

"Do you hear yourself? If you are the all knowing, then you would know exactly why I have a hard time believing there is a man in the sky who decides who deserves what in our time on Earth."

"That's what I'm telling you, Amelie." He took my hands in his and I tensed. "You are the decider of where your life goes. God? Well he might guide you but ultimately you are a Bloch. Do you know what Bloch means in the old language?"

"No?"

"It means foreigner. Someone who wanders but isn't lost. Someone who decides where to plant roots and paints the world around them with their minds, their dreams. You are the final part of the prophecy that God set for the Bloch family when he sent us to Earth. The greatest love he ever created. It was too powerful, so he split your heart in two to find the other when the world was ready. Your life? It has been a great test, and you have passed. You made it here. You found me, you found him." Al pointed to Kiaran. "You can decide your own fate. The High Priestess has a lot of power in the physical world, that part is true,

"But you have Morgenstern and Bloch blood racing through you. You have a spiritual side that can manifest any world you want, and an elemental magic that his Coven has wanted a piece of since the beginning of time. Don't you see?"

I didn't see, I was so excited to sit with my family tonight and find a sense of normalcy I never had nor might I ever have again. Now I wondered how much of my life was my own undoing. My own negativity. I wondered if my father was so happy because he knew exactly what his place in the world was and he made it better by bringing art to it. If my dreams could've been my reality, if I hadn't been waking up every morning only praying for the worst not to happen.

Since I'd arrived here, my dreams were lovely, usually playing out within days of having them. Life felt like it was worth living, there was a reason to wake up in the morning and it wasn't just to say I survived one more day.

Kiaran's hand was making comforting strokes around my lower back.

"You okay?" he whispered into my ear. I lied and nodded.

"So what now? I have less than twenty four hours and this was not a part of my plan."

Al turned even more to face me fully, tightening his hold on my hands.

"It's already a part of you, Amelie. You know exactly what to do. Stop worrying so much and enjoy this time with the boy."

My tiny friend came waddling through the trees in the distance. I wondered if the bonds Kiaran spoke of between us could form between friends, because when I needed my friend, she was somehow always there.

Ethel was making a bee line for our fire but I needed space so I released Al's hold on my hands and patted Kiaran on the knee before standing, "I'm going to speak with Ethel. Can we go soon?"

Kiaran nodded as I turned to run to my friend.

"Oh!" she squeaked as I squeezed her tight. "I'm happy to

see you too, girl." I felt a tear slip from my eyes, the weight of tomorrow finally crushing me beneath it.

Ethel combed through my long hair as more tears fell.

"Shh…" she coaxed. It wasn't a sob and I wasn't sad. It was a release.

"I'm okay. I just…" I leaned back and took a seat on the ground with her. "I'm scared about tomorrow."

Ethel smiled at me. "I'd worry greatly about your sanity if you weren't."

"What if I fail?" I sniffled, laying all the way back to admire the stars in the night sky.

"What if you don't?" she offered, laying next to me. My hand was wrapped between her chubby little fingers and I breathed in her words.

If I didn't fail, if I finally got it right, then maybe I'd get my happily ever after.

If I dreamed of it, willed it into existence, then was it meant for me? Al said I'd been in charge of my own fate this whole time, that God had only been a guide, so where did my choices end and his paved road begin?

Hesitant footsteps approached us and I'd recognize them anywhere.

"Ready?" Kiaran's soft voice floated through the air. Tilting my head to see him, the orange light gave him an angelic silhouette.

"Ready."

CHAPTER 32

Kiaran

When I was ten, I got to participate in my first Winter Solstice celebration. Mother let me and Mia stay up all night, the music in our palace was boisterous and made the night feel like the high noon sun. All members of the Coven were in full garb, the High Table wearing their headdresses while mingling with all the commoners.

Emmin, Leo and I were running around like fools on a major high from all the sugar we'd consumed. We made a complete mess of the estate garden, picking all of the winter flowers that fit in our little hands and making bouquets for our mothers. I couldn't find my mom when we went to give them away so I gave them to Mia, she was thrilled. Her smile was gapped from her week of losing baby teeth, it was the cutest thing. The chubby cheeks that only got chubbier when she beamed making it well worth giving her the flowers over my mother.

As upset as mom was about us destroying her garden, she agreed that a bouquet was a great way to celebrate Solstice. So, when I woke up this morning, I left a sleeping Amelie in my bed dreaming of today, and went outside to begin picking two bouquets. One for Amelie, and one for my mother.

After I'd filled my arms to the brim, I found one last pale blue one and tucked it into the center, then went back to the cottage. As I approached, I heard a tone deaf Amelie singing to herself..

Happy birthday to me,
Happy birthday to me,
Happy birthday dear me,
Happy birthday to me.

It was quiet, almost like she didn't want to be singing it at all and my heart hurt. It was her birthday? I never thought to ask. After your first hundred years, you kind of stopped celebrating it. Amelie would be twenty-five though. Only twenty-five birthdays in her lifetime so far and she didn't tell me about it.

As I walked through the threshold, flower petals spilling over, her back was to me but she let out a breath and smoke dissipated through the air in front of her.

"Morning," I said, interrupting her moment. She turned to face me and behind her sat a small piece of cake with a candle in it.

"Oh!" she startled, trying to move in front of said cake. "I didn't know you were back!"

"It's your birthday?"

"No." She laughed out, waving her hand around in the air at nothing.

"Why were you singing happy birthday to yourself then?"

"It's uh…" She thought of her lie quickly, though it was a bad one. "My favorite song." Amelie looked to the ceiling, giving our spirited home a look, clearly asking for help.

"Your birthday is on Winter Solstice?" I asked again, not giving her the chance to avoid it.

"Seems that way," she admitted. The High Priestess didn't miss a single fucking detail of the day.

"Why didn't you say so? We've talked about today for… months?"

"My birthday isn't of much importance as it stands now is it?"

She got me there. I supposed the reason for our conversation around the day didn't offer much room for celebration. But now that I knew, we'd be spending every minute celebrating her until tonight. If anything, it would keep her from spending the day over the cauldron in some last ditch effort to get us both killed.

"Well that's enough of that attitude. It's your birthday, let's enjoy the day."

"Really, it's not a big deal. I just want to have this piece of cake and be done with it," she replied with a hung head.

"We have all day, Amelie. We can do whatever you want. I'm sure we can think of something much greater than just a slice of sugar." I laughed off the comment but Amelie's face continued to drag deeper into something more than just sad.

"The cake is more than enough," she said quietly. I wasn't sure if it was even meant for me to hear or if it was to convince herself that it was enough. A fleeting thought of her little brother crossed her mind, I plucked it the second it appeared. A little boy's voice, *someday I'm going to make so many cakes for all the birthdays we didn't get one for.*

I took three long strides to close the distance between us, the flowers being the only thing keeping us apart. Reaching around her, I laid the second bouquet on the table and asked Orla to tie up Amelie's.

Pressing the pad of my index finger under her chin, I lifted it to make her look at me. A large arrangement of blue and purple flowers bunched in my other hand. She must not have noticed them before but her sapphire eyes sparkled as she took them in now. A smile slid across her face as she looked back to me.

"Are these for me?" she asked hopefully.

I nodded, giving her a kiss to her forehead as she bent forward to smell the freshly picked bouquet.

She took the flowers from my hand, setting them on the table behind her before wrapping her tiny frame around my body, a gesture I returned happily.

Since our night on the roof, there had been a distance between us that neither of us knew how to close. The anticipation for tonight hanging over us had been a rainfall that we couldn't find each other through. Holding her in my arms now felt like maybe the rain was dissipating. It knew that it could be our last bit of sunshine and the world was okay with giving us that.

"I have an idea." The thought crossed my mind when I heard the little boys voice and without thinking it through, I took Amelie's hand and led her to her room. She plopped down at the edge of her bed and I opened the chest that sat at the foot.

Rummaging through it, I noticed a new dress. The pale blue color that I knew she loved, I was sure Orla knew that too. Pulling it out, Amelie's eyes glistened with unshed tears. The long sleeves were flowy, the inside lined with a soft fleece so it could be worn in the winter. It was long enough to graze the ground, the skirt puffed slightly with tulle layering it. The neckline plunged, and I'd be lying if I wasn't excited to see that on her. It was perfect.

"Come here." I stood, draping the new dress over my shoulder and started undressing my girl. Her once frail arms, now toned with muscle, were raised above her head, I laced each side of the dress over them. It wrapped around her body, a perfect fit. I bunched her long locks into my hand and pulled it from inside the dress to let the waves settle across her back.

Wrapping my arms around her front, she tilted her head into the crook of my elbow. "Want to fly again?"

She turned to face me, stars streaked across her eyes in shades of gold. "Yes!"

Amelie pressed a kiss to my cheek and nearly skipped out of the cottage. I called after her, "I'll be out in a minute!"

I adjusted the knife sheathed in my boot. Before I left this morning, I asked Orla for it. It was stabbing into my ankle but if tonight was going to go how I planned, it needed to stay there.

Grabbing one of Amelie's loose journal pages, I sat down at her desk and wrote her the words I knew she would need come the morning sun tomorrow.

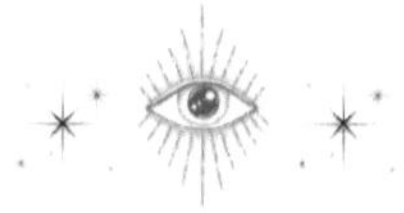

HIGH IN THE air above the canopy of the Forest, the palace that ruled her former life came into view. Amelie's body tensed at the sight but today wasn't going to be a bad day. I positioned us at the edge of the trees before the hole in the Earth that took you right into the belly of the Holleberg ruler's home. My short conversation with Al last night playing on repeat in my mind as we regained our balance.

"No," Amelie said as soon as she got her footing, taking steps back into the brush away from me. "I won't spend my last day here."

"You're not, pretty girl. Come here." I reached a hand out to her, letting her come on her own free will. Orla allowing me freedom had given me purpose to use my magic again. One of my favorite past times in Avonya was sending Mia away through portals I would create, she always came back. Amelie's explanation that magic was mostly manifestation gave me confidence that I knew exactly where she would go.

Casting a Witches gate that took the view of the palace away from her, her eyes softened as her tears began to fall. "Do you trust me?" I asked her, still giving her time to decide.

"Yes."

"Then what is it? Why are you crying?" God, I hated when she cried.

"I've dreamed of this. Of you, this." She waved her hand in front of her at the glowing gate in front of her. "I dreamed of it often before I met you. You always came back for me." She took a few hesitant steps toward me, slowly extending her hand to meet mine.

"Well, then all I ask is for you to come back for me this time. Call for me when you're ready." She took my hand and stepped into my chest.

"You're not coming with me?"

"No, this one is all for you." I pressed a kiss to her lips which she returned with fervor.

"I want to spend today with you."

"I'm trusting you. About having a tomorrow." I lie, knowing she needs this. "Now go." I gave her a light smack on her ass earning a giggle from her. The gold in her eyes sparkled at me as I admired my strong girl stepping through the portal to see her family again.

CHAPTER 33

Amelie

My stomach dropped as the magic from the portal took my breath away. Like my soul detached so two separate entities could rejoin on the other side.

In front of me, a cream stone cottage sat with colorful flowers cascading down from the windows. Hills rolled behind it for miles, behind me was a large open prairie where two children ran playfully, chasing each other with sticks. The sky was as blue as a winter sky could be and the few clouds that floated about blended in with the snow on the tippy tops of the hills.

I heard two voices coming from the inside of the small home and as my feet moved without permission, my ears registered just who those voices belonged to.

"Mom! Dad!" I yelled too loud for how close I was to the house but as if they knew who was approaching too, both halves of my blood toppled through the door with wide eyes.

"Amelie!" they shouted as they rushed to me to cover me with their arms.

"Ammy!" A smaller voice sounded from behind them and through the small space between limbs I saw my littlest brother waddling toward us too.

My parents loosened their hold on me so I could bend down to catch Tildan. I wrapped him so tight a little squeak left his mouth but he hugged me back just as tight. More little steps were running up behind us and now I knew who was chasing the other with sticks. Wren caught my back first, then Hansel. My boys were wrapped around me like vines on a tree.

The collective amount of tears being shed amongst the six of us could've created a new river. The beaming smiles could've created a new source of light. Sheer joy flowed through my family, all together again. My father scooped Tildan up and my heart cracked wide open. He never met Tildan, but Tildie clung to him just like the rest of us knew how to.

"How did you find us?" Wren asked. My scorned, rough around the edges little brother looked like a boy now. The wear around his face from scowling his whole life had faded much like the darkness that usually followed him.

"It's…" I hesitated, wondering how much time I had to spend explaining the last few months. "A long story. The better question is, how did you all get here?"

I looked around at each of the faces of my family landing on my father's last. "And papa? How are you here?" My father tucked my mom into his side and smiled.

"Bloch blood, but you know about that now, don't you?" My chest heaved forward, the idea of talking so openly about what he knew took me by surprise.

"You knew?" I asked.

"Always."

"You didn't tell us." Gesturing to myself and my brothers.

"It's a complicated thing to have such knowledge, we all come to it in our own way. But I hope you're here because you heard my message." Always a wise answer from him. He spoke so casually of it, just as Al did.

"What message?"

"That you were doing everything right."

My mind reeled for a moment. There were a lot of things I was working on for tonight. Things that Kiaran wasn't privy to. I eyed my father cautiously, not wanting to spend our short time together discussing the heaviest battle I was ever going to face.

"Get out of that head, Amelie. You've been dreaming of it for weeks, your entire life, really. You know exactly what to do." He gave me a wink and pressed a kiss to my mother's head. They both looked at me with proud eyes. It was exactly what I needed to hear from him. I knew he'd been in my dreams for a reason. I felt it to the innermost parts of my soul.

It hit me that my mother was upright, beautiful and lively in front of me, then an Earth shattering weight lifted from my shoulders.

"Mama…" I sunk into her arms. "How are you all here?"

"The guards came late that night you left, Arthur and Liam. I'll admit it was terrifying and I surely thought it was over for us. But they brought us here, where your father was waiting," my mother said.

Wren piped up next, "Daddy's been here the whole time. He called Uncle Arthur a grave robber."

My eyes widened and slid to my father's. He was laughing to himself and if I survived the night, I'd have to come back to that later.

"Happy Birthday, by the way," Hansel interrupted.

"Thank you buddy." I pulled him into my side.

"Why couldn't I come with you?" My tone was pathetic, like a little girl who was left behind. Though in a sense, I was.

"Haven't you figured out why?" my father answered with a confused expression spreading across his face.

"I literally just found out you're all alive," I retorted.

"You've met the Prince, though?" He tried again a different way.

"Kiaran?"

My father's face lit up at the mention of my complicated relationship with the cursed, three hundred year old Witch from the enchanted Forest. A reaction I wouldn't have, in a million years, anticipated from my father.

"Where is he?" he asked.

"He said this was for me," I answered defensively, feeling jaded that I was here and my father seemed to be more excited about my... boyfriend?

"Very thoughtful of him." His eyebrows popped like he was impressed, "Please bring him back, we'd like to meet him."

"What?" I shrieked. "No, that's okay."

"Amelie, bring the boy here. It's only right to have your father's blessing," my mother said now.

Relenting, I called to him.

Are you there?

His response was quick.

Always. It's only been a few minutes, though.

Open the gate.

It appeared immediately and my brothers' faces looked like they just struck gold. Magic was such a normal thing for me now, but the wonderment in my brothers' eyes was priceless.

Stepping through, my head spun again, but as promised, there he was.

"What-"

Without wasting time, I grabbed his hand and pulled him through with me. It took him no time to recover, but now I was doubly spinning. He steadied my shoulders and then finished his sentence he tried to say before I brought us back.

"What's going on?" he asked.

"My family wants to meet you."

"Oh." His face paled and his fingers started rapidly tapping against his thigh.

"Yeah." My family seemed to be very cool with my new

magical life and my parents obviously already knew about Kiaran. I decided that if this was the last time I saw them, or the last chance they'd have to meet the love of my life, then I'd take advantage of it.

I took his hand and brought him toward four beaming faces. Wren's face was steeled.

Kiaran was the complete gentleman, the eagerness of his hand nearly pushing me to the ground as he stretched it out to my father.

"Mr. Bloch." He offered first, shaking my dad's hand. "Mrs. Bloch, it's no mystery where Amelie's beauty comes from." He bowed slightly to her and I couldn't help but smile at the nerves I felt flowing from him.

"Thank you, Kiaran. We are so happy to meet you." My mother's sweet voice sounded as she tucked a piece of her long hair behind her ear.

It was so strange to see her upright, put together, and talking again. All of them were plastered with happiness and it made me feel so content to know this was how I'd leave them.

"Come, let's eat," my father said before turning back toward their home with my mother in hand.

Three little bodies bounced in front of Kiaran and I. Kiaran leaned down to meet Tildan's height. "You must be Tildan." My youngest brother's face lit up at the recognition and he wrapped his tiny arms around Kiaran's neck. Butter-flies were set free in the lowest part of my stomach at the baby being cradled in Kiaran's big arms.

Fuck, he'd be such a hot dad. Not a hope I needed to have right now.

But then that little girl I saw last night when Kiaran kissed me popped back into my head, my stomach churned as my heart tried to take flight. *Our* girl.

Tildan wasn't planning on letting go so Kiaran stood with the little monkey hanging on to him and moved to my next brother. "I assume this little reflection of Amelie is..." He tapped a finger against his chin but he knew exactly who he was, and Hansel was loving it. "Hansel!"

"Yup, it sounds like handsome, which is very accurate," my silliest brother replied. My smile spread wider somehow at how natural this all felt. Kiaran pulled Hansel into his side and hugged him as best he could while holding Tildan.

Then he turned to meet my first friend in this world. "That leaves you, the strong, adamant one, just like his sister."

"Wren," my brother said before Kiaran could finish, his arms were crossed and his chest was puffed out. He was trying his best not to be excited about the big, strong man he was in front of right now. Wren may have his boyish features back, but he was just like me and he didn't trust easily. My smile was about to cross the boundaries of my face as I relished in the thought that some things never changed.

"What are your intentions with my sister, Mr. Witch?" Wren asked in his most mature voice. I stifled the laugh that tried to escape me. Kiaran steeled his features and cleared his throat to meet the seriousness of Wren's questioning.

"Well, someday I'd like to marry her." Wren and I both jolted at that, but Wren collected himself much quicker. I couldn't take my eyes off of Kiaran though and my smile turned into a dropped jaw. "But I'll have to deserve her first, so I'm not sure when that day will come."

Jesus Christ, *this man.*

Wren nodded at his answer, then turned to face me and cocked an eyebrow. I shook my head, and started for my parents house with my brother at my side, the other three behind us.

"Pretty ambitious fella you have there, Amelie."

I turned my head to Wren. "You're tellin' me."

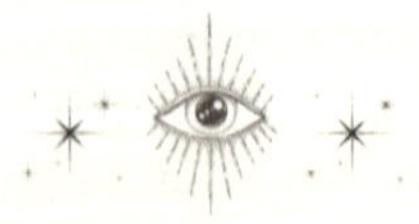

THE REST of the day was spent reminiscing with my family and Kiaran becoming privy to all the embarrassing stories from my life. A crash course in Amelie.

They even told him about the time that I climbed onto the porch roof when I was nine and couldn't figure out how to get down but I was too stubborn to ask for help so I slept up there. Kiaran quipped back that it sounded like I hadn't changed much.

The sun was beginning to set and so was the panic of the night to come.

"I'm going to step out for a moment," I called out as I approached the front door that was painted with a mural of our family in front of our home in Holleberg. "We should go soon," I whispered to Kiaran and he agreed with a nod.

Stepping outside, I took a seat at the table to the right of the entryway. Staring out at the sky, it was a perfect moment between night and day. Towards the setting sun, a blend of orange, pink, and deep purple spread across the horizon and met with the deep blue into black where the moon was rising.

The metaphor wasn't lost on me and it only made my stomach tic tighter into knots. We too, were in an inbetween, Kiaran and I. My birthday being the day of Kiaran's ritual was all too fated and I hoped it meant good luck. Who dies on their birthday?

I knocked on the wooden table at the thought just as the front door creaked open and my mother appeared on the other end of it.

Her smile was a beacon to a home I always wished for.

"We've missed you, Amelie." She covered my hand with hers. "And your father and I are so proud of you."

The heavy weight on my heart felt like a constricting snake now. It was so hard to hear that. My fate depended on tonight, as did Kiaran's. But with all the information between my mother and father's families made me feel like everyone's fate relied on me. For one day, I just wanted to not be needed.

Even if it was the most uncomfortable day of my life, the unburdening might do my soul some good.

"I've missed you all too."

She thumbed the top of my hand, her touch being such a comfort that I wanted to shrivel up right now so it was the last thing I ever felt.

"He's a very good man."

I met her gaze and for the first time I noticed how the gold in her eyes danced like mine.

"Kiaran?"

She nodded.

"Yeah.." I smiled at my own memories of him. "I like him."

"How are you?" Her question gave me pause. I wasn't sure she'd ever asked how I was. Not because she didn't care before, she just didn't have the capacity to.

"I'm okay," I told her honestly. It was the best word I could come up with for how I was feeling.

"You've always been such a force, Amelie. Do you know that? It's okay to admit you can't take on everything and I think that boy in there might be the one who wants to help you."

I gave her a half hearted smile, she was right. But I didn't want her to know just how much was riding on me that he couldn't, rather, wouldn't help with.

"Please let him," she added before the door opened, summoning the man in question.

"Sorry." Kiaran shied away from the private moment my mother and I were having, "Do you need another minute?"

His face was fresh. I couldn't imagine how long it'd been since he'd been surrounded by family. One specifically that didn't incur such a massive pressure as his own. Seeing him in this light hurt, I wanted to stay here forever with him. Let him feel what it was like to have nothing to your name but your family. We were always just the Bloch family, within the four walls of our deteriorating home, it didn't matter what was happening outside of it. As long as we had each other.

"No, we should go."

My mother and I stood from the table, my brothers and father stepped out behind Kiaran. My family held Kiaran and I in their arms, random squeezes coming from all over the group hug. I let one tear fall down my cheek then hung my head back to keep from allowing anymore, my father caught me.

"I love you so much, my special girl. Don't you ever stop dreaming," he whispered to me.

And for some reason, in that moment, I prayed that everything would be alright.

Prayed to the God I wasn't sure ever listened to me, but hoped for the first time he heard me.

I know it's been awhile. It didn't seem necessary to pray to you anymore. Funny how we only bow to you when things are bad. Do you hate that? Only hearing from your children when all they have left is to speak into your void? Plaguing you with everything that's going wrong for them? Maybe your to-do list on fixing people's problems is so long you just haven't gotten to mine yet. Either way, I'm sorry for not having faith in you. I need you now more than ever, if that doesn't tell you how dire this is, well… I guess I'll know you've never been listening.

Please let me have a tomorrow with Kiaran. A forever. The prophecy clearly said that a love so powerful was created in your image long ago, that Earth was not ready for it so you separated it. Made one heart, two halves of it and destined them to find each other. As wild as it seems that I am one half of that whole, I feel it every time I'm near Kiaran. The clandestine pull to one another, the colors that tie us together. If your word is true, your prophetic path for me and Kiaran was carved into the stars, I beg for your guidance tonight.

Amen.

CHAPTER 34

Kiaran

Amelie was quiet from the moment we left her family until we saw the soft glow through the windows of our little cottage come into view.

"Is someone at the cottage?"

I hadn't mentioned to her that the High Priestess would be joining us tonight, there was already too much weighing on her. But there was no avoiding it now. Whatever Amelie had been plotting, she had no time to work on it today. Selfishly, it was part of the reason I wanted to get her out of the cottage. I needed her to stop fixating on solving a problem that had no solution. I had no idea how the night would go, I stopped thinking about it the moment Amelie pulled me through the portal to meet her family.

I decided it didn't matter. If the High Priestess killed me before I killed myself, Amelie would continue to live. If she took Amelie from me, I would lay my life down with her. So either way, Amelie would find happiness. Whether it was with me on the other side or without me and set free from the shackles of my curse.

"Yes. Some of the Coven members will be joining us tonight."

Amelie's eyes widened, my decision to not tell her that detail suddenly feeling like the wrong choice. Too late now. We landed in the clearing and I felt Amelie retreating. I could smell her fear. It was overpowering her usual vanilla and strawberry scent and it wasn't something I'd picked up on her since she first escaped into the Forest.

Reaching my hand out to her, I waited for her to be ready. She wouldn't look at me. Instead she was staring through the window attached to the kitchen, trying to catch a glimpse of the woman sitting in Amelie's spot at the table.

"Amelie..."

There wasn't much to say, she knew what was coming and maybe it had just hit her that she didn't have a fully thought out plan. For my girl to not be in control, it would crush her. I needed her to be with me or the thought of her panicking would destroy me.

She took a brave breath and then my hand. I didn't need to lead her though, she met each of my strides and walked with me to the den of Coven members waiting for us.

Kiaran, please let me try. I'm not ready to lose this.

Amelie pleaded to me. Before the ritual started, I would offer my life in place of Amelie's. I didn't need to know her plan because no matter what it was, one of us wouldn't rise with the sun tomorrow. It would be me.

Do not try anything.

I warned, but the pain she wore on her face told me she wasn't listening and I joined in her concern, knowing whatever happened tonight was out of my control. She wouldn't listen to me and whatever she had planned would get her killed.

Standing in front of the door, Orla gave us the opportunity to speak before she opened it for us.

"It's time." I thought I might be anxious in this moment but I wasn't. Sacrificing myself for Amelie would be the only good thing I ever did in my life, and I was okay with that.

Tears had already found residence in her water line but she kept a brave face.

"You are everything to me. Do you know that? This,"—bringing her hand to my heart—"beats for you. No matter what the morning sun brings, unless you are at my side alive, there will be nothing worth living for." A lie by omission. She didn't need to know the state I would be in when the sun rises. That being by my side in the morning didn't mean what she thought.

I would stay by hers though. I will follow her until the end of her days. I'd find her, dead, alive, or a Lost Soul. Every single fucking time. When she woke in the morning, I wouldn't be here to console her. I needed her to know that all that I was, was because of her.

"I can't begin to—"

"Please don't," she whispered through the cracks of her broken heart. "Please don't say goodbye right now."

A few tears betrayed her strong iron walls and spilled on to her cheeks. I used my thumb to brush them away.

I love you, magic man.

I love you more, pretty girl.

The door creaked open and the sheer power of magic in the room whooshed passed us.

I took a step in and Amelie quickly stepped beside me.

"Father didn't want to join us?" I asked, closing the door behind me and stepping up to the kitchen table. No one said anything in response.

In my periphery, Amelie's gaze slid to me as realization washed over her. I could feel her begin to shake, her palm going cold yet sweaty. She squeezed my hand, trying to pull my attention from those gathered around our kitchen table.

"Mother," I addressed the woman who bore me in the most disrespectful way I could. She was here as the High Priestess of Avonya's Coven, but I would not give her the satisfaction of being named by her place in it.

"Kiaran," she replied, "lovely to see you again." The twitch under her eye a dead giveaway that I got under her skin for a moment.

Amelie leaned into me and I knew exactly what was making her blood boil beneath her skin, "Mother?" she whispered. I didn't take my eyes off the wicked Valla McCalmont but I nodded to Amelie all the same.

My mother palmed the table and stood with all the grace of the Devil.

"Well, it's high time we begin."

AMELIE SAT NEXT to me at the table, my mother was across from her and Adan and Mia sat on either side of her.

When the three of them visited a few days ago, Mia and Adan's faces was covered by their High Table black veils. I could feel my sister in the room that night, but I didn't want to believe she was working with our mother in this way. Seeing Adan's unveiled and burned face from Amelie's dream was nothing less than satisfying, but seeing my once sweet little sister's was not. She was supposed to be better than this. I wished on every star I saw that our mother's wicked ways wouldn't poison her, but as she sat next to her tonight, it was clear there was little difference between them now. Down to every feature, they were the same.

Mia used to look at me like I hung the moon but tonight, she looked at me like my mother always had. A disgrace. A failure. I noticed my little sister was wearing the apprentice version of my mother's garb. A High Priestess in training.

Amelie was quiet as my mother pressed her on the events of the last few months. It was customary to share a last dinner, though I'd hoped it could be just Amelie and I. She was trying so hard to keep her face steeled and her fears hidden but I felt them. Instead of answering my mother though, my girl just kept offering more wine to the table, which everyone happily accepted.

"It's quite fitting for my brother to find someone who knows how to only cause destruction," Mia said as she sipped the last drop of her third glass. "Not even the herbalists could bring back the garden to its *full* glory."

Amelie burned holes through my sister's eyes as she returned to her seat next to me and her eyes were glowing embers, ready to light the world on fire.

"Your brother has been lovely company," she bit out, ignoring the insult to both of us.

"Kiaran? Lovely company?" Adan sputtered as some of his wine flew from his lips.

Amelie stared at him in disgust and my mother didn't miss it.

"I'm sure you're feeling quite thankful tonight, Amelie," she said. Amelie's eyes sparked further to life.

"Thankful?" she scoffed, falling right into my mother's antagonizing words.

"Sure. To not be fated any longer with my family. It seems you find my son's siblings to be unfit for your home."

Amelie's eyes widened but her brows lowered. I braced for the fire in her eyes to ignite the room. But instead, took a long, exaggerated breath then rolled her lips together before replying.

"I just expect our guests to be polite. Have manners. Seems the least you and your children could do seeing as you've laid a death wish upon your own blood's fated mate." Her nostrils flared, then she darted her eyes between my mother and Mia. "How exactly is that not a *clear* violation of the Witch's Oath again?" Amelie's head tilted and she painted a fake, sweet smile on her face.

My mother's lips quickly formed a tight, triumphant smile.

Her eyes squinted in amusement that she found the right button to press with Amelie.

"I see why you like her," my mother said to me. "Fire-y, just like your mother."

"I am nothing like you," she punctuated each word. I rested a palm on Amelie's knee hoping to calm her, but I knew we were far past that.

"It's insulting of you to assume I would break my Witch's Oath to my Coven." My mother brought the crystal wine glass to her mouth and sipped.

"*That's* what's insulting you?" Amelie laughed in a layered, sinister rhythm. "If only you could hear the things I think of you, then you would have reason to be insulted."

Mia cringed to herself at that. No one spoke to our mother like that. Not us. Not the Coven. No one.

Adan was laughing to himself, seemingly here for entertainment alone.

But my mother stared daggers into Amelie now. Behind her cold eyes was a threat and I couldn't bear it any longer. It was in that moment that I realized it was never about punishing me. For all the hatred my mother may have felt for me, for killing her baby girl, this was about the Morgenstern woman I loved.

Please trust me. My girl's sweet voice caressed the ridges of my mind.

"Mother, I would like to make a request under my Oath," I blurted out. Desperation reeked my voice. Amelie stood and grabbed the glass decanter filled with her homemade wine, then topped off everyone's glasses once more.

"Go on." My mother tilted her head in wait.

"Take my life, not Amelie's."

There was no reason she couldn't accept it. If she wouldn't, it would confirm that all of this was to finish her generation's old agenda against Amelie's ancestors.

"Absolutely not," Amelie interrupted the request. A huge

no-no in the Coven. These conversations were not up for debate nor was anyone besides the Witch requesting and the High Priestess allowed to speak unless otherwise directed. My request was between my mother and I.

"I'm ready." Amelie stood from the table, chewing on her cheek. She was trying to hide something that threatened to show on her face. "I just need to use the washroom."

She rushed off, slamming the door behind her, leaving me alone with my blood.

"My request?" I asked as we all stood from the table. My feet weren't steady and it seemed neither was anyone else's. Amelie's wine was strong.

My mother didn't respond. Instead, Mia spoke for her.

"The High Priestess denies your plea." She hardly spared me a glance before joining Adan and our mother in the sitting room. The three of them stood around the table with bored eyes and evil souls.

My only other option was currently stabbing into the side of my foot. I reached down for the knife.

Just as I was about to wrap my fingers around the handle, a swirl of bright colors and an assortment of scents whirled around through each McCalmont family member. Mia's veil lifted and landed haphazardly around her shoulders, Adan's greasy curls barely moved save for the ends of the ringlets and my mother's pin straight hair became snarled.

"What was that?" Mia shrieked. I was sure it was Orla, but I didn't want them to know about that.

"Just a draft. As I'm sure you've noticed, this isn't the family estate."

Amelie finally stepped out of the bathroom, a confidence emanating from her as if she wasn't about to be sacrificed.

"Mother, please take me," I tried once more.

"It's okay, Kiaran," Amelie said. *Pinky promise.*

She spoke through our bond as she discreetly locked my pinky with hers for a fleeting moment.

"Come." My mother's tone was sharp as her patience wore thin. She twisted her hand and pointed toward the sitting room. Our cozy living area transformed in front of our eyes into a replica of the High Table's ceremonial platform. A large stone table sat in the middle with a trough underneath it.

My stomach churned, I had to stop this. *Now.*

Amelie approached my mother, taking her hand willingly.

What are you doing? I called to her but she didn't waiver. My mother must have put a spell on her, veiled Amelie into complying. What the hell was she doing?

I tried to reach for the sharp blade again, but my body wasn't listening to my brain. I tried to speak but I was mute, I tried to move but I was stone. The only alternative I had if my mother did not accept my offer was this blade slicing through my neck and bleeding out, effectively ending my curse. But I couldn't get to it.

My mother was always a few steps ahead. She took away any chance at my interference.

I watched as Amelie and my mother entered the sacrificial stage.

My chest heaved as my heart thrashed hard against my rib cage, begging to be set free. To get to its other half that was being prepared for sacrifice.

Amelie…fight it…

Adan scooped Amelie up, laying her flat on the table. She turned her head to look at me. There was no fear in her eyes. They were oceans of sapphire and gold, bright and submissive. My girl had found a reason to live. This forest, her power, her friends, *me.* She showed up with bruised eyes and a broken soul, stitched it all back up on her own and now was willingly laying her life down for me.

Tears pooled in my eyes as I fought for my voice, my throat felt like there were knives being shoved down it. My stomach wound tight into a ball of a thousand knots.

I was trying to scream. Air left my lungs but the sound of

my voice went nowhere. Mia and my mother stood on either side of the table, tying Amelie's arms down on the board that Adan placed underneath her. It looked like a cross that would hang in one of Amelie's churches.

She wouldn't take her eyes off of me. If she was trying to speak to me, the magic my mother had working right now wasn't allowing it.

I kept willing my body to move toward her, but I was stuck.

"Kiaran, recite the curse." My mother's voice struck me, throwing my head back for a moment before a jolt of energy allowed my voice to come back.

Without permission from my brain the curse I'd come to now like the back of my hand sounded through the room as the magic of unveiling rumbled the ground beneath me.

"You are bound to the cottage in the mortal realm, in an enchanted Forest. In order to break your curse you will need to make an impossible sacrifice. You must offer your Coven something of value to you on Winter Solstice. You will have one chance, each year to be untethered. It must be of such value that handing it over to us will cause you unimaginable pain. If it does not mirror the pain that you caused, it will not suffice.

Let the longest night approach and with it, the weight of your choice. Let your mind fill with every other option you think you have and may you find no reprieve. You will spend eternity there, Kiaran McCalmont. Until you feel the curse lock into place, you will be alone."

My soul unlocked, coming unbound from the curse that had been weighing me down. It unbound from *her.* My feet were moving before I knew where I was going, but I landed in front of a trembling Amelie.

Fear shook her to her core as she finally met my eyes. The gold in hers was firing, blood began to drip from her nose. Grabbing her face, I noticed water dropping onto her face.

Tears. My tears.

"Amelie!" I roared so loud I wasn't sure the magic in the room was the cause of its shaking anymore.

Her back started slamming against the stone table, her eyes rolled, showing only the ghostly whites around her iris. Blood sputtered from her mouth. I couldn't see her clearly through the blur in my eyes and my hands were slipping against her face. The metallic smell of blood was taking up every bit of space in the room.

A sob wracked from me, I let my tears soak her chest as I laid over her heart. I tried to pull her to me, hold her, but the ties around her wrists wouldn't allow it.

"Come on, pretty girl, come back to me…" I rasped, unable to catch my breath. Her shirt was soaked. I lifted from her chest, hoping to see life still fighting in her eyes, but her entire body was red.

Blood.

So much blood.

From her ears, it was coating my hands.

From her eyes, her *beautiful* eyes.

From her nose, steadily flowing. An unstoppable river.

From her stomach, as if she'd been slashed straight down the middle.

It was purpling her beautiful blue dress she'd worn today, her birthday dress. Her fucking *birthday* dress.

"Someone grab towels!" I couldn't breath. "Mia, please. Help me!"

Somewhere in my frantic state I thought I could cup her blood back in my hands and give it back to her.

Amelie, here. Please, you need this.

"Mother, she won't have any blood left!" I screamed out loud, but my mind said *that's the point.* That's what the trough was for. That's what the sacrifice was.

"Please!" I cried. "Have mercy on her…"

Blood stained her eyes, the blues and golds disappeared into a haze of bronze as she stared lifelessly at where I was standing before.

The last thing she saw in her short life was me unbinding myself from her world, from her.

"Mama…" I begged my mother again. No longer speaking to her as a member of her Coven or the cursed McCalmont son. Just as a boy to his mother.

I wouldn't withstand the pain.

I didn't *want* to.

I shouldn't *have* to.

I reached for the blade, at peace with laying my Earthly body next to Amelie's and walking into whatever the afterlife could look like for us.

But before I could, a powerful hand laid upon my shoulder, I kept cover over Amelie with my body. They didn't deserve to see her. Not like this. Not like anything.

My crimson painted hands stuck to the tulle of her dress.

"When we get home, mommy will take all the pain away." My mother's voice was a siren song.

"I don't want to go home. Please, let me stay with her." I sobbed into Amelie's neck, pressing kisses into her blood soaked hair. My mother blocked my reach to the only way I could end this suffering.

I had to bury her. She couldn't be left here like this. Ethel and the Fae would come, the Lost Souls would come, they… she can't be left here like this.

"She's gone. A life for a life," she repeated those fucking cursed words to me.

"Then take mine! Bring her back." I turned, shouting into my mother's face. My voice rumbling like a boom of thunder at the end of a storm.

"What's done is done. It's time to go."

She couldn't be gone. It couldn't end like this, I checked once more for my girl to show me that she was still in there.

Wink at me…

I needed to see her wonky eyes try to wink one more time.

She'd never gotten it right. She had to learn how to wink before she could die.

This was her grand fucking plan I wouldn't fucking listen to?

I shook her shoulders, her head scraped against the stone. Pressing my face to her heart, I quieted everything that wasn't just me and her. I listen for the *thump, thump, thump* that should be there but there was no beat. No song of life.

Nothing.

"Time to go."

Amelie was dead.

Amelie died.

This wasn't how the fate was supposed to cross.

Al said it would be okay, Ethel told her it would be alright. Orla showed her our future. *We* had a future.

We were going to have a tomorrow, the day after that, forever.

You pinky promised. I reminded her, but it was dead quiet on the path from her mind to mine. My words went nowhere.

Today wasn't supposed to be her last day. *Our* last day.

I didn't get to kiss her one last time. She said she had a plan, why didn't she do it? I would never kiss those lips again.

I would never hear her sweet voice, or the one she used when she was pissed at me. I would never get to say the wrong thing and then show her I was worth another chance again, even if I wasn't. She'd never challenge me to be better again.

I let her down. I failed, *again.* I was supposed to protect her. She shouldn't have to bear the weight of my life. She'd taken on too much from every fucking person she'd ever met. She took care of everyone, all I had to do was take care of this and I fucking failed.

She was my first real friend, my only and best friend. The first person to not acknowledge my darkness and instead bring it into the light. She took my tattered soul, burned the edges of it off, then sewed new pieces of herself into it. Pieces I didn't want anyone else to see now that she was gone. The threads of color between us that were normally vibrant and winding, a mirror of Amelie's soul, were fading to black, a mirror of mine.

"I love you so fucking much, pretty girl."

I kissed her forehead, leaving the imprint of my lips stained in her blood.

Standing on weak legs, I turned to face my family. Adan was picking at his nails but Mia had tears in her eyes. The first sign that the little girl I once knew might still be there somewhere. But my mother, she was standing tall and proud. She'd defeated the Morgensterns once and for all. The smile that was painted on her face could have made the Devil himself weep. Then, she lifted her hand and snapped her fingers.

Compliance. She was compelling me.

I fought it only long enough to stride to the counter where Amelie's bouquet laid. I plucked the pale blue one I put in the middle then walked back to my girl and placed it over her heart. My head whirled as I fought my mother's spell.

I took a deep breath, rolled my shoulders back and stuck my chest out to keep the sob that was threatening to wrack out of me tucked deep beneath the shell that only one person was ever successful in getting under.

"Take me home."

Epilogue

The curtains were tied back against the oak window frame, allowing me a perfect few of the garden below. If Amelie's fury in this room threatened to once burn the McCalmont Family Estate to the ground, there was no proof of that now. The herbalist did a great job restoring it, I don't know what Mia was talking about. The roses were bright red against the stark white of snow. A walking path had been made between each of the rows.

Where Amelie and I watched our dream-selves first make love to one another, was the only shrub that was green and untouched by winter's evidence. Like her dream was cemented to life among the winter chill.

The knob of my bedroom door slowly turned and Mia popped her head in. "She's ready for you." Her tone was apathetic. All of them were unaffected by the events that unfolded tonight, but me? I was broken.

Amelie was dead. I didn't stop calling to her mind, hoping I would hear anything back. Any chance that she might still be alive. She had to have done something.

It wasn't right. It didn't *feel* right. So much of it looked like what Amelie described church to look like. Her Sunday services and how their leader was positioned on a cross to die for them.

Why did they lay her like that?

I replayed the events over in my mind, when my family and I arrived back in Avonya, I came to my room first. Hoping it was all a dream and Amelie would be waiting for me in here, when she wasn't, I took another shot in the dark and stepped to the window, she would be in the garden.

But she wasn't.

Amelie had been in hysterics in the days leading up to the ritual, pleading for me to help her with her plan. Not only did I not entertain helping her, I didn't even know what she was planning. She kept repeating *"Mirror, it has to mirror the pain."* but to that Amelie would've had to go to sleep, we all would've needed to sleep alongside her to be pulled into her dream.

She hadn't practiced the dream portals Orla wrote about in her journal, had she? If she did, she would've been terribly underprepared. That was Bloch…*magic.* Unprecedented and unpredictable. But that sounded like the definition of Amelie.

My chest ached and I knew I had to go, but my mother was waiting for me in the grand sitting room.

I left the window and took a seat on my bed. They could wait one more minute. The covers were rumpled as if to mimic the way Amelie and I slept the night before. Tears pricked my eyes as the smell of vanilla and strawberry filled every bit of me. I pulled the pillow from her side and buried my face in it. The smell of her hair suffocating me.

Tell me you're okay.

I strummed my fingers on my thigh.

No response.

Come on, pretty girl. I know you didn't give up that easily.

The gold in her eyes was so lifeless.

Amelie, please.

A tear fell from my eye, my stomach felt like it was being punched over and over again with every flash of her cold, dead body in my mind. Her puffy, pink lips were pale and cracked. The perfectly wavy curls in her hair she donned prior to dinner were frizzy at the ends and stuck to her forehead at the top, printed in blood.

My beautiful girl. My perfect, fated mate.

The pain was too great. I hinged at my hips, putting pressure on my chest in hopes of feeling any relief.

"Fuck!" I screamed, the room rumbled in response.

Crying into my lap, I rocked back and forth trying to shake this feeling. The tether between should've snapped by now, the heartbreak was one thing but that tie between life and death would shatter me completely. I needed it. If Amelie's God had a say in where I went after death, I'd tell him I want to be with her in purgatory, or Heaven or even that fucking cottage. I didn't care, as long as I was with her.

A knock at the door had me trying to suck the tears that were in free fall back in.

"Let's go." Adan was taking a straight line to me, grabbing me off the bed and pulling me back to the long hall that led to the grand sitting room. We were the same size, tall and broad, but Adan's freedom over mine in the last two hundred years made him stronger. I couldn't fight him with the weight of my shredded heart holding me down.

We rounded the corner and standing at the long oak bar pouring herself a mug of cider, was my mother. The High Priestess of Avonya.

Mia sat in full High Table garb with her apprentice pin attached right in the middle of her jewel covered epaulets. Her face was covered now with the traditional black veil worn only when operating under Coven orders.

"Oh Kiaran, you look exhausted. Drink?" My mother's tone was flat as she finished stirring her own drink, popping the stir stick into her mouth to take every last drop off of it.

"No, thanks." Taking my arm back from Adan, I went to sit by Mia on the couch. Though she was clearly not the sweet, kindhearted little girl she once was, she was the only thing that made me want to come home all those years.

My mother sashayed over to us, her long hair and High Priestess gown swaying as she handed me the drink she just made.

"Just take it. It was a long night." She ran her knuckles over my cheek, studying my face.

My lips pursed, nostrils flaring, and I wished I had Amelie's fire to set this place ablaze right now. "What the fuck do you want from me?"

Mia said when we arrived back that our mother wanted to hold a family meeting in a half hour. I wanted to be anywhere but here but I hoped when Amelie's soul crossed to the other side that I would be alone to feel the tether snap.

"Drink," my mother commanded.

I took a sip. Notes of berries and apples slid over my tongue but left a rancid taste sitting at the back of my throat. It was dry and aromatic, going straight to my head.

My mother slowly nodded at the mug, urging me to keep drinking. Adan was standing at the balcony doors, fidgeting with the floor length drapes, not paying attention to the rest of us. Mia's face was still covered. Traditionally, when you sat at the High Table and were operating on orders from the High Priestess, your face would be covered by the veil. It united the Witches working together.

Mia said this was a family meeting, but she was working under High Priestess orders right now.

I set the mug at my feet, leaning forward on my knees and lacing my fingers together to get a better look at my mother.

Something was *wrong* about all of this.

"Finish the drink, Kiaran."

"What are you playing at?" I questioned my mother.

She tilted her head to the side, then smiled, sending chills up my spine. Keeping my mind clear of any thoughts she might try to pluck from me, I focused on her.

I sifted through each ridge of her mind, hoping to find the answer to what she wanted from me in this moment. What exactly she was playing at.

"Ah… my son. You won't find what you're looking for in here." My mother used her pointer finger to tap gently on her temple, her long sharp nails clacking against her headdress. "Drink."

It was an order.

My body was compelled by it. I picked the mug back up, my mind competed for control but lost. Tipping it back as it reached my lips, the rest of the cider slid down my throat, three gulps and it was gone.

"Good boy," My mother assured me.

I wasn't sure what she was talking about.

"And the girl, how are you feeling about that now?" she asked, grinning in wait of my response.

"What girl?"

TO BE CONTINUED…

Acknowledgments

First of all, holy shit. I wrote a book. Second of all, you read my book! So for that, I thank you endlessly.

I'm sure I left you feeling a little pissed off, oops! I promise I am working to get the second book in this duet, *Through the Woods*, completed and in your hands ASAP. Make sure you are signed up for my newsletter so you don't miss the exclusive content coming soon.

Trevor, thank you for encouraging me, letting me be your background music while you played video games and I wrote (while singing every part of every song on the Over the River playlist). If it weren't for you, I'm not sure I could've created a book boyfriend like Kiaran. Thank you for being my best friend, always giving me grace when my head is in the clouds, and healing wounds that you didn't inflict.

Next, my son. My little baby boy, the inspiration for Tildan, and the tiny hands that often slammed my laptop shut on my hands. I love you so much chicken butt. I'll never let you read this but thanks for being your weird self.

To Noemi, Rachel, Katie and Cierra—I literally couldn't have done this without you.

C, if you hadn't been the first one to read my book, I'm positive I never would have let anyone else read it. I trusted your unfiltered opinion and if it weren't for you this would not be a published book.

Noemi, my girl, I'm so glad our stars crossed on the *for you* page and brought you to me. The day I met you, was the day I started feeling like a real writer. To have such a fast friend and confidant—thank you. For answering every voice memo with one equally as long, for letting me be apart of your author journey, for your advice and being a voice of reason when I wanted to scrap this whole thing. Just, thank you.

Rachel, the best hype girl. Again, I couldn't have done this without you. Though we met at the end of both of our books, I still don't think I would have had the confidence to let this find people's hands if it weren't for you.

Katie, you were literally the first person to know I was even doing this and while you could've called me crazy, you told me you couldn't wait to read it. I wouldn't have written the first word of this book without ya girlfriend.

That goes for all my hot mom friends, thank you guys. For more than just your support on this journey but for your friendship since we all found each other during pregnancy.

To Kylah, my editor. Where do I start? Handing my book off to you was one of the scariest days of my life. I was ready for it to be ripped to shreds, torn to complete and utter pieces. But instead, you empowered me with every suggestion, were so incredibly kind with my book baby and made it the version it is today within these pages. Thank you for becoming another fast friend and understanding me through my words. Thank you!

Mama, thanks for never telling me to come down from the clouds I live in and always encouraging my imagination. I love you. Also, thanks for giving me a baby brother and the inspiration for Hansel.

And last but certainly not least, my beta readers. THANK YOU. Your feedback was invaluable and knowing I have a group of cheerleaders waiting to get their hands on this book is the best feeling.

Beta Readers for Over the River:

Bri, Abbey, Noemi, Cierra, Rachel, Meridith, Madeline, Sydney, Sydney, Sydney, Sharleen, Katie, Lindsey, and Natalie

About the Author

Taylor is a wife, mom to a crazy baby boy, and dog mama to a sweet black lab named Hazie. Her love for books began with Amelia Bedelia and Judy Moody, eventually evolving into fantasy and romance novels. When she's not reading or writing, Taylor enjoys music, golfing, and (almost always) winning at Overcooked! against her husband. Summers are spent lakeside with family—the people who mean more to her than anything in the world.

Follow along:
@taysgonnaread